RENNO—His blue eyes startling in his sun-bronzed face, the reknown White Indian is young in years, mature in wisdom, and proud in his heritage as Sachem of the Seneca—but now he faces a foe so hideously evil that even the Manitous may not be able to save his family . . . or his life.

BETH—Beautiful, British-born wife of Renno, she has pledged her love to this virile Indian, but her desire for wealth and society life may lead them both to doom.

HODANO—The satanic horror of his soul is mirrored in his maimed face and split tongue; his awesome power is aimed at the destruction of Renno's body . . . and enslavement in a living death.

ADAN BARTOLOME—Crafty Captain of a black ship, he flies the skull and crossbones above his vessel . . . and hides an outrageous secret in his greedy heart.

EL-I-CHI—Shaman brother to Renno, he journeys into the white man's world to discover the brotherhood that unites all men . . . and the power of a woman's love.

MINGO—Massive in size and great of courage, this leader of Jamaica's runaway slaves has a price on his head, hatred in his heart, and a tie of blood with the great Sachem.

The White Indian Series
Ask your bookseller for the books you have missed

The White Indian Series
Book XVI

MANITOU

Donald Clayton Porter

™

Created by the producers of
**Wagons West, Children of the
Lion, Stagecoach,** and
Winning the West.

Book Creations Inc., Canaan, NY · Lyle Kenyon Engel, Founder

BANTAM BOOKS
TORONTO · NEW YORK · LONDON · SYDNEY · AUCKLAND

MANITOU

*A Bantam Book / published by arrangement with
Book Creations, Inc.*

Bantam edition / July 1988

*Produced by Book Creations, Inc.
Lyle Kenyon Engel, Founder*

ISBN 0-553-27264-0

Published simultaneously in the United States and Canada

Bantam Books are published by Bantam Books, a division of
Bantam Doubleday Dell Publishing Group, Inc. Its trademark,
consisting of the words "Bantam Books" and the portrayal of
a rooster, is Registered in U.S. Patent and Trademark Office
and in other countries. Marca Registrada. Bantam Books,
666 Fifth Avenue, New York, New York 10103.

PRINTED IN THE UNITED STATES OF AMERICA

O   0 9 8 7 6 5 4 3 2 1

New York
N.H.
Boston
Ma.
Ct.
RI
Lake Erie
Northwest Territory
Pennsylvania
Ohio River
Philadelphia
N.J.
New York City
MD.
DE
Virginia
Nashboro
Knoxville
Asheville
North Carolina
Cape Fear River
South Carolina
Wilmington
Georgia
Charleston
Florida
Grand Bahama
Gulf of Mexico
Bimini Islands
Bahamas
La Habana
Great Exuma (Georgetown)
Atlantic Ocean
Cuba
N
Haiti
Port au Prince
Jamaica
Kingston
Caribbean Sea
©BOOK CREATIONS INC. 1987
R. TOELKE '87

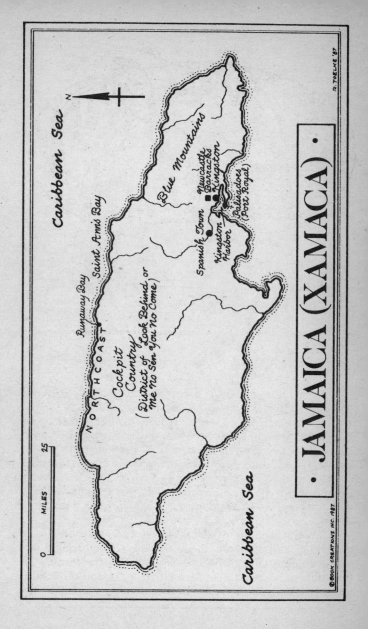

· JAMAICA (XAMACA) ·

Caribbean Sea

Caribbean Sea

N

MILES
0   25

R. TOELKE '87

© BOOK CREATIONS INC. 1987

NORTH COAST

Runaway Bay

Saint Ann's Bay

Cockpit Country
(District of Look Behind, or
Me No Sen You No Come)

Blue Mountains

Newcastle
Barracks
Kingston

Spanish Town

Kingston Harbor

Palisados
(Port Royal)

Chapter I

The air was so cold and still that it seemed to freeze sound, to make the ring of ax on wood sharp and brittle. The new snow had become encrusted, but that crust broke with the weight of Angus McCoon's boots as he repositioned himself and swung the ax once more. One blow, two. He was sweating inside his sheepskin coat. The small, barren branches at the top of the tree shivered as if in dread. There was a sharp crack of sound and a groan as the tree leaned and fell with a whoosh to smash crust and small limbs in a tangle of sound.

McCoon leaned on his ax handle and took deep breaths of the biting, achingly pure air. Across the new clearing a wavering column of smoke was emerging from the lean-to. In the stillness he could hear a sweet, rising sound of childish laughter. His face softened. He checked the sun, low in the

1

west. The light was still brilliant, but the heat of the sun left
the cold untouched. He swung the ax, buried its head partially in the stump of the tree he had just felled. It was early,
but there were advantages to being on one's own, days from
the nearest settlements: if a man decided that he wanted to
quit work before sundown, there was no eye to see, no one to
raise an eyebrow.

The storm from Canada had moved in a week past with
heavy snow, and now the air that followed enveloped the
Ohio Territory forests with an iron cold that penetrated even
the temporary shelter that McCoon had erected for his wife,
Mary, and their four children, ranging in age from one year
to seven. It would be cozy inside, however, with Mary using
the last of the dried apples to bake a new-year's treat, with
the kids sniffing delightedly at the aroma, their mouths wa-
tering in anticipation.

He examined the fallen tree. It was of the proper size to
take its place in the rising walls of a log cabin under construc-
tion near the lean-to. The limbs would go onto the woodpile
to help slow what seemed to McCoon to be an almost magical
diminishment of the firewood supply.

So that the walk to the lean-to would not be wasted, he
bent, loaded his arms with cut firewood, and trudged toward
the laughter, warmth, and smile of his wife. His feet crunched
through the crust on the snow, and he sank so deep that he
had to lift his legs high. Perhaps it was merciful that the first
arrow struck him at the base of the skull, penetrating flesh,
bone, and sinew to snuff out his life as one would blow out a
candle with one strong puff. As he fell the firewood scattered,
making crisp sounds as it bounced on the crusted snow.
Another arrow glanced off his spine, but he was dead before
that second impact.

A shadowy form moved through the clearing that had been
opened so laboriously by Angus McCoon since his arrival
north of the Ohio River in early summer of the past year. The
silhouette resolved itself into a fur-clad man who glided over
the crusted snow on moccasined feet without breaking through.

Mary McCoon, only twenty-two years old but thickened
and aged by work and by having borne four children, bent
into the crude, stone fireplace inside the lean-to and, using a

scorched pot holder, lifted the lid of the metal pot suspended over the fire. A heavenly aroma of spices, precious sugar, and baking fruit wafted out, drawing the children, three girls and the eldest, Andrew, to her side.

"I like it hot," piped Faith, second eldest, almost six years old.

"But we do like them cooked, don't we?" Mary teased, smiling fondly.

When Mary heard the door open behind them, she replaced the pot's lid and put one hand on her side to ease the ache in her back as she straightened and turned. The smile was already forming on her face, a special smile that she kept in reserve—although she was unaware of that fact—for her husband, the father of her children, the man who, she felt, had more ambition and courage than most. Not many men were confident enough of their own ability to protect their families and to venture into the Northwest Territories.

Mary loved the weather-toughened, somewhat craggy face of Angus McCoon, and she trusted the man behind that face. Although many had warned them against settling north of the Ohio, in a wilderness where white blood had been shed by wild Indians, she had had no hesitation in sharing Angus's dream of being among the first settlers, of taking and holding and working enough land to make their children independent in the future.

Her smile froze on her face when she heard Faith cry out at her side. Although Faith was the eldest girl, she was more timid than her younger sisters. Mary saw a blur of motion in her peripheral vision but could not take her eyes off the thing that stood in her doorway.

He was silent, motionless, his face shadowed by a thick cowl of wolverine fur. He smelled of the outdoors, of the trackless forests. The knife in his hand was bloodied to the hilt, and a sodden mass of red hair hung on a belt tightened around his bearskin coat. Mary could not fail to recognize the hair, but she couldn't scream, couldn't speak, couldn't move. It was as if the malevolent eyes glowing from the shadows under the cowl had mesmerized her.

Young Andrew had reached his father's musket, leaning against the wall next to the fireplace. He was making sobbing, frightened sounds as he leaned back to get leverage and raised the heavy weapon.

The cowled man vented a shrill, falsetto shriek, and his arm whipped strongly, sending the bloody knife flashing, catching the glint of firelight in the dimness of the room. The knife buried itself in Andy's throat, and blood pumped past the blade as the musket clattered to the floor.

The cowled man growled, a guttural, eerie sound. Two oddly painted Indians slipped past him. One of them seized Mary and, when she struggled, stilled her with a powerful blow to the face. The other lifted the one-year-old baby by the left foot and swung her around as she let out one shrill cry, to thud her head against the stone of the fireplace. The second-youngest girl was dispatched quickly, with one swing of a tomahawk.

The cowled figure had moved swiftly to lift Faith out of the path of his fellows. She screamed and twisted violently to free herself. A sound like the hiss of a snake came from the shadowed mouth, the words in English, ordering the little girl to be silent. She obeyed only because sheer terror drained the blood from her brain in a blessed faint.

One of the painted Indians was ripping at Mary's clothing while the other skillfully lifted scalps from the three dead children. Mary's exposed body was very, very white. The man who crouched over her looked up at the cowled figure to make an obscene motion.

The cowled one snorted in disgust. "She is yours," the shaman answered, "and all this. I have what I want."

But rather than leaving immediately, he stood to watch the painted warriors spend their passions quickly on the white woman, then to nod in satisfaction as blood spurted from Mary's throat after one quick slash of a knife.

When he entered the forest with the unconscious six-year-old under one arm, the lean-to was burning behind him. He paused, slung the limp body of the girl over his shoulder, then traveled deep into the wilderness.

His breathing was still long and slow, in spite of having covered miles at a swift gliding pace, when he halted, listened, then advanced carefully. He made a full circle around the Seneca longhouse, listening carefully to be certain no one was inside. The longhouse was well hidden in forest depths and many feared him, but all, he knew, were his enemies. Some even said he was mad. He thrust out his tongue. It was slit, forked, like that of a snake. He hissed and entered the longhouse, tossing the still-unconscious girl onto a pile of sleeping skins.

It took a few minutes to stir the coals of his fire and coax the dry branches into flame. He shed his outer clothing and began to make preparations. He brewed a strong herbal tea over the open fire and filled a small drinking bowl. The girl was breathing evenly, and he used his finger to dip drops of the strong tea into her mouth and stroked her throat to cause her to swallow.

Faith screamed once as her eyes opened. Her captor had pushed back his cowl. His face was a thing of horror, thin to the point of being skeletal, one eye a ruin, the other red. His cheeks were horribly scarred.

He sat her up and forced her to drink. The tea's herbs caused her limbs to jump and her eyes to dart wildly. Although she emitted odd gasping sobs, she was stimulated enough for the rite to begin. He knew she would not faint again. And a strong, healthy girl-child, properly stimulated by the strong herbs, could live long with excruciating pain. He had picked his subject carefully from among the four children, having previously scouted the clearing and dwelling of the foolish white man.

In the giving of pain he was not inexperienced. Long ago he had dedicated himself to the darkness. The ceremony that he performed in the longhouse, miles from the nearest Indian village, was almost routine. The screams of the agonized child were sweet to him, and the shaman accompanied them with guttural chanting: his pledge to darkness, his prayer to his evil ones.

He tied her well to the stake and brought forth a few more moans of anguish before, timing it exactly, he sucked the life from her last, gasping breath, his wide mouth covering hers, eating her spirit as it flew from her body.

He felt the familiar surge of power, knew an exaltation that seemed to lift him from the packed-earth floor and send him soaring. He closed his good eye and called on the powers of darkness to come to him, to give him sight, to send him a vision of triumph. He conjured in his mind the hated image: a tall man, pale with white blood, skin bronzed by sun, with hateful light hair. He chanted his pleas for guidance, but there was only a blankness, with the image of Renno, the white Indian, smirking, in his mind.

The shaman screamed out his frustration and his rage, kicked the bloodied, bruised corpse of the girl, then smashed a pottery vessel in his torment.

"I have given myself to you!" he shrieked, the sound of his voice escaping the walls of the longhouse and dying in the deserted wilderness, which was colder now in the black of a winter night. "I serve you with my life, yet you desert me."

He fell exhausted onto the sleeping skins. His horribly disfigured face poured sweat. His eye was unfocused and his mouth slack. It had all been for nothing. Not even the spirit of a white child, a virgin and tender, had appeased his evil spirits or opened their wisdom to him.

He jerked to his feet, his hand going to his tomahawk as he heard footsteps crunching the frozen snow. He snarled when a voice called, "Allo, Hodano!"

The tomahawk was in his hand and his arm muscles quivered with the desire to greet that hoarse, French-accented voice with the blade when the footsteps reached the skins covering the entrance to the longhouse. But then he relaxed with a visible effort.

"It is I, Toulouse," the voice called.

"Enter," said Hodano.

"I greet you, Shaman. I, Paul Toulouse, bring a gift." The Frenchman extended a bottle of rum.

"And why does Cochon, the pig, bring a gift?" Hodano asked.

"Eh," the Frenchman said, "we have been friends, have we not?" Toulouse was smiling, but he, like Hodano, would have preferred to greet the other with a blade. The shaman, at one time a member of the Seneca tribe, had been the one who stole his name, for in the Northwestern Territory he was no longer Paul Toulouse, trapper. Thanks to Hodano he was Cochon, the pig, renegade from justice in Quebec. Now he even thought of himself as Cochon, but that was all right, for he was a man, and one day he would have his revenge on the ugly shaman.

Hodano took the bottle of rum, pulled the cork with his teeth, and poured the fiery liquid down his throat to make a warm spot in his stomach. "The rum is good," he said.

Cochon had turned and was licking his lips as he stared at the naked, small, thin body of Faith McCoon. "Eh, I thought you were my friend," he complained, "and yet you kill the little *poulet*. Why did you not keep her alive, at least for a little while after you had your pleasure, so that Cochon might have had a small measure?"

With an eruption of fury Hodano swung the rum bottle, and Cochon escaped injury only by ducking quickly.

"Hold!" Cochon yelled as Hodano drew his tomahawk. "What is wrong with you?"

Hodano controlled his anger with difficulty, telling himself that a man of Cochon's mentality could not be expected to understand. Had an idiot such as the trapper gotten his hands on the white child, he quite expectedly would have used her in a different way.

Cochon crouched warily, his hand on the hilt of his knife. Hodano had always been a little crazy. Who didn't get a little crazy in the midst of a long, frigid winter in the wilderness? But he had never seen the shaman quite so touchy.

"I would not dishonor my spirits by taking sexual pleasure from a gift to them," Hodano explained with elaborate patience.

Cochon relaxed, reached for the rum, and took a swig. "Medicine," he said, lifting the bottle in salute.

"A weak, foolish word," Hodano said.

"Did you gain by this gift to your spirits?" Cochon asked.

"You would not understand," Hodano replied, sitting down.

Cochon sat on a log beside the small fire. His belly strained at his clothes. To his left the child's mutilated body hung on the ropes that bound her to the stake. "You have pretty good medicine," he admitted. "That evil eye of yours can wilt a warrior in full stride. And yet . . ."

"And yet?" Hodano asked.

"There are those—those I have seen—who do real magic."

"You have not told me why you are here," Hodano said angrily.

"Just passing nearby," Cochon said offhandedly, unwilling to admit that he had been lonely, that the trapping had not been going well, and that he had felt the need to see another face, even one so nearly inhuman as Hodano's. "Perhaps I will tell you of the magic of the voodoo masters of the islands to the south."

Hodano snorted but did not protest.

Cochon laughed. "There they would say of this"—he pointed to the dead child—"that you have sacrificed the goat without horns."

"And who are these masters of magic?" Hodano asked.

"Black men, who have brought the ancient magic to this new world from Africa. And with the magic, the voodoo gods. I have seen a voodoo master leave his own body, and his soul enter the body of a goat."

"If that is magic—"

Cochon threw his head back and laughed. "Ah, but if one could send his spirit into the body of a goat, what else could he do? The powers of the masters are not to be despised, *mon ami*. With your magic increased by theirs . . ."

Hodano was interested in spite of his doubt. He grunted.

"There is a voodoo god or spirit so powerful that only a few know his name, and even fewer can pronounce it and live. With that spirit harnessed to do your will, you could do anything," Cochon said. "The masters can control this one. They say they put god in a bottle."

"I will clear this away," Hodano said, thinking that what Cochon was saying was nonsense. He untied the child's body and dragged it into the night, leaving it atop the snow a short distance from the longhouse. The wolves would do the rest.

"You don't seem impressed," Cochon ventured after Hodano had returned to the longhouse and was heating a cornmeal mixture over the fire. Hodano remained silent. "And yet you cannot make yourself invisible. You cannot fly."

Hodano made a sound of disbelief.

"But this I have seen," Cochon insisted.

Unbidden visions of Renno flashed into Hodano's memory. It was bad enough that he had been defeated by the white Indian, but he also had been humiliated by Renno's brother, El-i-chi. His magic was made to look impotent; his reputation among the northern tribes had been damaged.

"Lies," he accused.

"No, I swear," Cochon said. "Eh, you hate the white man, *non*? I know that you have been organizing the raids on the whites who are stupid enough to move into this territory. But it will take more than that to keep them out. Your medicine won't do it. All the warriors you can muster won't do it."

Although he was not educated in the white manner, Hodano knew enough of the history of the Indians of other tribes to hear a ring of truth in Cochon's statement.

"You have seen these things with your own eyes?" Hodano pressed.

"What did you do with the white girl? Medicine. Spirit eating, *non*? Well, I have seen a voodoo master not only take the spirit from a living man but keep that man moving, although he was dead, a slave, a zombie, as such beings are called."

Another flash came to Hodano, and for a glorious moment he could envision his enemy, dead and yet alive, without will, doomed forever to obey the wishes of Hodano. Ah, yes, that would be a fitting punishment.

"Already it is getting too crowded for me here," Cochon continued. "The good trapping is in the past. Too many tribes in one area have depleted the game. There is no place for me in Canada, with the British. I am caught between the British and the Americans. Once France ruled, and a man could roam as he pleased and the beaver were as thick as hens in a chicken run. Now there is only this."

The howl outside of a prowling wolf, the sigh of the wind, seemed to belie Cochon's claim that the wilderness contained too many people, but Hodano understood. Little by little, mile by mile, the whites were extending their civilization into the wilderness.

"Why do you not go south, back to the islands in the sea, then?" Hodano asked. "You complain of the cold and the snow. I have heard that there are lands that never know snow or the chill of the north wind."

"I have thought about it," Cochon admitted.

"Go, then."

"Maybe you should go with me. Maybe you can learn some real magic, eh?"

Hodano snarled, but as he began to eat, not offering food to the Frenchman, his mind was working: to be able to fly, to soar over his enemy and attack from the sky . . . to be invisible and attack without any hint of warning . . . and to be able to suck the spirit from his enemy and leave him an empty husk to do his own bidding, ah.

"I do not know how to do this," he said.

"You'd have to dress as a white man, or at least as a member of one of the conquered tribes, to get through the Americans. This I could teach you."

"I will go with you," Hodano declared.

"I'll be damned," Cochon said, quite surprised.

"And if you have lied, if these masters of medicine you speak of do not exist, I will kill you and eat your spirit, although it would produce only the weakest kind of magic."

Cochon laughed, but as he tried to fall asleep on his skins spread on the dirt floor of Hodano's longhouse, he wondered just what he had brought onto himself.

The winter in 1788 had not been unusually severe in Knoxville. There had of course been snow in the mountains to the east, but it had not been too bad, so the mails had continued with something approaching regularity. It was a beautiful day with the temperature well above freezing under a bright sun when a packet of letters addressed to Renno came in care of Roy Johnson.

Roy paced the floor, the packet of letters clutched in his hand. Nora, his wife, looked up from her knitting and sighed. "You've been looking for an excuse to see the grandchildren."

"Yes, I suppose I have," Johnson confessed with a laugh. "Look, the weather is fine and appears as if it will hold. Why don't you come with me?"

"No, thank you," Nora said. "The cold seeps into my bones too easily. But you go."

"I think I should. Renno will be pleased to have the letters from Beth."

"Roy . . ." Nora said, then paused.

He looked down at her. Neither of them was young anymore, but in spite of her sometimes fragile health she was the girl he had married. Her graying blond hair was lifted into a loose bun at the back of her neck. Her skin was still smooth and unwrinkled. It was only around her eyes and at the neck that she showed any signs of aging.

"Hate to leave you alone," he said.

"Oh, don't worry. I'll be fine. But Roy—"

"Yes?" When he looked directly at her, he could see the sadness in her eyes. He doubted that she had ever fully recovered from the death of their only child, their Emily, who had married a man Nora felt was beneath her, a white man who was in his heart and mind a Seneca warrior.

"Ask him when we may have Renna with us," Nora finished.

"I will," Roy promised.

It took him only a few minutes to prepare for the journey, and so eager was he to see his grandchildren that he would not wait for an early-morning start but left Knoxville late that same afternoon.

"You'll simply have to sleep in the open," Nora protested.

"Be good for me. Been cooped up too long as it is."

It had been a long time since he had known the freedom of being alone in that wilderness, which was slowly being peopled by white settlers coming over the Great Smoky Mountains from North Carolina, Virginia, and Kentucky. It gave him a feeling of being renewed and allowed him time to think. He let the horse pick its own pace, a slow, comfortable walk, for it was pleasant when Knoxville was left behind. The great forests enclosed him from all but the pleasantly chilly air, the sun dappling through evergreens and the bare limbs of hardwood trees, and the disturbed squirrels scurrying about.

As he rode, Roy contemplated the changes he had witnessed in that land beyond the mountains that he had chosen to be his home. He and others, Governor John Sevier chief among them, had once dreamed of founding a new state of the Union, a state named for that most sensible of the founding fathers, Ben Franklin. But the United States government— such as it was—had refused recognition of Franklin as a state.

Roy's spirits sagged a bit as he thought about Franklin. Two sets of officials had been claiming authority in the would-be state, and now, in 1788, Johnson feared that his friend Sevier faced final defeat. Sevier's term as governor expired this year, and there were some—little men, Roy felt, with little minds— who were calling Sevier an opportunist, even a traitor for his ambitions.

But to be fair about it, the problems of the territory west of the Great Smoky Mountains were insignificant when compared to the challenges facing the country as a whole. The young United States lived day to day with the threat of armed intervention from one of the major European powers, or being caught in the middle of the continuing power struggle between Spain in the south and the British in the north.

The United States economy was in a shambles, burdened by vast public and foreign debts. Thus the fledgling country was in no position to be firm with the European giants as they bickered over territory and trading rights. If the new nation sided with Great Britain, Spain would undoubtedly attack in the south. If she sided with Spain, then the British would be more overt in their attempts to control and maintain the vast, rich territory north of the Ohio where, it was rumored, they were up to their old tricks, inciting the Indians to violence against American settlers.

Yep, Johnson thought as the horse clip-clopped along, a man could worry himself into a fret thinking about things that could happen. But Johnson had always been an optimistic man. He figured that most of the things a man worried about never came to pass, and he had little control over the few things that would happen, so what the heck. It was too pretty a day, and sometime tomorrow he'd be seeing his grandchildren.

He made a dry camp about halfway to the Seneca village where his son-in-law—or to be technical about it, since his Emily was dead, his former son-in-law—was sachem. The distant howl of a wolf was music in his ears as he drifted off, to sleep like a lion and awaken with the sun making jewels of the moisture that had accumulated on the trees during the night.

Before he saw the village, he could see the smoke of the chimney pots in the log cabins that some of the Cherokee had been building after the white man's style. He was riding along, having urged the horse into a faster walk, grinning to himself in anticipation, when he was whacked in the chest by a small arrow with a blunt point. His reaction was instinctive. He threw himself off the horse and sought cover while pulling his pistol. He looked around for his attacker, but the forest was still. The horse had continued a few paces, then halted, and was now looking back at him in a puzzled way. Roy remained behind a tree, trying to see movement.

"It's all right, Granddad," a boyish voice called. "I got you."

Little Hawk, son of Renno and grandson of the man who had been got, materialized as if by magic from the trees. Roy grinned proudly in spite of himself. The boy was a chip off his father's block, already possessed of wilderness skills. If the boy had been a hostile adult with a real bow, Johnson would indeed have been dead.

"You scamp," Johnson admonished fondly, rising and putting away his pistol. "Get yourself over here."

Little Hawk came on the run, a lively, handsome boy, dressed in buckskins and moccasins. He threw himself high into Johnson's arms and allowed a squeeze before he began to squirm.

Johnson put him down. "Yep, you got me good."

"It was easy," Little Hawk boasted. "You should be more careful, Granddad."

"When I am in the lands of my friends and family?"

"Well," Little Hawk said, "it doesn't hurt none to practice."

"How is your little sister?"

Little Hawk wrinkled his nose. Johnson could see in that small face his own daughter and the best features of Renno as well. "Come," Little Hawk said, "my father will be pleased to see you."

"And how about you?"

Little Hawk grinned widely. "I'm glad to see you too." He became serious. "I wonder if you have brought anything, *ummm*, special, Granddad."

Roy answered the grin. "As a matter of fact . . ." He pulled a bag of hard candies from the saddlebag and hefted it in his hand.

Little Hawk went into a delighted war dance, prancing around and puffing and whooping. Roy grabbed him by the shirt, hoisted him onto the horse, and mounted. They rode into the village with Little Hawk's cheeks distended roundly with hard candy.

Johnson's other grandchild was playing in front of her grandmother's longhouse. A tidy little bundle in a buckskin shirt and skirt, Renna, almost two, had the pale hair of her mother. Johnson's heart seemed to stop as he halted the horse and watched. He was seeing Emily all over again as a baby, with a sunny smile and that pale-gold hair. For a moment he wished that Nora could see the child as she was, unaware of his presence, lost in her make-believe world.

"Ha, Renna!" Little Hawk yelled. "I have candy."

Renna did not remember her grandfather, and she was, at first, a little shy. But candy and the warmth of love flowing from Johnson solved that problem, and soon he was holding the little girl on one arm, telling her that she would have to come and see her grandmother Nora soon.

Toshabe, Renno's mother, came out to usher him into the longhouse after greeting him with Seneca formality and politeness.

Inside the longhouse a scorched coffeepot held a chewy brew. Toshabe chatted with Johnson for a while, but their conversation suffered from the excitement of Little Hawk and Renna. Renna's shyness was totally gone, and she delighted in sitting on Johnson's lap, something to which he did not object at all.

"The men have not gone far," Toshabe said, rising. "I will send some young one to tell Renno you are here."

"No hurry," Johnson said.

Toshabe smiled, knowing what he meant. "I will send just in case, knowing men. Perhaps you will be so kind as to keep these two from destroying everything while I am gone?"

"Sure." Johnson caught an attack from Little Hawk with his arm and rolled the boy onto the floor to tickle him severely.

Roy spent a pleasant hour with his grandchildren. The sack of candies suffered devastation. He was pleased to find that Renno was teaching Renna English as well as the Seneca language. Little Hawk could chatter in both languages, plus some pretty respectable Cherokee, and when he saw that his grandfather was impressed, he even threw in a few words of Spanish, saying that his father was also teaching him that language. Renno had learned Spanish from Beth Huntington, Little Hawk soberly explained.

At the mention of Beth the boy's face sobered. "Granddad," he said, "my father says that she is my mother."

Roy felt a moment of sadness. He understood why Renno would tell his son that Beth, who, after all, was Renno's wife, was now his mother, but there was a small stab of pain nevertheless. It was a bittersweet experience to look into the faces of Little Hawk and Renna and see so much of his own daughter. He had never been able to understand why it had been God's will to take Emily from them while giving them the little girl, Renna.

"Yes, son," Roy said. "And she's a fine woman."

"My *mother* lived with us," Little Hawk continued stubbornly. "She made good things for us and played with us."

"With *you*," Roy corrected. "She died when Renna was born."

"Yes, but you know what I mean."

It was a delicate situation, Roy knew. His Nora had little patience with the idea of Renno's wife living in Wilmington, weeks of traveling time away from Renno's village. He himself could rationalize Beth's concern for her ailing father, but in spite of that he had to agree with Nora that a wife's place was with her husband.

He did not blame Renno for having married Beth. A man doesn't like to live alone, and the Englishwoman was beautiful. But he had been guilty of questioning Renno's wisdom in choosing to marry a sophisticated woman such as Beth, a woman whose only experience in living as Renno *would* live was on that one journey to the Southwest.

"I 'spect that Beth will live with you one day," Roy said. "When her father is better."

"Or dead," Little Hawk declared with the matter-of-fact acceptance of the very young.

"Your father loves Beth very much."

"Girls," Little Hawk said disgustedly as he launched another surprise attack that was barely parried by his grandfather.

Renno entered the longhouse with a breath of cold air following him. His smiling face was unpainted. He seemed to loom larger than in the past, or, Roy wondered, was it that he was becoming more mature? Johnson deposited the two children on the floor and rose to take Renno's hand but was seized instead in a bear hug that drew him to Renno's chest.

"It is always good to see you," Renno said, and the look of pleasure on his face left no doubt in Johnson's mind that Renno was sincere. But still Roy felt regret that Emily could not be alive to see her man in his prime, to feel proud of the way he commanded the absolute respect of his Seneca and the Cherokee, not to mention that of many important men of the territory and the United States.

Renno was dressed fairly lightly for the weather in buckskin trousers and fringed shirt. His golden brown hair was long, tied into a pigtail at the back with a leather thong. His piercing blue eyes were warm and friendly as he laughed, listening to Little Hawk and Renna, who were clinging to his legs, competing to tell him about the candy Granddad had brought.

"I told her to save some for you," Little Hawk announced, "but she ate the last piece."

Soon the longhouse was filled to crowding. Renno's brother, El-i-chi, added his warm greeting. Renno's sister, Ena, and Rusog, her husband, stood next to Toshabe's new husband, Ha-ace, the panther. And Ha-ace's budding young daughter, Ah-wa-o, the rose, was happy to see Roy, whom she had met only once, and briefly.

Hunting had been good, so there was a venison stew cooked in that particular Seneca way that Johnson enjoyed so much. Then to everyone's delight Johnson produced yet another bag of candy and passed it around, the adults seeming to enjoy it as much as the children.

Toshabe and Ena took the children to the far end of the longhouse while the men sat and smoked and exchanged news. Things were peaceful and prosperous with the Cherokee-Seneca group.

"Too quiet," El-i-chi, always the eager one, complained. "I think it is time for my brother to—"

"Start a war so that you can count coup?" Ena asked from across the room.

"Perhaps Roy would enjoy a hunt," Renno suggested.

"I would," Roy admitted, "but I'd best not. Nora's health, you know. Guess I'd better spend a day or two with the kids and then head back to Knoxville." At that point, reminded of the purpose of his trip, he rose, took the packet of letters from his saddlebag, and handed them to Renno.

Renno immediately recognized the neat, stylish handwriting, and his heart rate accelerated. He lifted a letter to his nose and caught a faint hint of the scent of her, of Beth.

"Now he will want to seclude himself to read," El-i-chi teased, without disapproval.

That, in fact, was exactly what Renno wanted.

"Go on," Johnson urged. "I've had a long ride, so I'm turning in."

Chapter II

By the light of the fire in his own house, Renno organized Beth's letters by date and began to read. The first letters had been written starting the day after he had left Wilmington, and scarcely a day had passed that Beth had not talked to him on paper in her neat, feminine hand.

Cedric Huntington's health, Renno discovered as he read, had improved steadily, but only under a dictatorial regimen instituted by his strong-willed daughter.

"God knows I wanted to be with you," Beth wrote, "but I feel, and the doctors agree, that had I not been present to insist upon rest and quiet, my father would most probably have done serious harm to his physical state. He is a restless and stubborn patient."

As he read, Renno felt the pang of being separated. It warmed him to know that Beth, too, felt that sadness.

17

"How I do miss you," she wrote, "and curse the circumstances that keep us apart."

She spoke glowingly of the time when he would come for her and take her to his land. She would, she promised, work hard to be a good Seneca wife and a worthy mother to Little Hawk and Renna.

"In the meantime, my darling, although I know that you, too, have your duty to your people, if things are going well, would it not be possible for you to come to Wilmington, to be with me until my father has recovered enough to be left alone?"

Renno was still a young man, only in his twenty-fourth winter, although his maturity and wisdom seemed to belie his youth. Responsibility had been thrust upon him early by the death of the great Ghonkaba, his father. The weight of duty did not usually press him down, but there in the longhouse as the fire flickered, he had one fleeting moment when he wished that someone else had come into the leadership of the southern Seneca. That weakness was quickly crushed, for he had the blood of Ghonkaba in his veins, and his ancestral line went back from Ghonkaba through Ja-gonh to the original Renno. His great-grandfather had also come prematurely into responsibility, and he had never faltered. Neither would the great-grandson. A man with the blood of such great ones would never betray the trust of old Ghonka, who had reared a white boy as his own and had seen that adopted son attain greatness. Even though Ghonka's Seneca blood was not flowing in young Renno's veins, there was in his heart everything for which Ghonka had stood. He was Seneca in spite of his fair hair, his blue eyes, his sun-bronzed white skin. He was Renno, sachem of the Seneca, and now he had not only a responsibility to his own people—those Seneca who had followed his father into the southlands—but he felt a heavy weight when he thought of the parent tribe, the Seneca of the north woods.

Far away, in the land where he had been born in the year 1764, in the lake district that was the hunting ground of the Seneca, good men faced a crisis. Roy Johnson had obtained for him a copy of the Northwest Ordinance of 1787, in which it was stated officially that the lands between the Ohio River and the Great Lakes belonged to the United States.

The ordinance provided for division of this vast wilderness
territory into five units, each of which, as white settlements
developed and the white population grew, would become a
state. The inhabitants of the new territory were guaranteed
freedom of worship, trial by jury, and the protection of ha-
beas corpus. Presumably such guarantees would apply to the
Indian tribes, some of which had already been forced, some
more than once, to move westward from their ancestral lands.
The problem was that such white man's rights meant little to
an Indian whose way of life depended not upon clearing the
land for farming, but in having a vast, unpopulated region for
hunting.

Blood had already been shed in the Northwest Territory,
and more would fall, for there were those among the Indians,
chiefs of ability, who were determined to fight. Such a war
would have an effect on the northern Seneca, and Renno
prayed to his manitous that men of wisdom, such as his friend
Cornplanter, would prevail and hold the Seneca aloof from
the coming carnage.

So, as he read the correspondence from the flame-haired
Englishwoman whose appearance in his life had been foretold
by the manitous, his thoughts were a mixture of knowledge, a
sense of duty, and a burning love that would be cooled only
by holding Beth in his arms.

He felt a powerful urge to leap to his feet, prepare his
travel kit, and run toward the east. Once he actually stood,
letter in hand, his heart pounding in rhythm to Beth's words
of love, but reason prevailed for a few more minutes as the
dates on the letters began to measure more and more time
following his departure from Wilmington and Beth's longing
for him became more apparent.

The fire had been replenished several times before Renno,
in no hurry to devour the letters since they gave him a
feeling of being near Beth, which he wanted to prolong,
reached the bottom of the stack. There he found an envelope
of a different sort. It bore the seal of Lord Beaumont and was
addressed to Renno in care of Beth by the sweeping, mascu-
line hand of William Huntington, Beth's brother. William
had been—and still was in spite of the distance that separated
them—a good friend. He had been brave and dependable,
and he had fought well in the Southwest when Renno had

led a small group in search of gold. Ordinarily Renno would have been delighted to hear from William, but now the letter seemed intrusive. He wanted nothing to impinge on the mood created by Beth's words of love. He put Beth's letters into a deerskin pouch to protect them, left the letter from William unopened, and went out into the early morning cold. The stars, bright lights in the sky, glistened sharply. The absence of a moon seemed to deepen the loneliness he felt.

The impulse to move, to use his muscles, to feel the ground passing beneath his feet became strong in him. He ducked back into the longhouse and seized his weapons. The English longbow presented to him by William was slung over his shoulder, with a quiver of arrows. The Spanish stiletto hung in its ornate sheath at his side. His tomahawk, the blade always honed to razor sharpness, took its place with a pistol and a powder-and-shot bag. The long-barreled musket was left behind because he would travel light.

He made one stop. El-i-chi, still grieving for the wife he had loved for so short a time, no longer shared a house with other young warriors but had his own house on the edge of the village. Renno woke him carefully, giving the call of an owl from his doorway. One did not carelessly awaken a warrior as tightly strung as El-i-chi lest one was quick to dodge the defensive swing of a tomahawk or a knife.

El-i-chi sat, wrapping a bearskin around himself against the cold. The light of dawn was just beginning to penetrate the darkness inside the lodge.

"My brother is awake early," El-i-chi said. "Does he have something in mind?" His tone was hopeful.

"My heart cries out for the solitude of the forests," Renno said. They spoke Seneca, a language that was more expressive than English, in which he would have said, "I need to get away for a while."

El-i-chi sighed, his hopes that Renno had decided to do something exciting dashed. But he understood. "I will tell the others." He had seen the large packet of letters from Beth, and because he himself had loved, he knew the fire of longing that must be burning in his brother. "Roy won't mind. It'll give him some time alone with Little Hawk and Renna."

Then, where Renno had stood, there was only the empty

darkness, even though the skins that covered the doorway had scarcely moved. El-i-chi sighed again and nestled back into his bed. As far as he was concerned, unless a hunt was scheduled, there was absolutely no reason to greet the dawn.

Renno put distance between himself and the villages—the smaller village of the Seneca, which almost joined with the larger Cherokee village, where more and more log cabins in the style of the white man were appearing. He ran very near capacity, his moccasined feet seeming scarcely to touch the frozen ground. Since he was in friendly territory, he ran for speed and release, not for silence, and as the sun rose, his chest was heaving, his lungs billowing, his breath making panting sounds.

He ran at full tilt down a slope of browned grasses, leapt a small stream on the fly, and drove himself up the opposite slope. There he eased his pace. Gradually his tortured lungs pumped more easily, and his heart slowed to match his steady, ground-covering warrior's pace.

He ran to the southeast, but his heart ran directly toward the sun, toward the distant blue line of mountains beyond which was North Carolina and a journey through white towns and settlements to the Cape Fear River and Wilmington. He could punish his body. He could stretch every muscle to capacity. He could cover ten miles, a hundred, a thousand, but if those miles were not traveled in the direction that led to Beth, he would feel the same: incomplete.

It was midafternoon before he halted long enough to drink from an icy, clear stream. Then he was moving again, cautiously, silently, his legs gliding in the pace that could move a well-conditioned Seneca raiding party sixty miles in a day and still leave them the strength and energy necessary to win battles.

There were a few Cherokee homesites in the area through which he traveled, but he avoided them. All around him were Cherokee lands. To the northeast were Knoxville and the spreading white settlements. To the south were the hunting grounds of the Choctaw, but he would not be traveling so far. To the east lay the mountains. Around him were the virgin forests. He struck the spoor of a deer, but he was not on the hunt. He startled and was startled by a covey of quail and leapt into a pose of combat readiness even as he laughed at himself. The explosive rise of those small, sturdy birds was always a surprise.

He ran into a small valley between two hogbacked ridges. A stream sparkled there, meandering through a mixture of evergreen, pines, and cedars, and barren, winter-stripped hardwoods. In one spot the stream had carved out a sandy, pebbly nook enclosed by cedars, the pebbles strewn with deadwood drifted there during times of flood. He cooled his racing heart and hot, coursing blood by walking, a silent wraith moving like a shadow among the trees, to scout out the immediate surroundings. He gathered the deadwood and built a fire, then gathered evergreen branches and placed them under the bank of the little cove. He was dressed lightly, wearing only buckskins and no skin robe. A weather change was in the making, the feathery clouds moving swiftly toward the northeast as fitful winds came and went. He had not brought food. Provisions were the last thing on his mind. But he had water from the stream.

His thoughts ranged far as night closed in with the rise of a cold wind and a darkening of the sky that hid the stars. Sleet began to rattle down onto the pebbles. The temperature had dropped precipitously since sundown. Renno arranged his evergreen limbs under the overhang of the bank, and the sleet became a cascade of sound, hissing as it melted in the campfire. The cold was a thing with fangs, digging into his body so that he shivered involuntarily. He added deadwood to the fire.

He had punished himself by running hard, and now the spirits were cooperating by sending him miserable weather—since it seemed that his desire was to be punished for having a longing that ran counter to his duty as sachem.

A grin showed his strong white teeth. He sat with his legs crossed, his long hair brushing against exposed roots on the underside of the peaty overhang. *Yes*, the white Indian told himself, *if the desire is to be punished, then enjoy it, for you are being blessed with a night of it*. He relaxed, ignored the cold, and let his mind idle. He saw in his memories the frozen, deep-snowed wilderness of the North, where his forefathers had lived and hunted and fought; remembered the brotherhood that had been extended to him by the Seneca there and reviewed his talks with the wise sachem Cornplanter; and then he saw a vision of Hodano, evil shaman of the split tongue, avowed servant of the dark spirits. The wind howled as it gusted, blowing stinging barbs of sleet into Renno's face.

He tensed and had his hand on his tomahawk, for in the swirl of sleet he had seen other movement. It was there . . . and yet it was not there. He squinted and leaned forward.

An area of calm formed on the other side of the fire, an area free of wind and sleet. There was wispy movement that seemed to solidify, and Renno cried out in spite of himself, for he saw the old, beloved face of his grandmother Ah-wen-ga, who had gone to the Place Across the River during the winter before.

"Grandmother!" he cried happily.

She smiled. Only once before had the spirits come to him without his first having fasted and meditated. Ah-wen-ga extended her hands toward him. He understood: the gesture was one of love and encouragement, but she did not want him to approach.

"I am troubled, Grandmother," he admitted.

A gust of wind swirled the sleet and whipped the struggling flames.

Her voice, so familiar, seemed to be more from inside his head than from out of the air. "The wisdom of Ghonkaba, of Ja-gonh, of the first Renno, are yours. You have done well."

"For this I am thankful. Without the guidance of my ancestors—"

She silenced him with an impatient gesture. "It was your wisdom that decided it is not yet time to take our people back to the ancestral lands of the North."

There was a long silence, and he feared that she was gone, for the wind howled and the sleet clattered loudly around him. Already the ground was covered with the unmelting icy beads.

"Other matters distress me," he confessed. "Grandmother?"

She was there, smiling as she had in life, and he could imagine her as she had been when he was a child, a beauty with enormous dark eyes, so beautiful that the king of France had desired her.

"The old order is changing," the spirit said without sadness. "Others will join us soon, beyond the River."

Renno felt a stab of loss, for he was very much aware that two he loved and respected were at the age of being called: Loramas, who had been but a husk of a man since the death of his beloved Ah-wen-ga; and old Casno, who had fought with Ghonkaba in the War of the American Revolution.

"Do not be sad," the spirit counseled. "They have earned their rest. And do not feel guilty about your love for the flame-haired woman. Her coming, foretold by the manitous, has a purpose in your life. That purpose is not yet fully accomplished. Drink in her love, Grandson, and thank the manitous for your happiness."

A flood of warmth came to Renno. For a moment he felt as if nothing would do but to leap to his feet and dance a dance of victory, but he saw the vision fading and reached out a hand. "Guide me, Grandmother."

"We are with you," the spirit soothed.

A clash of war came into Renno's mind—the scream of a wounded horse, the shrill cries of attacking warriors, the terminal groan of a dying man—and around him he felt, as he had at other times when death was everywhere and men struggled against other men, the army of the manitous, the spirits of those who had passed to the Place Across the River, for, he knew, a Seneca warrior never marched alone.

"Not true," the spirit contradicted, her voice fading. "Not true. The truth of this is far away, and the living march alone in distant places."

Blowing sleet stung his face. The campfire flickered as it fought the onslaught of the sleet.

"We watch," the fading voice warned as Renno strained to hear. "We can only watch."

"Grandmother," he said softly, but the manitou was gone. The little cove was shrouded in sleet, and the wind howled.

Renno endured a night of cold that saw ice form along the edges of the swift-flowing stream as the sleet piled to a depth of inches. He had only his fire, which he carefully tended, then gazed into its flames and embers, trying to see the future. But he was only a man, who had not the gift of the manitous to see. He pondered the words of the spirit of his grandmother. Once he loosed the challenge of a bear, a guttural roaring, as if he sought reassurance through an an-

swer from that most potent of his clan's totems, but there was
only the sleet hissing in his ears.

The day dawned foul and dark, and the sleet turned to a
freezing rain that coated the branches of the trees in a sheath
of ice diamonds. Still he sat, hoping for clarification, praying
for further guidance. Then, chilled and aching in every limb,
he moved through the icy rain, soon risked the warrior run,
and reached his village after midnight, his feet finding inse-
cure purchase on the ice-covered ground.

Someone had tended his fire so that he had only to add
wood, and with his great bear robe wrapped around him, he
stopped shivering.

At last he opened the letter from William Huntington and
felt a sense of foreboding as he unfolded the sheets of paper
inside. He looked around quickly—it was almost as if a spirit
of evil had touched him, but he accepted it as a warning.

He had known that a change was coming, that he would be
leaving the village. He had been certain of that from the time
Ah-wen-ga's spirit had come to him, for the manitous did not
speak to him in times of calm. He began to get an inkling of
the meaning of Ah-wen-ga's warning as he read William's
letter:

If I ask too much, forgive me, for I know you have
responsibilities of your own.

It was almost as if Renno could hear William's voice, deep
and warm, with that crisp English accent. He could envision
William's face and see him standing beside Estrela Isabel de
Mendoza, the woman he had rescued from the Apache, then
married.

William Huntington stated his request simply. Roberto,
Estrela's only living sibling, was missing, kidnapped by pirates. Roberto de Mendoza had set sail from the New Spain
port of Vera Cruz, aboard a Spanish merchantman with a final
destination of Spain. But Roberto's plans to visit that country
had been dashed when the ship was seized by pirates. As a
supplement to William's letter, there was a neatly written
ransom demand for a great deal of gold, with instructions as
to how to make a rendezvous with the kidnappers.

Renno skipped over the instructions and concentrated on

the problem. William's letter stated that he had sent the ransom to Beth on the same ship that carried his letter:

I'm sure that you found yourself in the same position as I, for I know of your wonderful plans for helping your people with your share of the Apache gold. My share diminished quickly. The debts piled up by my lovable but profligate father took most. I had to scrounge deeply to raise the ransom money.

Renno put the letters aside and stood, hands at his side, his eyes not seeing the walls of the lodge but great distances—the sea. And he seemed to hear the words spoken by the spirit of Ah-wen-ga: "The living march alone in distant places. We can only watch."

Part of him was rejoicing. He would see Beth, for he would have to travel to Wilmington to get the ransom gold and to use one of Beth's ships. He would see her and hold her and be with her. Ah-wen-ga's warning, however, had not been given lightly. To do this thing for William meant leaving his children and his people. And it was not as if he would be setting out on a land journey. A man of the wilderness, he never lacked faith and confidence with his feet on dry land, whether it be the sunbaked sands of the southwestern deserts or the forests of far Canada. Now he was being asked to leave his country, to take to the sea, an unfamiliar territory governed by the caprice of the elements and dangers he could not anticipate.

But William was his friend, and he would see Beth.

Roy Johnson was playing with Little Hawk and Renna in the central compound when Renno awakened from an exhausted sleep. The weather had turned once more, and a benevolent sun brightened the sky and had begun to dry the earth of the swiftly melting ice and sleet. The children greeted Renno warmly, but it was evident that, although they loved their father, they were having entirely too much fun with Granddad to bother with Renno. He tugged Renna's pigtails lightly and patted Little Hawk on the head and walked on, alone with his thoughts. He found himself in the Cherokee village, near the lodge of Se-quo-i. The young Cherokee was at work carving a new false face for the coming celebration of spring's renewal, a Seneca ceremony that had caught the fancy of many Cherokee. The mask was for Little Hawk, who, as son of the sachem, was entitled to wear it and join older and wiser men in the rites.

Renno's thoughts were too distracting to allow for an enjoyable visit, so he excused himself shortly after entering Sequo-i's lodge.

When Renno arrived back at the house of Toshabe and Ha-ace, the family was at the midday meal. Renno took his place and, to the pleasure of his mother, did justice to the good venison stew and corn soup. When the meal was finished, Renno spoke, telling them the contents of the letter from William Huntington. Ha-ace, a worthy warrior but not a sachem, kept his silence. Toshabe, sensing that her son's mind was already made up, merely nodded.

It was Roy Johnson who spoke. "You would, of course, go first to Wilmington."

"Yes," Renno answered.

Johnson smiled. He could not totally submerge his futile desire for Emily to be alive, to share the love of this man whom he had come to love and respect so greatly, but Emily was dead, and Renno had another wife.

"Do it, Son," Roy encouraged. "Take Renna and Little Hawk with you to Wilmington."

Toshabe looked up quickly, a frown of disapproval forming.

"This one is as wild as a buck," Roy continued, tousling Little Hawk's fair hair. "And Renna needs to learn a bit of the ways of the whites. Beth is a fine woman. She's going to make a good mother to these two. They can stay with Beth while you're exchanging the ransom for the Mendoza boy. You shouldn't be gone long."

Toshabe had reconciled herself to having to share the children with Roy Johnson and his wife and knew that sooner or later Renna especially would have to spend time in Knoxville. But this new threat caused her to speak. "I see no reason to expose two as young as these to the dangers of a long journey."

"Grandmother—" Little Hawk began. He was silenced by Roy with a hand over his mouth.

Renno spoke quietly, as became the sachem. "I will be

with them." It was a simple statement, but it said more than was immediately apparent. Even though Toshabe was his mother, she knew that the issue was decided, that she should speak no more. But she spoke, for she was a woman, and a grandmother.

"Then you must take a woman along to care for them on the trail and to be a known face when you leave them alone with Beth in Wilmington."

Renno did not want to be burdened with a woman on the trip. He wanted to travel fast. But he knew his mother, so he nodded agreement.

Ah-wa-o, daughter of Ha-ace, had been doing her duty by serving the elder members of the family and was still eating. When she heard Toshabe's words, she swallowed quickly and said, "Mother, please, I have wanted to see more of the world."

"Yes, let's take Ah-wa-o," Little Hawk piped. Both he and Renna loved the girl in whose care they were often left. As for Renno, he had accepted Ah-wa-o as the sister she had become when his mother married the panther. She was young—what was she, fifteen?—but she was a solid-minded Seneca girl steeped in that nation's traditions by her father.

"With your permission, Ha-ace," Renno said, "it will be Ah-wa-o who accompanies us."

Ha-ace looked at his daughter with a fond smile. "Just so she doesn't see too much of the white man's world and begin to get ideas not becoming to a Seneca maiden."

"Oh, I won't," Ah-wa-o promised.

Ah-wa-o had rejoiced when she had become a part of the family of the sachem. It was an honor beyond her dreams to be sister to the greatest warrior who had ever lived, for that was how she viewed Renno. She was also sister to El-i-chi, a man she thought was the most handsome of warriors, even more handsome than Renno. It was odd the way she felt about El-i-chi. With Renno she was a proud younger sister, eager to please him, always trying to discover something that she could do for him. With El-i-chi she became years younger and miles shier, almost unable to speak in his presence. El-i-chi, who was a great man of twenty-two years, a shaman, a war leader, and an exceptional warrior, had the habit of patting Ah-wa-o on the head, as if she were a child like Renna, and teasing her fondly.

"What should I pack?" Ah-wa-o asked eagerly.

"It will be cold during the first part of our journey," Renno said, "but we will travel as lightly as possible."

"I will handle the packing," Toshabe declared.

Roy went outside to enjoy a pipe of the rich local tobacco. Renno followed him, and they discussed the route the white Indian would follow, taking into consideration that the mountain passes could still be snowed in deeply. Then the young man went to his lodge to see to his weapons and his clothing. With Renno, a decision once made was quickly put into action. They would leave immediately after the feast of the new beginning.

It took only hours for the news to reach the ears of almost everyone in both villages. Winter was a slow and unexciting time, so any news traveled swiftly. Renno was honing the edge of his stiletto when El-i-chi burst in, his usually stoic face brightened by a grin.

"Don't deny me," El-i-chi said.

Renno answered the grin and shrugged. "It is not a job for two warriors."

"I will go," El-i-chi said.

"If your hunger to be back among the pale faces is so great . . ." Renno acquiesced.

El-i-chi let out a whoop and was gone. Renno thought he was returning almost immediately, but the face that appeared in his door was that of the young Cherokee Se-quo-i.

"Sachem," Se-quo-i said, "is it true that you journey to the sea?"

"It is true." Renno tried to hide a smile.

"I have been working this winter with the books of the white man," Se-quo-i said. "I have gone as far as I can. I would travel among them, to gain their wisdom—for what it is worth—and to study their ways."

Renno rose and put his hand on Se-quo-i's shoulder. "I could ask for no more worthy a traveling companion."

"Thank you, Sachem," Se-quo-i said with a glad smile.

"It might be a good idea to pass the word that Renno's traveling party is complete, lest so many decide to make this journey that the people of North Carolina go up in arms to repel an invasion," Renno suggested.

He was uneasy as night came. The evening meal was enjoyed, and Renna stayed with Toshabe and Ah-wa-o while Little Hawk slept with his grandfather. Renno was alone. He had difficulty falling asleep. Even with the assurances from the spirit of his grandmother and Roy that he was doing the right thing, he would have preferred to remain in the village, at the head of his people.

He daydreamed about leading his Seneca west into new lands, but it was only idle speculation, for such an action would mean war with the tribes already living in the western territories. One day perhaps he could lead his people north and reunite them with the Seneca, but that was where white expansionism was exerting the greatest pressure on the ancestral hunting grounds of many tribes. Try as he might, he could find no solution to the problem he faced each day of his life—the danger of the relatively small band of Seneca being assimilated into the Cherokee culture by association and intermarriage.

And when he finally slept he did not find peace. Night terrors came against him. Faceless giants attacked him in his dreams. Eerie animals threatened. He would sit bolt upright in bed time after time, covered with sweat and his fists tightly clenched around the hafts of nonexistent weapons, and tell himself that they were only creatures of a dream. But when he slept again, the terrors sought him out.

He took his prescribed part in the traditional rites celebrating the victory of good over evil, the new beginning when the forces of darkness, embodied in winter snow and ice, were once again defeated by the forces of good, the sun and coming spring. But on the night before leaving the village he fought sleep. He had fasted for three days and had sent his chants for guidance to the manitous, but it was not his manitous but the spirits of evil who visited him there in the dark of his lodge in the early hours of a winter morning. In his dreams he searched for help, for the great stone ax and the spirit knife that had been sent to him by the manitous and had seen him through terrible dangers, but the ax had been returned to the spirits and the spirit knife had crumbled to dust, its job done.

He had only his strength against monstrous animals and evil spirits. In his bed he sweated, rolled, and managed to survive, but throughout the attacks, as he relived the onslaught of spirit wolves and battled against unseen threats from the unknown, flashed the brooding, evil face of the shaman Hodano. The wolverine cowl was thrown back to expose the full horror of Hodano's scarred visage. The one good eye gleamed red with hatred.

The vision was still with Renno when he awoke. He chanted, asking explanation from the manitous, but there was no response.

The trip was to be made on horseback. One packhorse was needed just to carry cooking equipment and spare clothing for Ah-wa-o and the children. Roy rode along as far as Knoxville. In a cheery camp with a blazing fire Ah-wa-o proved her womanly skills by feeding all of them well. When Renno retired to his sleeping skins, he slept soundly and awoke refreshed. It was as if the evil dreams had been left behind. He was on the move again, and travel always pleased him. He had seen more of the wilderness and more of the settled areas of the United States than most men, but there was always in him that desire to see more, to travel to the next river, to the next range of mountains.

There was a bit of potential unpleasantness when, in Knoxville, Nora Johnson discovered Renno was taking her two grandchildren all the way to the North Carolina coast, over three hundred miles of hard travel, most of which would be done in winter's cold. Roy spoke firmly to his wife, telling her that the trip would be good for the children. In private Nora wept and had to be reminded that Renno was, after all, the children's father.

On the morning of a crisp, clean day Roy escorted the group—Renno, El-i-chi, Se-quo-i, Ah-wa-o, Little Hawk, and Renna—some miles from town. He told them good-bye there, then rode back to Knoxville, where he held Nora in his arms and reassured her that Renno was fully capable of taking care of his own and that the younguns were tough little nuts who would not be adversely affected by being out in a bit of weather.

The miles could not be covered quickly enough for Renno.
The journey was just begun, the Smoky Mountains were still
to be crossed, but he was Renno again—the alert master
hunter who consistently and successfully hunted fresh meat
for his little band.

Now the tortuous trail led up, up, winding in and around
the western approaches to the main Smoky Mountain range.
As the trail followed the French Broad River up a narrow
valley, the group saw signs of deer and bear in the snow, and
once Renno, in the lead, caught a glimpse of black as a bulky
animal crossed the trail ahead of him. He halted and waited
until the others came abreast. He motioned for silence and
lifted his head to give forth the hunting call of a great bear. A
moment later the answer came from the other side of the
river. The bear had moved fast.

"We don't kill bears," Little Hawk stated importantly.

"No, we do not," Renno confirmed.

Little Hawk turned to his sister, who was riding with
El-i-chi, so bundled that only her bright blue eyes and slightly
reddened nose showed out from her warm furs. "Renno talks
with the great bears," he said, "for the bear is the chief totem
of our clan. We are Bear Clan."

His uncle El-i-chi laughed. "It is one thing for Renno to
speak with bears," he said. "If *you* see one, small warrior,
you will run like the wind, for it might be a bear who doesn't
realize that he is a totem."

Little Hawk cocked his head. "No bear would harm one
with the blood of the original Renno."

"Nevertheless," Renno warned, "you will stay in your position in the group, and you will not wander alone into the
forests."

"I hear," Little Hawk said.

A few Cherokee braved the winter in the high mountains,
most of them living in log cabins. Many were known to
Renno, and he to them. Thus it was that a few nights were
spent comfortably sleeping on rough plank floors in front of a
fireplace, the travelers paying for their meals and comfort
with news from the main body of Cherokee to the west and
with tales of war, for all Indians loved a good story. And
when a warrior of the stature of Renno or El-i-chi told, for
example, how El-i-chi had used a combination of white man's

fireworks and Seneca lore to defeat the evil Hodano, it was not a brag but a fact, and worthy of the listening. In return the isolated mountain dwellers warned the travelers of obstacles ahead—for example, how deep the snow had drifted in a certain pass. The highest passes were still ahead, and the trip was delayed for two days by a snowstorm. The Cherokee who had offered his hospitality urged them to wait for a few days, for a thaw was due. Winter was, he told them, having its one last victory.

Each mile traveled put Renno closer to Beth. He led the group out into the fresh snow, which came several inches up on the legs of the horses.

"This is not snow," El-i-chi told Little Hawk and Ah-wa-o, who seemed always to be near. "This is but a sprinkling of snow. In the north where our ancestors lived—there you see real snow, so deep that a horse could not walk."

"I like snow," Little Hawk responded. "When I am a man I will go see these northern snows."

"Snow cold," Renna added.

Chapter III

White settlers moving west had found the Great Smoky Mountains to be a formidable obstacle, effectively separating the settled areas in the would-be state of Franklin from the more populated areas of the Old North State, North Carolina. Cherokee hunters and loners, however, had traversed the convoluted mountains and steep gorges for generations. Renno's party did not always follow the established trails but often took an alternate route in order to make travel time shorter, skirting gorges and mountains instead of bulling through or over them in the stubborn manner of the white man.

It was cold, but for children of the wilderness the cold was familiar, something that was accepted, something to which even young Renna had become inured. To an observer from another place or time, it might have seemed that those who rode through the knee-deep snow were also inured to the natural beauty of the gleaming, snow-covered mountains, the pines wearing formal gowns of white. No one rhapsodized the beauty, but not one of them was unaware of it. Ah-wa-o was all eyes, unable to see enough, alert for each new vista as a ridge was topped.

The going was slow, and this chafed Renno. Soon they would be at the highest point of the route, in a pass where the snow gleamed with a brightness that hurt the eyes, and he looked forward to telling the others that the worst was past. He made camp beside an ice-fringed stream, and soon cheery fires were burning, and the aromas of food and coffee, that one white man's habit that had been adopted by Renno, filled the little glade. As he lay in his sleeping skins, the stars were so bright that they seemed to sing to him, and when he awoke, the sky was cloudless, the day perfect.

Their climb began immediately after breaking camp. The trail made great switchbacks as it scaled the sheer side of a mountain. Renno was in the lead, walking, leading his and Little Hawk's horse. The boy perched on the back of the horse, snug and warm in a bundle of furs and skins, now and then offering advice to his father about the route. Se-quo-i was carrying Renna in his arms while leading his own horse. Walking behind him was Ah-wa-o, also leading her horse and once again managing to take the position nearest El-i-chi. He brought up the rear, leading both his horse and the packhorse.

Wind had partially denuded the trail of snow so that the going was easy except where ice had formed from the runoff of some earlier thaw. To the right a steep drop stretched down a snow-covered slope to a thin band of trees, which began a hundred feet down the slope. The mountain, dense with pines and spruce, towered over them and seemed, to Ah-wa-o, to be insurmountable, endless. She was looking up, wondering if they would ever reach the summit of these imposing heights, when she stepped on ice and felt both feet going out from under her.

The horse snorted in fear as Ah-wa-o fell, tugging on the reins. She made just one startled sound before losing the reins and sliding feet first over the drop.

Renno froze when he heard El-i-chi's sharp yip-yip of

warning, then turned to see a form sliding down the steep
slope. "Stay exactly where you stand and do not move," he
told Little Hawk. He ran back down the trail.

El-i-chi had moved quickly. Even as Ah-wa-o was sliding
down the snowy slope at an ever-increasing speed, he was
searching for a way to get down to her without taking the
dangerous slide that could send him hurtling into a tree down
below.

Ah-wa-o moved in silence, not screaming, her hands claw-
ing, trying desperately to find purchase in the snow to slow
her fall. She crashed into a small bush, and the impact caused
her to gasp in shock, and then she glanced off the bole of a
tree and crashed into low-growing brush.

Renno stood directly above the marks of Ah-wa-o's swift
passage down the slope and realized that there was only a
narrow band of evergreen trees and low brush between Ah-
wa-o and a vertical drop into the gorge—a fall that would,
should she somehow slide through the band of trees, kill her
instantly. He saw El-i-chi leave the trail at an angle, leap,
bury his feet into the snow, leap again, going down in great
strides. There was no need to send two men after the girl.

"Where Ah-wa-o?" Renna asked Se-quo-i, who, awestruck
by El-i-chi's rescue attempt, could not respond.

El-i-chi missed his footing, and he tumbled and rolled to
come up short against a tree trunk, but at last he was down
the steep slope. He felt his side. It would be bruised, but
there were no broken ribs. He began to make his way down,
clinging to trees and brush. He followed the marks of Ah-
wa-o's passage through the snow, and as he neared the end of
growth and looked out over the sheer drop of hundreds of
feet to the gorge, a strong cold wind blasted him in the face.
He saw nothing of the girl. He edged closer and called her
name.

She was gone. The world fell away dizzyingly just ahead of
him, and the marks of her slide dropped out of sight over the
edge. His heart leapt when he heard Ah-wa-o's voice.

"I am here," she told him. "Hurry."

He threw himself down, dug into the snow with his hands
and toes, pulled himself forward carefully. He looked over
the drop, and there was one more ledge below, short of the
cliffs. He still could not see her.

"I can't hold on much longer," she added, her voice quite calm.

El-i-chi knew from her labored breathing that he had only moments. Moving to the edge of the cliff, he jerked the tomahawk from his belt and smashed it hard into the snow, sinking the blade into the frozen earth. He tested the strength of its hold and eased himself out toward the edge of the ledge. There he used his knife to cut footholds, then braced himself. Jerking the tomahawk's haft to free it, he drove it again into the frozen earth, this time to lower himself onto the small, narrow ledge below.

He looked down. Just below that steep, snowy platform there had grown one stunted seedling pine, and it was to the bole of that small tree that Ah-wa-o was clinging, dangling precariously over the gorge.

He was near enough now, if he lay with his body stretched along the ledge, to reach down to Ah-wa-o. As he did so, he realized that the seedling pine was in danger of being ripped out of the cliffside by the girl's weight. He extended his arm and could touch her hands on the tree.

"Can you take my hand?" He kept his voice very calm.

"I'll try."

As she moved a little cascade of snow fell from around the base of the tiny tree, but she clasped his hand and he squeezed tightly. Her hand was small and cold in his.

"Now take your other hand off the tree and clasp it around my wrist."

It was done. He pulled. She tried to crawl, but that sent a clatter of hard snow and ice down the precipice. "Just relax, Sister," El-i-chi advised her. "Let me pull you."

Stretched as he was, with one hand clinging to the tomahawk, the other reaching down as far as possible, it was a strain, but he pulled steadily and she was able to gain the ledge with her knees. Then she was lying beside him on that narrow platform, her fingers digging into his flesh from the intensity of her grip on his hand and arm.

"Now," he said, "come closer to me. Use my body as a stepping-stone, and stand up until you can reach the brush."

For a moment they were face to face, noses only inches apart, her large dark eyes looking into his. "You are brave, little Ah-wa-o," he commended. "You can do it."

He had never really seen her before, he realized. She was quite beautiful, the Seneca maiden personified, young, vital, just coming into her period of greatest appeal. But it was no time for the appreciation of the beauty of his sister. He urged her on. He dug his hand into the snow when she released it and clung instead to his body, pulling herself up, putting her weight on him. Then she pushed on slowly until she was standing on his back.

"I can pull myself up now," she said.

"Carefully," he encouraged.

He felt a push of her feet against his back, and then she was scrambling up, and snow was falling atop him. He waited for a moment.

"I am secure," she said.

He moved slowly and carefully, using the tomahawk for purchase, and breathed easier when he, too, was off the ledge and clinging to sturdy brush. It took a while to guide Ah-wa-o upward to the trail, for they had to travel at an angle. He pulled her onto the trail about fifty yards below the point where the others waited. She stood and looked up at him, her lips parted and her eyes full of tears and an expression that puzzled El-i-chi for a moment until he realized that he had seen it before, in the eyes of Holani. It was a look of pure adoration. He felt rather guilty, for Ah-wa-o was, after all, his little sister.

She collapsed slowly, so slowly with the little smile still on her face that he was easily able to catch her before she hit the snow. He lifted her into his arms. Even through the furs and buckskins, he was aware of the form of her, the softness. He stood for a moment, looking down into the most beautiful face he had ever seen. He glanced up toward the others quickly, as if they, even at a distance, could read his thoughts and know the swift pleasure he felt. Then he submerged such thoughts and walked up the trail.

He carried her for an hour, then she was conscious and able to sit on her horse. Nothing seemed to be broken, but she was badly bruised. Her right ankle was swollen and painful. It was not practical to stop and treat her injuries in the windy, cold pass, and El-i-chi was proud of the way she endured her pain. At last, late in the day, they made camp in good shelter at the bottom of a gorge.

El-i-chi was, after all, a medicine man, a shaman trained by old Casno. He knew how to ease the pain of a man wounded in battle and could set broken bones and lash them into place with splints. He had never examined a young girl closely, however, for the treatment of injured or ill females was left to the women. At first, when the fire was warm and he had constructed a shelter for Ah-wa-o, he merely examined her swollen ankle and determined that it was sprained.

"You will not be able to walk on it for a few days," told her.

"It does not hurt too much."

El-i-chi knew pain when he saw it. In spite of the cold a beading of fine perspiration was on Ah-wa-o's upper lip and forehead. "Something else bothers you," he said.

"Bruises, that's all," she said, not able to meet his eyes.

"Tell me where."

She turned her head away.

"Where?"

She burst into tears.

El-i-chi spoke sternly. "Ah-wa-o, we are far from home. There are no women here to help you. I am skilled in such things. Tell me where you are hurt."

In answer she rolled onto her stomach. El-i-chi was about to speak more harshly, thinking that she was turning away from him, when he saw that she was pointing to a spot on her left buttock. He bent closer to see a rip in her buckskins and the brown stain of dried blood. He opened the rip in her clothing a bit and saw more dried blood.

"I will have to take a closer look," he said.

She made a sound but did not move. He loosened her belt and pulled down her buckskin trousers as she lifted her hips to help him.

El-i-chi had been married, and his brief time with the spirited Chickasaw girl Holani had been a time of happiness. He was a man of some experience, and he was a medicine man, but his lips went dry as he saw the budding, delicate form of Ah-wa-o. Since the death of his wife he had felt no urge to seek out another woman and no desire to express his natural passions. He told himself that his strong and unexpected reaction now was nothing more than appreciation of feminine beauty. After all, he told himself, Ah-wa-o was his sister.

But only by marriage, a small voice seemed to whisper to him.

The moment of weakness passed. He took control of himself. He melted snow and kept it on the fire until the water was warm. Then he washed away the blood from her buttock.

A dry, brittle stick had penetrated her flesh. It was, at the surface, about a quarter inch in diameter. It had broken off, leaving nothing more than splinters protruding. Her skin was swollen around the point of entry and turning an angry red.

"Lie still for a minute," he said, covering her bared rump. He placed his knife in the fire for a few moments and then went back to kneel next to her. "This will hurt."

"I know that you will not hurt me more than necessary," she whispered.

He tried to be gentle, using the cooled point of his knife to pick at the large splinter, but the brittle material just broke away. He clenched his teeth and with one quick motion lanced into her soft flesh. Blood welled up and her muscles tensed in pain, but she did not cry out. He picked the exposed splinter out with the point of his knife, then washed away the blood to be certain that no part of it was left deep inside.

"It is almost done," he soothed, covering her once again.

He heated the point of his knife white-hot in the coals of the fire. He removed a rawhide bracelet from his wrist and told Ah-wa-o to put it in her mouth. "Bite hard," he told her.

White-hot steel sizzled in blood and flesh as he cauterized the wound. Ah-wa-o made one small sound, a mixture of gasp and sob, and then she was still. He applied a soothing balm to the wound and pulled her buckskin trousers back over her shapely rump.

"Do you hurt anywhere else?" he asked gently.

"Praise the manitous, no."

He laughed. "Where are you bruised?"

"Where am I not?"

He was more professional now. He started with her legs and worked up, finding her bruises as she winced. She had a growing black-and-blue spot on her shoulder, exposed as he

opened her shirt, but the skin was not broken anywhere, and
there were no broken bones.

"With some food I think that you will live," El-i-chi announced. He started to rise.

She seized his hand. Her whisper could not have been
heard by the others. "You know my body as no man has ever
known it."

El-i-chi felt himself flushing. He left her, returned with
food and coffee, but he was silent. He could not help but
note that Ah-wa-o's eyes followed his every move.

With the morning the girl was stiff and sore. She tried to
walk, but the pain was too great. "I can't walk and I can't
ride," she told Renno.

"If this were a war march," Little Hawk teased, "we would
have to leave you behind."

"Well, this is not a war march," El-i-chi said, not appreci-
ating his nephew's humor. He busied himself rigging a sling
that was tied over his hips at the back of his waist and
extended down to the front. He asked Se-quo-i to lift Ah-
wa-o into place, her feet pushing down into the sling and her
arms around his neck as she perched on his back. He carried
her all that day, in spite of offers from both Renno and
Se-quo-i to relieve him. All that day he had her body pressed
to his back, her warm breath on the back of his neck, on his
ear. On the third day she managed to sit a horse gingerly,
and he was not entirely grateful to be freed of his burden.

Renno skirted away from the town of Asheville. The traveling was easier now, and the weather was moderating. There
was a sameness for days as the eastern foothills of the mountains were left behind. Now and again they passed home-
steads or encountered white farmers on the muddy roads. All
but Renno and El-i-chi looked at the whites with as much
curiosity as the white people exhibited toward the Indians.
Ah-wa-o came to believe that most whites were hairy, dirty,
and pale. She wondered if Little Hawk would look as untidy
as these white men when he grew up, but then she glanced
at his father and his uncle, clean-shaven by virtue of scraping
their faces with a well-honed knife each morning, and had
hope.

Little Hawk, who was just beginning to realize that although he was Seneca, he was different, was very puzzled when a white woman, bundled into dark, dirty-looking clothing, leaned out of a passing buggy and said loudly, "What air them filthy Injuns doin' chere?"

While traveling through a state as old as North Carolina, it was impossible to avoid all contact with the population. "We are not here to fight," Renno reminded El-i-chi, who was steaming after a series of insulting remarks and rude stares.

"There are times when I think we should go north, join with Little Turtle, and fight all whites," El-i-chi growled.

"Against men like Roy Johnson and George Washington?" Renno asked.

The discussion was to continue for many days. After passing the growing city of Charlotte, Little Hawk said, "White people are pretty strange."

"There are good and bad white people," Renno replied, "just as there are good and bad Indians. If we were traveling through Chickasaw lands, we would be faced with more than curiosity and insults."

"But why do they hate us?" Little Hawk asked.

"Because they fear us," El-i-chi said fiercely.

Unlike the others, Se-quo-i took every opportunity to converse with white farmers, travelers, and storekeepers. Some treated him rudely; others, impressed by his command of the English language, exchanged information and answered questions, so there were times when Se-quo-i, delayed in conversation, had to ride hard to catch up with his companions.

They rode into spring in the flat, piney, marshy reaches of eastern North Carolina, and there were times under blue skies when Renno fancied he could smell the sea. They had been eating white man's food for some time, and no one was particularly happy with that diet. Camped among pines, with great swamps on both sides, Renno made a brief excursion and killed a four-foot alligator. He had encountered alligator tail as a food while among the Seminole in Florida, and the fresh meat was a welcome addition to their rations. Nothing would do for Little Hawk but to hear, once again, Renno's story of his Florida adventures, so it was relatively late before the children were asleep.

The stars did not seem as bright there, so close to the sea. They were dim and distant, and the air was heavy with moisture. Little Hawk's bed was near his uncle El-i-chi's. El-i-chi, still awake and restless, was in turn quite near Ah-wa-o. Since her fall down the mountain, Renno had noted that his brother had always been at the girl's side, treating her with a deference that was new to him. Renna slumbered peacefully beside her father, so Renno, sensing that something was on Se-quo-i's mind, made himself available to the Cherokee, sipping one last cup of coffee by the fire. Se-quo-i, too, was drinking coffee.

"So we adapt to some of the white man's ways," Se-quo-i said without introduction, sloshing coffee around in his mug. "If all things came as easily . . ."

Renno grunted to acknowledge that he heard and understood the meaning.

"We can never live side by side with them," Se-quo-i continued, "and their numbers shame the stars."

"There is some little time left." Renno was in an optimistic mood, being so near his destination and to Beth.

"But the time will come. They uproot the very trees, whereas we supply a village with vegetables and corn and leave the forests relatively untouched. They rip and tear, and the mountains will not hold them back for long," Se-quo-i insisted. "Once I thought we could live with and among them, but now that I've had firsthand experience with the white man on this trip, I'm not so sure."

Renno was silent. Se-quo-i had come to consider a problem that had already plagued the Seneca sachem for a long time.

"We must cultivate the men of goodwill among them," Se-quo-i declared. "Men such as your friend, George Washington. We must convince them that we must have our own lands, perhaps a Cherokee state, as a member of the Union."

"As a state we would be open to settlement by all," Renno pointed out.

"This soil here is poor and sandy," Se-quo-i said. "And yet how many farms have we passed in the last few days? When their masses learn of the rich earth of our lands, will we be able to stop them?"

"Only by learning their ways," Renno answered. "By becoming citizens of the United States so that we have the same rights as they, and by developing our own lands. The time of the hunt will pass, for the presence of people will drive the game away, and then we will have to live by planting the land and by taming cattle, as the white men do."

"Many will fight instead," Se-quo-i warned. "Our traditional ways are too ingrained. Can you see Rusog behind a plow?"

Renno laughed.

"And yet there must be a place for us."

"Where, if we are pushed from our present lands?"

A new voice came into the conversation. "Think of the Mohegan, the Pequot, the Wampanoag, and in this immediate area, the Roanoke, Croatoan, and Pamlico." El-i-chi, the consummate warrior, did not often reveal that he, like his brother, was a student of history. All the tribes he had named were wiped out by the white man, pushed out of their ancestral lands to blend with and become lost among other tribes farther inland. Often those tribes to the inland had, in turn, been killed or pushed farther west.

"Have you heard the history of North Carolina, Se-quo-i?" El-i-chi inquired. "When the white man first arrived, he was met in friendship. He brought death by disease, greed, guns, and cannon. We are probably the only Indians within a hundred miles of Wilmington. When the peaceful tribes rebelled against white aggression, two brothers named Moore marched up from Charleston, in South Carolina, and exterminated all the Indians along the Cape Fear River. *All.* Without exception. Men, women, children. The lands were good for growing rice and indigo, and the Indian makes a poor slave."

"You paint a bleak picture," Se-quo-i said.

"I am not a deep thinker, as you and my brother are," El-i-chi confessed. "I see things simply. In the end it will come to this: either we kill enough of them to discourage them, or they will kill us."

"Perhaps," Se-quo-i allowed.

"Once we were one people," El-i-chi said, not even aware of the irony of such warlike words coming from a man with light-brown hair, blue eyes, and fair skin. "All Indians have a common ancestry. The Seneca and Erie in the north are blood brothers to the Comanche, the Apache, the Osage, and the Choctaw. If we could but bring all tribes together—"

"As Little Turtle is trying to do in the Northwest Territory?" Renno asked.

"All. *All* tribes," El-i-chi said. "It would mean that we might have to fall back, to move to the west, to the buffalo plains where the Comanche live."

"Would you volunteer to take the news to the Comanche that thousands of Seneca, Cherokee, Creek, and Choctaw were moving into their hunting grounds?" Renno asked mildly.

El-i-chi chuckled. "That is why, Brother, I say that I am not a deep thinker. I don't know how to unite all Indians. I merely submit the idea as an ideal solution."

"And the war leader of the grand confederation of tribes would be El-i-chi," Renno said, laughing with his brother although he saw no humor in the talk.

"Well, the final war will not come before morning." El-i-chi yawned. "And soon we will see the river and the great sea."

The last leg of the journey skirted grand plantations where black slaves worked in rice and indigo fields. Hoards of biting insects made life very uncomfortable. The group arrived on the western bank of the Cape Fear River, where there were a few marine-commerce buildings, storehouses, and wharves. Renno looked across the water to the neat little town that began at the water's edge with warehouses and wharves and climbed the bluffs to the south, to the residential area where Beth's house overlooked the river from the height. He saw a great ship tied up to the Huntington wharf and recognized her as the *Seneca Warrior*.

They took a ferry across the river. In that bustling seaport they attracted fewer curious stares than among the inland folk, because ships from all over the world sailed up the river to trade for rice, indigo, cotton, grains, and naval stores from the forests on the west side of the river. Sun-browned, oddly dressed sailors mixed with businessmen. Black slaves in tattered rags seemed to ignore all who came and went on the busy docks. Renno left the others in a compact group and walked to the end of the wharf, where he hailed the *Seneca Warrior*. A familiar face peered down at him, and Moses Tarpley, who had shown his leadership and bravery in the rescue of Beth from the British in Canada, shouted a glad greeting and leapt onto the wharf to seize Renno's hand.

"Mistress Huntington is going to be very pleased to see you," Tarpley said, still grasping Renno's hand. "She was here just an hour ago, but I think she went back to the house. The old man's still supposed to be mostly abed, and she has to keep a close eye on him."

"First I must arrange for a stable for the horses," Renno said.

"You go on about your business," Tarpley urged. "I'll have a man see to the horses. And I'll get a buggy to haul your things to the house."

"That won't be necessary," Renno said, extricating his hand.

"Fine, fine," Tarpley said. "We'll have a talk later. I know you want—"

But Renno was gone, taking long strides toward his destination while beckoning to the others to follow. He led them from the wharf area onto busy Front Street, where they dodged horses and wagons as they crossed Market Street. El-i-chi and Se-quo-i, carrying Renna, joined Renno in the lead. Little Hawk, all eyes, dashed about, now ahead, now lagging behind with Ah-wa-o. It was, to those who saw, an odd procession: three Indian warriors in trail-bedraggled furs and buckskins, a tiny girl, a buckskin-clad boy brimming with curiosity, and an Indian maiden following dutifully.

A lacework brick wall enclosed the front garden of the Huntington house. A wrought-iron gate opened to Renno's eager hands just as the front door burst open.

Beth flew down the steps and onto the brick walk. She was wearing a serviceable black dress touched with white at the throat, and she exposed dark-stockinged legs as she lifted the heavy skirts to run into Renno's arms. Her hair fell a bit during her mad dash down the walk so that it touched her shoulders, a miniature sea of flame. Her green eyes were wet with tears of joy. Her lips had the taste of all that was good, all that was worthwhile.

Renno's companions waited patiently, averting their eyes from the reunion. Finally, flushed, filled with happiness, Renno disengaged himself from Beth's arms and turned. Beth then hurled herself at El-i-chi, squeezing him hard. She grasped Se-quo-i's hand, and then held both of Ah-wa-o's hands in hers as Renno explained that the young girl was his sister, daughter of Ha-ace, who had married his mother. At last Beth turned her attentions to Little Hawk, for Renna had fallen asleep in Se-quo-i's arms. She kneeled, took the boy's shoulders, and looked into his face. "You, young man, are a very handsome warrior."

"She is very pretty," Little Hawk said in Seneca to his father.

"Thank you," Beth said, smiling. "The first time I met you, you wanted my red hair and offered to scalp me." She spoke in the same language, causing Little Hawk to do a double take. "But you were just a little boy then, and I'm sure you don't remember."

Little Hawk blushed very red.

"But now we must get in out of the sun," Beth said, leading the way into the house. Cedric Huntington, the former earl of Beaumont, was resting on a bed in the drawing room. It had been installed there so he would not have to climb stairs. There were greetings and introductions, and then Beth was turning Ah-wa-o and the children over to a servant to be directed to their rooms.

"Knew you'd come, by heaven!" Cedric waved Renno over and patted the bed for him to sit. "Knew we could depend on you, although I question William's sanity in sending good gold after a Spaniard."

"Father . . ." Beth ordered.

"Stop fussing, girl," Cedric said. "It isn't every day we see Renno."

Servants were told to prepare food. Se-quo-i and El-i-chi went to the dining room in their wake. Renno stood, following Beth, unable to get enough of her into his eyes and heart. She came to him in the hallway and clung, lips on his. Then she led him into the dining room and pushed him into a chair. He wasn't hungry, except for the sight of his wife, but he began to eat as she talked.

Cedric Huntington's health was much improved, but his weak heart would allow little physical activity; even walking to the dining table tired him. The shipping business was thriving. Beth had purchased two new ships. The *Seneca*

Warrior had been refitted, with the addition of more fire-power. The only cloud on the horizon was William's request.

Se-quo-i and El-i-chi sat patiently, having finished their meal, listening to Beth's recital of the news. "White civilization has one advantage," El-i-chi said, running a hand through his hair. "As I remember it, there is a fine bathtub in this house."

"Oh, please excuse me for being thoughtless," Beth said. "If you gentlemen want to retire, the servants will show you to your rooms. Please do make yourselves at home."

At last he was alone with her. She sat next to him, reaching to hold his hand. There was a long silence as they looked at each other. "I would have done anything to get you here," she admitted, "and it took William to do it."

"Whatever the reason, I am glad," Renno assured her.

"You're not leaving here without me." She smiled. "Whether it be by ship or by land. The servants can look after my father during my absence. I deserve a short rest."

He had anticipated her intention to accompany him, and his arguments were ready against her going to sea to deliver the ransom money. That, however, could wait.

"Little Hawk has grown so much," Beth said. "He's the proper little warrior now, and Renna is so beautiful. She must look like her mother."

"Very much so," Renno confirmed.

"I think Little Hawk likes me."

"How could he not, when his father feels the way he does?"

"I do so want them to like me, to love me, because we're going to live together as a family, and soon."

"I pray so." But Renno did not feel optimistic. She had said that Cedric's weak heart would be a continuing problem. Would their being together have to wait for her father's death? And what of her thriving shipping business, which she had built through sheer force of will? Would she be content to leave it? He looked around at the lavishly decorated, beautifully furnished room. How long would she be content to live in a Seneca longhouse with dirt floors and skins over the doorway to block the cold of winter, to cook over an open fire as Emily had done, to live in the style of the Seneca?

All those answers would have to come sooner or later, but now he was content just being with her, hearing her voice as she, quite womanlike, told him all the things she had done, felt, and thought since they had last been together.

They left the dining room so the servants could clear the table and prepare for the evening meal. They sat outside on a wooden bench overlooking the river and talked the afternoon away. He came to the table for the evening meal in the same clothing he had worn on arrival. The meal was good, the talk spirited. Cedric came in to join them, and he was in fine fettle, entertaining Little Hawk with tales of life in England.

"At last I have a grandson," Cedric enthused. "And when that nagging daughter of mine allows out of the house, young man, I am going to take you fishing."

"I looked at the water of the river," Little Hawk said. "It's too muddy to spear fish."

"Well, there are other ways," Cedric said.

It seemed an eternity before Renno went up the stairs with Beth on his arm. She had ordered the bathtub filled with hot water and, to Renno's soon-evident pleasure, insisted on washing him. And then they were lying side by side on Beth's huge bed, and for a night Renno had no concerns.

When he awoke, he was alone. He heard the sound of childish laughter coming through the window. He rose lithely, naked, and looked down into the garden at the rear of the house to see Beth and his children. Little Hawk was himself, in buckskins, but Renna's hair was brushed and arranged, and she wore a frilly little dress in light blue that fluffed out with petticoats.

"Can't run, Beff," Renna complained.

"But you look very pretty," Beth told her. "You'll get used to wearing a dress."

Renno knew a moment of uncertainty. Renna was Seneca. She was out of place in a frilly frock and white man's shoes. But then he smiled. Her mother and her grandmother Johnson would approve. His children had to be at home in two worlds, and judging from the way Beth was getting along with both of them, she was going to be a good teacher.

He dressed and went below, wolfed down coffee, beefsteak, eggs, and biscuits, and then walked to the back of the house. He was just getting ready to go out the door when El-i-chi, Se-quo-i, and Ah-wa-o came around the house into the garden. El-i-chi halted in his tracks when he saw Renna in the clothing of the white man.

"Pretty dress?" Renna asked.

"Yes, pretty," Ah-wa-o said.

"We're going shopping later, Ah-wa-o," Beth said, flushed from her play with the children. She was smiling, happy with the world. "I'd like you to come along. There's a gown at the clothing store that will look lovely on you."

"No," El-i-chi said, his voice low, forceful. "My sister will not wear the white woman's clothing."

Renna broke the tense moment that followed by walking stiffly toward El-i-chi. "Can't run," she said, "but pretty."

Chapter IV

The *Seneca Warrior* had just returned from a profitable winter voyage to England. She had braved the winter storms of the North Atlantic, although there had been some damage to the rigging. Beth and Renno inspected the ship with Moses Tarpley. The captain said it would take at least ten days to have the *Warrior* repaired and reprovisioned for her trip to the islands. Beth, always the businesswoman, was planning to load the ship with rice, pitch, and turpentine to be traded in Jamaica for coffee so that the voyage to rescue Roberto de Mendoza would not be wasted.

Although Beth did not voice it openly, Renno perceived that she was of the opinion that Roberto was already dead—it had been months, after all, since his abduction from the ship traveling toward Spain.

The stay in Wilmington was a sweetly pleasant time for

Renno. He and the others were entertained several times by his distant cousins, Nathan and Peggy Ridley. At these affairs Renno was distinguishable from other whites not by his dress—he had donned white men's clothing—but by his bronzed skin and alert, athletic poise.

Se-quo-i humored Beth by allowing her to provide him with shoes, that pinched his feet and trousers, waistcoat, and linen that constricted his breathing. El-i-chi, however, allowed no compromise, appearing everywhere in buckskins. Little Hawk protested sufficiently to rid himself of shoes, wearing his moccasins with the gentlemanly clothing Beth purchased for him. Renna was becoming quite the little lady in a wide assortment of dresses that Beth delighted in buying.

It irritated El-i-chi to find that Ah-wa-o's dark beauty attracted much attention. To his disgust she seemed to enjoy it. Yet she had made no protest against his pronouncement that she would wear no white woman's clothing.

The presence of Little Hawk and Renna in the house did more to improve Cedric Huntington's health than the combined efforts of Beth and the doctors. Beth had given up trying to keep her father in bed at all times. The physician had allowed that mild exercise might be beneficial, and the old man seemed careful not to overdo it. He took short strolls with the children and sat in the back garden watching and advising as Little Hawk measured how far he could hurl a pebble down toward the river.

Renno noted that exertion made Cedric pale and breathless, but there was progress. One day Cedric requested that he be allowed to visit the company office at dockside. Renno accompanied him and left him chatting quietly with a small group of sailors in the office, only to return from an inspection of the work on the *Warrior* to find Cedric laughing loudly, talking boisterously, and participating energetically in a game of dice for small stakes with the sailors.

When Moses Tarpley announced that the *Warrior* would be ready to sail in two days, Renno knew that it was time to get a few things settled; Beth still assumed that she was going with him. Her reasoning was sound: William's influence in England had obtained for her an exemption from the British Office of Trade, enabling her to bypass the blockade that was still being imposed on American shipping by the powerful British navy.

When Renno took her into the back garden and explained that he was not going to allow her to be exposed to danger by going on the voyage, she proved calm and persuasive.

"But this is important, Renno. It's not just a voyage for our company's profit. It will benefit the United States and be a small wedge into the blockade."

"You have become quite prosperous," Renno said. "You don't need the money."

"Honestly, I'm interested in more than just doing it to make money." She smiled. "I won't give the profits back, of course. But there's also a great deal of prestige to be gained. And this exemption for the purpose of trade may very well inspire the governments and merchants in the Caribbean to put pressure on the British government. It's senseless to prevent the United States and the islands from exchanging goods and to force us to send our ships all the way across the Atlantic to England."

"Are you sure you can leave your father?"

"For a short time. Look, we'll reach the Bahamian island quickly and pay the ransom if Roberto is still alive. Then it will require a matter of only a few weeks to go on to Jamaica." She squeezed his hand. "You like your coffee, my proud Seneca warrior, and don't deny it. Just wait until you've tasted coffee brewed from Blue Mountain beans."

The issue was not closed, and Cedric added his argument during dinner. "This is business, Renno, and my girl is a sharp trader. I promise to behave myself, and I'll have the servants here to care for me. Besides, Little Hawk and Renna will see to it that I observe my bedtime and eat my food, right, Little Hawk?"

"I will be with my father," Little Hawk corrected him, looking at Renno with an unspoken plea in his blue eyes.

"Another one," Renno said, rolling his eyes but smiling. He had been dealing all along from a position of weakness, and he knew it. Actually he did not want to be separated from Beth so quickly. The days in Wilmington had been made golden because of her presence. It was as if he had left all his heavy responsibilities behind. He knew they would be waiting for him when he returned, but for a short time he had only to concern himself with Beth, the pleasant company of Nathan Ridley, and the talks with men of knowledge and substance—but mostly Beth, Beth, Beth.

"Sachem," Se-quo-i ventured, "if it would be of help to you in making your decision, I am willing to stay here and assist Ah-wa-o in tending the children."

Renno nodded, knowing what that offer had cost Se-quo-i, for the young Cherokee had been eager to see as much of the odd world of the white man as possible.

"Shipboard life does not agree with me," El-i-chi announced. "I stay. Se-quo-i goes."

Renno caught his brother's eye. El-i-chi held his gaze steadily.

"Unless," El-i-chi said, "my brother thinks he will need El-i-chi's fighting arm."

Renno was relieved. He had been a bit uneasy about leaving the children in Wilmington with only Ah-wa-o to look after them. He had hoped that Se-quo-i would offer to stay. Se-quo-i had already made profitable use of his time in Wilmington, going almost daily to the library, in his Cherokee-style buckskins, to borrow a variety of books that had librarians whispering behind their hands in amazement. Although Se-quo-i had proven his considerable worth, El-i-chi was El-i-chi, and there was no man in the world better qualified to keep the children safe in Renno's absence.

"Good," Renno said. That was settled.

"Without El-i-chi you will need another warrior," Little Hawk suggested.

"You are absolutely right," Renno agreed, and Little Hawk, wanting to whoop for joy, remained stoic instead. He straightened himself and looked around the table with such an expression of stern pride that Beth had trouble controlling a giggle. Ah-wa-o was smiling but not at Little Hawk. Her eyes were on El-i-chi, and her heart was full, knowing that he was to stay in Wilmington.

There remained only the packing and loading of Beth's personal things. That was delayed, as was the departure, by a pleasant and unexpected event: there appeared on the river the next morning a sleek, well-armed four-master, which showed the salt-encrustation and wear of an Atlantic crossing. Moses Tarpley brought the word, and an excited Beth hurried everyone to the waterfront to watch the graceful ship being nudged to dockside. Her figurehead was an Indian with golden hair. The name on her prow was *Seneca Chieftain*.

"You see," Beth explained, "I have named all my ships in honor of my sachem."

"Renno," Moses Tarpley said, "I know it'll cause a further delay, but I'd strongly suggest that we take the *Chieftain* instead of the *Warrior*. The *Chieftain* is newer and stronger. Those oaken planks of hers will deflect anything short of a point-blank direct hit by a cannonball. She's got more guns—bigger guns. If we run into trouble, I'd feel more secure with the decks of the *Chieftain* under me."

The *Chieftain* had made a record crossing, with brisk winds behind her all the way. No one had expected her to be back so soon. She was an impressive ship. Renno agreed to the switch, trusting the judgment of Tarpley.

Only one man didn't like the idea. A short, broad, dark-faced man leapt down to the planks of the dock and grasped Renno's forearm in greeting. The mood of Billy the Pequot, the captain who had pushed the *Seneca Chieftain* across the Atlantic in record time, changed quickly from pleasure at seeing Renno again to glum acceptance when the news was broken to him that he would take the *Warrior* to England with a cargo of indigo and cotton while the *Chieftain* went south.

"But if there is a chance of trouble," Billy protested, "I should be with you also."

"Billy," Beth said, "there's no one else I would trust with the *Warrior*, and this cargo for England is important."

Billy brightened only a little when he was told that there would be a large bonus for having brought the *Chieftain*'s cargo of English manufactured goods to Wilmington weeks before it was expected.

The delay was not long. Good-byes were made. Renna seemed to be perfectly happy to be staying with her uncle and Ah-wa-o. The ship made her way down the Cape Fear, past the tall, magnificent pine forests of the western bank, the forests that had made Wilmington an important port, for England's ships needed the tall spars made from the pines and the pitch made from their resin.

Beth pointed out the ruins of old Brunswick Towne, burned by the British early in the war, and once the site of a British fort near the mouth of the river. Then the low but wooded barrier islands were passing on either side, and the ship

began to move with the restless energy of the sea as she
sailed over the bar and pointed her prow to the southeast.

As winter lingered in the virgin forests extending in every
direction from the Cherokee-Seneca village, Toshabe was
discovering that nothing leaves a hole in one's life like the
absence of two lively beloved children and Ah-wa-o. She did
not let a day pass without thanking the manitous for having
given her Ha-ace. The spirits had blessed her with two hus-
bands. She still honored the memory of Ghonkaba, for he had
been great, but she unreservedly gave her love to the worthy
warrior who now filled her life with his manly presence, his
lusty passion. In the privacy of their bed Toshabe often felt
like laughing aloud, for the young ones considered her to be
old. She did not feel old in the arms of her panther.

In that time after the ceremony welcoming new beginning,
one could anticipate the warm, glorious days when the women
and the young ones ventured forth to gather the new wild
greens of spring to augment meals. Soon the women would
be planting.

But there was sadness as well. The winter fevers had
taken their usual toll of the old and the weak: Loramas, great
chief of the Cherokee, father of Rusog, was dead. Many of
those who had made the long march south with Ghonkaba
had joined their ancestors in the West, and as winter died,
Casno the shaman was dying.

That Casno's death had been foretold was known only to
Renno, for he had seen no need to burden others—not even
his mother—with that knowledge. Of course the old man
knew, and he did not lack for care. Toshabe, Ena, or another
Seneca woman was with him constantly, feeding him broth,
trying to soothe his fever with cold cloths, massaging his
aching, desiccated old limbs to try to restore circulation.

Casno crossed to the Place Across the River as many others
did, in the cold, still, silent hours before dawn. Toshabe was
awakened by a young girl sent by Ena. She hurried to Casno's
lodge. Ena looked at her and shook her head sadly.

"He asks for you, Mother," Ena whispered.

Toshabe knelt beside Casno's bed. "I am here, old friend."

". . . black," Casno whispered. "The shaman in black.
Renno."

"Rest," Toshabe said. "Be easy."

"Renno knows . . . black," Casno gasped. "Little Hawk. Tell him. Tell him."

"Tell him what?" Toshabe asked, becoming a bit frightened. Casno had been familiar with spirits. What was the significance of his words? What dangers faced Renno and Little Hawk that Renno should be warned?

"Tell Renno . . . shaman in black . . . spirits of evil. Tell him—" Casno said a name, but neither Toshabe nor Ena understood. "Vow to me," Casno pleaded, "that you will tell him."

"Yes," Toshabe promised. "Yes, we will."

With a surprisingly strong voice Casno began to chant the praise of good, of the manitous, of the all-powerful, of orenda. And then his voice ceased, as did his heart and his life. Ena began to sing the song of mourning.

"And so the old ones go," Toshabe said tiredly. "Pass my greetings, spirit of Casno, to the others who have gone before. Give my greetings to Ghonkaba, and to Ja-gonh and Ah-wen-ga, and all the others who have crossed the River."

It was midmorning when the women had finished preparing Casno's body. Then Toshabe voiced her fears. "Was he in communion with the spirits? The warning was vague, and we could not understand all the words, but he asked for a vow."

"Mother," Ena said, "you know how the mind wanders as death approaches."

Rusog nodded. "Renno can take care of himself, Toshabe. By now he is far to the east, perhaps even aboard the great ship that will take him to the southern islands."

"He asked for a vow," Toshabe persisted. "And he feared for Little Hawk as well as Renno."

"I will go," Ha-ace decided. "I will make the run. If he has not left for the sea, I will overtake him."

"Honored Panther," Ena said, "you made the long march from the north as a younger man. Remember those great distances. It is not so far to the sea, but it is far, and my brother will be eager to complete his task for his friend in England. You would not reach him in time."

"Ena is right," Rusog said. "Old Casno's mind must have been clouded by the nearness of death."

"Ena," Toshabe said, "when Casno mentioned the name of

the black shaman, did it not sound to you as if he said Hodano?"

"Perhaps," Ena said. "I can't be sure."

"Hodano is a shaman of the far north," Rusog said. "It is not likely that he would be in a white man's town on the coast of North Carolina."

"True," Ha-ace agreed. "And yet Casno asked for a vow."

"I would go with you," Rusog offered, "if it were possible to reach him in time, but it is not."

"Hodano is not a creature of the sea," Ena said. "Perhaps Casno's warning pertains to the future."

"We will send a letter," Rusog suggested. "Ena will write it. I will take it to Knoxville to Roy Johnson, and he will send it. It will be waiting for Renno when his ship returns."

The letter was written and sealed, and Ha-ace accompanied Rusog, who held a particular sensitivity against the whites. And yet Toshabe's fears were not stilled. In the absence of Ha-ace, alone in her bed, she prayed fervently to the manitou for the safety of her family.

The death rites were performed for Casno, and the village seemed changed by his passing; his death diminished all, and his spirit had taken with it a vast store of Seneca lore.

Far away on the island of Haiti, where there was no winter, where the rank jungles fought root against root and leaf against leaf for space in the sun, where the sun was sultry and the rains came with dismaying regularity for one who had lived his life in the forests and around the lakes of the northern lands, Hodano sat, sweating profusely, while he watched a wrinkled, toothless black man sing to a full-bodied young black girl.

Hodano was not pleased. The voyage had not agreed with him. Not once but many times he had emptied his stomach, until there was nothing left in him but bitter bile. The heat of that tropical place enervated him. Sweat stung his one good eye. It was too hot for his wolverine cowl, and he was forced to improvise a cloth garment that would hide his scarred visage from the probing, accusing eyes of strangers. The march overland, through the stinking, steaming jungles, left him praying to his evil spirits for relief.

The French trapper Cochon was at Hodano's side, his eyes

glittering with lust for the naked young black girl. Sweat glistened on her skin as she gazed into the old master's eyes. She seemed to be dazed.

Hodano snorted when a goat was led into the small underground chamber, a widening of a cave leading back into a jungled ridge. Thus far he had seen foolish, juvenile mumbo jumbo. He had, for example, seen a voodoo "master" bite the head off a living chicken. Hodano was unimpressed. He was beginning to suspect that Cochon had led him astray, perhaps for his own vile lusts, for at the voodoo ceremonies agile black girls danced naked, and in the frenzy of their "trances" their bodies were available to any man. Hodano had determined that Cochon would not leave Haiti alive—that his vile spirit, whatever it was worth, would pass to Hodano, eaten.

The voodoo master's voice was rising in the singsong, repetitive chant. Hodano had learned some of the words: he recognized the name of the leading "god" of voodoo, Damballa Ouedda, repeated over and over. There was no magic there—only the ignorance of people worthy of nothing but slavery, people from a backward, primitive, faraway land, who did not have the intelligence of a rabbit.

The young girl was swaying in time with the master's chanting. The drums were picking up the tempo, and in the darkness beyond the light of the small fire, women sobbed and moaned as if in ecstasy. Already some were coupled with men in the shadows, the musk of their bodies making a stench in Hodano's nostrils. He tensed his legs to rise, to leave this place of inane superstition that had no connection to the dark powers of evil that were his mentors.

A silence fell, causing Hodano to delay his departure. A gleaming knife had appeared in the voodoo master's hand. The young girl was moaning, her eyes glazed. Then she bleated like a goat. Hodano snorted with disdain. Supposedly the soul of the girl was now in the body of the goat, and vice versa.

Killing Cochon would be small revenge for a wasted trip and the discomfort he had endured.

But his attention was riveted as the master made a quick slash with the razor-sharp knife and a leering, red smile came to the soft throat of the girl. Blood gushed, pumping, and at that instant the goat fell to its knees, a woman's scream loosed from its throat. Hodano leaned forward and felt the spirit leave the body of the dying girl. It was not a human spirit.

"Ah," he said, relaxing as the drums increased to a frenzy and people leapt to lave their hands in the gushing blood of the dying sacrifice.

Hodano, the master, and Cochon sat around the dying fire. Cochon, who understood the bastardized French of the master, served as interpreter. Hodano posed the questions. The body of the sacrifice had been removed. The worshipers were slowly leaving the cavern.

"This magic, can it be taught?" Hodano asked when the three of them were alone.

"It is a gift from Damballa Ouedda."

"Can it be given to me?"

"Only if you give yourself."

"Teach me, Master," Hodano asked.

"And in return?"

"I will teach you to put new life in your old limbs with the swallowed spirit of the dying."

Twice, three times in darkest secret—it would not do to instill too much fear with frequent sacrifice of a human being— the old voodoo master drank of a spirit. Invigorated, he began the instruction.

The blacks of Haiti were a simple people, and the basic beliefs of their dark religion often seemed childish in Hodano's eyes. And yet there was power, a power he wanted and needed. He watched as the old master took the spirit of a young man and then put a semblance of life back into the body, thus creating the first zombie Hodano had ever seen. The Indian shaman's entire being ached to see the great Renno in such a state, his spirit eaten, his will gone—a walking dead man to do the bidding of Hodano.

Hodano could sift through the mumbo jumbo of the voodoo belief and discard the useless bits of ritual, like using after-birth and umbilical cord for making charms. He was not, however, above other beliefs: eating the heart of an enemy to add to one's own courage or rubbing the brains of an enemy on a gunsight to give the gun accuracy, for example. But he felt that such practices had more value in their dramatic effect than actual results. He was interested primarily in taking possession of a man's spirit. It was not enough to suck away the living spirit of a human being, for that gave only a moment's exaltation. He wanted to *control* that spirit and, most importantly, to be able to keep his enemy's body in a state of walking death, so that he would be able to savor his victory for long, sweet years.

For sheer enjoyment and entertainment the *petro,* or blood-sacrifice ceremony, was fine, but Hodano wanted more than amusement. First he learned how to charm and handle deadly snakes, the sacred symbols of Damballa. Then he chose as his personal voodoo god the bloody warrior Ogoun Badagris. He learned how to put a woman in a deep trance and as a reward to Cochon, did so often, leaving the helpless, sleeping woman to be used by the Frenchman.

As the weeks passed he tried and rejected a voodoo master's technique for gaining strength by first mesmerizing a child, then sucking blood from needle holes sunk into the child's arms. The taste of fresh blood was repugnant to him, and he gained nothing from that practice. He listened with growing interest to the older masters, who traced the practice of voodoo back to Africa and who spoke of all the old, black gods as living, dynamic beings. He witnessed the power of the art—or was it suggestion?—when a voodoo priest punished an errant man by casting a spell of death. The victim fought helplessly and died within three days of no apparent cause.

He combined his own evil magic with voodoo and was a sensation at a voodoo ceremony when he caused snakes to crawl from his own mouth.

He learned that the blacks, like Indians, were a tribal people, hanging on to their tribal names even in slavery. The most powerful magic had come from the Dahomey nation. The master who tutored him in the making of a zombie was Dahomean, of the African Yoruba tribe. He drank blood with the master to seal his lips, vowed over the death of a young child to keep the precious secret, and then he was ready. One final gift was given him—the name of a god so fierce, so feared, that only masters could mention it. This did not impress Hodano, for invocation of that dreaded god, Bakulubaka, added nothing to his increasing power.

"You have learned well," the old master commended when Hodano announced that he and his friend would be leaving Haiti. "You are powerful. You could face the she-devil Marinette of the dry arms and sucking lips and live through her caress. She would not be able to eat you."

"I will honor you, Master," Hodano intoned.

"The enemy you will face is powerful," the old man foretold, his toothless gums smacking as he spoke. "He has been armed by powerful spirits. He has his own magic."

Hodano spat but did not disagree.

"There is one other, a master known to me by reputation and told of by travelers. He lives on an island to the west. Although it is far and the journey to his cave is difficult, go to him."

"What power could he teach?" Hodano asked.

"To be invisible," the old man answered. "To be able to soar above one's enemy and attack from nowhere, unseen."

"The old man speaks of the island of Jamaica," Cochon translated for Hodano after listening a few more minutes to the master. "But this place he tells of is far inland, in difficult country."

"How far can it be on an island so small?" Hodano asked, studying a chart of the islands. "We go."

The destination of the *Seneca Chieftain* was a tiny cay southeast of the Bimini Islands. Moses Tarpley had the course charted, and the great ship coasted southward under fair skies and favorable winds into the waters off Spanish Florida. For Renno and Beth the trip became the honeymoon they had never had. Only once in the weeks required to reach the area of the islands, with the *Chieftain* sailing within sight of Grand Bahama, did Renno have his terrifying nightmares. Although the political situation in the United States was a favorite subject for table talk, the problems seemed far away.

Little Hawk proved to be a fine sailor. Not once did he experience seasickness. He became like an appendage of the big, bearded Moses Tarpley, who found that his young student had a keen mind that absorbed the esoteric lore of the deep-water sailor. Se-quo-i, always reaching out for knowledge, studied the art of navigation.

After reaching Florida waters Tarpley began to tighten

discipline aboard the ship. The age of piracy was past, and the captain was surprised that a pirate vessel had taken a Spanish ship and kidnapped Mendoza. There were still potential dangers, however, and he explained to Renno why he was standing round-the-clock watches on the guns.

"English power and English ships did away with the freebooters," he said, "but that force was severely eroded by the American war. Toward the end of the war England had half the world fighting her. One reason why the Americans won their independence was that England had to pull most of her naval power back to home waters. They're still there, protecting against threats from Spain and France. Maybe there are Spanish pirates operating again because there aren't enough English ships in these waters to protect every sea-lane."

Renno was pleased with the efficiency of the crew during drills to determine battle readiness. Through his reading he was already familiar with England's difficulties in the New World: a brilliant British naval victory against great odds had saved England's island possessions from the French in 1782, but the French still had ambitions in the islands. And old Spain, although tired and glutted into complacency with the gold and treasures of New Spain and South America, still posed a threat. As the *Chieftain* continued southward under her huge white sails, Renno often stood on the deck, scanning the distances, adding his own eyes to those of the lookouts.

The uncertainty in the Caribbean was known to the sailors as well, and they spent their off-duty hours telling tales of days gone by, when men like Long Ben Avery, William Kidd, the dreadful Teach, and the greatest and most successful pirate of them all, Bartholomew Roberts, sailed the Caribbean.

Little Hawk loved to hear the tales of piracy and high adventure. Once a sail was sighted at a great distance, and the little warrior rushed onto the deck, armed with his miniature bow and an arrow ready to fire, only to be disappointed when the ship passed to the north without drawing closer to the *Seneca Chieftain*.

That sighting prompted Renno to reread the letter of instructions telling him how to arrange a meeting with the captors of Roberto de Mendoza. This voyage held many potential dangers, among them the upcoming encounter with the roving criminals of the high seas.

The *Chieftain* was to anchor in a secluded cove off a small, unnamed, waterless cay. There a man would tell them where to rendezvous with the ship on which Mendoza was held captive. Renno asked Tarpley if it might be unwise to sail the *Chieftain* into a cove where she could be blocked from the open sea and deprived of maneuverability.

"We're a match for any ship short of a man-of-war," the captain said, "at anchor or in free movement. We'll keep an eye open. If one ship tries to block us in, we'll sail into her teeth with all our guns firing and she'll change her mind in a hurry."

As the time for action drew near, Renno began to regret having allowed Beth and Little Hawk to come along. He knew that Tarpley was a capable captain, and he approved of the well-trained crew, but his wife and his son were precious cargo.

"At the first sign of trouble," he instructed Beth, "you will take Little Hawk below and stay there until any fighting is over."

The Bimini Islands were to the west now. The weather was holding nicely. Spring, Tarpley told Renno, was a good time to sail Caribbean waters, whereas fall was the worst, for that was when the storms called *huracáns* by the Spanish swept the islands.

"Well," the captain said, surveying the blue distances and stroking his bushy black beard as Renno, Se-quo-i, Beth, and Little Hawk also enjoyed the splendid morning, "we should sight our destination today." He turned and called up to the lookout to keep a sharp eye. Beth and Renno walked with Little Hawk to the bow to watch the *Chieftain's* hull slap down into the sparkling, clear waves. A school of porpoises surfaced and began to keep pace with the ship as if playing a game, pleasing Little Hawk with their grinning snouts and flashing speed.

"I wish I could swim that fast," Little Hawk said.

Beth and Renno smiled at each other, then down at the boy. The peaceful moment was disrupted when a call came down from the lookout.

"Sail ho!" the voice shouted. "Sail off the starboard beam."

"That means on the right," Little Hawk squealed. "It's pirates."

Renno jerked his head around and shaded his eyes. Within minutes he saw the tips of the sails of a large vessel. He walked to midship, where Tarpley was studying the distant sails through a telescope. "She's big," the captain remarked, "and fast. She's on a course to intercept us."

"Can she overtake us?" Beth wanted to know.

"Too early to tell," Tarpley answered. "We'll hold course for an hour or so, and then we'll be able to judge her speed better."

Within two hours it was evident that the ship off to the west was both larger and faster than the *Chieftain*. Dressed in all her sails, the newcomer was closing on the *Chieftain* with surprising ease.

Renno paced the deck, fully armed and ready. Little Hawk walked beside him, his face set in an imitation of his father's stoic expression. Tarpley motioned to Renno.

"We have two choices," the captain said. "We can run eastward, try to beat her to Great Harbour Cay, and if successful take cover behind the island. Or we can continue on this course and pray that she isn't looking for a fight."

"Would we beat her to the cay?" Beth asked.

Tarpley shrugged.

The decision was determined by a shout from the lookout. "Cap'n! She's flying the battle emblem of the British navy."

Tarpley relaxed visibly. "Well, that's that, then. No problem. We have the proper papers. No English captain is going to give us a hard time with the documents Mistress Beth has from the Office of Trade." But he did not cancel his orders for battle readiness as the British ship loomed larger and larger.

As the hours passed and the British ship made clear that her intentions were to close on the *Chieftain*, another cry came from the lookout. The unnamed cay that was the *Chieftain*'s destination lay dead ahead. Tarpley ordered the sails shortened. The *Chieftain* began to slow. The British ship came booming onward—an impressive sight, rather beautiful, Beth thought—under her full spread of canvas.

Renno made out the details of the ship with his naked eye, saw the open gun ports, and counted an impressive number of guns. He remembered Tarpley's comment: "We're a match for any ship short of a man-of-war." And this was a man-of-war, a British ship of the line, bearing down on them.

As the white Indian watched, a puff of smoke came from a forward gun on the British ship. He tensed and asked Beth to take Little Hawk below as the sound of the cannon came booming across the water. The shot splashed far ahead.

"I get the idea that he wants us to heave to," Tarpley said, then gave the appropriate orders. Soon the *Chieftain* was rocking softly, dead in the water. Sails were being furled on the British ship as she came around and heaved to a hundred yards off the *Chieftain*'s starboard.

"Standard procedure," Tarpley commented. "You see, the English have appointed themselves the guardians of the world's oceans, especially in the area of their land holdings. They'll send a longboat over, and we'll show them Mistress Beth's documents. Then we'll be on our way. I only hope that her being here doesn't scare away the fellows we're supposed to meet on that little cay."

Something had been bothering Renno, nagging at his mind since the chase began just after dawn. To a landsman most ships looked much alike, but there had been something very familiar about the vessel that was now furling sail and beginning to lower a longboat. Now it came to him.

"The *Assiduous*," Renno said, an edge to his voice.

He knew her well. He and Billy the Pequot, with the help of a great whale, had ripped the rudder off the *Assiduous* in the cold waters of the bay of St. Lawrence, above Quebec.

"By heaven it is!" Tarpley exclaimed incredulously as Beth came back on deck. "And if our old friend Captain Horatio Jaynes is still in command . . ." He turned to a seaman. "Pass the word quietly to the men to stay alert. We may have to fight yet."

Chapter V

Captain Horatio Jaynes had started his day in the usual way, with a fencing session with his first mate, a lad of good breeding and some skill with the foil. His crew considered Jaynes to be an odd duck, preoccupied with improving his skills with bladed weapons. He was better than any in shipboard competition with the foil, and his improvement with the cutlass had impressed even the salty old bosun's mate, who was the acknowledged master of that weapon. But only Jaynes knew the devil that drove him to daily practice.

When a sail was sighted by the lookouts, Jaynes noted the time in the ship's log and waited for a couple of hours before taking a look through a telescope. He recognized the rigging as being American, and a smile split his thin, elegant face. Nothing would please him more than seizing a Yankee ship having the audacity to sail into a restricted British trade area.

He suspected that it was the interbreeding with foreign blood—French, German, Dutch, even Indian—that had reduced good Englishmen to savages in America. He hated them all.

The *Assiduous* was a taut ship with a good crew. She had been repaired and refitted after the disaster in the bay of St. Lawrence when, somehow, a whale had become entangled in the rudder and ripped it away. Jaynes let his men relax during the better part of the day while the *Assiduous* closed on the armed American merchantman. He hoped there would be a fight. He would much rather kill Americans than wet-nurse them to a British port where they would be impressed into the British navy.

When the *Assiduous* heaved to with the Yankee within good gun range, Jaynes straightened his cocked hat, checked the cutlass at his side, and climbed into the longboat, standing firm and well balanced as it was lowered into the small waves. He was feeling better and better because he had noted the name of the vessel, the *Seneca Chieftain*, and her home port, Wilmington, in raised, carved letters on her stern. He fervently prayed that she was the sister to another ship with the name *Seneca* in her title, a ship that had been ripped from his grasp by a man who had humiliated him, beating him badly with his own weapon, the foil, in front of the British governor in Quebec.

Jaynes remained standing as the crew of the longboat bent to their oars and closed the distance quickly. He ordered two sailors to clamber up onto the *Seneca Chieftain* first; then he followed. He threw back his shoulders, straightened his coat, laid his hand on the hilt of his cutlass, and looked around disdainfully. A smirk curled his lip as he looked into the eyes of the man he had been praying that he would meet again. There, standing with his arms crossed on his chest, was the very man who had shamed him. And at his side was the flame-haired woman, Beth Huntington.

His pulse throbbed at his temples. His every impulse was to draw his cutlass and have his revenge at that very moment, but he had only a handful of men with him. Once he had a crew on board the Yankee vessel, he would put a cutlass into the hands of this man who was neither Indian nor white but a mixture of both, and then he would toy with the freak, cutting him down slowly, slowly.

"Who is captain of this vessel?" Jaynes demanded.

"Captain Moses Tarpley at your service, sir." He stepped forward, a leather folder in his hand. "You will want to see my papers, sir."

"Yes." Jaynes sneaked a look back toward the *Assiduous*. Three longboats were halfway to the Yankee ship, each loaded with armed men. The guns of his own ship were primed and ready to deliver a smashing broadside to the *Chieftain*. His face was set as Tarpley opened the leather folder and extracted the official document that gave Crown permission to the Huntington Shipping Company for the purpose of trade at the port of Kingston in Jamaica.

Jaynes took the paper, unfolded it, squinted at it. A flush of anger darkened his face for a moment. The papers were in order. He glanced at the approaching longboats. They were very near; he was thousands of miles from the government offices in London; as master of an English ship of war he had broad latitude to make split-second decisions on the spot. He would not let a mere paper deprive him of the joy of revenge on this man called Renno.

The longboats bumped against the hull of the *Chieftain*, and armed men poured up over the rails. The crew of the *Chieftain* were grouped strategically. Tension was etched on their faces.

With a grim smile Jaynes turned, walked to the rail, and held the official document high so the wind would carry it from his hand. It sailed out and away, falling to the sea. Jaynes turned, took the folder from Tarpley, looked inside, turned it upside down, ran his hand across its interior, then tossed it aside.

"I see no papers giving you the right to invade British waters," he protested. His men had fanned out around him, weapons ready.

"Captain," Beth said evenly, her face flushed with anger, "I am a British subject, sister of the earl of Beaumont. Your behavior is inexcusable."

"This ship is seized in the name of the king," Jaynes announced. "Any man who resists will be dealt with harshly. Those who submit will be treated fairly." The look in the blue eyes of Renno was making him a bit uneasy. He looked around. His force on the *Chieftain*'s deck was outnumbered by the ship's crew, but his men were all well-trained veterans. Moreover, he had the guns of the *Assiduous* behind him.

"I want that man"—he pointed at Renno—"put in chains."

Moses Tarpley cast a stricken glance at the white Indian. It was meant as an apology. While the first longboat had been making its way to the *Chieftain*, Renno had recognized Horatio Jaynes. "We must not allow that man to board us," Renno had said.

"Not even Jaynes can deny the permission given to us from the Office of Trade," Tarpley had countered. Then he had pointed out the ready guns on the *Assiduous*. "One broadside from that range, and we'll be seriously damaged. The British respect their own law. Jaynes can't ignore the documents."

Renno's hand was now on his tomahawk. As four men moved toward him cautiously, Beth said sharply, "Captain Jaynes, if you persist with this folly, I will see to it that you are ruined."

Renno was not a man to submit meekly to being put in irons. And yet if he fought, he would be endangering Beth's and Little Hawk's safety. But to fight was the only honorable way. Little Hawk was Seneca, and as such he would have to face danger. Beth was his wife. In marrying him she had accepted him for what he was, a warrior. It would not be the first time that a Seneca wife had been caught in the middle of a battle.

But the guns of the *Assiduous* gave him the most concern. They would not be used, he felt, as long as Jaynes and his men were on *Chieftain*. The only hope, then, was to kill or overpower Jaynes's force of armed men and keep Jaynes alive on the theory that his first mate would not fire on the *Chieftain* while his captain was aboard.

The tomahawk flashed a deadly message as it cleared his belt. From Renno's throat came a low growl, the challenge of a great bear. The four seamen who were approaching him faltered, drew their cutlasses, and continued onward. One met the steel of Renno's tomahawk with a parrying thrust of his cutlass, then died swiftly as the blade of Renno's weapon glided along the blade of the cutlass to the man's throat.

With his peripheral vision Renno saw Se-quo-i leap into the battle, knife in one hand, tomahawk in the other. Beth had sensibly withdrawn. The second British sailor lunged, his cutlass whistling down Renno's chest and slashing fringe from his shirt.

"Take them!" Jaynes screamed, drawing his own cutlass.

With men closing on him from two sides and others rushing forward, Renno pivoted to a new angle, his tomahawk slashing in an uppercut to take a British seaman under the chin. The Spanish stiletto in his left hand reached out in the opposite direction to slide between a man's ribs, the tip reaching the heart. He then leapt to Se-quo-i's side. Tarpley was already there. The first group of the *Chieftain*'s crew, drilled in the maneuver by Renno himself, moved as a body, presenting an impenetrable wall of blades.

This was a time for killing, and Renno's mind and body merged into a fighting machine that needed no time to make decisions. It reacted in an instinctive way that was the result of long training. He, Se-quo-i, and Tarpley formed a wedge to face the British crewmen, who advanced in a ragged line. Steel came closer to steel in a breathless, timeless instant that would end with the clash of blades and the slash of steel through soft human flesh.

The sound of low thunder swept across the quiet sea, rolling, deadly, and from the corner of his eye Renno saw cannonballs strike the upper rigging of the *Assiduous*.

Jaynes yelled in dismay when the smashed foremast of his ship began to topple, carrying rigging and canvas with it in a thunderous chaos to the deck.

"It seems we have friends," Tarpley whooped, pointing with his cutlass.

She lay broadside to the *Assiduous*, a sleek, deadly black ship with white sails, and even as Renno took time to glance past the *Assiduous* to see their unexpected ally, the British man-of-war erupted with fire and smoke as another broadside swept its rigging.

Renno's attention was then totally on the men who faced the point of his stiletto and died from the crushing, slicing blows of his tomahawk. Beside him Se-quo-i was splattered with red—the gushing spurts of a British sailor's lifeblood.

The encounter was brief and deadly. Two men, two Indians, had done the most damage. The few British still standing now lowered their arms and begged quarter. Only Horatio Jaynes had his weapon raised, and Renno leapt lithely toward him. Both glanced away as the guns of the *Assiduous* roared, for she was far from finished. The shots into her rigging had not lessened her firepower, and the first broadside sent wood flying from the black ship.

"At least I will kill you," Jaynes snarled, a smirk on his lips. He raised a pistol with his left hand and fired. The smoke and the roar came together as Renno threw himself to one side and heard the ball pass his ear with that distinctive percussive sound of a near miss.

If Jaynes's actions had not imperiled Beth and Little Hawk, Renno might have spared him, but there was no forgiving the threat to those he loved. The white Indian smashed Jaynes's cutlass aside and with one satisfying blow buried the steel blade of his tomahawk into Jaynes's skull. He felt the bone give way, and as the blood welled up around the blade, he jerked it away and prepared to deliver another blow. But the white ooze of brain matter leaked out of the aperture, and Jaynes went totally limp and began to fall.

The sea battle was continuing. The *Assiduous* was in action, and the British were not known as rulers of the sea for nothing. There were good men there, Renno knew, experts in naval warfare. The *Assiduous*'s guns were hurting the black ship severely, even as that ship's shots continued to batter into the larger vessel.

"Gunners!" Renno shouted. "Fire at will."

The *Chieftain* shuddered and lurched sideways as the starboard guns let loose with a roar and a cloud of black smoke. The guns were aimed just above the waterline, and most found the mark. The *Assiduous* shuddered with the impact.

Not expecting an attack from the Yankee trading vessel, the *Assiduous* was slow in answering. When her port guns did retaliate, they fired a split second after the force of the second broadside rocked her, causing the shot to fall short, splashing water over the *Chieftain* but doing no damage.

"Hold fire," Renno ordered, his strong voice carrying to the gun bays.

A broadside from the black ship smashed the last of the rigging on the *Assiduous*. Masts and spars and canvas fell in a roar. The ship was listing badly.

"Take me closer," Renno told Tarpley, and the captain bellowed orders. The *Chieftain* closed on the *Assiduous*.

"Stand ready to board," Renno shouted to the crew.

"Our mysterious friend is closing as well," Tarpley pointed out. Indeed the black ship, sails holed and one mast atilt, was moving toward the *Assiduous* from the other side, but she was farther away.

Renno took a place forward, and when he was within hailing distance, he cupped his hands and shouted across the gap between ships. "Strike your colors, and we will put you ashore at the nearest British port."

The reply came to him faintly: "I will hear that order from my captain."

"Your captain is dead. Strike your colors," Renno shouted.

"Never."

"Then we will stand by to pick up survivors when your ship sinks." Renno saw no gain to be had from a battle on the decks of the *Assiduous*. He had not set out to conquer, only to defend himself and his.

"An excellent decision," Moses Tarpley said with a sigh of relief.

The black ship, however, had different ideas. She closed fast. Grappling irons flew, and after strong arms drew the ships together, lines fastened them in an embrace of death as men poured from the black ship.

Renno, not accustomed to watching battles without actively participating, felt his blood grow hot as a tall, agile man led the attack. He wielded a cutlass with great power, cutting a swath of blood through the valiant men of the *Assiduous,* many of them showing wounds received during the bombardment.

"He fights like a man who enjoys the work," Se-quo-i commented with admiration.

One by one or in small groups, men aboard the *Assiduous* began to lay down their arms. The tall, dark man led the assault that overcame the last of the opposition.

A silence descended, broken only by the groans of the wounded and the sigh of the wind strumming the rigging.

"For what?" Beth asked in an awed voice. She had come back on deck to stand beside him, Little Hawk's hand in hers. The boy's eyes were wide. "For what? Because of a little man's ego?"

"Are they pirates?" Little Hawk asked.

"I think not," Renno answered. "Spaniards, perhaps."

"Now might be a fine time for us to take our leave," Tarpley suggested.

"No," Renno decided. "They fought well at our side against a common enemy. I will speak with their captain."

Before Beth realized what he was doing, he had pulled off his shirt, stepped to the rail, and launched himself over. He clove the water cleanly and surfaced, swimming hard toward the sinking *Assiduous*.

When he pulled himself up over the rail, he heard laughter and boisterous talk. The ragtag crew of the black ship, many with dark, Spanish faces, had begun to loot. A stream of supplies and foodstuffs were being relayed upward from the storage areas. The tall, dark leader saw Renno and came striding toward him, a smile showing gleaming, white teeth.

"You fought well," Renno complimented him in English.

The dark man extended his hand. "As did you, from what I could see of the action on board your ship."

Renno grasped the hand. The man's clasp was hard and firm but a bit slippery with blood. There was something familiar about his face. He had piercing black eyes, dark, curled, almost feminine lashes, and heavy dark eyebrows. The lips were well shaped, the nose long and strong. Altogether it was a likable face, and it was beaming in friendliness.

"Captain Adan Bartolome, of the good ship *Mano Negra*, at your service." He bowed with an elegant sweep of his arm.

"I am Renno, of the Seneca."

"Ah," Bartolome said. "Well, then, we can continue this conversation later, if it pleases you, for now I think that we must act swiftly or have slightly wet feet."

The *Assiduous*'s decks were tilted. Bartolome's men were busy transferring loot to the black ship.

"We will take the British survivors aboard our ship," Renno offered.

"If that pleases you," Bartolome responded. "I had intended leaving them to their longboats, since they can make the nearest of the Bahamas easily."

"We will take them," Renno repeated.

"I have said you may, if it pleases you." Bartolome's voice lost its warm tones. "Now I have business." He turned away.

In Spanish Renno said, "Thank you once again for joining us in this fight."

Bartolome turned to answer in the same language. "But we did not join the fight to save your skins, my friend."

The wounded were transferred first. Their able-bodied crew mates helped, then climbed onto the *Chieftain* to watch glumly as the once proud ship slid down into the waves. The black, deadly-looking *Mano Negra* sat fifty yards away.

"*Mano Negra* means black hand," Little Hawk said. "Beth told me."

A longboat was lowered from the black ship. It moved toward them swiftly, and then Adan Bartolome and two shifty-eyed men were on *Chieftain*'s deck.

"You thanked me," he said to Renno. "Now I thank you, for *Assiduous* had too many guns to allow us to take her alone." Then he turned and favored Beth with a wide smile. Upon being introduced, he bowed regally and showed great charm in brushing Beth's hand with his nose. He grasped Little Hawk's hand with elaborate seriousness.

"Are you a pirate?" Little Hawk asked.

"But of course." Bartolome walked to the rail with a cocky, swinging stride, made a wide motion with his arm, and a flag was run briskly up the lanyards to unfurl in the breeze. On the black flag was a white skull and crossbones.

"Why, Captain," Beth said, "a man as charming as you? A pirate?"

Bartolome shrugged delicately. "A man must make a living for himself as best he can in these troubled times."

"Walk with me," Renno invited. Bartolome nodded and fell in at his side. Renno led him past the gun bays. He did not speak, but he did make certain that the pirate became aware of the manned guns, all primed and ready.

"Luckily we escaped damage," Renno said casually.

"My friend," Bartolome said, "I get your meaning. The sinking of a great ship is a melancholy affair. It serves to remind us that we, too, sit on a frail, man-made platform in the middle of a great ocean. We have seen enough blood for one day."

Renno grunted, satisfied. He led the way back topside.

"My friend Renno has been giving me a lesson in strategy," he told Beth. "He has shown me a fighting ship, well manned and well gunned." He grinned. "But still, how can a self-respecting pirate keep his crew content when the takings from the *Assiduous* were so paltry?"

Beth laughed, not sensing any real danger from this charming man. "*If* you could take her," she said, "the *Seneca Chieftain* would be even more disappointing. The major portion of our cargo, being naval stores, is not edible. And the only gold on board is in this necklace." She reached up, striking a pretty pose, and removed the necklace. "Since you fought so well for so little, please take this as part of your booty."

"I have never preyed on beautiful ladies or on their personal property," Bartolome said. "But your ship would make a fine prize when delivered to an open port. Even her poor cargo would bring some money, I am sure."

Renno's face warned Beth. She laughed, knowing that her husband was thinking of the ransom gold stored in their cabin, and she knew that he would rather fight to the death than submit.

"Captain Bartolome—"

He interrupted with a raised hand. "Do me the great honor of calling me Adan."

" 'Adan,' then," she said, liking this smiling, dark man. "It's quite a nice name."

He bowed.

"Now, Adan," she continued, avoiding Renno's eye, "you and I both know that piracy is no longer a viable way of, as you say, making a living. Aside from certain, uh, insecurities, there are no longer opportunities to take the great galleons that once brought gold and emeralds from South America. I can offer you honest work, carrying cargo. I need ships, and yours is a fine ship."

Adan smiled. "It is a generous offer."

"But?" she asked.

"Have you heard or read about Captain Bartholomew Roberts?" Adan asked.

"As a matter of fact, yes."

"Then you know that he captured more than four hundred ships. Still, he was a moral man. He allowed no alcohol to pass his lips. There was no gambling aboard his ship, and he allowed no women. A great man, indeed. I had aspired to better his record."

"But he died fighting," Beth noted.

"How else should a man die?" Adan asked.

"Once the navies of the world combined to crush piracy," Beth reminded him. "Should you show success, others will emulate you, and then the great nations of the world will forget their differences long enough to crush you. You will face ships from England, France, the United States, even Spain."

"But in the meantime I'm afraid it is my duty to myself and my crew to ask you to surrender peacefully," Adan persisted. "I will put you ashore unharmed, along with the Englishmen about whom my friend Renno was so concerned."

"Wait," Beth whispered as Renno reached for his weapons.

She smiled at Adan. "Do you really want to become, under law, *hostis humani generis*?"

"What's that?" Little Hawk asked.

"Enemy of the human race," Adan translated. "Yes. I have chosen to act with *animo furandi*." He winked at Little Hawk. "With predatory intent, for *causa lucri*. That's profit," he told Little Hawk. "And to avenge great wrongs." He raised his hand and pumped it twice, and immediately two cannon roared from the *Mano Negra*, the balls striking close enough to shower water over the *Chieftain*'s stern. He then turned quickly to face Renno, who, stiletto in hand, was advancing.

Renno was not amused by the man's charm. His eyes were deadly.

"Many will die aboard this ship," Adan warned, his voice revealing uncertainty.

"Since you will already be dead, you will find small consolation in that fact," Renno retorted. He inclined his head toward the two seedy men from the *Mano Negra* and said contemptuously, "You will send them to tell your men to sail away. They can pick you up in a few days on the cay that lies on the horizon. If they make one hostile move, you die."

"We seem to have arrived at a stalemate." Adan took a step backward. "If I am killed, my men will fight. Don't underestimate them; they are hungry for riches and all have reason to think unkindly of those who possess riches and power. Now here's a suggestion: let us return to the days of chivalry and glory, when wise men settled disputes in a manner that limited the shedding of blood. I speak of single combat between the Seneca and me. The winner takes all. All of the *Seneca Chieftain*, that is."

"Not fair," Little Hawk protested. "If you lose, you lose nothing."

The adults turned to stare at the child, startled by his quick grasp of the situation.

"My life is nothing?" Adan asked Little Hawk with a sad little smile.

"This is nonsense," Beth said.

"What say you, my friend?" Adan pressed.

Renno humorlessly smiled as he said, "Choose your weapon."

"For me to choose would be very unfair," Adan said, "for I would choose the cutlass, and I happen to be a master with that weapon."

"So," Renno said, taking Tarpley's cutlass. He moved to the open deck and stood, cutlass in hand, a silent figure of death.

Adan drew his cutlass and moved toward him.

Renno was still motionless.

"Is there really any need to fight to the death?" Adan inquired. "I'm afraid that I've rather come to like you during our short acquaintance. Would first pinking suit you just as well?"

Renno's answer was an explosion of motion as he lifted his cutlass and leapt to the attack. He smiled with pleasure when his thrust was parried neatly. Tired of all the talk, he was ready for a fight. Jaynes had died too easily. This man, however, was truly a master of the cutlass.

The force of the blows struck by the two opponents hissed through the hot tropical air. Steel rang on steel. Sweat soaked through Adan's silken, flowing shirt and also gleamed on Renno's sun-bronzed torso.

For one of the few times in his life Renno found himself being forced into a defensive posture. He had indeed come upon a skillful and brave opponent. The white Indian gave ground, studying the techniques of the Spaniard, concentrating on parrying, blocking, and looking for an opening. He could hear Little Hawk yelling out encouragement, the boy's voice pipingly clear over the harsh, excited cheers of the sailors. He had now analyzed Adan's basic style. Renno feigned weakness, fell back, and as he saw confidence light up Adan's face, he launched an attack of such ferocity that the Spaniard's eyes went wide in alarm.

The pirate successfully skipped backward to escape the deadly blade.

Renno now used the cutlass in the manner of a foil, stabbing through Adan's defenses to leave a long, clean slash in Adan's silken shirt.

"*Madre de Dios,*" Adan gasped. He literally had to run backward before Renno's onslaught. Then he found secure footing, braced himself, and let a potentially deadly thrust slide down the blade of his cutlass to be forced harmlessly aside.

Toe to toe they stood, the pirate slightly taller, slimmer; the other golden haired and athletically muscular, a splendid example of manhood at its prime. Renno decided that it was time to end the duel; he had already discovered Adan's one weakness: the pirate tended to turn into a swinging slash aimed at his left side, moving toward the blow in order to catch it with his parrying cutlass. Renno feigned the blow, but instead of following through to bring the blow home, he lifted the arc of the swing, and the blade whistled over Adan's head to hiss downward.

Adan recognized the change of tactics too late but managed to hop backward. Instead of being severely maimed by the blow's landing full-bladed on his shoulder, the tip of the cutlass sliced downward along the side of his sword arm. Blood wet the silken shirt immediately. He staggered back, the cutlass dropping from his nerveless fingers; his face gone suddenly pale.

Renno lunged, pushed the tip of his cutlass into Adan's neck. Both men stood motionless. Blood dripped down onto the back of Adan's hand and from there spotted the deck.

Renno did not fight for sport. The fire of death was in him. His muscles tensed to send the blade biting into Adan's throat.

"Renno, let him live," Beth cried.

"He's no good to us dead, Renno," Moses Tarpley said.

With effort Renno relaxed.

"Thank you," Adan said, his entire body rippling with emotion. "It is true that I would be of no use to you dead."

"You live only if your crew honors your agreement," Renno warned.

The ship's sawbones, a graying, somber man whose body

looked ravaged by consumption, led Adan to a hatch cover and pushed him down. The cut was not deep, but it was bleeding freely.

"I'll have rum and a needle," the old sawbones said over his shoulder, and the requested items were fetched. "This will smart a bit," he warned as he poured the fiery rum over the cut.

Adan's face went pale, but he made no sound then nor when the old man used a sail-mending needle to stitch the cut closed with catgut.

"Very fine work," Adan croaked, watching as the needle first made a puckered mark on his skin, then penetrated. "When you've finished here, I have a pair of breeches that need mending."

"I can do that too," the old man said without cracking a grin. "Makes no never mind—skin or cloth. Principle's the same."

When the job was finished, the old man wiped the needle on his sleeve and stuck it into the crown of his cap. Adan stood, and his knees buckled. Tarpley caught him before he fell. Two seamen carried him below.

The sails of the *Chieftain* went up. The black ship, with men working frantically in her rigging to repair the damage done by the *Assiduous*, trailed behind.

"I don't think we want to go into a cove with that one behind us," Tarpley said. "I figured we'd sail past the cay and maybe lose them during the night."

Night came with the suddenness of the tropics. The *Chieftain* showed no light, but with the morning the black ship was still close behind. Adan came on deck, his right arm in a sling. He nodded greetings to Renno.

"I see that my lads stayed close," he said.

"Which presents a problem," Renno remarked.

"One easily solved," Adan said smilingly. "If you will allow me my longboat and my men to row . . ."

Renno was silent.

"I'm sure you have your doubts," Adan continued, "but you have my word. At any rate I have business back at the cay we passed last evening." He watched Renno closely for reaction. There was none.

"I somehow got the impression," Adan said, "that you, too, had business at the cay." Adan waited for a reply. When it came his eyes showed surprise.

"In the early-morning light I used a telescope to take a close look at the ship you call the *Mano Negra*," Renno said. "On the stern it looks very much as if another name has been painted over. Could that name have been *Santa Beatriz*?" The *Santa Beatriz* was the ship on which Roberto de Mendoza had set sail from Vera Cruz.

Adan laughed. "I have to admit that I didn't pay close attention to the name of the ship when I seized her."

"Might your business on the cay have to do with collecting ransom?"

Adan laughed again. "You have found me out. I admit that I had hoped to seize the ransom without delivering the object of the ransom to you, for I have grown accustomed to the company of Señor de Mendoza. But now . . ." He shrugged. "I have known, of course, since I came aboard and was introduced to Mistress Huntington, sister of the man who married Mendoza's sister, that the charming lady did not tell the whole truth about what the *Seneca Chieftain* carries."

"So we were well met not only in the matter of fighting the British warship," Renno said.

"Well met indeed. Now, I suppose, there remains only the matter of exchanging gold for Señor Mendoza. My longboat can carry the gold. It will return with Mendoza."

"Two longboats will set out at the same time. Mendoza in the one from your ship, you and the gold from the *Chieftain*."

Adan turned and looked upward into the sky. White, billowy clouds were forming to the west. He cleared his throat. "You have caught me out again, my friend. Actually Mendoza is not aboard the *Mano Negra*. He is being held—in comfort, I might add—on an island in the Bahamas."

Renno, more and more certain that his suspicions were correct, said, "I fear that you have caught *me* out as well, for as Mistress Huntington has said, we carry no gold. There was no time to get the gold from England, and Mistress Huntington had no such assets. We carry our cargo to Kingston, where it will be purchased with gold, and that gold is to pay the ransom."

"*Sangre de Dios,*" Adan breathed.

"So it seems, my friend," Renno said with sarcastic emphasis, "that our business transaction will have to wait."

"You do want Mendoza alive?"

"We do."

"Then I will give you one last chance. As previously arranged, I will leave men on the cay. Meanwhile I will sail to my island, retrieve Mendoza from his comforts, and have him here in, say, one month, which should be ample time for you to accomplish your business transaction in Kingston. Is it agreed?"

Renno nodded.

Beth stood by Renno as they watched Adan Bartolome being rowed toward the *Mano Negra*.

"Why didn't you arrange to pick Mendoza up as quickly as possible?" Beth asked.

The longboat had reached the black ship. Soon the sails were trimmed, and the black ship turned away from the *Chieftain*'s course, presenting her stern.

Renno handed Beth a telescope. "Closely examine the name at the stern."

"I don't see— Yes! I see! A name has been partially obscured but not totally painted out."

"The name that is painted over is *Santa Beatriz*," Renno said, "the ship on which Mendoza sailed from Vera Cruz. The pirate who holds Mendoza is sailing the very ship on which Mendoza took sail."

"Perhaps it was a better ship than his own," Beth suggested. "His own vessel might have been badly damaged during the fight."

"And perhaps Mendoza is dead. If he is not, our laughing friend will be here when we return. If he is, I think we've seen the last of Bartolome."

Chapter VI

~~~~~~

In a time of peace and plenty the day-to-day life of the Seneca village required no strong leadership. The most pressing problem seemed to be restraining the rising spirits of young boys invigorated by spring, and the firm hand of the Seneca mother was fully capable of accomplishing that small task—at least within reason. There were those who felt that being surrounded by a whooping horde of imaginative warriors ranging in age from two to eleven was nerve-racking, but if so, there was always the calming solitude of the wilderness.

The warming waters of the streams encouraged the migration of hulking fish, welcome targets for spearing, later to be baked in clay with herbs. The spicy taste of poke greens spelled spring to the palate. There was an overabundance of volunteers for far-ranging hunting trips. The community of longhouses, lodges, and log cabins in the Seneca-Cherokee villages was opened to the fresh air by the women. Sleeping furs and skins were shaken out and hung to freshen in the sun. Agricultural implements were sharpened, and the smell of newly turned earth was pleasant.

The sadness of winter was behind them now. Casno had been sent to his Place Across the River with all the honors due to him. In the absence of the sachem and the shaman who had inherited Casno's duties, several senior warriors shared in the rituals of honoring Casno in death, being advised by Toshabe, now a sort of elder stateswoman in regard to the observance of Seneca ceremonies.

Rusog, sachem of the Cherokee since the death of his grandfather, Loramas, had felt the call of spring and was somewhere in the west. His excuse had been a combination of the hunt and a defensive scouting excursion, just to be certain that the Chickasaw were behaving themselves and staying in their own hunting grounds, which extended to the great Mississippi.

Ena, in whose veins ran the blood of the white Indian, whose sun-darkened skin, fair hair, and blue eyes matched those of her brothers, Renno and El-i-chi, was troubled. She had always enjoyed perfect health, but now something was wrong. Being vaguely ill was a new and somewhat frightening experience for her, but it was not her way to complain—she had endured long marches at the side of warriors, had braved the wilderness alone, and had distinguished herself as a scout and a woman warrior who could hold her own with most men.

Being the firstborn of Ghonkaba and Toshabe, Ena was two years older than Renno. Now twenty-six, she was proud that her figure matched those of maidens in their late teens. Lately, however, she had discovered that the sun-squint lines at the corners of her eyes did not disappear when she relaxed.

Rusog's absence gave her the opportunity to spend more time with her mother. The two women sat outdoors in the pleasantly warm sun, working the new deerskins that had been taken during the winter, preparing to provide themselves and their men with new clothing. Ena thought about telling her mother about her malaise but decided against it, not wanting to worry her. Instead they talked about almost everything else under the sun, some of lesser import than others, in the manner of women everywhere. They spoke of Renno, El-i-chi, and Ah-wa-o, speculating on where they were and trying to imagine how it would be for them on the sea and during the long journey homeward across North Carolina.

Ena longed to be with her brothers, but she had chosen her life. Her Rusog was a man of great honor, a chieftain worthy of the daughter of Ghonkaba, and she had no regrets . . . save one.

That regret was illustrated to both Ena and to her mother by the approach of a little girl dressed charmingly in minia-ture buckskins. The toddler was pure Seneca, dark eyed, round faced, and solemn until Ena seized her in a hug and tickled her. The tot giggled and squirmed in delight.

Toshabe knew Ena's thoughts as the little girl waddled laughingly back into the arms of her young mother. The manitous had willed that Ena be barren. That fact was evi-dent, but it was not a matter for conversation. It was never mentioned.

Turning back to her work of softening the skins, Ena felt a moment of unease. She swallowed hard, leaned back, and stretched; then Toshabe glanced up and continued a well-known story of the time when she was young and a handsome warrior sought her hand. Ena never tired of her mother's stories. She liked to imagine Toshabe as a full-bodied young girl and got pleasure from picturing her father in his young manhood. Ena smiled as Toshabe told of her union with Ghonkaba.

In the midst of the tale, however, Ena's eyes went wide as her stomach churned. She leapt to her feet, and the need for privacy propelled her behind the lodge. Toshabe followed her there to find her bent over and retching, her face pale and sweaty.

For a moment in her misery Ena was a child again, grateful for her mother's cool hand on her forehead. She leaned on Toshabe as she was helped into the lodge.

"The new greens of spring do not agree with me," Ena explained as her mother eased her down onto a bed.

Within minutes Ena felt better and was back at her work. No further mention was made of her brief illness, but when it happened the next morning and the morning after, the second time in Toshabe's presence, questions were finally asked. "How many times has this happened?"

"I am never ill," Ena said.

"How many times?" Toshabe insisted.

Toshabe had once again taken Ena into her lodge. Ena was lying weakly on a bed, her stomach still uneasy.

"I don't know."

"Ena!" Toshabe said sharply.

"Several times, two weeks. Not so bad at first."

Toshabe sighed. "How is it with the flower of blood?"

This was a subject that was almost never openly discussed, pertaining to that monthly event common to women.

Ena's eyes went wide. Perhaps because she was so strong, so active, the monthly time had never been a burden for her, the blood flow often so light that it was scarcely noticeable, and she never experienced cramps or pains.

"Think, girl," Toshabe said.

"I—I—don't know."

"Did you flower with the last moon?"

"I don't remember. No. No, I'm sure I did not."

Toshabe sat down. She laughed. "You are going to be the mother of your first infant at your age?"

Ena swallowed. She sat up, her eyes wide, a glow of sweet hope on her face. "Could it be?"

"Twenty-six winters, and she does not know when she is carrying the seed of a warrior," Toshabe said, but she was smiling.

Ena put her palm flat on her solidly muscled stomach. "Could it actually be?"

"Unless your memory is gone completely and you did see the flower of blood at the last moon. Unless for weeks you have been eating worms."

Ena made a sound of disgust, but she was beaming. "I must find Rusog. I must tell him."

"Hold," Toshabe advised. "Be sure first."

"But how?" Ena's expression was so young that Toshabe's heart went out to her.

"When the flatness of your stomach goes."

The morning sickness continued. Ena's face seemed to bloom. She spent much time with the young ones of the

village. One day when Toshabe entered Ena's lodge in the
Cherokee village, she surprised her daughter, standing with
her skirt down, gazing at and feeling her flat stomach. Ena
blushed when Toshabe laughed, but she allowed Toshabe to
feel her exposed stomach.

"It is still too early," Toshabe told her.

"But I'm sure it is not so flat as it was. And another moon
is here without the flower."

"It will be a son," Toshabe declared. "To carry Rusog's
blood, and yours. Renno concerns himself about our being
slowly absorbed into the Cherokee tribe, but now, the manitous willing, Seneca blood will run in the veins of a Cherokee
sachem."

Rusog came home with fresh meat and with his spring
fever subdued by swift and far travel. He thought that Ena's
passionate greeting, her radiant face, were merely a response
to his return, but when he heard—the women were sure
now, and their experience was not to be questioned—he
whooped as loudly as a ten-year-old playing war games. The
sachem of the Cherokee nation then danced around the lodge
like a drunken war leader preparing for a raid on a Chickasaw
outpost.

At twenty-six, Ena was going to be a mother. The manitous
were indeed good and kind.

In spite of El-i-chi's training at Casno's feet and in spite of
having the same blood as Renno, he had never had a spiritual
experience. El-i-chi knew the Seneca lore and the magic
tricks, had memorized the oral history and the legends, and
could recite the myths that extended far back into the dim
distance of time when all Indians were of a family. But he had
never been advised or visited by a spirit.

When it finally happened, El-i-chi found it to be an awesome thing. The vision came to him not long after Renno's
departure aboard the *Seneca Chieftain*. He was lying in his
bed in the Huntington house, not fasting or meditating but
thinking that Ah-wa-o was only a wall away, sleeping with
Renna in the room next to his. The visitation from old Casno
came without warning, causing the icy-nerved warrior to jerk
into a sitting position in his bed. It was only a wisp at first,
then a seeming solidity. The spirit did not speak.

"Casno?" El-i-chi whispered.

The spirit raised one hand in benediction. There was a smile on the face that *was* Casno's, without doubt. There was the scent of spring in the room, the feeling of well-being, and then the spirit was gone. After his first startled moment El-i-chi felt only a great sense of loss, then peace. He knew with an undeniable assurance that Casno had come in spirit to say farewell and to give his successor his blessings.

"Casno has gone to the West," he told Ah-wa-o the next morning.

To Ah-wa-o's credit she accepted his statement without question. "May he be content with his ancestors," she whispered.

In spite of his fears to the contrary, the days had not hung heavy on El-i-chi. Ah-wa-o was partially responsible. She had proven to be a creature of immense curiosity. She had cajoled El-i-chi into taking evening walks, with Renna of course, around the residential neighborhood of Wilmington. She had shown El-i-chi the house where the British general Cornwallis had wintered before marching north to his final battle at Yorktown. She had become knowledgeable about a variety of subjects, and when El-i-chi questioned her about the source of her information, she said she was learning to read with the help of an elderly woman who lived next door to the Huntingtons.

El-i-chi had not even tried to come to grips with his new feelings about this flowering child, this sister-by-marriage. He knew that he was most happy when she was with him, even if engaged in one of the little tasks she took upon herself around the house. Her sunny face, her vibrant enthusiasm, and her slim beauty pleased him—and he did not want to delve any deeper than that into the matter.

But undermining his best intentions was the fact that Ah-wa-o blossomed more with each new day. El-i-chi had begun the trip from the Seneca-Cherokee village with a child, and he had treated her as a child. Now she was a woman, and so beautiful a thing that she drew his eyes with a look, a movement. He began to fight the growing attraction, spent more and more time away from her, away from the house, but it was there.

In the Seneca society, as in most, there were of course strict taboos against intermarriage by close family members. Ah-wa-o was his stepsister. It was fitting for him to consider her beautiful. He often cast a proud, brotherly eye on the splendid figure of Ena and considered himself lucky to have such a beautiful sister. It would have been perfectly acceptable if his eye looked on Ah-wa-o as it did on Ena, but he became aware that Ah-wa-o meant something different to him.

There was the fact that she was his sister only by marriage. He thought again and again about all the laws of the tribe as taught to him by Casno and other elders. He could not remember a case that concerned a brother- and sister-by-marriage. The question simply had never arisen. Surely in the lore of the Nun-da-wa-o-no, the great hill people that was the Seneca tribe, there was precedent. He missed Casno's wisdom, for the old man would have known. There were stern guidelines of course from antiquity, from the time when the great League of the Iroquois, the league of the Ho-de-no-sau-nee, was formed. The people of each of the united Indian nations had been divided into eight clans, designated by their principal totem—wolf, bear, beaver, turtle, deer, snipe, heron, or hawk.

Under the old traditions a Seneca of the bear clan recognized, for example, a Mohawk of the bear clan as his brother. To a Seneca every member of the bear clan, whatever his or her nation, was a brother or sister, as if born to the same mother. Originally, before the coming of the white man and his wars, there was a more complicated law of brotherhood that made wolf, bear, beaver, and turtle brothers and thus forbidden to intermarry.

Hawk could intermarry with bear, as in the case of the great sachem, Ghonka, who was bear, and his wife, who was hawk. Thus the original Renno was bear and hawk, and that mystical relationship to the totems existed to the present time, when Renno's sometimes eerie affinity to hawk and bear often exhibited itself.

As the white man's wars began to disrupt the league and decimate its numbers, some of the old rules were relaxed by necessity. But any who violated the ancient laws of marriage still incurred the deepest detestation and disgrace.

All the lore was known to El-i-chi, and except for his mother's marriage to Ha-ace, he would have been free to admire Ah-wa-o's budding beauty to his heart's content. He was a man of just twenty-two years. At fifteen, going on sixteen, Ah-wa-o was entering the age when she would marry, and it was not only acceptable but desirable for a young girl to marry, if at all possible, an established warrior a few years her senior. Ha-ace was of the beaver clan. Bear could marry beaver. But could brother- and sister-by-marriage marry?

There was one fact that gave El-i-chi some hope: he fancied that he saw the subtle hand of his mother acting as a matchmaker. Toshabe had never been thrilled by his love for the Chickasaw maiden, Holani. Since Holani's death during that journey into the far Southwest, Toshabe had been open about her efforts to put El-i-chi into contact with available Seneca maidens of the proper clan. Had Toshabe deliberately chosen Ah-wa-o to accompany them on the trip to the sea with the hope that Ah-wa-o's blossoming beauty would inspire El-i-chi to forget his loss of Holani?

Oddly enough, once he had come to accept the idea that, yes, he was being manipulated by his mother, his attitude toward Ah-wa-o underwent a temporary change. He rebelled against the role she had assumed as mistress of Beth Huntington's house. He came deliberately late to some meals and missed many entirely. He tried to return his relationship with Ah-wa-o to that of easier days, when she was a child, but he ran head-on into female wisdom. If he slighted her, she ignored it or answered his sharp words with a smile. If she was irritated by his being late to meals, she hid it well, bringing him warmed-over food from the kitchen.

All of this confused El-i-chi. No woman could be so even tempered, so long suffering. Was it simply because she looked upon him as a big brother?

Now that *was* disturbing. For if she looked on him only as a brother . . .

In desperation he borrowed a boat, took along a wharf loafer who had the reputation of being a fine fisherman, and went off down the river on a trip that lasted for a week and saw the catching of more fish than he and the other man could eat. Throughout that entire time he could not get Ah-wa-o's face out of his mind, and when he came back and entered the house, a bit aromatic from days of sitting in the sun in the same set of buckskins, Ah-wa-o smiled and said, "I thank thee that thou art well, Brother," in traditional Seneca greeting. "There is a bath drawn for you."

He did not even ask how she knew to have a bath ready. Women, he felt, were of another tribe entirely and lived in a mystical world all their own. But he was pleased by the sight of her, and he would not be going off on another fishing trip soon.

Cedric Huntington was another reason why the days were never dull for El-i-chi. Beth had extracted a promise from El-i-chi to keep an eye on her father, and that was often an interesting task, for the old man was invigorated by company, especially Renna's. He liked to have Ah-wa-o dress the child in something pretty, frilly, and feminine in keeping with her age, and then take her for a ride in his personal carriage, with an enclosed cab and a driver's seat perched up front. To Renna's delight he sometimes drove the carriage himself with the little girl on his lap, letting her help to hold the reins.

"This is my pretty little granddaughter," he would say at every opportunity.

At other times Cedric would take himself off to the waterfront, where El-i-chi would see him gambling with sailors and longshoremen. At first this concerned El-i-chi, for he knew that the former lord Beaumont's compulsive gambling had depleted his fortune in England and left him in danger of losing his estate. As if in answer to his unspoken concern, Cedric confided laughingly that he was on a tight rein, that Beth had seen to it that he couldn't put his hands on large amounts of money, and that the deeds to the Huntington property in Wilmington were inaccessible to him as well.

The gambling seemed to do no harm to Cedric's health, and he did have enough willpower to refrain from strong drink, something warned against very sternly by his doctor.

El-i-chi didn't object to the company Cedric kept—mostly sailors between voyages, waterfront characters of dubious morality, and workmen building new additions to waterfront properties. Each man had his own story to tell, and El-i-chi was a good listener. He was Indian to the core in that respect, always willing to hear a rousing tale. He listened and learned and imagined himself weathering a typhoon off the coast of old Cathay, or on shore leave in Bombay, where a man's throat might be sliced through for the sake of a penny. He heard

tales of England and France and countries of which he had
never heard—of pygmies and cannibals in Africa, a continent
still so little known that it excited his attention. One day, he
mused, he and Renno would go there to hunt. With English
longbow and musket they would face animals so fearsome, so
huge, that he almost could not believe the sailors' descriptions.

Ah-wa-o, on the other hand, was not pleased when Cedric
brought his cronies home to dinner. Although the eating
habits of the Seneca might not match the formality and ceremony of guests at, for example, the table of Nate and Peggy
Ridley, they were civilized in comparison to some of the
men Cedric sat down at his daughter's table. Moreover, it
upset the matronly old black kitchen slave to have Cedric
show up at dinnertime with three or four ragged, dirty sailors
on his heels.

El-i-chi was both amused and pleased when Cedric's
unpredictable behavior showed him a new side of Ah-wa-o's
character, revealing the same fire and pride El-i-chi had seen
in her father, the panther, over the years.

The table had been set for four: El-i-chi, Ah-wa-o, Renna,
and Cedric. The old black cook, who ruled the kitchen with an
iron hand, had prepared one of Ah-wa-o's favorite dishes,
chicken and rich, thick, chewy dumplings. They had waited
fifteen minutes for Cedric to return from the office on the
waterfront, and Ah-wa-o was getting vexed from having to
deal with Renna, who was hungry and fussy from smelling
the good, steamy aromas. Ah-wa-o was just about to tell
El-i-chi and Renna to take their seats when they heard loud,
boisterous men coming up the walk. The front door burst
open, and Cedric led a group of four sailors, all except Cedric
slightly in their cups, into the entry hall. They faced a small,
shapely girl in neat buckskin shirt and skirt standing with her
hands on her hips, regarding them with evident disapproval.

Ah-wa-o's English had improved greatly, and she had
begun to pick up the English accent that still remained the
mark of people of substance. "Sir," she said, her dark eyes
looking upward to Cedric's florid face, "this is really intolerable."

"Beg pardon?" Cedric asked, taken aback.

"I realize, sir, that this is *your* house as well as the house of
your daughter, but I would remind you that your grand-

daughter is present, and I question exposing a young child to such men as these."

"Now see here, girl—" Cedric sputtered, his face getting redder.

"That's all right, gov," one of the drunken men mumbled. "We warn't all that hungry."

"Cook and I will be happy to feed your friends on the back porch," Ah-wa-o said. "In the meantime, sir, I suggest that you see to your toilet and join your granddaughter at the table."

Cedric looked at his hands. They were soiled from a spirited game of dice on the floor of the office. He opened his mouth to protest, then looked around as if seeing his companions for the first time.

"Chaps," he said, "take yourselves around back, and we'll stoke the inner furnaces for you."

The four men backed out the door. "Ain't that an Injun?" one of them asked.

"Whatever, she's got fire in her eyes," another said.

Cedric, a bit subdued, joined the others at the table. He waited until his plate was served with a heaping helping of chicken and dumplings, and then he looked across at Ah-wa-o. "Thank you, lass." That was the end of it.

When Queen Isabella of Spain asked Christopher Columbus to describe the island of Jamaica to her, he answered by crumpling a sheet of paper into peaks and valleys and tossing it onto a table before the queen.

Lying south of the mountainous eastern end of the much larger island of Cuba and almost directly west of the western-extending lower limb of Haiti, Jamaica was a green jewel in the Caribbean. As the *Seneca Chieftain* seemed to be wafted along on warm, favorable winds, the green mountains rose from the sea. As the ship neared, those aboard her could see beautiful beaches. The soaring mountains rose from a narrow coastal bed of flatlands to heights of as much as 7,400 feet. Renno could readily understand Columbus's illustration of Jamaica's topography with the crumpled sheet of paper.

The *Chieftain* was making for the port of Kingston, east of the capital of the island at Spanish Town. As she entered the harbor, she sailed past the ruins of the once notorious city of

Port Royal, which had been devastated by an earthquake in 1692. Everything had been destroyed except the remnants of a stone fort. Little Hawk asked question after question, for he had heard tales from the sailors about Port Royal and the pirates who once frequented the city of sin.

Port facilities had been reconstructed farther up the natural harbor, away from the exposed flatness of the Palisadoes. Under British rule the port was flourishing. As the *Chieftain* was nudged to wharfside, Renno noted that there were several merchant ships carrying the British flag in the harbor.

A cold-eyed British colonial customs official appeared almost immediately, backed by armed redcoats. A United States ship appearing in Kingston harbor was a potentially profitable event for the customs man if he were the first to seize her for having violated the blockade. The man was disappointed when he was told that there would be papers on file in Government House showing that the *Seneca Chieftain* had Crown permission to trade in Kingston. But he played it cautiously, quarantining the *Chieftain* while a messenger made the trip to Spanish Town to return with the word that, indeed, William, earl of Beaumont, had forwarded a copy of the official document that had been destroyed at sea by Horatio Jaynes. The messenger also brought an invitation from the governor for the owner and captain of the American ship.

Moses Tarpley declined the invitation, explaining that he was not cut out for social graces and would stay behind with Little Hawk. Renno, dressed in full Seneca regalia, drew not a little attention as he crossed the docks with a formally dressed Beth on his arm. A carriage took them over rutted dirt roads through a profusion of tropical growth to the governor's impressive house in Spanish Town.

Sir John Peter Grant, newly a widower, proved a charming host who set a fine table, resplendent in silver and fine Wedgwood china. Grant had known Cedric Huntington personally and had, he chuckled, won several wagers from Lord Beaumont.

"I have limited this meeting to the three of us," the governor said when they had been seated and the first course served, "because I wanted to be able to speak openly. You know, Mistress Huntington, that it is quite irregular for a ship of the United States to be trading in Jamaica or any other British possession."

Grant had not quite figured out the relationship between this beautiful, flame-haired Englishwoman and the white man who dressed as a wild Indian, but after all, Beth had introduced herself as owner of the *Seneca Chieftain* and the holder of permission to trade. He assumed the Indian was the ship's captain.

"Let me state," Grant continued, "that I am pleased by this development. We on this island lack many of the necessities of civilized life, and it seems idiotic to transport them all the way across the Atlantic—at great expense and risk, I might add—when we could obtain many of them from you."

"That, sir, is why I am here," Beth said.

Renno listened to the talk of business and trade but did not participate. He became more interested when Grant began to talk about Jamaica itself after he and Beth had concluded how much Blue Mountain coffee would be a fair exchange for Beth's naval stores and rice.

"Rice," Grant said. "We need tons and tons of it. Best and most economical food for slaves, you know. We have to be concerned not only with feeding those who work here, but with the transients. Kingston is a clearinghouse for blacks fresh from Africa. They're shipped from here all over Spanish America, and I suspect some of them might find their way to the United States as well."

The very idea of slavery made Renno restless. "It is, Sir John, a shameful trade," he said.

"Yes, yes, admittedly," Grant said quickly. "But I fear we're stuck with it, my boy." He seemed eager to leave the subject of slavery. "What do you know of our island, Mistress Huntington?"

"Very little."

"It has an interesting history," Grant said, warming to his subject. "Old Columbus stumbled onto it during his second voyage in 1494 and spent some time on the northcoast at the end of his fourth voyage, when he put his ship aground there. There was a native American population, the Arawak, quite peaceful, living in what amounted to a Garden of Eden, where one could pluck food from the trees. But the Spaniards, as usual, weren't interested in tropical fruits. They killed or worked to death the natives and began to import blacks from Africa."

"I am familiar with the pattern," Renno said distastefully. "There were efforts by the Spanish to enslave American Indians, but they soon found that we did not make good slaves."

"I can imagine." Grant took a long look at his dinner guest. "Well, to make my story short, old Oliver Cromwell sent a military and naval expedition into the Caribbean in 1655, and by 1660 the Spanish rascals had been totally expelled, leaving behind them a large number of ill-treated, half-wild slaves who promptly sought out the most inaccessible parts of the island, where they encamped and began to raid English settlements. They've been a pain in the neck ever since. Call themselves Maroons. They say they fight for freedom, which, when translated into English, means loot and rape."

There was a silence.

"Nasty lot, those Maroons," Grant continued, "but never fear—they confine their hit-and-run raids to isolated areas. Wouldn't dare come near a well-protected place such as Kingston. No. They hide out in the most godforsaken spots on the island, northwest of here—Cockpit Country it's called—and worship their old heathen gods from Africa."

Renno was examining the room in which they were dining. It was as if a piece of old England had been picked up intact and set down in the New World. The walls gleamed darkly with varnish on the wood panels. The candelabra were good English crystal, the furniture decidedly English and therefore uncomfortable.

Beth drained her wine.

"Our maps of Jamaica are far from definitive." The governor nodded to a servant, who refilled Beth's glass. "No surveyor has measured, for example, the convoluted folds of the Blue Mountains, which run from Newcastle to a height of over seven thousand feet on Blue Mountain peak. There are many places where no white man's foot has ever trod—Spanish or British." The governor paused to let this sink in. "Although roads of a sort connect the north coast settlements at Ocho Rios and Runaway Bay with the capital and Kingston, away from the main roads the interior is almost as unknown as the interior of the dark continent, Africa."

Renno nodded and looked at Beth. There had been no roads on their expedition to the Southwest. And the white Indian had made his way across thousands of miles without a road. He was not impressed.

"Now and again," the governor continued, "a few hardy souls venture into the interior in search of the magnificent caverns that have been formed over the centuries in the substructure of limestone that underlays the island. And ambitious white families are slowly building homes and plantations at greater and greater distances from the coast in most areas, save one—one vast stretch of land covering about two hundred square miles lying mainly within Trelawny parish. It's listed as 'unknown' on our maps." He chuckled. "There are names for the area, but ordinarily the names do not appear on maps. It is referred to as the Cockpit Country or, more colorfully, as the Land of Look Behind, or Me No Sen You No Come. But to get back to a more important subject, I trust that this trading relationship will continue."

"If it is profitable," Beth said.

"I think we can make it worthwhile for you," Grant ventured. "We can offer sugar to go with our coffee."

"In the United States," Beth said, "almost every community has at least one cane press."

"I see. Cacao, then?"

"All right," Beth agreed, "but mainly coffee."

"Rum, of course," Grant suggested.

"I hesitate to trade in such a beverage," Beth answered.

"Spices?"

"Yes, and I do think that coconuts would travel well."

Grant, without a hostess at his side, had become more and more infatuated with this flame-haired beauty with the good head for business. Such a woman, he knew, would be an asset to a man in his position. He smiled at her and said, "I assure you that the welcome of this house is extended to you at any time. Perhaps you could stay, and we could discuss our mutual interests more fully." He glanced meaningfully at Renno to tell her that, of course, the savage was not included in the invitation.

Beth leaned from her chair and put her hand on Renno's shoulder. "That would be up to my husband," she said, smiling sweetly. "And I fear that he's eager to see more of

your country and to get back to look to the off-loading of our
cargo."

"Well," Grant said, nonplussed. "Well, then." He had
been prepared to offer the wench the comforts of the house,
instead of condemning her to the doubtful quality of the
hostels in Kingston or the cramped space aboard ship. But he
was not at all inclined to extend that courtesy to an Indian
whose first words in his house were a condemnation of slavery, which had made the settlement and development of
Jamaica possible.

It was late in the day when the carriage returned them to
dockside in Kingston. Tarpley was still supervising off-loading,
the manual labor being done by black slaves of both sexes.
Se-quo-i sat moodily on the rail of the *Chieftain*. He came to
join Renno and Beth on deck.

"A sea of black faces." Se-quo-i waved his hand to indicate
the bustling wharves. "Slaves."

"So," Renno said.

"The white man's world is truly a strange and contradictory
one," Se-quo-i mused. "Not long ago your people and mine
fought to help the colonists win the right to live by their
definition of freedom. And yet these and others like them,
even in the United States, are property."

"It's not just the English," Beth said a bit defensively. "The
Spaniards brought slaves here first. If the French invasion
had succeeded in 1782, they would have been doing the same
thing—working slaves for their own gain."

Se-quo-i nodded, then brightened. "I am told by those
who live here that one can escape the heat by traveling only a
short distance into the mountains."

They all looked northward. Beyond the city the mountains
rose abruptly and greenly to the clouds that topped them in
white splendor.

Renno, having been cooped up on board ship for so long,
felt an immediate need to stretch his legs, to see what lay just
beyond those green peaks that faded into blue near their
summits.

"Hold," Beth said. "I'd like to see the mountains, too, and
God knows I'd welcome a bit of respite from the heat, but we
have an appointment with a certain Spanish gentleman to the
north in a matter of weeks."

In Choctaw, a language Beth did not speak, Renno said, "You see, my friend, what happens when one marries."

Beth hit him playfully on the shoulder. "I didn't understand that, but I can guess."

"I told him," Renno said, "that I was fortunate to have a wife who is not only beautiful but practical."

"I don't think so," Beth said, "but I'll accept that."

Chapter VII

Renno had experienced higher temperatures than those prevailing in Kingston during the summer, but there was something about the combination of heat and the heaviness of the air that made the days seem more oppressive than those arid, blazing, sun-filled days he had seen in the deserts of the Southwest. He found buckskins to be entirely too hot. He was constantly soaked with sweat. He noted that the slaves—and indeed the white sailors and others who worked along the wharves—stripped to bare essentials. He set an example for Se-quo-i and Little Hawk by reducing his daywear to loincloth and apron, the gleaming Toledo-steel stiletto and his tomahawk secured around his waist with a leather belt. He convinced Beth to sleep with him on skins on the open deck.

During the day Beth noticed that the wharf was a popular

place for a carriage ride by the ladies of the city, and she suspected that the golden, mostly naked warrior was more of an attraction than the ship, which was, after all, only another ship. If Renno noticed, he paid no heed, and Beth smiled behind her hand and politely inclined her head in answer to the curious stares of the touring ladies. One of the customs officials assigned to supervise off-loading and loading told them that they might enjoy watching the upcoming slave auction, the largest of the year. The man was a walking repository of numbers, constantly quoting tonnage of cargos moved through the port and other statistics, including the fact that over 610,000 slaves had been sold through Jamaican markets since the arrival of the British on the island.

For lack of something better to do, they walked the littered, foul-smelling streets to the slave market and found an advantageous spot from which to view the proceedings, by virtue of the strong shoulders of Renno and Se-quo-i pushing through the crowd.

Beth had become known to many as the owner of the fine American ship, the flame-haired woman who was the wife of a rather odd man. The auctioneer, a Britisher of impeccable dress and accent, nodded to her. "We welcome our American neighbor," he said. "Madam, I'm sure you'll find that our merchandise is of highest quality. I suggest that you pay particular attention to a collection of young girls of the Fon tribe, known for their tractability. They would offer no difficulty of transport and would, I'd venture, fetch high prices in the United States."

Beth smiled and nodded noncommittally. She had no intention of entering the bidding.

The old and the weak were first on the block. The bidding was slow, with a white-haired Spanish gentleman taking most of those who had not yet recovered from the trauma of transport from Africa in the holds of the slavers.

It took only a few minutes for the parade of black shame and misery to sicken Renno. His disgust quickly turned to anger as the first females were put on the block for inspection, their clothing removed. Now the bidding was spirited, for it was a choice lot of mature women, good for breeding. Several times men stepped up onto the block to examine teeth, to probe and test the firmness of breast and buttock.

"We go," Renno growled, and he roughly pushed his way through the press of bidders and onlookers to the open air of the streets, his entourage behind him, Little Hawk hanging on to Renno's belt. The white Indian had dressed for the outing in the town and he was hot and sweaty, and that fierce anger burned in him. Not even a pleasant trip by carriage to a nearby beach, where Little Hawk played in the clear, small waves and Beth gathered seashells, could dissipate his fury at the injustice. He sat on a log and chopped fiercely at a coconut with his tomahawk.

"Renno," Beth said, sympathizing, "an end will come to it someday."

"I can't fight it alone," he said.

"No, but there are good men of Christian morals in England who fight slavery even now." She put her hand on his. She could feel his tension. "We'll be heading home soon. The coffee beans are already being sacked at the plantations in the hills."

"So." Renno looked at Little Hawk, who had been upended by a wave, and smiled. He deeply empathized with the black captives who poured through Kingston to Spanish masters from Florida to South America. But he knew that a man had to know when to resist the temptation to scatter his energies. As Seneca sachem he knew his duty lay to his own people, for there was always with him that sense of urgency, that sure knowledge that years of crisis were coming.

The outing in the sun had made Beth pleasantly tired and had acted as a sleeping potion for Little Hawk. The boy fell asleep immediately after the evening meal, taken on the open deck. Beth hid a yawn. Renno accompanied her to the cabin, held her for a few moments, and left her crawling sleepily into bed. Se-quo-i was on deck, leaning on the rail. The lights of the city twinkled before them.

"Come," Renno said. He led the way down the gangplank, off the docks, and into the narrow, littered night streets of Kingston. From a waterfront pub the sound of a concertina accompanied raucous voices belting out an off-key sea ditty. A carriage rattled past, wheels splashing water from puddles formed by an afternoon rain and household sewage. The two restless warriors walked on, leaving the business areas and entering a section of shacks—homes of slaves and perhaps a few freemen. Now the narrow streets were dark. A starving dog came from the doorstep of a shack to bark cringingly. They passed a slave pen, guarded by three armed ruffians who glared at them with suspicious eyes by torchlight.

"Those are the untamed ones left from the auction today," Se-quo-i said.

All the slaves inside the pen were male, some large and well formed. Their eyes gleamed whitely in the guards' torchlight.

The walk in the city had done nothing to lighten Renno's black mood. He was ready to suggest that they return to the ship when a tightly grouped formation of six men rounded a corner ahead of them and moved toward them. Se-quo-i, a warrior of common sense and caution, started to move toward the side of the street, for the six men approaching were marching directly down the center of the narrow alley. When he saw that Renno was not going to give way, he shrugged mentally and moved back to Renno's side.

"Here, you!" one of the approaching men shouted as he saw Se-quo-i's dark face, made darker by the dimness of a moonlit night. "Halt and explain yourself."

Earlier, as full darkness had cloaked the city and the night-time curfew for anyone with a black face went into effect, a dark shadow had begun to make its way silently through Kingston's outskirts, seeking any available cover. The man was six feet tall, his gleaming black skin covered with a makeshift assortment of rags. His right hand hovered close to the hilt of a razor-sharp machete thrust into his sash. He moved with the silence of a night-prowling predator and the grace of a hunting cat. He blended in with the smallest shadow, so that as he approached the slave pen that held those newly arrived males deemed too dangerous by the bidders, he had attracted no attention.

He stood unmoving in the darkness as his eyes measured the distance from his place of concealment to the slave pen, where three white guards lounged, smoking pipes. He estimated the number of black bodies inside the pen, some sleeping on the barren earth, some standing with hands clenched onto the wire of the pen, one pacing back and forth like an imprisoned lion.

The tall, bulky body of the prowler moved without sound, slipping from shadow to shadow, circling to approach the slave pen from behind the idling guards. He covered the last few yards crawling on his belly. He froze for a moment when he realized that he was seen by the man pacing inside the pen, and to that slave's credit, he paused only momentarily, then continued.

The first guard died silently, his head almost severed from his neck by one powerful stroke of the machete. The second guard's cry of alarm was cut off by the flashing blade as it found his throat, slicing through his voice box. The third had his pistol swinging upward, and he managed to cry out "Help! Help!" before the machete crashed down on his head with stunning force and broke open his skull.

The liberator jerked a key ring from the sash of one of the guards and fumbled with keys until he found the one that fit the lock. The men inside the pen crowded up around the gate. The liberator whispered in an odd, guttural language, and there were answering whispers. Then six slaves were following the shadowy figure into the street, bare feet making scarcely any sound.

"We have a blackbird who ignores the curfew," taunted the leader of the six-man patrol that now faced Renno and Se-quo-i in a dark street.

"You are making a mistake." Renno's icy voice gave a meaning to the words that, at first, the slave patrol did not understand.

"You," the leader said. "You may have white skin. Before I crack your skull, you have three seconds to identify yourself."

"This is my identification," Renno countered, his tomahawk appearing in his hand, the steel blade reflecting the light of the moon.

"I see either a half-breed renegade or an albino helping a slave to escape," the leader snarled, moving forward to begin a swing with his truncheon. He almost lost a hand to Renno's tomahawk. The man clutched his wrist and screamed, "Shoot them!"

Renno signaled Se-quo-i with the harsh cry of a hunting hawk, and two tomahawks whistled through the air as a shot rang out. The ball went harmlessly skyward as Renno's blade sank deep. He retrieved the weapon, whirled, and using the blunt edge of his blade to crack a skull, heard the sharp sound of breaking bones. He jumped sideways to avoid a shot from another pistol and as a reward sent an incapacitating blow into the stomach of the man who had fired. Beside him Se-quo-i was fighting to disable, not to kill. He had left one man on the ground behind him and was closing on another who had drawn a cutlass.

The man whose wrist had been almost severed used his left hand to land a glancing blow with his truncheon on Renno's back, and Renno, in retaliation, spun on one heel to add power to the blow of his blade with the spinning motion of his body. The man died.

Blood streamed into the foul gutters. Of the six, three were dead, the other three in no condition to dispute passage to two men, one of whom had a dark face that could be mistaken for black in the night. A white-eyed black face peered out a glassless window and ducked back after seeing the carnage on the street. From a distance Renno heard the sound of running, booted feet.

"For once," Se-quo-i said, "I advise retreat."

Renno's anger, so quickly translated into bloodlust, was cooling. He stood, waiting, as four redcoats pounded around a corner and came to an abrupt halt, their long-barreled muskets at the ready.

"Stand and hold," came a British voice in cold command.

"We stand," Renno said.

"Drop your weapons," the voice ordered. Renno had recognized the voice of a British sergeant who commanded the omnipresent guard force on the docks.

"My weapon has a delicate edge." Renno thrust the tomahawk into its place in his sash instead.

"You're the Indian from the American ship." The sergeant moved forward. "What in blazes is going on here?"

"These men mistook us for escaping slaves," Renno explained mildly.

The sergeant moved forward cautiously. He whistled low as he counted the men lying on the street. "Slave patrol . . . My friend, I fear you will have to answer to the governor for this. It just isn't polite for guests to kill the men who keep order in the quarters."

"I will be found on board the *Seneca Chieftain*," Renno said.

The three soldiers with the sergeant had moved forward. Renno walked toward them, headed in the direction of the ship, Se-quo-i by his side.

"Here, that won't do at all," the sergeant sputtered. "I'm going to have to hold you for the governor."

Renno's tomahawk was back in his hand. He was not more than two paces from the sergeant, who had lowered his musket. "If the governor wants to question me about this, he will find me on the ship," he said evenly.

"I can order my men to shoot you," the sergeant threatened.

"Before the order is out of your mouth, you will be dead," Renno responded. "We have no quarrel with you."

The sergeant considered. He wondered if he could get his musket up before the wild man had scalped him with that gleaming weapon. He decided on prudence. "Nor I with you. I will tell my commanding officer that you will be available for interview aboard your ship."

The British officer arrived shortly after dawn. A few hours' sleep had improved Renno's attitude. Perhaps, he admitted to himself, he had overreacted.

The officer, a young lieutenant newly arrived from England, was finding Kingston's summer to be oppressive, and he was already regretting the ambition and patriotism that had convinced him that the army would be an excellent career. The rising sun carried with it a hint of the heat to come.

Beth was still sleeping, as was Little Hawk. Renno met the officer at the gangplank and invited him aboard. The young man took in Renno's dress, or the lack of it, and asked politely for an explanation of the events of the night. Renno made it simple. He concluded by saying, "Perhaps our reaction was overly severe, but when two men face six, five of them with drawn pistols, the choice of delivering an incapacitating blow instead of a fatal one is sometimes denied by the desire to live."

"Most disturbing, this," the young lieutenant muttered. "I must say, sir, that killing slave patrols is highly irregular. I shall have to send a report to the governor, you know. He'll make the decision as to whether or not to take action."

When Beth heard the story from Se-quo-i, her face went pale and tense. She found Renno with Little Hawk, on deck, both gleaming with perspiration as Renno conducted a lesson in the use of the tomahawk.

"In view of what happened, perhaps we should leave," Beth suggested. She knew British justice and was concerned for Renno.

"Without even so much as a pound of that splendid coffee you promised me?" Renno teased.

It was midafternoon before the young lieutenant returned, his uniform wilted by heat and sweat. He was alone, and this made Beth feel better.

"The governor has decided," the officer stated, "that the encounter in the streets was a natural mistake on both sides, and that although the results were most unfortunate, your reaction was in self-defense."

"So," Renno said.

"Actually," the lieutenant confided, "not much loss, considering that those fellows who hire out as slave patrol are the dregs of society, which, in this place, can be quite, uh, dreggy."

"So," Renno said.

"The governor did suggest, sir—and madam—that it might be beneficial in many ways, for your health and, uh, for the health of anyone else who might mistake the noble face of our, uh, red friend for something else, if you would be guests of the government at the summer camp of the army for a few days, until your cargo is gathered here and loaded. You'll find Newcastle"—he turned and pointed to the range of mountains that rose abruptly behind Kingston—"to be a pleasant relief from this sea-level heat. Quite pleasant, as a matter of fact."

"Yes," Beth urged, "let's do go."

Renno nodded.

"As it happens," the lieutenant continued, "I'm sending up a contingent of troops tomorrow morning, so you can be guided by them. I shan't say that you will be protected, for, apparently, you need no such protection."

Renno, Se-quo-i, and Little Hawk were only too happy to

have a chance to explore the mountains. Beth was relieved
that the deadly affair in the streets had ended so calmly. She
was the first one ready the next morning, and she was smiling
and happy when Renno helped her into the seat of a military
dray that had been sent for them.

The route led them past the slave quarters. A group of
twenty soldiers had earned the right to escape the heat on
the cool heights, but there was a price to be paid, a long,
weary march that climbed a tortuous switchback road into
jungle hills. Several times Renno and Se-quo-i, urged on by
curiosity and by their training never to try to move a large
body of men without scouts out front and to the flanks, left
the steep, rocky road and tried to penetrate the jungles. They
found the going to be impossibly rugged; the thick jungle
soared above them on precipitous slopes and fell away below
the road hundreds of feet to equally dense jungle valleys.

The sergeant in charge, the same man who had decided
that it was the better part of valor to allow Renno and
Se-quo-i to return to the ship, assured Renno that the road
was perfectly safe, that the eastern half of Jamaica was free of
any troublemakers.

The party made camp atop a ridge in a clearing that was
maintained for that purpose by dint of constant battle with
the jungle. The curious troops clustered around the Americans. The young men were awed by Beth's beauty and eager
to exchange information with the Indian with blue eyes. The
army rations were supplemented by a variety of fruit that was
readily available for the gathering. Little Hawk greedily sampled pawpaws and sweetsop, a small type of banana, and a
fruit called akai, which, the soldiers warned, was poisonous if
eaten unripe.

Their first view of the impressive summer camp of the
British army showed a line of gleaming white, red-roofed
buildings slanted down a ridge with the jungle in the fore-
ground and the green, purpling mountains rising behind.
They looked across a defile after having climbed from swel-
tering, tropical summer to what Beth thought to be a touch of
England itself with pure air and cool temperatures, even in
the middle of the afternoon, in the low seventies.

Beth had shown great interest in the dense, widely varied
vegetation. The sergeant, it seemed, was a self-made author-

ity. He confided to Beth that he planned to settle in Jamaica when his tour was finished, to become a landowner. He pointed out to her the beautiful flowers of the lignum vitae tree, with wood as hard as iron; great stands of West Indian ebony and Caribbean pine; at least twelve species of palm; and a huge silk-cotton tree, its buttressed trunk having a girth of some thirty feet.

Renno, however, was disappointed. Although it was good to be away from the heat and stench of the city, the hunting in Jamaica was miserable. He learned that bats made up the greatest variety of Jamaican wildlife, and the only native land mammal was a small rodent called the cony. There were hummingbirds with long, split tails, and pigeons and parrots, which were quite tasty when roasted over an open fire.

The streets of Newcastle Barracks were raw and red, but the coolness and the view—there was Kingston, far down and away, and beyond the city, the blue of the bay and the whiteness of surf on the outer bar of the harbor—were magnificent. They were given rooms in an officers' billet, where they were served by black slaves, one of whom specialized in native dishes. Little Hawk especially liked akai fruit cooked with scrambled eggs.

Unknown to the army or to Renno, another group of travelers had left Kingston for the mountains on the night of the swift and deadly battle with the slave patrol. Led by a tall, strong black man, the newly arrived slaves had taken a far more difficult route than the rough road constructed to allow relatively easy access to the rest areas at Newcastle. These men, who spoke no more than a few words of barely recognizable English, toiled up perpendicular slopes so thick with jungle growth that the leader's machete had to cut a narrow path. They lived off the land, eating fruit. They traveled long hours, from first light until darkness stopped them. They slept where they fell.

Four days after escaping Kingston, they rested atop a ridge while the leader went forward to meet a group of black men armed with a variety of weapons. They were also dressed in a colorful mixture of near rags. The language was a bastardized form of Spanish.

"I have brought six," the liberator reported. "They are Fon, and strong."

"You have done well, Libertador," a young, strong black answered.

An older one warned, "But one day, Libertador, you will go into the English den once too often."

The huge, strong man called Libertador showed his teeth. "On that day many white dogs will die before me."

"We go," the young man stated with an air of leadership. "We have observed the coming of redcoats, twenty of them—with two oddly dressed ones—a boy and a woman with hair like the sunrise."

"Are you afraid?" Libertador needled. "The English do not venture into the mountains from their camp save to walk up the peak near the camp, to see the pretty little birds."

"I fear nothing," the young man retorted, "but I avoid cannon and muskets out of good sense."

"You say," Libertador said, "that there was a white woman with red hair?"

"A toothsome morsel," the old man said.

"One for the master?" suggested Libertador.

"We go," the young man repeated. "We came to help you gather new ones, not to invade the very lair of the lion."

"We have come a long way," Libertador said. "The gods will bless us for what we have done, but we would accumulate luck with a gift for the master. We will see this red-haired woman, at least."

To two travelers from the northern forests of the United States, the Cockpit Country presented a face of isolation and ruggedness unlike any previous experience. Well-watered by tropical rains, the junglelike growth covered countless conical hills and roughly circular pits, glens as deep as five hundred feet with nearly perpendicular sides. It was from the pitlike glens that the area took the name applied to it by white explorers, for the pits reminded men of the arenas constructed for watching cockfights, although these cockpits would have been more fitting for battle between giant, mythical birds.

Hodano and Cochon had made contacts in the small village of Falmouth, on the north coast of Trelawny parish, and had been guided into the wilderness by a wizened, cynical old black who was sure that he was leading these two foreigners to their deserved deaths.

To penetrate the Cockpit Country the travelers were required to carry their own food and water. It was a trip of long, grueling days traversing winding, slippery trails past frightening crevasses and sinkholes formed by the collapse of underground limestone. Some pits hidden well among the lush green growth seemed to be bottomless. It would be necessary to hack their way for miles with machetes through the vegetation. There was an abundance of bloodsucking insects. Quite often the trio marched through tropical downpours that began and ended with suddenness.

Cochon was all for turning back almost immediately, but Hodano, having had a taste of the power of voodoo on the island of Haiti, burned to meet and exchange secrets with the man who, said the masters of Haiti, was the master of all.

Communicating in a barely understandable version of English, the old guide, pressed for information, described the inhabitants of Cockpit Country as freemen.

"We kill English for hundred years," he bragged, "and white governor Trelawny beg peace. We give peace on paper, but they no come, 'cause we no sen."

Once the old man asked, "Who sen for you?" in a way that made Cochon nervous.

The savage appearance of the black people living in the settlement that was their final destination, deep into the Cockpits, made Cochon wish that he was back on Haiti or in the north woods. They were immediately surrounded by huge, armed, fierce-looking men.

Hodano was prepared. In that wild and dark country he had felt his power growing, as if his evil spirits were physically with him.

"I have come to consult with your master," he announced imperiously. "Take me to him."

A black warrior laughed and made a playful stab at Hodano with his spear. Hodano lifted his arms and began to chant in a voice that stilled the laughter and caused the Maroons to step back a pace. An eerie, unnatural darkness descended on the glen where the black ex-slaves had built their village. A woman wailed in terror. The blackness deepened, and into that came something even darker, a forbidding shadow with a voice of thunder and doom. The words were in a language previously unheard by Hodano.

Terrified women prostrated themselves. The Maroon warriors stared upward at the black, menacing shadow, their eyes wide in fear.

"Let the master come to me," commanded a frail, piping old voice.

The voodoo master had appeared from the mouth of a cave fringed by ferns and growth. He wore a loincloth of animal skins, and his body was wasted, his bones covered only by a thin layer of translucent black skin.

Gradually the eerie darkness lifted. Hodano, his face concealed by his cloth cowl, strode forward.

"I bring you greetings, Master, from your peers in far lands, in Haiti," Hodano said.

"The master who brings the dark is welcome," the old man replied. "Come."

Hodano and Cochon sat cross-legged in a special chamber lit by fire and torch. The old man—he seemed to have no name save Master—chanted softly to a full-bodied naked woman who knelt before him. The woman's eyes became glazed, and she swayed, her pendulous, full breasts making soft motions. The master penetrated her flesh with a long needle. He turned to Hodano to show his toothless gums in a grimace of a smile. "Does the visiting master have this power?"

Hodano nodded. "I have come to you, Master, for more than simple tricks, for more than this easily obtained mastery of will over believers."

The old man snorted, then clapped his hands. Hodano's interest soared as a small, weeping white lad of about five years was half-dragged, half-carried from a recess of the chamber.

The old black master whispered to Hodano. "Come into my head and feel how this is accomplished." He pointed to the white boy and said, "This kind is rare."

Hodano gazed into the black master's eyes and felt himself sharing the old man's thoughts. The boy's death was painful, lingering. Before the boy breathed his last, his throat was hoarse from screaming and begging. Hodano felt disappointment when the old black man leaned forward and gulped the boy's departing spirit. Had he come so far to be shown something he already knew, spirit eating?

Then he cried out in surprise as the voodoo master floated slowly from the cavern's floor, keeping his cross-legged pose, to disappear into thin air. To Hodano's excitement he had felt the transformation of thought and will that had given the master the power to soar and to become invisible. That, he knew, was a power worth having.

It was long minutes before the old man reappeared and sank slowly to the floor. Hodano's face was transformed into an expression of awe.

"Is this worthy of the visiting master?" the old man asked.

"It is worthy, Master," Hodano whispered.

"Then teach me the power of the descending darkness."

"Look into my mind," Hodano said.

It took the old man only minutes to darken the cave to the point where the blazing fires and the torches were mere pinpricks of light in a blanket of sightless night. When it lightened, he chanted his thanks to his dark gods.

"Now . . ." Hodano said.

"First you must have the sacrifice," the master said. "Some of the men will travel with you to the white man's lands."

Hodano, severely disappointed, nodded. "What manner of white is best?"

"The young," the master answered, "for they do not understand the reason for the pain, and their spirits suffer more. Next, a white woman."

"And an adult white man?" Hodano asked.

The old man shrugged. "For a master of your powers, a white man would serve the purpose—with more difficulty, however."

"May I have the unquestioning aid of four of your warriors?" Hodano asked.

The old man nodded, made motions, and four Maroons came to kneel before the two masters.

"This man." Hodano indicated Cochon.

"For God's sake, Hodano." Cochon smirked. "You're joking."

"Tie him and prepare him," Hodano ordered, and on a nod of confirmation from the black master, the warriors leapt upon Cochon and quickly subdued him.

Cochon's eyes were wild. He was bruised by the struggle. He could not believe that Hodano was serious. "Eh, *mon ami?*" he pleaded.

"I don't need a translator anymore." Hodano shrugged. "Be rewarded by the knowledge that your death will contribute to my power. From your death will come the means for the destruction of our enemies."

Early in his stay in the north woods Cochon had once witnessed a ceremony during which a warrior of an enemy tribe had been given glory by a slow torture, mostly by the women of the Miami tribe. The warrior's death had been slow and without doubt, since knives, fire, and sharp splinters had been utilized, quite agonizing, but the warrior had smiled and taunted his torturers until his spirit flew. For long minutes Cochon determined that he would deprive the treacherous Hodano of the pleasure of hearing him scream. Perhaps if he died silently, he would deprive Hodano of the power to be taken from torture and sacrifice.

Cochon's determination faded, however, as his flesh sizzled with a hot iron, as Hodano's knife skillfully did irreparable things to him, as his stomach was opened and he could look down and see the writhing, bloody entrails pouring out. He screamed. He begged. And he died, his spirit being sucked into the rapacious mouth of Hodano, a mouth made more horrifying by the split tongue, by the sharpened teeth.

Hodano felt the power come into him. He willed himself to soar and felt his body rising slowly. He looked down on the chanting, writhing audience of blacks, saw men and women celebrating the exhibition of power with bodies joined, with wild grunts and pantings. He willed himself to fade from sight and heard a rewarding gasp from those who watched, which told him he had succeeded.

Around him black, sooty clouds roiled. He pierced them with his all-seeing eye. He saw the island spread before him, saw the distant cities, saw a tall ship at dockside, and then his eye was soaring upward, upward, to the heights above the city, as if he were a bird. He saw a grouping of white, red-roofed buildings drawing nearer. His blood froze as he began to distinguish individual forms on the ground below: red-coated English soldiers and a man in buckskins, a man of golden-brown hair and pale, sun-bronzed skin. At his side was a flame-haired woman, a woman Hodano had once tried to kill, only to be denied by the white power that had emanated from this man, and from the brother of this man.

His mood soared, and he chanted thanks to his dark spirits, for his enemy was *here*. Renno of the Seneca was in *Jamaica*. Now he knew why his guiding spirits had sent him so far from his hunting grounds, had sent him first to Haiti, where he gained power, and then to Jamaica, where the ultimate power became his.

Renno. He hissed the name with his split tongue, and around him the dark clouds began to form, and they were laced with black lightning as he drifted slowly to feel his body make contact with the ground inside the master's cave.

Chapter VIII

Renno bolted upward into a sitting position, shaking off a terrifying nightmare, his spirit escaping dark horrors that had no face. His body was soaked with perspiration. Beth slept peacefully beside him, covered against the pleasant coolness of the mountain night. He tried to recall his dream, the first evil one he'd had in some weeks, and he searched for the reason. Try as he might, he could remember only a feeling of terrible threat.

He got up quietly, wrapped a blanket around his naked body, and walked into the Jamaican night. Birds unknown to him made soft night calls. The wan moon was in a morning position to the west. The sky was spectacular, with the stars larger, more brilliant, than those of his own land. Below, far away, only a few lights twinkled in Kingston. He could make out the dock areas and the bay and the sea. He dropped the blanket and felt the chill of the night. He lifted his arms to the lights of the sky.

"Manitous," he chanted, "of what am I being warned?"

He remembered the words of the spirit of Ah-wen-ga, that the living march alone in distant places, that the manitous can only watch, and he felt truly alone.

"I have noticed, my brother," said Ah-wa-o, "that we are not being overwhelmed with invitations or with friendliness."

El-i-chi felt quick anger. In spite of Nathan and Peggy Ridley's continued warmth toward them, he too had felt shunned by the people of Wilmington. That didn't bother him. His anger was aroused because he knew that such behavior was hurtful to Ah-wa-o, who was looking more the rose with each passing week. He himself was aware of the reasons.

"The malice of the white man is not new to me," he replied. "Ignore it, Sister. Be assured that any person of true worth would be kind and friendly to you."

"I am not bothered," she replied. "I have little patience with the talk of the white women—the talk of clothing and gossip about their friends and acquaintances."

"The white women are not reacting to you as a person," El-i-chi added. "You know the guilt most whites feel because of the treatment they gave the Indian. The peaceful Indians of this region were exterminated or driven out long before the war for white independence, and in this backwater of the United States there are no men such as Washington and Franklin who know the contribution our people made to their war."

"*I* know that people are people," Ah-wa-o said, "but some don't. Some who look down on the black slaves seem to class me as being only slightly above them."

"There is reason for that as well," El-i-chi said. "The greatly weakened tribes, pushed into the interior, tried to replenish their numbers by taking escaped black slaves into their communities. Indian blood was mixed with that of the African."

She came to him and put her hands on his. "I have troubled you without reason," she whispered. "Soon Renno will return, and we will go back to our own."

"Yes," he said, thinking, *Just let any man, white or otherwise, insult this woman.* His hand itched for his tomahawk.

Sensing that she was disturbed by the ostracism in spite of her protestations to the contrary, he felt his heart going out to her. Her hands were still on his. He was looking down into her young, beautiful face. Her eyes slowly changed, going wide and becoming deeper, and it was the most natural thing in the world for him to pull her into his arms and find her mouth with his.

He was totally unprepared for what happened then. The manitous sent thunder and lightning into his blood. His heart raced.

In his arms Ah-wa-o was tense at first, and then she seemed to melt, to mold against him. Her lips, never having known the kiss of a lover, knew not what to do, but his instructed so that they were closer, and the sweet warmth of her mouth was his, and then, with a gasp, he pushed her away. Her eyes were closed. They opened slowly, widely, and there was a look of awe and surprise on her face.

"That was not a brotherly kiss," she whispered in a child's voice.

"No, it was not," El-i-chi confirmed, "nor are my feelings for you any longer that of brother to sister."

She gasped and turned, as if to flee. He took her arm. "It is too soon for me to declare myself to you, for you are my sister. There will be no more of this—after this." He pulled her to him again, savored the slim strength in her body and the taste of her mouth, then gently moved her away from him. "I must talk with the old ones, the wise ones, to see if there are any traditions that apply to this."

Ah-wa-o, shocked to find that her own passions, which had given her feelings of guilt for the very reasons mentioned by El-i-chi, had been matched in his heart, could not speak. In spite of the fact that her eyes feasted on El-i-chi at each opportunity, she had always felt that she was being foolish, for he was her brother.

"When we are at home," he said, "we will seek the approval of those who keep the tribal traditions." A sudden thought came to him. "Or have I shocked you, insulted you?"

"No," she answered quickly. She giggled. "Had my father

not married your mother, you would have counted me among the maidens who pursued you."

He smiled. "Pursue not, little rose, for in this case I will be easy prey."

Now it became torture not to be near her, pain not to be able to repeat those two burning kisses. He told her, "I want to be near, to touch you, but we must wait, and so I must not be near you always."

"I understand," she said.

El-i-chi left her to tend Renna. He wandered aimlessly for a while, then found himself on the riverside near the Huntington shipping office and warehouse. He entered through the warehouse, where workers were consolidating the inventory in preparation for the return of the *Seneca Warrior* from England with a cargo of manufactured and luxury goods. Cedric had told El-i-chi that the cargo of Beth's third ship, which already had been off-loaded and sold, had added much to the Huntington coffers.

The door to Cedric's office was closed. El-i-chi, walking softly in his moccasins, was extending his hand to the doorknob when he heard an angry voice from inside. He listened for a moment. Unable to understand all the words, he heard just enough to recognize the threatening tone and to know that a large sum of money was involved. Whatever was happening in the office, he reasoned, had to do with the firm's business, and that was no concern of his. He turned to go, but then he heard Cedric's voice. It was raised, and his words were gasped. It was not the words but the pain, the gasping, that sent El-i-chi's hand back to the doorknob. He opened the door softly.

Cedric sat behind his desk, his face pale, one hand clutching his shirt over his heart, his forehead beaded with sweat. The man who stood before him was powerfully built and dressed roughly in the manner of a seaman.

"No man welshes on me," the man was saying. "Don't think because your heart is going to kill you that that will satisfy your debts."

El-i-chi walked quietly to stand behind the man and tapped a finger on his shoulder. The man whirled, his hand going toward a pistol in his belt, but El-i-chi's hand was faster, seizing the man's wrist in a grip of steel. For long moments they stood toe to toe, eyes glaring and muscles straining. The man was unable to move his arm toward the pistol. He relaxed, and the momentary advantage was his, so that a blow glanced off El-i-chi's head from the man's other hand. But then El-i-chi was moving, thrusting his hands under the man's arms and up over his neck in a neck-breaking hold. He applied pressure and considered finishing the job, but remembering that he was in white man's country, he merely applied pain and pushed the bent, grunting man toward the door leading onto the wharf, then thrust him out, seizing the pistol from his belt as he fell.

He disarmed the pistol, then tossed it into the lap of the fallen man, who glared up from baleful, pale eyes and vowed, "You're dead."

El-i-chi's tomahawk leapt to his hand, and he took a step forward before he was able to control himself. "If you have business with Mr. Huntington, you will conduct it in a manner that does not aggravate his illness," he ordered, and the tone of his voice silenced the man.

Cedric was still gasping for breath, but he looked better, with a bit of color returning to his face. El-i-chi brought a tankard of water and waited until Cedric's breathing was almost normal.

"Thank God you came when you did," Cedric breathed.

"What happened here is none of my business," El-i-chi said, "but on behalf of my brother and sister, I am at your service."

Cedric tugged out a handkerchief and mopped his face. "I am a bedamned old fool, my boy," he admitted.

El-i-chi waited. He had glanced through a window to see his opponent walking powerfully away down the wharf without a backward look.

"Perhaps we can start with that man's name," El-i-chi suggested.

"Hollinger, Spade Hollinger."

"A friend?" El-i-chi prompted when the old man fell silent.

"Hardly." Cedric sighed. "We began as friends—or at least I thought so—playing friendly games with small stakes."

El-i-chi nodded encouragingly.

"I should have stuck with my sailor friends, but they were insulted when we turned them away from the house." Cedric waved his hand. "I'm not blaming anyone. I was wrong to bring them there. But I had no one to game with, so I started dicing with Hollinger. I won small amounts, and he insisted upon a chance to get even. The stakes got higher. I'm a fair man, El-i-chi. I don't gamble to take large amounts of money away from men. I play because—" He paused. "Because, damme, of the excitement of winning or losing. The amount doesn't matter. It's the game that matters."

"I heard Hollinger mention a large sum," El-i-chi said.

Cedric put his head in his hands. "And so history repeats itself."

"How much?"

"Enough to bankrupt the company," Cedric groaned. "As we played, I told him that I had no access to large sums of money. He said that money was only a way of keeping score. I was caught up in the excitement of the game. There were witnesses. A gambling debt, my friend, is a matter of honor, as legitimate a debt as if I'd borrowed it from the bank."

"What is to be done?"

"If I could get my hands on the proceeds of the *Warrior*'s cargo when she arrives, that would satisfy Hollinger for a time, I suppose."

"But it is not your money," El-i-chi reminded him.

"My daughter would—" He stopped. "El-i-chi, you would be doing me a favor if you'd take that sharp-headed hammer of yours and bash in my skull."

El-i-chi laughed. "Perhaps such drastic measures will not be necessary. I suggest that you go home now and stay there until you've recovered from your strain."

"Excellent suggestion." Cedric rose weakly.

El-i-chi, no authority on debts of honor or any other kind, sought out his kinsman Nathan at Ridley's shipping company. He was greeted warmly and ushered into Nate's office, where a pot of coffee brewed constantly on a small stove, even in the heat of summer.

"I guess we're becoming thoroughly Americanized, El-i-chi," Nate said as he poured a mug for his visitor. "Not long ago this would have been a teapot, heated only at teatime. Now we swill this vile dark beverage all day or get irritable because none is available."

"White man's evil conquer Indian too," El-i-chi said in

comic imitation of a white man's idea of how an Indian should speak.

Ridley laughed. "Peggy wants you and the girls for dinner on Sunday. I'm glad you stopped in, since I was deputized to relay the invitation."

"Thank you. It is always a pleasure. I came for a reason, though. What do you know of a man named Spade Hollinger?"

"*Hmmm*," Nathan said. "I hope you're not involved with that nasty fellow. He has a little coastal sloop but never seems to have any cargo. Has a crew that looks as bloodthirsty as any gang of reprobates I've ever seen. No one seems to know what he does for a living."

"Gambling?"

"Haven't heard that," Nathan said, "but it wouldn't surprise me."

El-i-chi briefly told how Cedric had been coaxed into gambling beyond his means.

Nathan looked grave. "Such men take their gambling debts seriously. Tell you what: I'll put out a few feelers, learn what I can about Hollinger, and give you my report on Sunday."

El-i-chi, however, was not willing to wait the two days. He was a familiar figure around the docks and knew many of the sailors and workers by name. His presence there was not remarkable, so as darkness fell and all worthy sailors were hoisting tankards of rum at a waterfront pub, he was able to snoop around the area. He saw that Hollinger's sloop appeared to be left without a watch aboard. He leapt to her deck lightly and waited until the motion caused by his weight had ceased, then probed into the small crew's quarters and the captain's cabin to find strong odors of old cigars and regurgitated rum. He lifted a hatch and was assaulted by a stench unlike any he'd ever experienced, even on a battlefield where enemy dead lay rotting.

He had to seek out a ship's lantern, for the space below was too dark. He lowered himself through the hatch, lit the lantern, and tried to hold his breath against the horrendous odors. The entire hold was laddered with raw wood bunks, with not much more than a foot's space between them. He estimated that if all the spaces were full, there would be over forty people crammed into the small area. The purpose was clear: Hollinger's sloop was a slave transporter.

El-i-chi extinguished the lantern and left the ship. He, like Renno, hated the institution that allowed a white man to make a beast of burden and labor out of a black man, although to date El-i-chi had little respect for the African. A Seneca, he knew, would have fought to the death against being enslaved.

Although El-i-chi could read, he was not the omnivorous reader that his brother was. He had heard Renno discuss the question of slavery several times and knew that the Ordinance of 1787 pertaining to the Northwest Territories specifically prohibited slavery. El-i-chi believed that slavery would die of its own accord. Men such as Washington, Jefferson, Madison, and Hamilton, all of whom had favored a prohibition against slavery in the Constitution, would prevail.

Unlike Renno, El-i-chi was unaware of efforts elsewhere, especially in England, to end the practice of slavery. He had never heard of Thomas Clarkson, who, in 1786, had inflamed public opinion against slavery by the publication of "Essay on the Slavery and Commerce of the Human Species," nor of Granville Sharp, who gave of his own fortune to establish a colony in Africa for freed slaves who had been taken out of America by the retreating British.

In short, although he hated the idea of slavery, it had never been one of El-i-chi's chief personal concerns. Now, after smelling the stench in the hold of Hollinger's ship, after seeing the coffinlike bunks in which men and women had to stay for weeks, he was angered and determined to learn more about Spade Hollinger.

Nathan had some information for him on Sunday. The two men retired to Nathan's library after a meal of fresh summer vegetables and melons, fish, and a wild turkey taken in the forests on the west side of the Cape Fear. Nathan lost no time beginning.

"Hollinger is a Massachusetts man, and the rumor is that he fled from there to avoid being imprisoned for murder. It is also rumored that he deals in slaves."

"He does," El-i-chi confirmed.

Nathan nodded. "He is said to make trips to the slave markets in the British islands and deliver slaves either to Spanish Florida or to the cotton producers of South Carolina or Georgia. I was quite discreet in my inquiries, but the general opinion is that Hollinger is not a man to be trifled with. He's known to have severely maimed two men with his bare hands, and at least two men known to have crossed him have disappeared."

"And his gambling?"

"Men were willing to talk about that quite openly. It seems that he has uncanny luck with the dice. I talked to at least four men who had lost their entire wages for a long voyage to him in an evening."

"Is it merely luck?"

Nathan shrugged. "One man hinted that he was suspicious. The others said nothing. I got the impression that they were reluctant to speak ill of Hollinger. And yet when they spoke of his luck, there was a certain look on their faces—if you take my meaning."

"That Hollinger might cheat at dice?"

Nate nodded grimly.

"How would a man go about cheating at dice?"

Nathan laughed. "You're asking the wrong man that question. Oh, I know the rules of the game. We might even have some dice around the house." He went out of the library, and El-i-chi heard him calling Peggy. When he came back into the room, he was shaking something in his right hand that made a clicking noise. In his left was a bowl of buttons.

"Dice are nothing more than cubes of ivory," Nathan explained, tossing two of them onto the top of his desk. "Each side has a number, from one to six. Certain combinations of numbers make for winning or losing. The dice have to be cut very precisely, perfectly square. I have heard that shaving one side—or weighting it—will cause certain numbers to come up more often."

El-i-chi took the dice and examined them as Nathan explained the meaning of the numbers and what he had to do to win. "Real dice players favor being on their knees," Nathan said, taking the dice and kneeling to bounce the tiny cubes off the baseboard. One die spun on its corner on the wide planks of the pine floor before it came to rest.

When Peggy and Ah-wa-o came into the library to see what was keeping the men from the after-dinner watermelon, they found the two men on the floor on their knees, the buttons being used in lieu of money.

"Just teaching El-i-chi the basic rules of the dice," Nathan explained, looking sheepishly up at his wife.

There had been no need for money in the wilderness until white expansion showed Indians the luxury and convenience of certain of the white man's inventions. Wishing to possess these goods, the Indians needed to deal in the white man's system of exchange. Some of the gold that Renno and El-i-chi had brought back from the Southwest had gone to buy cooking pots, blankets woven in England's textile mills, knives, and a few bright bolts of cloth for the women. But mainly the gold purchased guns, powder, lead, and molds to make balls. Aware of the necessity of having some money in order to travel through the white man's country, Renno had put aside a relatively small amount for such pursuits, and he had drawn on that store for the trip to Wilmington. He had left El-i-chi a few dollars in case of emergency, although food and necessities would be charged to Beth's various accounts with Wilmington merchants. El-i-chi retrieved a few coins from his small hoard, had them changed into pennies at the bank, and sought out dice games on the docks.

It was, he found, an exciting way to pass time. There was something vital and riveting in risking one's own money on the roll of two small cubes of ivory and the ridiculously inflated sense of accomplishment that resulted when he won. Over a period of a few days he played with several groups, using at least a half-dozen different pairs of dice. Luck was fickle indeed, El-i-chi decided, but he ended up with only a few pennies less than he'd had when he started. When he felt he had mastered the ins and outs of gambling at dice, he sought out Cedric.

The old man had been sticking close to home, fearful of encountering Spade Hollinger. El-i-chi had explained the situation to Ah-wa-o, instructing her to send a servant for him at the docks immediately if any stranger came around.

"I want to show you something," he told Cedric, going to his knees near the chair where Cedric sat. He cupped the dice in his hand and rattled them.

"I say! Not you too," Cedric said.

"Watch." El-i-chi rolled the dice to bounce off the baseboard. The result was a winning number.

"Jolly good! I'll wager a penny you can't do it again."

He did it again and again, until Cedric's eyes were popping and he demanded to look at those dice. He examined them carefully.

"Purchased just today from the general store," El-i-chi said.

"But it's unnatural," Cedric protested.

El-i-chi flexed the long, graceful fingers on his right hand. Casno and others had taught him that hidden deep inside every man are senses that he does not use. Hardened as they were by the use of weaponry, by a life in the wilderness, El-i-chi's hands could become an extension of his other senses, with a delicate sense of touch that had been developed over the years, working under Casno's teachings. He threw a winning number and tried to explain to Cedric that there was something in his fingers that allowed him to feel the exact moment to release the dice, to make them come up a winning number.

"But my boy," Cedric exploded, "you have the makings of a fortune in your hands! I'll arrange games for you. Mind you, you'll not be able to throw winner after winner—you'll have to arrange to lose, just a little, now and then."

"Could it be that Spade Hollinger used such methods when he was gambling with you?"

Cedric's enthusiasm left him like air from a balloon. "I've never seen anyone control the dice the way you can. Are you asking if he cheated me? I can't say. The dice took some peculiar rolls. In the end he did make seven straight passes. Odd, but not unheard of."

"How can I get into a game with Hollinger?"

Cedric's face contorted. "See here, I won't have you risking—"

"Does he play anywhere with regularity?"

"No. I've discovered that he plays mainly with strangers."

"So he is either very lucky on a consistent basis or he can influence the dice," El-i-chi declared. "Tell me where I can find him."

"Well, I can put out the word. I'm deucedly tired of staying in the house."

El-i-chi agreed to escort his elderly friend to the shipping office.

As it happened, things moved rapidly. When El-i-chi

checked in on Cedric later that afternoon, the old man was excited. "There's to be a big game this very night on board Hollinger's boat. The crew of that Indies schooner that docked this afternoon was putting out the word that they were looking for action. One of Hollinger's men arranged it."

From the shadows of the buildings on the land side of the wharves, El-i-chi watched men board Hollinger's sloop and soon heard their voices raised in the excitement of the game. He waited for a half hour, then boarded the boat. Hollinger was the holder of the dice when El-i-chi walked to the afterdeck to see several men on their knees, watching the tumble of the dice by lantern light. He edged his way to the gaming area, taking the place of a man who cursed in dismay as Hollinger threw a winning number and raked in a pile of coins.

Hollinger looked up into El-i-chi's eyes, and his expression froze. El-i-chi threw a pouch onto the deck. It contained all the money Renno had left with him, some gold, mostly silver. "I would try my luck."

Hollinger seemed undecided. The look in his eyes told El-i-chi that the man wanted, more than anything, to launch himself in attack, but the obvious weight of El-i-chi's money pouch won out.

"Well, gentlemen," Hollinger said, "let us see how luck treats the noble savage." He tossed the dice to El-i-chi. "Newcomer's dice."

El-i-chi felt the dice. They nestled in his palm, even, square. He threw and deliberately lost a small silver coin. The dice were passed. When others were rolling, El-i-chi noted, Hollinger's bets were careful and conservative as he bet the odds, often winning, sometimes losing. Hollinger acted as dice manager, often taking the dice into his own hands to pass them along or to return them to the shooter. El-i-chi watched the man's hands carefully. He saw nothing suspicious until it was once again Hollinger's turn. Careful observation revealed that Hollinger substituted a different pair of dice for those that had been in play. He threw out his bet against Hollinger's making a winning throw and lost. Hollinger made five straight points, doubling his bets each time until there was a large pile of coins in front of him.

"He'll never make six," a sailor muttered, shoving all his

money into the center. The number was a winning combination. The sailor swore and left the game. Two other players were bankrupt before Hollinger, with a deft movement, replaced the second pair of dice with the first and threw a losing number.

El-i-chi's turn lasted for a long time, and he made increasingly large bets as he won. Another sailor quit in disgust, and then there were only El-i-chi and Hollinger left, with Hollinger's pile of silver and gold much the larger.

"I find that I like this game." El-i-chi shoved gold to the center. "Let's make it even more interesting."

Hollinger matched his bet. El-i-chi threw a winning number, then said, "The bet is there," indicating the doubled pile at the center. Hollinger's eyes narrowed. El-i-chi threw a number that had to be matched to win, and Hollinger reached for the dice, deftly substituted another pair for them, threw them back to El-i-chi. The dice had a different feel to El-i-chi's delicate fingers. He used all his power of concentration and rolled, manipulating with his fingers and his mind to cause the number to match that one previously thrown. He raked in the money and looked at Hollinger, who was staring at him in disbelief.

"Here," Hollinger said, "give a man a chance to get even." He shoved a large amount of money into the betting circle. El-i-chi fingered the dice, which, he had decided, were weighted so delicately that a man without his ultrasensitive fingers could not tell the difference.

"I've heard that you are a man who is not afraid to gamble for high stakes," El-i-chi challenged. He shoved all his money to the center. Hollinger grinned wolfishly, counted the money, and matched it. The pay of a half-dozen sailors for an entire Atlantic crossing to England and back was in the circle, plus El-i-chi's original small stake. Determined to discover just how much he could disorient Hollinger, El-i-chi rolled a winning number.

Hollinger muttered oaths, reached for his stash in a leather pouch in his pocket, and brought out gold coins of France, England, and Spain. "Let's see if *you* are afraid of high stakes," he taunted, matching the pot.

This time El-i-chi made it more interesting. He rolled a

number with high odds against repetition. "Care to increase the bet?" he asked mildly.

"Name it," Hollinger said.

"I have six horses in the stables. . . ."

"Write out a bill of sale and toss it on the pile," Hollinger said, for El-i-chi still had the weighted dice. Blind luck had saved the savage so far. The certainty of the dice's rolling a losing number would make up for all of it on the next roll.

El-i-chi took quill and paper from Hollinger and made out a bill of sale for six horses. Hollinger emptied his pouch to match the bet with gold. His eyes glittered dangerously as El-i-chi, his face impassive, rolled the dice, a winning number. Hollinger, in horrified disbelief, seized the dice and looked at them.

"They're your dice," El-i-chi said. "The same dice you used when you played with Cedric Huntington."

"You—" Hollinger leapt to his feet.

El-i-chi was calmly gathering up the winnings. He counted out his own original stake and put it into his leather bag.

"Wait!" Hollinger said. "I'd like one more chance to get even." He disappeared into the cabin and returned with yet another pouch of gold coin. No one could continue to win against his specially weighted dice. The money he now threw into the circle represented the money he'd need to purchase slaves at the Nassau slave market on his next trip.

"My pleasure," El-i-chi said, picking up the dice.

Hollinger was still standing. El-i-chi rolled the winning number and threw himself to one side as Hollinger's boot lashed out at him. He seized Hollinger's ankle and upended him, to be astride him as quickly as a cat. His tomahawk was raised in his hand, poised to deliver a death stroke.

"Would you say," El-i-chi asked conversationally, although the tomahawk, blade glinting in the lantern light, had been lowered to dent Hollinger's throat, "that the money on the deck would equal the paper you hold on Cedric Huntington?"

Hollinger's eyes squinted in thought. "Not quite, but if that is your goal, we can call it even." Anything, he was thinking, up to and including murder, to regain his seed money, for without money to purchase slaves, he was out of business.

"Get it." El-i-chi pulled the tomahawk away and got to his feet.

"Have it on me," Hollinger said, pulling Cedric's pledges from an inside pocket.

"I trust this is all of it," El-i-chi said, checking to see Cedric's shaky signature. He ripped the papers into pieces and let them blow overboard.

"No hard feelings, friend," Hollinger said. "In fact, I'd give a pretty penny to know how you managed that little trick."

"I had considered having you return the money you took from the sailors," El-i-chi said, "but when I pass the word that you were using loaded dice, perhaps they'll come for it themselves."

"Now look," Hollinger faltered, "you and me can make a lot of money. I'll show you my tricks, you show me yours, and we'll work together. We can take every gambler on the Atlantic coast from Maine to Georgia."

"Good night, Mr. Hollinger." El-i-chi had been watching his back. Four of Hollinger's men had been standing by the gangplank, perhaps unaware of what was happening on board. He leapt from the rail, thus avoiding the gangplank, to land solidly on the wharf.

"Get that Indian!" Hollinger shouted behind him, and the four men converged on him. He saw the glint of a knife, the bulk of belaying pins. He felt the surge of joy that precedes a good fight but let it die as he turned and ran. El-i-chi, running! But he ran not due to fear or cowardice, but because he was in white man's country, in a white man's city. He ran because of Ah-wa-o and Renna. He never doubted his ability to kill the four ruffians and Hollinger, too, if that scoundrel chose to join the fight.

Fate halted his flight as his foot hit a rotted plank and he tripped, turning in the air to land on his shoulder and roll like a tumbler to face the charging men. His tomahawk and knife were grasped firmly as he heard the air whisper with the force of a blow from a belaying pin. El-i-chi dodged under it and drove his knife into the soft bowels of one man. Then he slipped aside to avoid the straight-on thrust of a knife. His tomahawk took that attacker behind the ear.

Now two men circled him. One shouted a signal, and they came as one to see El-i-chi leap aside and swing backhand to crush a spine with his tomahawk. And then his knife flew through the moonlight to embed itself to the hilt in the stomach of his last opponent. He retrieved his weapon and looked up toward the sloop to see if Hollinger was going to join his men. But Hollinger was running up the docks, and soon the whistles of Wilmington's constable force sounded. One guardsman was on duty each night at the docks. El-i-chi, knowing he had been forced into the fight, decided to stay and face the white man's law.

The constable came running, with Hollinger behind him. The lawman's pistol was drawn. "Hold," he ordered El-i-chi.

"These men attacked me without provocation. I was defending myself."

The constable looked around. Dark blood stained the sun- and salt-faded planking. "Gawd," he gasped.

"This Indian lost at dice, Constable," Hollinger accused. "And then he tried to steal our money. My men were chasing him."

"Well, pal," the constable said, "it's the jail for you."

"Where is this money I am supposed to have stolen?" El-i-chi asked.

"In your pocket, in a small leather pouch," Hollinger said. "You can check it, Constable. You'll see that I'm right."

El-i-chi's nature urged him to kill the constable and Hollinger, but there were still Ah-wa-o and Renna to consider. It was his love for Ah-wa-o and his brother's daughter, his regard for Renno, that forced him to stand and argue.

"If I had been intent upon stealing, I would have taken all of the money, not just the few coins in my pocket."

"We'll let the justice of the peace sort it out," the constable said. "Now you come along like a good Injun before I have to shoot you."

A man groaned at El-i-chi's feet.

"You take him, Constable," Hollinger said, "and I'll see to my men. I'll get a doctor for them."

The constable waved his pistol. El-i-chi allowed himself to be disarmed, although this was the hardest part, gave a look of certain promise to Hollinger, and walked ahead of the constable up the docks. He consoled himself by remembering that his brother-by-marriage, Rusog, was once put into jail, falsely accused.

He was then shoved into a small cell with iron bars. Alone

in the cell, he dozed, then awoke a couple of hours later, while it was still night. He called for the jailer.

"When will I see the justice of the peace?" he asked when the man came in answer to his call.

"Speak when you're spoken to, Injun," the jailer snarled. "Don't bother me again. I'm trying to sleep."

Chapter IX

The Jamaican jungle was unlike anything Renno and Se-
quo-i had ever seen. The white Indian had experienced
moist heat and tropical growth in the swampy areas of Seminole country in Florida, but there the land had been flat. On
the heights above Newcastle the steep mountainside was an
impenetrable mass of rank green vegetation. A trail had been
carved out over the years by British soldiers who sought the
view from the peak directly behind the summer rest camp,
but to venture off that sodden, steamy, tunnellike trail meant
hauling oneself up the mountainside by clinging to roots and
bushes while pushing hard through a curtain of solid growth.

Ginger plants emitted an aromatic scent when crushed,
and there were bright, odd blooms in the trees from parasitic
plants. There were no signs of animal life—only the flittings of
curious, relatively large hummingbirds that often landed on

nearby branches, as if to investigate these strange beings invading their territory.

It had not taken Renno and Se-quo-i long to excuse themselves from the summer camp. They had begun the climb early, wasted some time in trying unsuccessfully to penetrate the precipitous jungle slopes, and reached a man-made clearing atop the peak after a climb up the trail. It was a fine vantage point: they could look down on the red roofs of the British installation, off to the east into a gorge far below that might have hidden a stream among the dense jungle. White clouds hung over the higher peaks, and from the deep, purplish color of the far mountains it was evident how the range had come to be called the Blue Mountains.

Renno had never felt claustrophobic, even when traveling through the densest of the virgin northern American forests; even in those areas that were made difficult by thick undergrowth, a man could slip through and make relatively good traveling speed. Here it would be a work of much time to travel even a few miles if one left the trails.

"I would see the stream in the valley," Se-quo-i said, looking down, down.

Renno nodded. "A difficult trek from the looks of it."

Se-quo-i shrugged. "My feet itch."

"Go, then," Renno urged.

"I will not come back this way. I will scale the lower slopes and approach the camp from the downhill end."

Se-quo-i disappeared quickly into the greenery, and soon the sound of his movements faded. Renno sat on an exposed rock. Although he was not at the highest point of the mountain range—to the north and the east there were higher peaks—he found himself at cloud level as a billowy, white mass moved to engulf the peak in fog. He felt oddly ill at ease: being inside the cloud cut him off from the world; the light was dim; objects became ghostly at a distance of mere feet, and beyond that there was only the milky white of the cloud.

He heard himself chanting to his manitous even before he realized consciously that he was doing so. He stood, lifted his arms to the unseen sky, and called out for an explanation of his forebodings. His voice seemed to be turned away by the dampness of the cloud. He felt a sense of frustration, for Ah-wen-ga's spirit had warned him that he would be alone, but he called out anyway, his voice low, guttural in the language of the Seneca, and from the mist emerged a form with brown skin that was lighter than that of most Indians, with that distinctive tone that comes from sun-coloring. On the figure's head was an odd cap of bright-red and gleaming-white feathers, and his only garment was a short skirt of the same feathers arranged in alternating white and red. He held a longbow in his left hand but carried neither quiver nor arrows.

The figure stepped closer in silence, and the ease of movement was explained when Renno noted that his feet did not touch the ground.

"Who are you, manitou?" Renno asked.

Now the spirit was joined by a female, graceful and slender, her round, firm breasts bared. She wore a slightly longer version of the man's kilt, also made of the same red and white feathers, but her headdress consisted of a band across the middle of her forehead from which protruded one single red feather. Around her neck was a double necklace of white seashells.

So sad. Their faces were so sad.

"Share your wisdom, Brother and Sister," Renno invited, "for once we were of one family."

Neither male nor female spoke, but in a fog more impenetrable than any Renno had ever experienced, he saw pictures and felt himself being transported to a happier time, when the beautiful and bountiful land of Xaymaca was the home of the Arawak Indians. It was a fair land. To eat, one had only to extend one's hand to pluck mangoes, avocado pears, plantains, pawpaws, sweetsop, and soursop. The sea yielded its bounty of fish and shellfish, and small arrows brought down the fat, delicious pigeons.

Then he saw the bearded Spaniards, perpetrating shocking acts of horror, raping, enslaving the gentle, unwarlike Arawak. He saw men and women under the lash of cursing Spaniards on sugar and coffee plantations, and he saw the Arawak die by the hundreds, the thousands, in the barren mines as the gold-greedy Spaniards punched holes into mountains. He watched in anguish as a group of the light-skinned, desperate Arawak ended their oppression in a mass leap from a high bluff into the sea.

"Why do you show me these things, manitous?" Renno
asked, but the spirits were silent. The woman lowered her
head and wept. The man's face expressed only pain and
sadness, and then they were gone.

Renno knew for a certainty that it was time to leave this
place. He did not know precisely what message was intended
by the spiritual visit of the long-dead brother and sister, but
he knew that he must take his family and friend away from
this land of heat and greenness and mountain wastes. The
lush island, he felt, had not changed since the Spanish first
enslaved the Arawak. Only the skin color of the master and
the slaves was different, and there was a sickness in the very
air. He made his way carefully toward the trail. In that
gloomy fog of cloud his usual infallible sense of direction
became confused, making him wonder if he moved at the
proper angle to enter the trail at the edge of the clearing.

He halted quickly as something tried to materialize from
the cloud. He thrust his head forward in an effort to see
more clearly, and gladness rushed through him, for he saw
the face of his grandmother. It was indistinct and weak, as if
the journey from beyond the river to the land of the living
was not quite complete.

"So you have come to be with me after all," he said, his
voice very warm, grateful.

Ah-wen-ga covered her face with her hands in an attitude
of weeping.

A cold chill made Renno shiver. "Speak," he begged.

Ah-wen-ga's spirit lowered her hands to reveal tear-reddened
eyes. Her voice drifted in and out, barely comprehensible.
"You will go far to the west."

Renno's heart thudded once. Was it his time, then? To go
to the West was not a fearful thing, except that it would mean
leaving Little Hawk and Beth unprotected on an island that
suddenly had become a place of menace.

"The mouse that flies will guide you in the end," the spirit
said, and was gone.

"Grandmother!" Renno cried out, but he was alone. His
mind raced as he found the path and threw himself recklessly
down the steep trail. He knew then that his manitous had not
been warning him of his own death, for no warrior needed a
guide to that Place Across the River. No, his travels would be

in the earthly sphere, and the danger was not, at least for the moment, to himself.

He ran out of the lowering cloud and slid now and again to the more-level ground of the slope where redcoats drilled. The rote orders of the drill sergeants seemed to belie the threat he had felt while covered by cloud on the peak. He did not slow until he reached the building where he and his family were quartered.

The large, sparsely furnished rooms were empty. He ran outside, found the black servant assigned to them emptying kitchen refuse onto a pile to be burned, and seized her arm. "Where are my wife and son?"

The woman's eyes showed fright. He released her and repeated his question more calmly. "Dey go." The woman pointed not toward the trail to the peak but to another, which angled across the concave slope to a point of vantage opposite but on the same level with the buildings of the camp. He ran in that direction and came upon the sergeant in whose company they had made the upward journey to the camp.

"Yes, I saw your wife and son," the sergeant answered. "I pointed them to a rather pleasant nature walk. Easy trail. Goes level around the upper end of the defile, there, and comes out exactly opposite. No danger. No danger at all. Favorite walk for dependents because there's no uphill going at all. Safe as houses."

Renno did not take time to thank the sergeant. He unleashed the power of his legs and ran at maximum speed. He was soon back on a tunnellike trail, his haste startling the birds. Several times he saw the impressions of Beth's walking boots on the soggy red earth. The trail curved, and he sped on. A glance confirmed that he was now on the opposite slope looking back across the relatively shallow defile to the drill grounds. He halted suddenly, for in the red earth he saw the marks of struggle. The marks of bare feet were mixed with the prints of Beth's boots and the small signs left by Little Hawk's moccasins. He found where a group had left the cleared trail. He pushed into the rank growth. The trail led upward, to the west.

Now the mountain jungle knew a sound it had never heard—the angry, blood-chilling roar of a great bear, a call that

reverberated to the drill grounds, where all men missed a
step and all heads turned toward Renno's location.

There was threat and promise in that roar, for sooner or
later whoever had taken the wife and son of the white Indian
would have to challenge his anger.

In his rage and his quick fear for Beth and Little Hawk, he
followed the trail, moving swiftly; then he cooled and turned
to run back toward the camp. He was armed only with his
tomahawk and stiletto. Now he added the English longbow
to his weaponry and left a note for Se-quo-i. The Cherokee,
he knew, would be many hours away, for it would take a long
time first to go down the steep slopes to the valley and then
to climb upward again to the camp. He was thankful that
Se-quo-i had made a study of the white man's written language, and for a fleeting moment he felt regretful that Se-
quo-i had not yet fulfilled his desire to reduce the Cherokee
language to written form, so that the message would remain a
private one between himself and Se-quo-i.

For hours the trail of those who had abducted Beth and
Little Hawk was simple to follow. It seemed that those ahead
of him did not fear being pursued. He had only to follow the
trail of slashed and bent undergrowth, which climbed the
slope of the ridge west of Newcastle, then dipped off the
ridge and angled down, down, into a defile. There, where a
stream cascaded hundreds of feet in a roar of white water, the
abductors had used the stream to obscure their trail. It cost
Renno some time, casting up and down the stream, to find
that the tracks led still westward, just as the spirit of Ah-
wen-ga had predicted.

The heat of summer had sent Roy and Nora Johnson to the
front stoop of their cabin in Knoxville. The sun was low, and
evening came as a relief. It was pleasant to sit there, Nora
rocking quietly as she knitted a pair of socks for Roy, to hear
the occasional sounds of voices from others who were also
taking the evening air. A group of ragtag boys swept past,
whooping like Chickasaw on a raid.

Johnson had a lot to think about, for great change was in
store for the territory west of the Smoky Mountains. A dream
was dead—the hope of having a state named after Ben

Franklin was gone. John Sevier's term as governor had ended, and no successor had been elected.

Man, Johnson felt, was a cussed animal, often blind to his own interests. The men of the territory could not come to an agreement, perhaps because too many of them wanted to be big frogs in a little pond. As a result the fate of the land Johnson chose to be his home would probably be decided by men in Raleigh or Philadelphia.

Musingly sad, a little angry, Johnson consoled himself with the knowledge that he had done his best. He knew that Sevier was a good man, a man with vision. He was trying to convince himself, not with great success, that there was still hope, when he heard the sound of racing hooves and looked up to see a horseman thundering through the streets at risk of life and limb—not only his but those of anyone not agile enough to leap out of his way. The man jerked his lathered horse to a halt in front of the porch, threw himself off, and ran to the steps.

"They've arrested Sevier," he gasped.

Johnson leapt to his feet.

"Charged him with treason! Charged *John Sevier* with treason!"

"Rest yourself, man," Johnson advised. He knew the fellow slightly from the militia. "Nora, get the gentleman a drink of cool water."

He stepped down, guided the spent man to the chair he himself had been occupying, and handed him a mug of water when Nora came back.

"There will be those who will fight," the messenger said between swills of water. "Be you one of them?"

Johnson heard Nora gasp. *That's all we need,* he thought glumly, *a civil war between settlers.* But John Sevier was his friend. He didn't know who among Sevier's political enemies had engineered an accusation as absurd as treason, but he realized that he would indeed be among those who would fight to prevent such injustice to a sincere and patriotic man.

"I'm gonna put you in the spare room," he told the messenger. "I'll gather up a few men. We'll ride with the dawn."

"Roy," Nora pleaded, clutching his arm. "We've more than just ourselves to think of now. We've got to think of Renna and Little Hawk. We're the only civilizing influence they'll have."

"Nora, I wouldn't consider myself a man, much less a civilized one, if I didn't come to the aid of an old friend unjustly accused." He moved her firmly aside and strode swiftly down the street in search of volunteers.

At dawn a group of just under twenty men left Knoxville with the messenger and Roy, moving swiftly and with purpose. It was a long and tiring journey to Nashville, where Sevier was being held. Along the way, as the news spread, the group, mostly members of the militia unit of which Johnson was colonel, was joined by others. Somehow, even in a newly settled wilderness, momentous news had a way of getting around.

The road between Knoxville and Nashville was halfway decent except in the rain, which they encountered in rolling hills, where horses struggled and slipped. During the days that it required to make the journey, no further news met them from Nashville, but Johnson's force continued to grow. John Sevier was not without friends. With a quick day's ride left before reaching Nashville, the group made camp to rest the exhausted horses and saddle-sore men.

A messenger arrived shortly after darkness had fallen, shouting out to the men around the campfires. This well-dressed emissary was a bit too dandified for the taste of the rough frontiersmen with Johnson, and when someone recognized the visitor as a longtime political opponent of John Sevier, there were hoots and jeers. No man who was a total coward lasted long in the West, however, so the gentleman from Nashville, while keeping his silence, dismounted, and then asked the whereabouts of Roy Johnson.

"I don't reckon the colonel wants to waste time with the likes of you," a man wheezed, standing in the visitor's face, leaning close to breathe the fumes of chewing tobacco.

"It's not for the likes of you to judge that," the politician said coldly, giving the frontiersman a solid push.

A growl of anger rose from those who had been watching, and the scene could have exploded with violence had not

Roy, having heard the exchange, quickly taken the visitor aside. He had never met the gentleman. "I'm Johnson. I'm sure you have reason to be here."

"I am to let you know that there won't be any resistance if Sevier is taken from the prison by a mob."

Johnson narrowed his yes. "As simple as that, is it?"

"Just get him out of Nashville."

"You haven't told me your name," Johnson said. "I'd also like to know the names of those who guarantee that there'll be no bloodshed."

"Names don't matter. Our concern is that your backwoodsmen don't go off half-cocked and kill innocent people. We don't want a fight, and we don't want to have to hold a man like John Sevier in prison. I don't agree with Sevier, but he's finished as a power and doesn't deserve to be cooped up like an animal."

"Just how would you advise this so-called mob to go about rescuing John?" Roy asked.

"Ride in whooping and hollering. Make it look like you're spoiling for a fight. You'll find that the street will empty right fast. Then you ride out with Sevier, and whether you whoop and holler on your way out is up to you."

"Well, citizen," Johnson said, "we'll consider your advice. I reckon you're hungry."

"I will eat on the road back to Nashville," the visitor said quickly, eager to get out of there.

Johnson called his men together after the man from Nashville had gone, and reported on the conversation.

"Roy," said a grizzled Indian fighter, "looks like a trick to me. If we go in acting like we're looking for trouble, I reckon they'll be some folks in there to give it to us."

"They could be jest trying to get us overconfident, like. We ride in expecting no opposition and, *wham!*" another veteran said.

"I think," Johnson said, "that we'll take a look-see first, and then maybe we'll do some whooping and hollering."

So it was that the militiamen drifted into Nashville in small groups ranging from two men to a half-dozen, approaching the town from all directions. Johnson rode in with three good men. His musket rested across his saddle in front of him. He looked relaxed and a bit trail worn, but his eyes were keenly alert. His eyes checked every movement: the lazy lope of a dog down the dirt street, a ragtag, towheaded boy carrying a cat, women going into and out of a mercantile store.

It all sounded too simple. He expected to see a hint of movement in a shadow or atop one of the plank buildings, and his muscles were tense, as if anticipating the thud of a musket ball in his back.

Up ahead he saw the sharpened points of the log palisade, the first structure to have been built in Nashville when the initial settlers expected Indian attacks at any time. That was where they would be holding Sevier, and that was strategically the strongest point in town. If there was going to be any shooting, it would begin from the protection of the palisade.

His little group joined with another coming down a side street. A dozen other men were riding in slowly. So far so good. The town was going about its business in a normal way. The buckskin-clad frontiersmen were not even drawing curious glances. Roy began to think that if the opposition planned treachery, they at least would have evacuated the women and kids from the street.

The log gate of the palisade was standing wide open.

"Well," Johnson said, "if it's a trick, we're gonna know pretty soon. Let's go get John." He gave a Seneca war whoop and kicked his horse into a gallop. Men converged behind him, and the group, sounding like at least a thousand blood-thirsty savages, poured into the compound behind the palisade. The area was empty. Men flung themselves off their horses and took firing positions, their muskets pointed at the windows and doors of the log-and-plank buildings inside the palisade. The shouting dwindled.

It was as simple as that. John Sevier, calm, unharmed, complete with a good horse and saddle, was delivered to the waiting militiamen. The ride out of Nashville was uneventful, the ride back to Knoxville tiring.

After a good night's rest, Sevier joined Roy on the front porch to watch the sunrise. It was Roy who broke the silence.

"What brought it on, John?"

"Plain stupidity," Sevier answered. "And maybe greed. Stupid people."

Roy grunted and waited.

"Well, we won't worry about it," Sevier declared. "It'll all be forgotten in time. I'll wager my best hat that I'll be general of militia again, even before the year's out. Meantime, you still hold your rank as colonel. They think pretty highly of you up in Nashville. Reckon, if you want it, you might take the generalship away from me. And if you do want it, I won't fight you for it."

"No thanks," Johnson said quickly, remembering what Nora had said. He had no ambition to be a general of an almost nonexistent force. He would keep an eye on things as a colonel and make sure that some idiot didn't go pushing into the lands of the Cherokee and the Seneca and stir things up.

"Yep," Sevier said after a long silence, "the times they are a'changing, Roy. We'll have statehood out here sooner than later, but the Lord only knows who'll be running it. Won't be North Carolina, much as they'd like to annex us. Northern states such as New York and Massachusetts won't stand for that for a lot of reasons, slavery among them. Me, I'm a little tired of fighting. Being governor of a new state has lost its appeal."

"Can't think of anyone I'd rather have in the statehouse," Johnson suggested.

"I'd like that," Sevier agreed. Then he sighed. "Maybe we'll round up a bunch of volunteers and ride up into the Northwest Territories when the war starts there."

"I think I'll sit that one out."

"Well, whatever suits you." Sevier shrugged. "Interesting times."

"Yep."

"We fight the French and Indians, and then we fight the Indians, and then the British and the Indians, with a skirmish or two with the Spaniards on the side. And a bunch of politicians off in Raleigh and South Carolina, or Boston, New York, and Philadelphia, they're gonna decide what becomes of us and what we'll be called. If the big Southern states won and we got hooked onto North Carolina, we wouldn't have any say in it, or even as to whether we're slave or free. One thing I do know: there are more and more settlers coming over the mountains from North Carolina and Virginia and down from Kentucky. They keep pushing and pushing until a feller doesn't have room to breathe."

"Good land," Roy said. "That brings 'em."

"And soon they'll start pushing down into the hunting grounds of your friends," Sevier remarked.

"I fear so."

"Then some of us are going to have to decide which is more important, race and skin color or friendship."

"John, there's enough land for everyone."

"I know you're pretty tight with the Indian," Sevier acknowledged. "By the way, how's that white Seneca, married to your daughter?"

"Renno. He's away at the moment."

"Good man. I'd hate to face him in a fight, and he would fight, wouldn't he?"

"Like no one you've ever seen. And I have to say, John, that I'm not sure that I wouldn't be on his side if it came to that."

"Figured as much."

There was another long silence. Around them the town was coming to life. A farm wagon rattled down the street, loaded with melons and roasting ears destined for the farmers' market.

"There's the future," Sevier said, inclining his head toward the street. "White farmers. They'll push into the hunting grounds an acre or two at a time, and then there'll be a toe-to-toe crisis."

"The Cherokee farm."

"Subsistence farming," Sevier dismissed. "Little garden plots tended by women with sharpened sticks. Nope, it'll come, Roy."

Johnson was silent. The man who sat next to him in Nora's rocking chair, a man who had killed many Indians in his early days as Indian fighter, sometimes seemed to have a knack for seeing into the future. Roy felt a jab to the heart as he thought about Little Hawk and Renna. How would they fare in some future crisis between white expansionism and the need of the Indian for great virgin stretches of land? On which side would his grandson fight?

Then he thought of Renno and El-i-chi, and he knew the answer.

* * *

The island of Jamaica was only 146 miles long, a lesser distance than that covered by Roy Johnson between Knoxville and Nashville. But the land west of the Smokies was not precipitous, folded, convoluted mountain terrain, and it was not covered by jungle. Actually Renno's track would cover fewer than eighty miles, but that as-the-crow-flies distance would be more than doubled by the necessity of skirting deep gorges, of trailing around instead of over the smaller peaks to the west of Newcastle.

At first the miles passed quickly as Renno moved along narrow but passable trails, through passes, into the valleys, and up and over jungle ridges. He ran when the trail was clear, was slowed now and then as those he pursued tried to hide their tracks. He skirted a coffee plantation, saw slaves laboring, and sped onward. He lived on fruits and the clear, sparkling water of the streams that formed numberless, roaring, white, cascading falls. The direction was generally to the northwest, and after days of travel he crossed a white man's road, where a sign pointed north to St. Ann's Bay. He had to cast around for the tracks, for his quarry had traveled for miles northward along the road, most probably at night. He was aided in spotting the trail by a scrap of color, a bit of material ripped from one of Beth's petticoats. He held the scrap to his nose, trying to capture the scent of her.

The tracks took him to the outskirts of another plantation. He moved through the cultivated acres of coffee trees, hearing from a distance the rhythmic work chant of slaves. Beth and Little Hawk's captors had passed through the cultivated areas during the night, he guessed, or else they would have been seen, for Renno had to duck several times to avoid being spotted by work gangs.

He could see the end of the planting ahead. A steep ridge rose high. He could not afford to move swiftly, for he did not want contact with the white overseers who roamed the cultivated areas. Any delay would be potentially disastrous; he estimated that he was already a full day behind his quarry. They could, at times, travel in the night, while he had to wait for light in order not to lose the tracks in the steaming jungles.

He was running, bent slightly, in the cover of a row of

coffee trees when he heard a cry, then sharp cracking sounds, followed by agonized female screams. He halted, peered out and down the slope, and trembled with anger as he watched a group of white overseers standing in a circle while another white man lashed a weeping, screaming woman with a long, evil-looking whip. Renno's blood ran cold.

An older black woman ran to seize the arm of the whip-wielding overseer, pleading for mercy for her daughter. With a shout of outrage another white man began to lash the mother.

For Renno that was too much. Caution told him to go; concern for Beth and Little Hawk told him to keep hot on the trail. But his basic humanity sent him down the slope between the rows of trees. He moved in deadly silence, so the first indication of his presence was when the flat of his tomahawk resounded against the side of the head of the white man who was lashing the older woman. He could announce his presence then, and he did so with the roared challenge of a bear as he leapt to send the man who had been whipping the younger slave into quick unconsciousness.

It had not been his intent to kill or to wipe out the institution of slavery by rushing to the aid of two black women. He was but one individual responding to the cruel punishment of the slaves. With the fall of the two overseers, he was finished, and a bit sorry he had revealed himself.

"There will be no more of this," he announced to the five overseers who stood dumbfounded. He began to back away, toward cover.

"Kill that scoundrel!" one of the men yelled, and another went for his pistol. Renno's hand flashed, and the Spanish stiletto penetrated a white, English throat, severing the spinal cord. The other four men, armed only with whips and clubs, rushed toward him. He downed another overseer with the flat of his tomahawk and knew that to avoid injury himself he could not be merciful. The white Indian unleashed a killing blow on a second man and jerked back as a group of black men overwhelmed the remaining two overseers from the rear, dispatching them bloodily with their bare hands and fists and feet.

The beating continued even after the men were dead.

Other slaves had delivered the same treatment to the two men Renno had rendered unconscious. Now there was a hush. The slaves moved slowly, cringingly, toward Renno.

"You sen?" one asked.

"I do not understand," Renno answered, then turned toward the uncleared jungle.

He heard the slaves running after him and turned, gesturing them back. He could not be encumbered with them.

"You sen for us?" a man asked. "Take to Me No Sen You No Come?"

"This one no Maroon," a woman told the man. "He white."

"I travel alone," Renno said, speaking slowly, keeping an eye open down the slope lest other overseers approach. "I advise you to go to this land of the Maroon, and quickly."

"We no know way," the spokesman said, his eyes rolling.

"There." Renno pointed toward the northwest. He was certain now that the abductors of Beth and Little Hawk were headed toward that dark country of which he had been warned, the impenetrable stronghold of the descendants of escaped Spanish slaves, the Cockpit Country.

"Take us, sar," a woman begged. "There our free brothers will help us."

"I travel alone. I will make the trail easy to follow."

"What we eat, sar?" a young girl asked.

"The fruits of the jungle," Renno said, and he dived into the green that threatened constantly to reclaim the coffee plantation and was gone.

He was far behind now. Frequent rains made the tracks difficult to follow. The distinctive prints made by Beth's boots were his most dependable clues, and he felt a rush of concern and a new anger when he saw that the soles of her boots had worn through. Once he saw a touch of blood on a rock where she had stepped, and he pushed himself hard, eating on the move, pausing at streams only long enough to drink deeply.

Little Hawk had been absorbing woodcraft all his young life from more than one excellent teacher, and Renno felt pride when he saw, at places where the trail was difficult to follow, signs left for him by his son: a broken branch, a scuff mark left by a small, moccasined foot.

After several more days of hard, tedious traveling, the country worsened as Renno reached the outskirts of the Cockpit Country. He found something that chilled his blood for its revelation regarding the character of those he followed: a black man dressed in an odd assortment of garments had obviously fallen from the narrow track and broken his leg on the rocks below. White bone protruded from the man's flesh. Ants were feeding on a dried pool of blood not from the leg but from the man's slit throat. It was evident to Renno that his wife and son were in the hands of savages, men who killed one of their own rather than leave him behind alive or help him to continue on.

He was moving with the first light of a new day. His feeling of urgency was growing. The terrain was gradually worsening when he heard the sound of axes in front of him, slowing him to move with more caution. The trail skirted a clearing being enlarged by a dozen slaves under the supervision of a hulking man who obviously had black blood. Renno watched for a few moments and decided that the workers were not slaves. They bantered, laughing, with the overseer. The crew's boss had no whip. All were dressed in a colorful assortment of torn and ragged garments.

Perhaps, he thought, he had reached the land of the Maroons. If so, these men might have information of value. He awaited his chance. The big half-breed overseer was talking with a young, muscular man. The man put down his ax and stretched, then started to walk toward a stream a short distance away. The overseer followed and caught up.

Renno skirted the clearing and ran as best he could through the tangle of growth, reached the stream, and made his way up it. The big half-breed was on his knees, cupping water into his mouth. The young man, lying on his belly, slurped directly from the stream. Renno moved swiftly and used the flat of his tomahawk on the skull of the big man, then seized the younger man by the head and laid the sharp blade of his tomahawk against his throat.

"I will not harm you."

A flood of words came from the frightened boy, and some of them seemed familiar.

"Do you speak English?" Renno asked.

The boy said something that sounded like, "No hablo."

"Español?"

"Sí, sí" the boy said eagerly.

Renno began to question him, telling him more than once to speak slowly, for the boy's Spanish was the result of decades of distortion, a mixture of English and various native languages of Africa. He asked if the boy had seen a group of Maroons with white captives, but the boy shook his head. "No, no."

"You lie." Renno put pressure on the blade.

"I see, I see," the boy blurted, a small trickle of blood running down his neck. "White woman. White boy."

"Where do they go?"

A gleam of defiance came into the boy's eyes. "They go home. You go?"

"Yes."

The boy showed spirit by trying to laugh, but the attempt was feeble. "Then my people will pick your bones."

"How far?"

"To the Land of Look Behind?"

"To the towns of the Maroons."

"Not far. Two, three days. For you, more maybe."

Renno released the boy. "Wake this one with water in his face." He indicated the fallen half-breed. "Do not try to follow me." He moved his tomahawk to indicate what would happen.

"No," the boy said, smiling happily. "Why should we follow? We walk many miles to find ground for planting ganja, so we stay. Libertador and the others will kill you or give you to the master as a plaything."

The land began to change rapidly, becoming the worst ground Renno had ever seen, even in the badlands of the Southwest. The trail was marked now and well traveled. No longer did his quarry try to disguise their tracks. Beth's boot holes left clear impressions, and Renno was able to move forward at a warrior's trot. But the miles were covered more slowly. Deep pits fell away from the curving, winding trail. Ferns, vines, ginger plants, and other vegetation clogged the deep pits and the almost-perpendicular walls.

Food was scarce. There were few fruit-bearing trees, and

most of them were barren except at the dizzying height of topmost branches, but Renno was not concerned with food. He felt that he was close to Beth and Little Hawk now.

On a clear morning he saw a hint of woodsmoke in the distance, and he moved forward at a run. The trail slanted downward, clinging to the side of a pit wall, into the glen. There was water there and, in a clearing beside the water, six large, oddly dressed Maroons, each armed with a different weapon—a spear, a machete, one pistol, an ax, a carved and a smooth club.

With a cry the man with the spear drew back his arm and launched his missile at Renno's heart.

Chapter X

Constable Abe Watts had first entered the city of Wilmington in 1781 as a British prisoner of war. His return to Wilmington in 1784 had been motivated by a plump, laughing girl who had promised to wait for him no matter how long it took. In order to enlist Abe had added fictitious years to his life, wanting to join in what he—as a sixteen-year-old boy—felt was a glorious cause.

Abe survived one of the most spirited actions to be fought in the Carolinas, when Lord Charles Cornwallis's veteran British and Hessian troops won a victory at Guilford that was so costly, it left Cornwallis no choice but to march first to Wilmington and subsequently to abandon the Carolinas in preparation for his "subjugation" of Virginia. That ended contrary to his hopes and plans at a place called Yorktown. Abe had been a member of the Fifth Maryland Regiment, a

new outfit made up of troops fighting their first battle. Abe
was among the leaders when British scarlet and steel conquered without firing a shot and the Fifth Maryland ran like
rabbits. Unfortunately Abe ran the wrong way, getting mixed
up with a bunch of Virginia Continentals who had come to
fight. He was wounded when Cornwallis, seeing his troops
getting the worst of it, ordered Colonel Donald Macleod to
pour grapeshot into a melee of American and British guards
and grenadiers. Grape is nonselective; Cornwallis was sacri-
ficing his own men, but the barrage of death that stopped
Abe Watts from running pushed the American forces back
and gave Cornwallis time to re-form.

Abe made a long, painful walk all the way to Wilmington
without dying along with some of the other American prisoners, but his shoulder wound went septic and was suppurating
vilely and he was delirious. He didn't know until much later
that he had been left behind to die when Cornwallis marched
northward. That he didn't die was the work of the plump,
laughing girl named Molly, who moved him into a broiling
attic room above the pub where she dispensed alcoholic drinks
and, some said, other favors and fought the infection in Abe's
wounds with a single-mindedness that allowed him, weeks
later, to start walking north, to be in on the end of it up there
in Virginia, maybe to make up for having run at Guilford.

"Yes, my darlin', I'll wait for you," Molly had promised him
tearfully. When he came back discharged, disgruntled, and
disgusted—as were most of the American cannon-fodder types
who had fought with such high ideals—he heard she had
waited only two weeks before heading south with an itinerant
fiddler. The land he and other soldiers like him had been
promised never materialized. The gold he had been promised
as his mustering-out pay turned magically into scrip that gave
birth to one of the longest lasting of American condemnations
of inferior things: in short, what Abe had been paid wasn't
worth a Continental. He was stuck in Wilmington with no
money and an old wound that ached like the devil when the
dark clouds moved in from the west, but without a plump,
laughing girl who had promised to wait.

To humor a nasty habit he'd acquired—eating—he sought
employment and considered himself lucky when he was made
a member of the town's constabulary. It didn't take long for

him to realize that the job would allow him to continue the
habit of eating, but that was about all. He lived in one musty
room, had to plan ahead to be able to afford a tankard of ale
at the pub where Molly once worked, and wondered what
had happened to him . . . and to all of them.

He had considered taking a wife, but he could not afford
one. He did manage to go without a meal now and then in
order to accumulate enough money to purchase the favors of
an even plumper girl who had taken Molly's place in the pub,
but such brief moments didn't promise much of a future. He
thought about going west, to try his luck as a trapper or
mountain man, but he didn't like the cold. It got cold, he
heard, out there in the western wilderness. He considered a
lot of things, but he was bound up in a sort of paralysis of will
that saw him knuckling under to his superiors and working
his duty night after night, week after week, month after
month, year after year, until he knew that his youth was gone
and he felt like an old man at age twenty-four.

Being a constable had some small rewards: he had matured
into a size that allowed him to subdue a drunken sailor with a
look; he liked the way the rowdies and the sailors stepped out
of his way when he stalked the docks and the streets; he
didn't take any direct pleasure in using his truncheon on a
man's pate, but he didn't mind doing it either. It was the
results of the truncheon's landing squarely on a sailor's
skull that changed Abe's life. He had subdued a fellow who
was making too much noise on Front Street in the early
evening. It was dark in the alley where he'd chased the
sailor, and he heard something jingling in the man's pockets
when he started to drag him to the jail. That something was
coin, silver coin, and—it being dark and deserted on the
street—Abe helped himself to just a little more than half of
the sailor's silver. He reasoned that the man would not know
how much coin he'd have left after a day of carousing, and it
worked.

Abe's new source of income had improved his life-style.
He was able to call the plump barmaid to his room whenever
he felt like it, drink three or four tankards of ale when he was
off duty, and begin to build a little stash. Since he always
took the money from drunks and never took all, he had been
getting away with it for over a year when he escorted that

white Indian to the jail after the fellow had killed two of
Spade Hollinger's ruffians and left two more in doubtful condition. Unfortunately Abe didn't have a chance to take half of
the Indian's coins because the fellow wasn't drunk and he had
witnesses.

But there had been some interesting things said there on
the wharf. The Indian had accused Hollinger of cheating at
dice. There had been mention of money, probably a goodly
sum of money, and Abe hadn't come away with any of it.

He thought about that sad situation while he was walking
the predawn streets, and he turned his way back to the jail
with a look of determination on his round, bovine face. He
told the jailer he wanted a word with the prisoner and took
the keys. The jailer, having been awakened from his sleep
twice, was snoring again even as Abe went back toward the
cell.

El-i-chi's anger had cooled in the intervening hours. He
had decided that there was nothing to be done at the moment. The bars were solid, the walls sturdy. He had considered the situation, shrugged, and was sleeping on the narrow,
odoriferous cot when he heard Abe Watts's club rattle the
bars. He was awake instantly and sat up.

"Constable," he said, "if you'll send word to Mr. Nathan
Ridley, I will be deeply appreciative."

"Well, ain't you a fancy talker," Abe said.

"I've told you," El-i-chi said calmly, "that I was attacked at
Hollinger's orders by those four men. I can prove that Hollinger
has been cheating at dice. I can prove that the money I have
is mine."

"How much money?" Abe asked, and in the flickering
lantern light that filtered in from the corridor, El-i-chi saw
avarice gleam in the white man's eye.

El-i-chi pulled out his little leather pouch and poured a few
gold and silver coins into his hand. "Not much."

"There jest might be a way I could get word to your
friend," Abe said, his eyes on the money. He rarely had a
chance at gold coins.

"If there's any way at all I can help . . ." El-i-chi raised his
hand as if to look more closely at the coins.

"Oh, maybe a goodwill gesture, something like that," Abe
replied.

El-i-chi knew he was on unsure ground, that an overt offer to bribe a law officer could be held against him. "I wonder if you'd hold this money for me, Constable. It might not be safe in here."

"Well, maybe I'll hold half." Abe didn't know why he said that, when the man was offering all. Habit, he guessed. And there was no real reason for him to open the cell door. He could have taken the money through the bars. He opened the door. He was thinking, *Why didn't I tell him all of it?* This was a savage. If anything came of it, it would be the word of a constable with a perfect record against that of a savage. He stood inside the cell, the door closed behind him.

El-i-chi extended his hand. "Hold as much as you want. Do you know where Nathan Ridley lives?"

"I do." Abe took a few coins, three of gold.

"Nathan Ridley will also be appreciative if you will get word to him quickly." El-i-chi had considered asking the constable to notify Cedric Huntington, but he reasoned that Ridley, being American and longer established in Wilmington, would know more about the steps to take to rectify the situation in which El-i-chi had found himself.

The constable made a sound that may or may not have been assent. El-i-chi turned to take the three steps back to his cot. Something huge and heavy fell on his head. His knees wobbled, and he felt the strength going from his legs. He went to his knees, shaking his head dazedly. The coins in his hand fell as his fingers opened involuntarily.

Abe heard the jingle of coin. It had taken a long time for the idea to penetrate that he could have all the money. It had been then that he lifted his truncheon as the Indian turned away.

El-i-chi fought against darkness. He could move his limbs, but it was as if he were enshrouded by heavy, clinging things. He realized dimly that the constable was on his knees, picking up the coins. His head cleared slightly, and he knew that he had been struck from behind. He tried to speak, but the result was a choking growl. He launched himself at the constable who had struck him, but he seemed to be moving in slow motion. Watts was able to scramble away, one hand full of coins, the other holding the truncheon.

El-i-chi had just enough awareness and strength to land

one blow—and open-palmed, pawing slap that jerked Abe's head to one side.

That impact triggered rage. He, the representative of law and order, had been struck by a savage. He swung the club, and it made a crunching sound as a rib broke, and then he was swinging almost blindly in his rage, the club following El-i-chi as he once again knew only blackness and crumpled to the floor.

"The Indian tried to attack me," Abe told the jailer, who was not at all happy about being awakened for the third time, all because of one dirty Indian. "I had to subdue him."

"Kill him?" the jailer asked.

"No, no. But he'll hurt for a while."

"Hope you didn't leave blood all over my cell. I'm the one what has to clean it up."

"Only a little," Abe said. "If he seems in a bad way in the morning, you might want to call in a doctor."

Abe went to his room when he finished his night's duty and spent a few minutes counting and examining his money. It didn't take too long to count it, but the gold coins were very interesting. He admired the design, tried to figure out the Spanish inscriptions, sampled the quality by biting the coins. There was a rich, pleasant softness to the gold that pleased him and set his mind working again. He could not stop thinking of something the Indian had said. He'd indicated that he had taken only part of the money on Spade Hollinger's vessel. And it just didn't seem reasonable that Hollinger would have tried to have the Indian killed for the small amount of coin that was now in Abe's possession. He decided that it might be interesting to have a chat with Hollinger.

Abe found Hollinger in the pub, having a breakfast of flapjacks and eggs, and waited patiently until Hollinger was finished and started toward the street. He fell in behind and called Hollinger's name when they were outside.

"Well, Constable," Hollinger said affably. "Have any problem with the Indian?"

"Had to talk a little sense to him," Abe said, swinging his truncheon suggestively. He didn't know exactly how to start the conversation he wanted to have with Hollinger. He didn't even have a clear-cut purpose in mind, only something vague that had to do with money. As it happened, Hollinger gave him the opening.

"Too bad you didn't kill him. I'll have to do the job myself if he persists in lying about my character."

"Ah," Abe said. "He did mention something about crooked dice."

"Lies."

"That's what I wanted to see you about."

Hollinger's eyes narrowed. If what he expected was coming, it wouldn't be the first time that an officer of the law had tried to put the bite on him.

"Let's walk," Hollinger said, heading toward the docks. Abe nodded.

"I'm a businessman, Constable," Hollinger said as they walked. "I'm not a gambling cheat."

"I know that, Mr. Hollinger," Abe said, finding a direction of approach at last. "I just wouldn't want some savage going around bad-mouthing a good citizen."

"Do you have any suggestions?"

"Well . . ."

"You're a hardworking man," Hollinger said. "Family?"

"No. Can't afford one."

"Not much money in being a constable, eh? But you seem to be a fellow of some ambition."

"I keep my eyes open for opportunity."

"Abe," Hollinger said, and the constable was a bit surprised to find that Hollinger knew his name, "I'm a law-abiding businessman, and I sure wouldn't want you to get the idea that I'm trying to bribe a lawman or cause him to have a conflict of interest with his duty. But you don't work all the time, do you?"

"I work at night."

"Now and again I need little things done," Hollinger said. "Say I needed something done during the afternoon, when you weren't working. Would you be able to take on a little job or two for me?"

"Just might. It would depend on what the job was and how much you were willing to pay."

"How much money would you like to earn?"

Abe laughed.

"*Hmmm*," Hollinger said. "Now this is just supposing,

Constable—I mean, Abe—just supposing. Suppose this Indian did get out of jail some way and started telling lies about me. Suppose I knew a man who was in a position to see to it that he didn't tell any more lies about me. Do you suppose such a man would do that little job for, say, a hundred dollars in gold?"

Abe swallowed hard. "Since we're supposing, I suppose some man would feed a half-dozen Indians in pieces to the catfish in the Cape Fear River for one hundred dollars in gold."

Actually Hollinger was not all that concerned about El-i-chi. His pride had been dented, and he was still puzzled about how the Indian did something that some pretty good gamblers had never done before—beat a pair of loaded dice—but he wouldn't have too much trouble replacing the men El-i-chi had killed or wounded. If the Indian went around accusing Hollinger of using crooked dice, it was just his word. He had been feeling Abe Watts out, because he had found in the past that it was good to have a lawman on the payroll. That situation opened up all sorts of avenues.

"Abe, you seem like a man after my own heart. I hate your wasting your time for pennies. Just how serious are you about making some real money?"

They had reached the edge of the wharf, and they stopped to look down at the swirl of water in the river. "Well, Mr. Hollinger, I fought and bled for my country. I was promised land and gold, but I got no land, and not enough Continentals to buy me a square meal. I been working here for a few years, and I can't even hire a nigger boy to shine my boots. How serious you want me to be?" He cleared his throat. "If that's what you want, I'll see to it that the Indian doesn't leave jail alive."

Hollinger made a dismissing motion with his hand. "I've got bigger ideas for you, Abe. How'd you like to have two thousand dollars in gold?"

Abe's breath jerked into his lungs.

"I just need to know you're serious," Hollinger said, "and not trying to trap me into something like trying to bribe an officer."

"I'll kill the Indian for you for free. I'll do it tonight."

"That would do it, but I wouldn't ask you to do it for free. You do that, show me you're serious, and then we'll talk."

"Tomorrow morning," Abe said.

"I'll buy you breakfast."

Hollinger watched the constable walk away. He lit a cigar and smiled. He got a little bored and just a bit ill—he wasn't cut out to be a sailor—making those trips over to Nassau to the slave market. He'd been considering a quicker and easier way of making money from the Spanish in Florida, and he reckoned that Abe Watts would make that plan possible. He started making the rounds, looking for a couple of men he knew, men who'd do just about anything for money.

Even before the Maroon launched his spear, Renno saw that it was coming. He saw the man's muscles tense, and as his arm went back, Renno was moving so that the spear whistled harmlessly past him. In an instant he had the English longbow in his hands, an arrow going into place. The deadly, steel-tipped shaft sang the short distance from the bow to the chest of the spear thrower.

Five Maroons launched themselves forward with wild cries. Renno narrowed the odds with another arrow, dropped his longbow, and then he was waiting, with tomahawk and stiletto, for the rush of the four survivors. A machete nipped a piece of skin from his buckskin-clad shoulder as he sent the tomahawk slicing through a throat and stabbed a mortal wound to the throat of another Maroon. A huge, studded club passed narrowly over his head, close enough to brush his hair, and the tomahawk flashed in counterstroke to crush bone.

The two survivors fell back and then, giving each other courage with their shrill yelps of war, moved in from opposite sides. Renno leapt far to remove himself from between them and charged low, coming up from the ground with a sweeping blow of his tomahawk even as he slipped out from under a downward slash of an ax. The force of his blow buried the head of his tomahawk in the Maroon's ribs over his heart, and as the man died, the tomahawk, still embedded, was jerked from Renno's hand. He faced the last Maroon with only his knife but ended the challenge quickly as his arm flashed and he threw the stiletto with all his strength. The Toledo-steel blade sunk to the haft in the man's stomach. The

Maroon, groaning in fear and agony, sank to the ground. Renno stood, breathing hard from the strenuous action, which had lasted less than two minutes.

One of the Maroons was still alive. Renno knelt beside the dying man and asked in Spanish, "Where are the white woman and the boy?"

The dying man spat into Renno's face. Then his eyes glazed and he was still. Renno stood, wiping spittle from his face, then crouched in sudden alertness as a deep, strong voice boomed from his rear, "You fight well, warrior."

Renno did not look behind him, knowing that he was a target for a spear or a knife. Temporarily without a weapon, the white Indian threw himself sideways, rolled, and came up leaping toward his fallen longbow. Only when he had the longbow in hand and was reaching for an arrow did he look up.

He saw a giant of a man, fully seven feet tall, a black man dressed much like those he had killed. The giant stood half in shadow, half in mottled sunlight, and Renno had the bow drawn before he saw that the giant was holding out both hands, palms upward. A huge spear, however, leaned against the giant's shoulder.

"You have killed six men as most men would swat flies," the giant complimented.

"Are you to be the seventh?" Renno asked, still holding the drawn bow, the arrow pointed to the giant's chest.

"If I wanted you dead, you would be dead."

"So," Renno said, slowly releasing the pressure to allow the bow to unbend, but keeping it ready.

"You are not white, you are not black."

"I am Renno of the Seneca."

The giant shrugged. He was a truly impressive sight. His hair was braided tightly in many little rows, and the braids glistened as if something oily had been applied. His head was, Renno thought, as big as a white settler woman's cast-iron washtub. His arms were heavy with muscle, as large as most men's thighs, and his legs were like tree trunks.

"And what does Renno of the Seneca seek in the land of the Maroons?"

"My wife and my son."

"I suspected as much." The giant nodded. "Perhaps you are already too late."

"If I am, many will die. Perhaps you included."

The big man laughed. "Mingo kills. Mingo does not die."

"So," Renno said.

Another voice startled both men. It came from the shadows of the jungle. "If the big one who calls himself Mingo had lifted his spear, he would have killed no more."

Se-quo-i, tomahawk in hand, emerged at Mingo's shoulder, looking quite small beside the huge Maroon.

A great burst of laughter came from Mingo. "So the little man who is of the Seneca—whatever that is—has help."

"You made good time," Renno told Se-quo-i.

"You left a trail that could have been followed on the run by a half-blind child." Se-quo-i looked at the huge Mingo. "What of this one?"

"I am curious about these small men, one with skin like an Englishman's, the other with skin like that of the natives who once lived on this island," Mingo declared. "Until I decide to kill you, I think we will be friends."

Renno, the bloodlust scarcely cooled, lifted his bow.

"I had no hand in taking your wife and your son," Mingo said, not out of any sense of threat. "Should you loose that arrow, you cannot miss, but I will be on you and kill you before you nock another."

"Let us speak not of killing," Se-quo-i suggested. "Since you had no hand in this, will you tell us where we can find the woman and the boy?"

"Follow your ears, that's all. The drums will chant soon." The big man actually shuddered. It made him seem more human, and Renno put his arrow back into the quiver and slung his bow over his shoulder. "But you go to your death, for the evil is all powerful."

"What evil?" Se-quo-i asked.

"The master and the one with skin like yours who comes from afar. They bring the darkness. They devour spirits."

"And Mingo does not like this?" Se-quo-i asked.

"I respect the old gods," Mingo explained, "but the sacrifice of children and young women saddens me."

Renno felt a chill in spite of the tropical heat. "This one

with skin like Se-quo-i's who comes from afar—has he but one eye and a face showing burn scars?"

"The same," Mingo verified. "And he brings more evil to us."

"Hodano," Renno breathed. He walked to stand in front of Mingo. He was not a small man, but he had to reach up to put his hands on Mingo's shoulders. "If Mingo is truly against evil, he will take us to the place of these evil ones. The one who comes from afar is my old enemy and he will die."

"He will drink your spirit, little Seneca."

"Will you guide us?" Renno asked, looking into the giant's deep, dark eyes, seeing the flat, huge nose, the big pores of a sheeny black skin.

"You have power against this evil?"

"Yes," Renno said, offering a prayer to the manitous.

"Then we go," Mingo said. He set a pace that had Renno and Se-quo-i at warrior's pace quickly. Before they had gone a hundred yards the drums began.

"We must be quick," Mingo said. "It is beginning."

Hodano had been given two young, nubile black girls. On the first night both girls had wept in shame and fear, for Hodano had created more awe among the Maroons by going about with his ruined face exposed. He had discarded the cloth cowl temporarily and had enjoyed the relief from the heat of it. The two young girls had suggested to each other that whoever was chosen for Hodano's bed first would close her eyes tightly so as not to see that horrible face, and then it might be bearable.

But Hodano, in a harsh voice, made it clear that their duties extended only to tending his hut and cooking his food. He did not give of his strength to that seductive orifice of a woman's body that was the downfall of so many men. He was conserving his power for that moment when he would find Renno in this hot and steaming land, end his quest for revenge, and go home to apply his newly gained power against the whites beginning to push their way into the Northwest Territories.

Hodano was beginning to understand the language of the drums made of human skin stretched over a section of hollow log. When he heard the drums speak from the outposts, he caught enough of the message to know that a raiding party was coming home. He gathered with the Maroons in the central compound of the village of huts and hoped that the raiding party came with white captives. He wanted to see if the old master had any more tricks powered by the spirit of a white sacrifice.

Hodano's was not an expressive face. One side of his face was ruined by the scars; the other was set in a half-grimace. But he came as close to a smile as he ever would when the Maroon senior warrior, Libertador, came into the village at the head of the raiding party with a small white boy in Indian dress and a flame-haired woman with her clothing in tatters. His heart soared. Once he had had this woman, the woman of Renno's, in his grasp, and his powers had failed him. Now she was *here*. And by all the evil spirits the boy with the golden hair would be Renno's son. Almost overcome, he fell to his knees and began to chant his thanks to the evil ones.

There was a cacophony of greetings, whoops of triumph, and jeers at the white captives. The slaves who had been freed from the slave pen in Kingston by Libertador were greeted with open arms and assigned to people who would give them food and a place to sleep until they could be integrated into the Maroon band.

Hodano had eyes only for the white woman and the boy. His mind savored thoughts of their torture and death and more, for he knew his enemy and guessed that Renno would not be far behind. This time, however, Renno was not in his own land among his own people. This time his spirit would be Hodano's.

He pushed close.

Beth, weakened by the forced march and bruised—although she had not been treated overly harshly, being of too great value to the master—looked into the scarred face and gasped.

"It is I," Hodano confirmed.

"He's Indian," Little Hawk said. He too was a bit bruised and battered, but he had withstood the march better than Beth.

"No, boy," Hodano said. "I am death."

The master appeared at the mouth of his cave as a drum began. The villagers turned as one. Libertador bowed toward the master and said, "These are for you."

The old man made an imperious gesture, and Libertador leapt to shove Beth and Little Hawk forward. Hodano fell in alongside. The master licked his lips and smacked his toothless gums, his beady eyes covering the flame-haired woman from head to toe.

"She has not been soiled?" the master asked.

"No, Master," Libertador said.

"Your reward will be great," the master said. "Take them to the chamber."

Libertador shoved Beth forward. Little Hawk went with her, at her side, into the cave.

The master cast his eyes on Hodano. "These will give me much power."

"Master," Hodano said, "these two are special. I would speak with you, alone."

"I look forward to the business at hand," the old man said. "Watch, if you care to. Learn."

"The flame-haired woman is mine," Hodano said.

The old man's eyes glittered. "How so? It was my warriors who brought her."

Behind Hodano, alerted he knew not how, warriors began to gather threateningly.

"She is *mine*," Hodano repeated, quickly devising an explanation, "because my spirits have brought her to me many, many leagues over sea and land. She is mine because the one I have told you about, the white Indian of the Seneca, kept me from claiming her far away. And now the spirits have sent her to me here."

"Kill him," the old man ordered calmly.

Hodano whirled and raised his arms. The blackness came so quickly that the two warriors leaping toward him with machetes were blinded and, in their fear and confusion, wounded each other. The black shadow of evil swooped down and howled, and even the voodoo master stepped back.

Hodano, still under the protection of his evil spirits, turned. His one eye glowed fiery red. "Old man," he intoned, "do not throw away an opportunity to share the greatest power you have ever known, a power you cannot even imagine."

Awed, the master said, "We will talk."

They sat on skins in the inner chamber. The fires were

being built up. Beth and Little Hawk, lashed securely, lay on a pile of filthy rags at the far side of the chamber.

"Wherever the flame-haired woman goes," Hodano told the master, "the white Indian will not be far behind. Even now he may be with us. I urge you to redouble your guard. Tell your warriors that this one is the match of many, and those who are overconfident or careless will die." He leaned forward. "But if we could capture this Renno alive, we could share a spirit that has the strength of many, through his manitous."

"I think that a few Maroon warriors will have no problem with one man," the master said.

"Listen to me," Hodano hissed, his split tongue extending in his intensity. "I have seen him kill a dozen men, and a pack of wolves. He will come through your warriors like a fine steel blade penetrating the soft belly of a woman if they fight his fight."

"You suggest . . . ?" the master asked.

"Overwhelm him with sheer weight. Have thirty, forty warriors close in. Tell them not to rely on their weapons, or many will die. Some will die anyhow, but there will be less loss if they simply swarm him and bear him to the ground with their weight. Then he will be alive, and we will share his spirit. When his is added to those of the white woman, who is mine, and the white boy, who is yours, we will be the two most powerful men in the world."

The old man was still doubtful. He licked his lips and wondered if his will would be stronger than the will of this mutilated man from across the great waters. He was tempted to fix his eyes on the one good eye of this man and use his powers, for Hodano, too, would have a powerful spirit. If the two of them could become the most powerful men in the world by sharing the spirits of the woman, the boy, and the warrior who came to find them, then how powerful would he alone be with all in his grasp, including the spirit of a man who could instantly summon the powers of evil?

But he was, in the end, too cautious and a bit frightened. Once he had thought the dark powers of old Africa to be more powerful than any, but that was before he had seen Hodano's spirits in action. In all his life he had never been able to find a voodoo initiate with the power to soar and become invisible, regardless of the number of sacrifices, the number of attempts. Hodano had achieved on the first attempt what had taken the master a lifetime.

Perhaps it would be best to share. He sighed. "It will be so," he said. "I will issue the orders. Fifty warriors will bear this enemy of yours to the earth, keeping him alive. We will share his spirit."

The fires were leaping up to consume freshly added dry branches. The drums had begun the rhythm of death. Men and women were gathering in the shadows. Many of them were drinking deeply of the potent coconut brew that was the alcoholic beverage of the Maroons, and one woman had already shed her clothing and was dancing sinuously in the flickering firelight.

"This one I will savor slowly," Hodano said, rising to walk and look down on Beth's face. He turned to the two young black girls who had been given to him. "Bring water and clothes. Wash her well and dress her in the white robes of a voodoo priestess."

Chapter XI

It was not like El-i-chi to stay away overnight without telling her his plans. Ah-wa-o had lain awake until almost midnight listening for his arrival in the room next to hers. She was young, and her days were filled with activity, so nature ended her vigilance and she slept. She helped Renna dress for the morning, chatted with the servants in the kitchen while breakfast was being prepared, and sent Renna upstairs to awaken her uncle.

Renna came back and said, "El-i-chi gone."

"Gone where?" Ah-wa-o asked.

Renna shrugged with both arms outstretched. Ah-wa-o went upstairs and saw that El-i-chi's bed had not been slept in.

Cedric was at the table with Renna when she came back down. He looked worried and lost his appetite when she told him that El-i-chi had not been in the house during the night.

He told Ah-wa-o that he would check around town and left the house. It didn't take long for him to hear of a fight on the wharf during the night. By that time of the morning the story had grown, as stories do when they are repeated, and it was said that at least six men had been killed and others severely maimed.

Cedric puffed his way up the streets to the police station. He had met the chief of Wilmington's constabulary force at various social occasions, and Cedric was the type who liked to go to the top when important matters were discussed. He was told by a sleepy-eyed constable that the chief wasn't in yet.

Cedric had learned, sometimes to his embarrassment, that his former standing as a peer of the realm had no weight in this raw, new country and that the very mention of titles and his citizenship of that country across the Atlantic seemed most often to draw down a curtain between him and others.

"Officer, I'm Cedric Huntington. My daughter and I own the Huntington shipping firm, you know."

"So?" the constable said. "What's your problem?"

"I'm looking for a friend, a guest of my house."

The constable sighed. He reached for quill and paper and said, "Tell me about it."

"He's a male, about twenty-two years old. Can't miss the fellow, since he wears frontier buckskins, has long, light-brown hair, and carries Indian weapons."

The constable turned and bellowed a name. The jailer, whose sleep had been interrupted three times during the night, was preparing to go home for a good day's rest. He stuck his tousled head in the door. "Gentleman here is looking for a wild man in buckskins," the constable said. "He the one who killed them men down on the docks?"

Cedric's faulty heart gave him a twitch of pain.

"Well," the jailer said, "Abe Watts did bring in a fellow wearing buckskins."

"Come on," the constable said. "Let's take a look."

Cedric followed the constable into the dim, stale jail area. When he saw El-i-chi lying on the floor of the cell, he rushed past the constable and seized the bars, calling El-i-chi's name.

"That's him?" the constable asked.

"What has happened to this man?" Cedric demanded.

The constable shrugged. "He must have tried to give Abe Watts a bad time. Ole Abe's a handy man with a truncheon."

"Open the door, please," Cedric said. The constable fumbled with the keys. Cedric knelt by El-i-chi's side and to his relief saw that El-i-chi was breathing. "This man has been beaten severely!" he shouted. "Why haven't you called a doctor?"

"Abe don't usually kill 'em," the constable rationalized. "But they sleep awhile after."

"I want a doctor immediately," Cedric said.

"The town don't have much money for medical treatment for prisoners."

"I'll pay for the doctor!" Cedric shouted. "And I want this man out of here. Now!"

"Well, sir, that's a matter for the magistrate," the constable said.

In the end Cedric had to haul himself, puffing and in some pain, down the street to summon a doctor. With the doctor on the way to the jail, he stopped at Nathan Ridley's office and, wiping his brow and having difficulty getting his breath, managed to gasp out what he had seen.

Nathan's face showed concern. "All right, Cedric, I'm going to have one of my men take you home in a buggy. I'll see to El-i-chi."

Abe Watts returned to the jail to prove to Spade Hollinger that he was serious. He told the constable at the front desk that he needed to question the man again.

"He's got company right now," the constable said.

Abe drifted back to the cell and saw two of the town's most prominent citizens in the Indian's cell—a doctor and Nathan Ridley. That puzzled him. What did a rich businessman such as Ridley have to do with a savage? He decided to find out. He walked to the open door and looked at the Indian with interest. Evidently he'd hit him on the head harder than usual, because the fellow was still out cold.

"Constable," Nathan said when he recognized the newcomer, "I understand that you brought this man here."

"That I did."

"You're going to have to explain why he has been so badly beaten," Nate said angrily.

Abe shrugged. "Some of it, I reckon, he got during the fight. Took on four, killed two."

"This man has been struck repeatedly with a blunt instrument," the doctor said.

Abe was getting worried. "Some of the men he fought had belaying pins."

"We need to move him to a place where I can treat him," the doctor said.

"Do you have any objection to that?" Nathan asked Watts.

Watts thought for a minute. He had a job to do. Ordinarily it would have been easy. He'd planned just to go into the cell and do something simple, like holding a filthy pillow over the man's face. It wouldn't have been the first time a drifter or a vagrant had died in a cell as the result of injuries sustained in a fight. If he allowed the Indian to be removed, it would complicate his plans.

"I reckon I can't say," he mumbled. "He killed two men. I reckon he'd have to be released by the magistrate."

"I'll see to that, Doctor," Nate said. He cast a speculative look at Watts as he moved past, a look that made Watts uncomfortable.

Nathan had no problem when he asked the magistrate to accompany him to the jail. The country was young, and the people still remembered the afflictions of having lived under a government that, over the centuries, had been insensitive to the rights and freedoms of individual citizens. The magistrate knew that he held his office at the will of the people. Nate Ridley was a citizen. That he was an influential citizen probably made the magistrate get his coat and hat quicker, but he would have come for any citizen, for he was a servant of the people.

Abe was still hanging around the police station. He wondered just what the heck was going on when Ridley came back so quickly with the magistrate. He tailed behind as Ridley took the magistrate to the cell.

The magistrate looked at El-i-chi's battered and swollen face and shook his head. He inquired for the arresting officer. Watts stood at attention.

"How did this man come by his injuries?"

"I told the gentleman, maybe some of them in the fight," Watts said.

"Did you have to carry him to the jail?"

Abe thought a minute. "No, no, he walked."

"Then the blows to the head came later."

Abe swallowed. But he knew he was within his rights. His was a tough job. He, one man, had to keep order in a rowdy waterfront area. "Well, sir, he resisted being put in the cell. I want to remind you, sir, that he'd killed two men and maybe two more will die."

"He resisted?" the magistrate asked.

"It is my opinion," the doctor said, "that this man has been struck on the head at least three times, for there are three different contusions. Any one of the blows would have incapacitated him. And he's been struck from behind."

"How many times did you strike this man?" the magistrate asked.

"I don't know," Abe said. "I guess maybe he was hit once or twice during the fight with a belaying pin. I just remember hitting him once."

"Were there any witnesses to this fight?" Ridley asked.

Abe took a little time. He decided that if he was going to work for Hollinger, Hollinger would have to stand up for him. "Matter of fact, Mr. Spade Hollinger saw the fight. He can tell you that the Injun was hit on the head once or twice." Now he'd have to get to Hollinger first and arrange to have their stories agree.

"We need to get this man to my office." The doctor stood and brushed off his breeches.

"Sir, he killed men," Watts said.

"It's a question of legality," the magistrate said uncertainly. "If the man's a murderer—"

"Tom," Ridley said, his voice low and intense, "I don't think you know who this man is. He's El-i-chi of the Seneca. He's the brother of Renno, the Seneca sachem who is welcome in George Washington's house. This man and his brother fought with Washington, and I assure you, sir, that if he dies, you'll have a lot of powerful men asking what happened."

The magistrate scratched his chin. "Well, in his condition he isn't going anywhere. Do what you have to do, Doctor."

With El-i-chi settled in the doctor's home, Nathan went to the Huntington house. The Indian girl took the news with

apparent calm. At least her face was calm, but when he tried
to talk her out of going to the doctor's house, he bowed to her
insistence and drove her there. The doctor had been working. The dried blood had been washed away, and there was a
tight, constricting bandage around El-i-chi's chest. The doctor was cleaning the cuts and bruises on El-i-chi's head and
face.

"Only one rib broken," the doctor told them. "It's the
blows to the head that worry me. His face looks worse than it
is, really."

Ah-wa-o slipped past the doctor, took El-i-chi's hand, and
whispered his name.

El-i-chi's eyelids flickered. His eyes opened. They were
unfocused, and then they moved and he tried to lift his head.
He lay back with a groan.

"I'll be damned," the doctor said, looking at Ridley. "Guess
that's the power of love."

Spade Hollinger listened with growing anger to Abe's account of what had happened at the jail. It was a hell of a time
for his luck to run bad. How was he to have known that the
Indian had powerful friends?

"I think you've got us in a pickle," he told Abe.

"Me?"

"You promised me something, boy," Hollinger said nastily.
"When a man promises me something, I expect him to deliver."

"Hell, Mr. Hollinger, he's at the doctor's, and he has half
the town with him."

"That's *your* problem. We've been pussyfooting around up
to this time, smelling each other out like a couple of stray
dogs. I'm gonna lay it on the line: you're in trouble. That
Indian walked away from the wharf on his own power, not a
scratch on him."

"But you have got to say that he was hit on the head by
your men," Watts urged. "I admit when he hit me I lost my
temper." He pounded his fist on his thigh. "Should have
killed him then."

"You should have. Look, if he's as bad off as you say he is,
they won't be moving him tonight. And there'll be no one in
the doctor's house except him and the doc."

"I don't think I can do that," Abe faltered.

"I think you can, and I think you'd better. If that Indian talks, he's going to tell everyone how you beat him in his cell when he was defenseless. These new free citizens of these United States are not going to like that. Too much like the good old days when the British were here."

"You have a stake in this too," Abe reminded him.

"Yes, I do. And I'm going to tell you how much of a stake I have, and where you come in. I can carry over forty slaves in the hold of my ship. A healthy male slave brings a thousand in gold in Spanish Florida."

Abe whistled. "That's a lot of money."

"I don't keep it all. It ain't all clear profit, because I have to pay about six hundred dollars a head in Nassau. Now, after I met you and sort of got to like you, I figured out a way where I could keep it all, every bit of the thousand a head. I was willing to cut you in. Remember I asked you how you'd like to have some gold? Let's say we took forty able-bodied male slaves down to Florida and sold them for forty thousand in gold. I reckon, since it's my ship and my business, ten percent would be a fair cut for a man's helping me."

"Four thousand in gold?" Abe asked, wide-eyed.

"For four thousand in gold can you pay a visit to a certain Indian tonight?"

"Yes," Abe said simply.

Throughout the day El-i-chi had brief periods of consciousness. The first thing he saw each time he opened his eyes was the calm face of Ah-wa-o.

The doctor, seeing that the girl was not inclined to be hysterical and that she could obey orders, welcomed her offer to sit with El-i-chi during the night. He explained that the only danger was that El-i-chi might begin to vomit and drown in his own vomitus. Ah-wa-o sat in a chair beside the bed, holding El-i-chi's hand. When he awakened shortly after nightfall, she stood and touched his face with her hands.

"You're going to be all right," she whispered.

"Knife," El-i-chi said, trying to raise one arm. "Knife."

"Your knife isn't here."

El-i-chi tried to push himself up, but he was in obvious pain.

"Wait. Lie still. I will find a knife." Ah-wa-o found a knife in the doctor's kitchen—a bone-handled carving knife with a blade that had been dulled by years of use. The knife seemed to satisfy El-i-chi. He clutched the bone handle; then, before going back to sleep, he slid the knife under his pillow.

El-i-chi awakened once more just before midnight. Ah-wa-o's eyes had become heavy in spite of her concern for him, and she was dozing in her chair. He turned his head and watched her face. He was still a bit confused. He couldn't remember exactly how he had come to this, to being in a strange bed with Ah-wa-o by his side and with his head so heavy, so painful. The only thought he could muster was in admiration of the beauty of his little rose. He slept.

Abe Watts entered the house through a set of French doors facing the river. He was armed only with his club. The house had that early-morning feel, the silence broken now and then by a creaking of a shutter, the crack of something contracting in the coolness of the night. He tiptoed toward the lamplight in the doctor's treatment room, then halted outside the open door to study the interior. The girl was sleeping, her chin on her chest. The Indian was still unconscious. It was going to be easy.

The presence of the girl did complicate things. It would have been better to find the Indian alone, but the rewards would justify the increased risk. Who would suspect a city constable of murder?

He crept forward slowly. He had heard and read about how alert and watchful Indians were. He'd never fought Indians himself, only the British. He figured Indians, especially an Indian girl, wouldn't be any more sharp than a British sentinel, and he'd once sneaked up on a redcoat on guard duty in the night and silenced the man with one quick slash of his knife.

He didn't want to kill the girl—no need for it. He used a delicate touch perfected over the period of his years as a constable on the docks and laid his club ever so lightly along the side of her head over her ear. There was a soft little thud and scarcely any change in her limp, sleeping attitude. Then he moved quickly to the bed and looked down into the bruised face of the sleeping Indian. He picked up a pillow carefully, slowly, and eased it down over the Indian's face, putting his weight on it.

In a dream El-i-chi was standing on a high cliff in a country he had never seen, a thickly forested land with steep ridges of barren rock protruding. Far below was a lake that held blue, deep water. The thing that attacked him was not seen, coming on him suddenly, without warning. It seized him from behind in clawed arms of incredible strength, and he felt himself falling, falling, to enter the water without so much as a splash and with no feeling of impact. Then he was sinking down, down, and his lungs were spasming for air, and he knew that to breathe would be death. The weight of the thing that had seized him from behind was still on him. He struggled. He felt the haft of his knife in his hand.

The Indian's body was jerking and bucking as his lungs fought for air. Abe kept his weight on the pillow. It would be only a minute or so longer. It was amazing just how long he had been holding the pillow tightly over the Indian's face, how long it took a man to die from lack of air. He didn't see the Indian's hand go up under the pillow and fumble around. He saw the arm jerk up and a glint of lamplight on metal, and then something penetrated the biceps of his right arm, and he yelped out in pain.

The arm was suddenly useless. He couldn't put pressure on the pillow with it, and the Indian had moved his head and had taken a huge gulp of air. Abe was afraid he was going to faint from the pain in his arm. He looked down and saw a kitchen knife being pulled from his arm and blood spurting. There was a roar of animallike intensity from under the pillow, and the Indian was surging up, and the knife was coming at him again.

He threw himself off the bed, upsetting the chair and feeling the slice of the dull blade on his right shoulder. The girl spilled from the chair and flopped limply to lie still. Abe scuttered across the pine floor on his hands and knees. The animal roared behind him, and he turned his head to see the Indian struggling with his bedclothes, rising up like some battered and bloody ghost. The blood, he realized with a whine of fear, was his own, for his arm was bleeding copiously.

He heard a commotion from upstairs. The noise had awakened the doctor. He had only one thought: to get out of there. He got to his feet and slammed out the French doors and ran until he was on the waterfront.

Spade Hollinger came from his cabin and looked at Abe disgustedly. The constable was clasping his right arm with his left and dripping blood on his deck.

"I take it you failed," Hollinger said.

"I didn't get him," Abe admitted, "but no one saw me, neither."

"You sure?"

"Dead sure. Help me to do something with this arm."

Hollinger packed the stab wound by lantern light in the cabin. The arm wasn't going to be of much use to Abe for a while. Hollinger made Abe repeat the story twice. When he was satisfied that Abe couldn't be identified as the man who had entered the doctor's house, he lit a cigar and leaned back.

"Well, maybe we can still come out of this all right," he said. "Depending on you. My plan depends on your being on duty on the dock at night."

"I can do that."

"They see you can't use that arm, they'll take you off duty."

"I won't let 'em know," Abe replied.

"That arm's gonna be sorer than a boil tomorrow."

"I walked from Cross Creek to Wilmington with a hole in my shoulder. Time I got here pus was running down to my belt," Abe said. "I'll be on duty. Tell me what I have to do."

"All right. You just keep your eyes open. Me and some of my boys will be making trips to my ship, and we won't be alone. It'll be up to you to cue us in so's we can get certain objects of contraband on board without being seen. Any sailors or loafers come around, you run 'em off. Got it?"

"This contraband," Abe said. "I think I can guess."

"Boy, there are a dozen plantations working slaves just across the river, some of them by the dozens. My boys and I have been laying this plan for a long time. We'll be snatching a few slaves from town here, and there'll be three boatloads of 'em coming from across the river."

"*That's* how you're going to be able to keep all the profit," Abe said. "You're gonna steal slaves."

"Bright boy."

"When you leave, I'll have to go with you."

"Figured that. It's gonna get too hot around here for both of us right quick," Hollinger said.

El-i-chi almost fell off the bed. He was still trying to get untangled from the sheets when the doctor ran into the room, wearing only a long, red nightshirt. He carried an old dueling pistol in his hand. He took in the situation and pushed El-i-chi back down on the bed.

"Whoever it was is gone, boy. Now you be still, or you're going to hurt yourself."

"Ah-wa-o," El-i-chi groaned.

"Well, if you'll quit trying to get off this bed, I'll take a look at her."

El-i-chi subsided immediately. He leaned on one elbow, looking down at Ah-wa-o. The doctor knelt beside her and lifted one eyelid. Ah-wa-o moaned and opened her eyes. Within a few minutes she was drinking tea and assuring the doctor that aside from a severe headache and a large bump over her ear, she was fine. El-i-chi, who had been going on adrenaline alone, felt the world sink out from under him again.

"He's a crazy man," the doctor was protesting.

The chief constable had been rousted from his bed. He had looked over the scene and brooded a bit as he saw the drops of blood marking the exit of the attacker. But he had no answers. It was now morning. Ah-wa-o's headache was almost gone, but there was a knot over her ear to remind El-i-chi that someone had attacked a girl he had come to consider his own, more than a sister.

"El-i-chi," Nathan Ridley pleaded, "be sensible. You're in no condition to get out of bed." Nate had stopped by on the way to work to check on El-i-chi and had arrived just as the Seneca was demanding his weapons and his clothing.

"We can handle this," the chief constable assured him. "And there's still the matter of murder charges against you, young man."

"Do you know who came in here and attacked you last night?" Nathan asked.

El-i-chi shook his head. He still wasn't thinking too clearly. Something was eluding him, and he could not say that he knew who had attacked him and Ah-wa-o. He had his suspicions, but he couldn't get his mind wrapped around that elusive bit of information that seemed to be hidden somewhere under the roaring in his ears.

"Man with a knife hole in him made by this should be easy to find," the chief constable said, looking with distaste at the thick-bladed kitchen knife. "Tell you what, Mr. Ridley. I'm going to put a man on guard here today for two reasons: one, of course, is for protection for these people. The other is because, legally, this man is a prisoner until he's been given a fair trial in the matter of the killings on the wharf."

"Lie down, El-i-chi," Ah-wa-o said sternly.

El-i-chi allowed her concern for him to be his excuse to lie down and close his eyes. He would not have admitted that he was simply too weak to get out of the bed.

From the top of a perpendicular wall of jungle Renno looked down on a village of rude huts in the circular pit below. Goats roamed and naked children played among the huts. There was a smell of food being cooked, the shrill gabble of women washing clothing in a clear, deep-looking pool of water at the glen's lowest point. Up near the far end of the glen the men had gathered, perhaps a half-hundred of them. They looked up now and then toward the fern-fringed entrance to a cave in the far wall. Most of them were smoking white clay pipes, but the smell that occasionally wafted to Renno's nostrils was not that of tobacco.

"I go," Renno told Mingo, who stood beside him.

"You would not make it halfway through the village," Mingo said. "Your white skin stands out like the sun peering through rain clouds."

"You say that my wife and son will be inside that cave?"

"They will be there." The sound of drums came from the cave's mouth. "The ceremony has started inside the cave. Listen to me, my friend. I go down first. The guards block the entrance to the cave. They have been alerted to something, and even now they are building their courage by smoking ganja."

"Is there a way to come down to the entrance to the cave from the far wall?" Renno asked.

"No. It is steep and slippery and you would be seen," Mingo said. "You say you have power over the evil that has been brought here to reinforce the evil of our own master. Perhaps I can give you a chance to use it, perhaps not. There are a few of us who chafe under the rule of the master. My father has long advised a halt to the raids into British territory for white sacrifice victims. Give me until the sun touches the hill to the west. If I have not signaled you, or if you hear the drums change to this tempo"—he drummed his fingers against his muscular, bare chest in a frantic rhythm—"then do as you must. Perhaps a swift dash through the warriors while they are preoccupied with their ganja would gain you entrance to the cave, where you might avenge the death of your wife and son before the guards could reach you."

Mingo plunged down a narrow trail leading into the glen. Renno watched him emerge into the cleared area and stalk toward a hut. An older man, large but not as large as Mingo, glanced once toward the rim of the cockpit as Mingo talked. Then they moved together toward the group of Maroons gathered near the entrance to the cave.

The drums did not change their rhythms, but Renno's blood was surging. Although he had not asked for details of a voodoo ceremony, he had heard enough from Mingo to develop a heart-stopping image about what was in store for Beth and Little Hawk. It took all his willpower to keep him from following Mingo into the village, all his weapons at the ready. He was realistic enough, even in his mental agony of fear for his wife and son, however, to know that not even Renno and Se-quo-i could hope to break through half a hundred warriors, each with his natural fear of death dulled by the drug called ganja.

Beth and Little Hawk had pulled themselves into a sitting position, backs against the damp wall of the chamber. The scene before them prompted Beth to tell Little Hawk to close his eyes. Directly in front of them, between them and the nearest of the fires, black men and women writhed and pumped in coupled abandon. Naked women danced around the fires. The drummers paused in their incessant efforts only to gulp intoxicating liquid from containers of baked clay.

"Don't worry, Beth," Little Hawk said. "My father will come."

"Of course he will," Beth replied, but she had seen the number of able-bodied men in the village outside. Even Renno would need help against so many.

She tried to pull away from the hands of women who came with water and robes. They held her and stripped away her clothing. Her soft, white skin gleamed in the light of the fires, drawing no particular attention from the gathered blacks but causing Little Hawk to turn his head away. When she was washed—not thoroughly but energetically—the women pulled a loose, baggy white gown made of coarse homespun over her head. Then they tied her hands and feet again and left her to join the others.

"What do you think they want to do to us?" Little Hawk asked.

"I'm not sure."

"Why have they dressed you like that?"

"Perhaps I'm to be part of some ceremony. I think they believe my red hair and white skin have some sort of magic." Beth spoke calmly, but her heart was pounding. She had heard the dark stories of voodoo sacrifice, but she'd never really believed that such horrendous things could happen.

Spade Hollinger's hired thugs had begun work early in the afternoon. They went by rowboat to the rice and indigo plantations across and down the Cape Fear from Wilmington.

Not all slaves were constantly penned or overseen by sadistic white men with whips. In the rice and indigo fields gangs of slaves often worked without supervision. Mainly they were treated fairly—or as fairly as a man who is denied his freedom can be treated. They ate well, and most slave owners realized that it was stupid to do deliberate damage to a valuable asset—slaves represented money in more ways than one—either through overt cruelty or by neglect.

It was relatively simple for the thugs in the three rowboats to isolate healthy-looking black men singly or in groups of two or three; slaves were accustomed to obeying whites.

As darkness came, more of Hollinger's men slipped quietly through the dark streets of Wilmington into those areas where trusted slaves had their own quarters. There were even a few black freedmen in the town, and more than one of them, accustomed to being able to move about without hindrance, fell victim to the clubs of the white men.

Soon after dark Abe Watts was patrolling his area. He moved onto the docks and used his authority to send loafing sailors and others on their way. Soon the docks were clear, and the first of the kidnapped freedmen was being dragged aboard Hollinger's ship.

Abe's right arm was as sore as hell and practically useless. He let it hang and tried not to move it, but there was no one to see that he wasn't the whole-bodied man he was passing for. He carried his truncheon in his left hand and told himself that he wasn't nervous.

The man who had been assigned to guard El-i-chi and Ah-wa-o in the doctor's house was a newly married man. He had been away from his home all day long, and he had become quickly accustomed to returning to his rooms and the eager arms of his young bride with the coming of sundown. He was restless. He had found during the day that the Indian girl was well-spoken and friendly. He'd spent a few hours listening to her talk about life in a Seneca village. The white Indian had not joined in the conversation much. He slept a lot, and when he was awake, he seemed restless but weak.

After dark the guard began to feel very homesick. His Sally was a goodly wench, full-bodied and so ripely passionate that his two weeks of married life with her had been the finest thing that had ever happened to him. He told the Indian girl about his wife and spoke with such longing that he caught El-i-chi's interest.

"You should not be kept from your wife," El-i-chi said.

"Well, it's my duty, you know."

"I have this." El-i-chi lifted the kitchen knife. "I will not be caught by surprise again. And since I am not yet able to move about, I will not go anywhere if you would like to go to your home and speak with your wife for a few minutes, just to let her know where you are."

It was tempting, damned tempting. "Well, I'm not here just to protect you."

"I killed in self-defense," El-i-chi reminded him. "I do not intend to become a fugitive from the white man's justice by fleeing. I can prove my innocence."

The constable lived no more than five minutes away. He pictured Sally waiting for him. She'd have food ready, but it wasn't food that drew him. "Well, I guess you ain't going anywhere."

"No," El-i-chi confirmed.

"Look, you wouldn't do anything to get me in trouble?"

"Have I the strength?"

"I'll be back in an hour," the constable said happily, leaping to his feet. "You keep an eye on him, little lady."

"I will," Ah-wa-o promised, wondering what El-i-chi had in mind.

She found out quickly. The constable's footsteps were crossing the porch outside and already El-i-chi was pushing himself up.

"No," she said, rising to put her hands on his shoulders.

"Here is what you will do." The tone of El-i-chi's voice left no doubts in Ah-wa-o's mind that, weak as he was, he was El-i-chi again.

Chapter XII

M en of substance universally recognized General George Washington as the unnamed head and the beating, vibrant heart of the continuing movement to make one nation of thirteen dissimilar provinces—the barely United States. Not perceiving himself in such a grandiose role, he had returned to Mount Vernon, but he had had little opportunity to enjoy the beautiful spring weather of 1788. Not a day passed without one or more visitors. They came on horseback and in various horse-drawn vehicles to seek out the advice and support of the man whom some cynics had already started calling King George.

Washington was tired. He had been in service to his country all his adult life, and he ached for privacy, for peace in his personal life. In spite of his achievements he considered himself to be a country gentleman, a farmer. But he could

not even take a morning ride to inspect his fields without
being chased down by some agitated seeker of favor or support or by a man carrying news.

The news of those days was a mixture of good and bad.
Since December 1787, when little Delaware had become the
first state to ratify the Federal Constitution, the other states
had begun to fall in line. The promise of a Bill of Rights had
delivered one of the giants, Pennsylvania. New Jersey, Con-
necticut, and Georgia ratified earlier in the year. Massachusetts had been close, with the old war-horses, Sam Adams
and John Hancock, being lukewarm if not privately opposed
to the Constitution. Maryland joined the Federalist side in
April, South Carolina in May.

In June, New Hampshire voted to ratify the new way of
law and life, and by majority rule the Constitution was law.
Without Virginia and New York, however, among the most
powerful of the thirteen states, Washington knew that the
Constitution would not be effective. Without those big states,
the whole thing would unravel like a ball of twine being
batted around by a kitten.

Washington, of course, supported Virginia's ratification.
He had some good men on his side—James Madison and John
Marshall among them—but to his concern, Thomas Jeffer-
son, the brilliant mind behind the wording of the Declaration
of Independence, was siding with the radicals from Virginia's
Piedmont. There'd always been political differences between
representatives from the Piedmont and Tidewater areas—Patrick
Henry, George Mason, and Richard Henry Lee.

In the spring Tom Jefferson was wavering, and Washington
had hopes that Jefferson would conclude that the addition of
the Bill of Rights would overcome Jefferson's doubts about
one generation's binding all those to follow with the Constitution. Since news traveled slowly, there was still hope that
Virginia would have the honor of being the ninth state to
ratify. New Hampshire, however, had already taken that
honor.

One visitor to Mount Vernon in early June was more than
welcome. A backwoodsman came trotting up the well-tended
lane on a hard-ridden animal with protruding ribs. A man of
the type that Washington respected highly, a man of the sort
with whom he could be most comfortable, the traveler found

the general sitting on a great black stallion as he observed work on a drainage project.

"Gen'ral," he said, putting one finger to his soiled, greasy coonskin hat.

Washington had been whittling on his misbegotten false teeth, trying to make them more comfortable. He looked up, his lips compressed by the touching of his gums, and squinted into the sun before he recognized his visitor.

"Well, Hobby!" Washington enthused. "By the name of heaven."

"Choppers givin' ye trouble agin, Gen'ral?" Hobgood Ryan asked. He was a tall, spare man with a scraggly red beard and red hair protruding greasily from under his cap. He had Erin-green eyes that had the faraway look of the frontiersman. Sun-squint wrinkles creased his forehead and around the green eyes, and his face showed the results of being baked in summer and lashed by frozen winds in winter.

"Devil take them," Washington complained, shoving his wooden plates with ivory teeth back into his mouth and making a face of disgust as he tried to seat them properly. "Hobby, what in the devil are you doing so far from the woods?" The last time he had seen Hobgood Ryan, the war was still in doubt and the Irishman had been a valued scout for his army.

"Wal, Gen'ral," Hobby said, " 'sides a little curiosity, wantin' to see this King George everyone's talkin' about—"

Washington's mouth showed his characteristic closed-lip smile. From another man, he would have taken the remark as an insult.

"—I reckoned they was a few things goin' on up north you might not know much about."

"You've had a long ride. Let's go up to the house and get some victuals into you."

"I've heard, Gen'ral, that there's those in Virginee who make some drinkin' whiskey most as good as the real thing."

Hobby seemed a bit ill at ease in Washington's study, but he sat on the edge of a brocaded chair when Washington delivered a drink that was, Hobby admitted, almost as good as the real thing.

"Well, Hobby?"

"Gen'ral, I just took me a trip in the foothills of the great St. Brendan."

Washington's lips showed that characteristic smile again. He had already heard the delightful nonsense about St. Brendan, over a campfire in the middle of a snowstorm a long way from the comforts of Mount Vernon, and from this very man. Every Irishman knew the tale, how Brendan the navigator discovered the New World in the sixth century and actually traveled inland as far as the banks of the Ohio River, where an angel had told him to return to Ireland. It made a spanking good tale for a cold winter's night, with the fire spitting at snowflakes and a man's stomach growling with hunger.

But the smile faded, for if Hobby had been on the Ohio, that was of interest to Washington.

"Mighty pretty country up there, Gen'ral. *Mighty* pretty, but it's full of the meanest damned Injuns I've ever seen since we got whupped at Fort Necessity in 'fifty-four. They're mad, Gen'ral, fightin' mad. You plan to send families with women and chillen into them northwest woods up past the Ohio, you better have a passel of soldiers with 'em."

"I don't have an army," Washington reminded him.

"I know that. But you got respect. You know where the skeletons are buried in jest about every state in this new union, and maybe a word or two from you might stop them Northern states from lettin' men bring women and kids out there to be scalped and worse. They's already people dyin' up there. And the bloody British are shippin' down guns and ammo and tellin' the Injuns to force us out o' the land north of the Ohio."

"You know for a fact that the British are enticing the Indians?"

"I've drunk their rum, and I've stolen their shot and powder from Injuns—dead ones, for sure. I've heard the Injuns talk."

"Hobby, in your opinion, could we come to an agreement with the Indians in the Northwest? Could we make them a fair offer of land and open up some of the territory to settlement peacefully?"

The frontiersman snorted and looked meaningfully at his empty glass. Washington nodded toward the bottle, and Hobby filled the glass to the brim and gulped before he answered. "What's fair? To the Injun it'd be fair for all of us to go back where we come from. Nope, they's some fire-

eaters at work up there. The war chiefs are sayin' to us,
'Hold. Enough. You whites have the lands all the way to the
sea, and you breed like maggots.' They'll fight this time,
Gen'ral."

"Hobby, I'm not active in government right now. I'm only
a retired general. There's a fight going on at the present
time that is demanding all the attention of the politicians
in the various statehouses. I'll have to tell you that I'm
pessimistic about anyone's being able to give protection to
settlers going into the territory. We moved too fast on that.
We opened the area for settlement by the Ordinance of 1787,
and many politicians believe that it will be up to the settlers
to protect their own families. The opinion seems to be that
since the people who take land there are the ones who are
going to gain most, let them do the fighting."

"And the dyin'," Hobby said unhappily. "Well, Gen'ral,
I jest wanted to let you know how it stands up there. Me,
I'm not goin' back. Come too close to losin' my scalp as it
was. Gettin' too old for Injun fightin'. I got me a place
up in the hills of Kaintuck, brought me back a Miami squaw—
sweetest little thing you've ever seen—and she's already
given me a boy child. Gonna plant me some corn and build
me a still and concentrate on drinkin' liquor and makin'
babies for a while."

Washington returned to his study after seeing Hobby off.
The old man had refused the offer of a bed for the night,
stating that he could be a few miles closer to his little Indian
moonbeam and his boy before nightfall. After some thought,
Washington took up a quill and paper. Some day, he told
himself, a man in Virginia will write a letter to another man
a few hundred miles away to the southwest and won't have
to wonder how many months it will take before the letter
is delivered. He was concerned about the Northwest Territory.
It was, he knew, a rich country, and in the end it would
become either a part of British Canada or the United States.
It was bad enough having the British to the north. To be
hemmed in from the west as well would be militarily un-
supportable.

The letter was addressed to the only man he trusted to go
into the Northwest Territories and bring back a detailed
report of the state of mind of the Indian tribes there.

*   *   *

Washington's letter to his old friend traveled first to the
Virginia Tidewater areas, then was put on board a ship in
Norfolk. It traveled by post rider from the port of Wilmington to the state capital at Raleigh, where it was showed
around a bit—it made some people feel good just to hold a
sample of George Washington's handwriting. There was some
speculation as to why the great general was writing to a
man with only one name in care of a colonel of militia in
a frontier area. The letter, along with an accumulation of
mail for relatives who had gone west, left Raleigh for Charlotte
and was delayed there while officials sought out a trader who
was known to make occasional trips across the mountains.

As the weeks passed and the *Mano Negra* covered empty
leagues of sea, sailing first north, then south, then eastward,
then westward, Adan Bartolome grew restless. He was far
more eager than his crew to see a sail. They, having had a
taste of British shot, powder, and steel, were sharing some
second thoughts about the gay life of piracy.

It was as if the oceans had swallowed up all shipping.
Adan reasoned that there had to be merchant ships out
there somewhere, lightly armed ships carrying valuable goods
to and from England or to and from Spain, but what had
happened to them was one of life's great mysteries.

The food supplies taken from the *Assiduous* were getting
low. When he put into a Bahamian port to replenish his
water supply, five crew members deserted him. He had
managed to sell the few negotiable items that had come as
loot from the British warship so that there was Nassau bacon,
fresh fruit, and a supply of beans and flour aboard, but
things were getting a little tense as the *Mano Negra* put
to sea and resumed her search for prey.

Adan made an inspiring speech to his crew, telling them
that the time was growing near for the return of the Americans
with gold. He told them that there would have to be a ship
soon. He tried to interest them in arms drills, but with
little success. A couple of weeks later he received a delegation
from the crew. The spokesman told him that the men were
wondering if it wouldn't be best to take up some honest
work such as, maybe, running slaves from the markets in
the islands to Spanish markets in South America.

"The men think we could sell most of the cannon and get a stake," the spokesman said.

Adan leapt to his feet, his face showing his fury. "Sell the cannon?" he bellowed. "What manner of men are you?"

But after another couple of weeks he knew that something had to be done. He was thinking about putting into George Town on Great Exuma, where he might be able to exchange the silver service in the captain's pantry for a few more weeks' food. He was about to give such an order early one morning when the lookout sang out the sighting of a sail. His heart soared. He roared orders, and the ship turned toward the sail. The distance closed rapidly, for the other ship was making for the sighting of *their* sails. The morning was not yet over when Adan could count more gun ports than he had ever seen on a floating object. He lowered his telescope, his heart doing a game of patty-cake. He lifted the telescope and began to count gun ports, but by that time the other ship was close enough for Adan's crew to do some tallying of their own.

Six men went running off, and the first thing Adan knew a British flag was run up, and the crew were tossing aside colorful garments such as orange head scarves and the naval uniform jackets looted from the *Assiduous* and were trying to present an impression of being ordinary seamen on an ordinary merchant vessel. Adan was shamed. Then he looked at the gun ports of that ship that flew the ensign of the British navy and didn't feel so shamed.

The British man-of-war was definitely intent on closing. Adan looked around for other telltale evidence and wished that he had been a little more stern in making the men keep the *Mano* shipshape. His only chance was to convince that ship out there that he was an innocent British island merchant-man on legitimate business. A belowdecks inspection would be his death warrant, because there were enough artifacts from the *Assiduous* marked with her name to give firm evidence of her fate.

The warship was making signals to heave to.

Adan looked around, worried. The men were standing about the deck alternating their gaze from the menacing monster out there to the captain. A line of showers was bearing down from the southeast, dark and roiling. The wind was picking up, blowing into the coming storm.

"Make signal," he ordered. "Will comply."

Men rushed toward the riggings without being ordered, and Adan shouted, "Avast there, keep your positions."

The signal was sent. The British ship was closing fast, and there was activity on her decks in preparation for lowering boats. Adan looked up at the advancing storm front.

"It's going to be a near thing," he told his first mate. "Have the men stand by. When I give the order, they're going to have to snap to fast—and I mean fast."

His head seemed to be on swivels, turning now to check the squall line, then to see that the warship's boats had been lowered and the boarding party was leaving the vessel. He waited until the boats—two of them, each filled with well-armed men—were halfway to the *Mano*.

"Hoist all sails!" he bellowed. "Rudder hard aport!"

The *Mano* heeled to the wind as the sails unfurled. She leapt like a stallion, and her bow began to pound into the seas as she turned. Adan didn't look back; he didn't want to see the puffs of smoke from what seemed like *hundreds* of gun ports. He'd hear the muffled roar first, and then the smashing sounds of countless balls tearing into his ship. A gust of wind hit him in the face, carrying with it stinging raindrops. There was blackness ahead. The sea was being lashed by a torrential downpour.

"Be slow," he was begging, picturing the British naval officers shouting and gunners training the deadly muzzles of *thousands* of guns on him.

The wind shifted suddenly, and the *Mano* leaned into the wind. Men scampered as he shouted orders, and then two roaring sounds came as one: the thunder of a tropical rain on the forward deck and the sound of the warship's guns.

He looked back. The *Mano* had changed direction and was tacking along on the winds of the squall line. Between *Mano* and death there was a wall of rain, a lovely curtain of it, so solid and so intense that he could see nothing of the British ship, not even her muzzle blasts when she let loose with another broadside that sent shot whistling and rumbling past the *Mano*'s stern.

"We've made it," he said, lifting his face to grin into the downpour.

"Sir," the first mate said, "I think we'd better shorten sail."

"I'll have the man's head who touches a sail!" Adan shouted. "Keep all sails set."

"We'll rip out her masts," the mate protested.

"Those British cannon will rip out her guts," Adan countered. "Prepare to come about."

He reversed course so that the *Mano* was sailing in the opposite direction. He hoped to confuse the British as to the *Mano*'s whereabouts. He stayed in the squalls, allowing the men to shorten sail only after a bitter, bruising afternoon of it. As night fell he sailed south, out of the weather, into a roiled sea under a clear, washed sky. No sails were visible.

"Mr. Williams," he said, "set course for Great Exuma, if you please." He had been convinced. The pretty lady from England, she of the glorious red hair, had been right. The age of piracy was dead, and after looking into the muzzles of the meanest ship he had ever seen, he could understand why.

The men, already having decided that piracy wasn't exactly their life's calling, began to spruce themselves up. One of them set up a barbershop at middecks, and the sea behind the *Mano* began to grow hair as the trimmings were tossed overboard. Clothing washed in salt water dried on the riggings. Where once the rousing chanties of the pirates had made the air ring with bravado and threat, there were tender ballads being sung.

Well, Adan thought, *so it goes*.

George Town was an old pirate port, and it still had the reputation of being quite a town for sailors. No longer a busy port, it had only three vessels of any size in its calm, still harbor when the *Mano* ghosted around a point. Adan put over two longboats, and the chanting of the rowing men carried far over the placid water as the *Mano* eased to an anchorage near a hulking merchantman that showed much wear. While he was anchoring the ship, the wind came up into a pleasant breeze, shifted a bit, and swung the *Mano* on her chains so that she was downwind from the merchantman.

"Land's sake," First Mate Williams said, "what's that stink?"

Adan had to grin. Funny how the formerly profane men of the *Mano* had changed even their language in so short a time. He, too, smelled the stench and wrinkled his nose. "Something dead."

Williams was examining the merchantman with a scope. "Worse, I think, Cap'n. That un's a blackbird, I'll warrant."

Slaver, Adan thought. He examined the merchantman more closely. The smell of her was a mixture of human excrement, long-dead things, vomit, and other things unidentifiable. The men were noticing it now, holding their noses, looking up in question to the captain.

"Well, Mr. Williams," Adan said, "I hate to ask the men to do the extra work—"

"We don't mind, Cap'n," yelled a seaman. "Just get us out of this stench."

The *Mano* was moved a few cable lengths upwind.

"Who was it that suggested we go into the slave trade?" Adan asked, grinning.

"Don't know," Williams said, "but if he suggests it again, I'll personally shoot him."

"Mr. Williams, if you've got your watch set, you may give shore leave to those not on duty."

"Yes, sir," Williams said with a grin. Within a quarter hour the boats were ferrying men to the waterfront, where they disappeared almost instantly into the sort of establishments sought out first by sailors: grog shops where the tankards were delivered by half-pretty girls who did double duty for men of the sea.

Adan didn't go ashore until later. It felt good to have solid land under his feet again, even if the dock did at first tend to take on the motion of the sea. He walked along the waterfront, chose a fairly decent-looking pub, and entered a room filled with smoke and the smell of rum and unwashed male bodies. He started to turn around and leave, for he guessed by the looks of the patrons that he had chosen the pub frequented by the crew of the slaver at anchor. But the sight of a large man seated alone at a table stopped him.

The man at the table was resplendent in a wine-colored swallowtail coat, a tall, black hat with a crown that diminished a bit at the top, a brocaded black vest with buttons of mother-of-pearl over gleaming, white linen that ruffled at his throat. One outthrust leg showed fawn-colored breeches and a gleamingly polished boot. Seeing Adan staring at him, the man bowed his head and motioned to an empty chair at his table. He gave the impression of possessing tremendous power—both personal and physical—that was carefully but barely restrained.

The sight of a man dressed not for the tropics but for the drawing rooms of old Europe aroused Adan's curiosity. He bowed in return and walked to the table. He himself had dressed in black breeches and a gleaming white shirt with ruffles at throat and hands, leaving off the jacket in deference to the warm evening.

"Join me, sir," the resplendent man invited in English, rising. A gold chain at his waist spoke of wealth. He clutched white gloves in his left hand.

"My pleasure, sir." Adan introduced himself with a curt bow.

"Bastian Vanderrenner at your service," the well-dressed man said. He snapped his fingers, and a maid appeared, rosy-cheeked and smiling, with a glass of potent rum for Adan.

"I think," Adan said, after a gulp and a wheeze, "that they scarce give this time to cool before pouring."

The Dutchman laughed. "The wines of Spain are smoother to the palate." He spoke English with a light accent and Spanish with hardly any accent at all. "I have not seen you here in our little paradise."

"First trip," Adan said.

"Ah, then I will be your host and show you the wonders of George Town. Fanny, there, is foremost among them." He indicated the maid who had served Adan. "Unless she has contracted the pox in the past few days, she is the most desirable practitioner of her craft on this island."

"I will keep your recommendation in mind," Adan said. "You live here, sir?"

"Twixt and tween," Vanderrenner replied. "Let us say that I consider this to be one of my home ports."

Adan guessed that one of the merchantmen at anchor was owned by the Dutchman.

"And you, sir?" Vanderrenner asked.

"I? I ventured out into commerce without, I fear, proper knowledge. I sit here with an empty ship at anchor, a crew that needs paying, and no trade contract to my name." He had decided, instantly, to test the waters. Vanderrenner, in spite of being dressed much too warmly for the climate, looked prosperous. Perhaps through such a contact he could find a paying, short-haul cargo to hold things together until he got his hands on the ransom money.

"I saw your ship enter the harbor," the Dutchman said. "She has Spanish lines, no?"

Adan shrugged. He didn't want to go into that subject too deeply.

"The British are touchy about who carries cargo to and from their ports," Vanderrenner informed him.

"So it seems." Adan didn't know what to say next, but he was given time, and food for thought, when a drunken seaman staggered toward the table, almost fell, and then stumbled over Vanderrenner's outthrust leg. The man fell heavily and came wobbling to his feet with a knife in his hand and a curse on his lips. Adan had not seen Vanderrenner move. There was a sharp blast of sound, and the seaman tumbled backward, a hole in his forehead from a ball fired by Vanderrenner's pistol.

There was a sudden hush. As men converged on the table, Adan prepared to bolt, not wanting to get caught up in someone else's fight.

"Take this carrion away," Vanderrenner ordered coolly, replacing the pistol under his coat. Men leapt to do his bidding. The dead man was dragged unceremoniously out the front door. Soon the laughing and talking had resumed.

Adan, stunned, examined Vanderrenner more closely. He had thick white-blond hair that was excellently trimmed. His smooth, boyish face looked younger at first glance than at second examination. His steel-gray eyes, Adan noted for the first time, almost never blinked. The lips were straight, cruel lines.

"He was living on borrowed time," Vanderrenner remarked offhandedly.

"One of your crew?"

"He *was*."

Adan gulped the fiery rum to cover his confusion. No one had been disturbed by the sudden killing. No lawmen came charging in. Vanderrenner touched his lips delicately with a napkin and drank. This, Adan knew, was no ordinary ship's owner.

"I see shock in your eyes, my friend," Vanderrenner said with a smile that scarcely moved his lips.

"It's just that I wasn't expecting—"

"He questioned my orders. So I had him flogged. It is my opinion that he tripped over my foot deliberately, looking for an excuse to use his knife." He waved a hand as if to dismiss the dead man. "Now, will you have Fanny? Or shall we find another for you?"

"My friend, I have seen the Spanish disease and what it does to a man. I thank you for your offer, however."

"Just as well," Vanderrenner said, pouring more rum in their mugs.

Adan felt his head spinning, but he was, he had to admit, fascinated by this man who could commit murder without a blink of his eyes and continue his conversation as if nothing had happened. He found himself opening up to Vanderrenner. He held back certain incriminating facts, but he elaborated upon his earlier admission that he had to have some profitable work or lose his entire crew and ship.

Vanderrenner listened without emotion. His lean, steel-eyed face was expressionless. "Have you ever seen Cuba?" he asked when Adan had talked himself out.

"Only from the sea," Adan admitted.

"La Habana is a beautiful city. And the land is rich. In general I find that the Spanish take a more sensible view of life than do the British. I have a little place there, you know."

Adan didn't know, but he nodded. His senses were a bit muddled.

"Of course I have to lie to the Spanish governor regarding the profits of my various enterprises," the Dutchman continued. "He knows I am lying, but he realizes that he should not kill the goose, as the saying goes. So he is content with his *mordida*, with his share, for he does not have to split with the Crown what I pay him. In return I am content with my little holdings there. Soon, perhaps after only two more voyages, I will cast my anchor there permanently."

"What is this little holding?" Adan asked.

"Sugarcane. Not much, only a few thousand acres and, oh, a thousand slaves. That's all."

Adan tried to clear his head. He wasn't sure he was hearing properly.

"I am waiting for you to ask how I have obtained this little holding and how I have earned the money to own a thousand slaves," the Dutchman said.

"I do not wish to offend with curiosity."

"I noticed that you moved from your anchorage downwind from my ship."

"Ah," Adan said.

"You see what I endure to earn my ease?" The Dutchman raised his white eyebrows.

"Does it smell like that all the time?"

"Oh, no. It is much worse when we are loaded and the wind fails so that the stench hangs over the ship."

"*Gaa.*"

"Soon, however, you will come to say, 'Eh, what stink?' That is the smell of money."

"I?" Adan asked.

"You are obviously Spanish."

"Yes."

"Of good blood and, I think, perhaps some influence?"

"Good blood, no influence."

"Well, no matter," the Dutchman said. "You have a ship, and I have need for another ship. Mark my words, my young friend: there may be only a few more years of opportunity for a man such as you. And then? Who knows? One day soon the British will take it upon themselves to halt my profitable voyages to and from the Bight of Biafra. The rumbling of the do-gooders is already being heard beyond the British Isles. You see, the British, who believe that they are superior to all, are slowly coming to think that the black African is actually as human as the rest of us." He shrugged. "There are those who cry that I am inhuman because I fill a need—the need for labor in the fields of the New World. If I could show them all the causeways of human bones built in Africa by the Yorubans so that they may carry their living prisoners of war to be sold to the slave ships tied up at the river docks . . ."

Adan shuddered.

"We can fit out your ship nearby." The Dutchman moved quickly. "I have excellent carpenters. I will advance you the money you need. We will alter your ship's hold thusly." He dipped his finger into his rum and drew a rough outline of a ship's hull on the wooden table, filled in bulkheads, and drew in dozens of marks representing human bodies laid side by side in rows, in stacks, in tiers.

"You see," he said, "the secret is to maximize profit by

carrying a maximum number of blacks. This lowers the per-head transportation cost. I'd estimate that you can carry three hundred after proper belowdecks refitting."

"No," Adan said.

The Dutchman ignored him. "For an easy voyage to the African coast on the easterly trades you'll need liquor, fire-arms, cotton goods, and some trinkets for trading purposes. I will finance that. I will conduct the trading for you because I have the experience and the contacts with the Yorubans. In return I will take fifty percent of your profit when we deliver our two cargos to the slave markets in La Habana." He rubbed his chin. "I wish we could take them to Brazil, but the Portuguese are touchy about that, reserving that trade for their nationals."

"But I'm not going," Adan protested.

"Don't be hasty," the Dutchman advised. "You sail a stolen ship"—Adan felt a chill—"and you are wanted for murder *and* piracy. And you were fool enough to sail openly into this harbor."

"No one was killed when my crew took our ship," Adan said.

"An old man died on the island where you dumped the crew and passengers of the *Santa Beatriz*," the Dutchman contradicted. He shrugged again when Adan looked at him, aghast. "Perhaps he would have died anyway, but he died after you stole a ship, and thus you will be hanged for his murder." He raised a finger. "Unless, my friend, you very quickly go very far away and stay long enough for things to cool down. A voyage to the west coast of Africa would require just the right amount of time."

Adan sat speechless.

The Dutchman rose. "Now I think you should round up your crew and explain the necessity of taking your ship out of this harbor quickly. I will tell you where to go. I have a place on a small island where the work will be done."

Adan was dazed by the rum and the Dutchman. He couldn't seem to think straight. "This is a British island."

"And the *Santa Beatriz* is a Spanish ship, eh? But you don't understand. The British and the Spanish have their differences, but not in their mutual dislike of pirates. The British will hand you over, my friend. Never think for a moment that they won't."

Vanderrenner waved a hand. One of the most villainous-looking men Adan had ever seen came running, a black man bare to the waist, with a scarred face of dark stone. His hair was a bilious red, his eyes flicked like a scorpion on a hot rock, and his mouth was a big-lipped pink maw of threat. "This is Noir," the Dutchman said. "He will help you round up your men and show you my island. He speaks Spanish, a bit of English, and a half-dozen African tongues. Keep him away from women."

"But— But—" Adan said.

The Dutchman raised one eyebrow in annoyance. "Do you have a choice, boy?"

"Now listen, men," Adan said pleadingly, trying to be heard over loud protests. His crew, some of them showing how quickly a seaman can get drunk after a long time at sea, were gathered on the deck of the *Mano Negra*. "It's as simple as this: we have no choice. One voyage, maybe two, and we can all retire ashore in comfort. They say Cuba is a beautiful land."

"Cap'n," Williams said, "once you get the smell of a slaver into the planks of a ship, it never comes out, not in a hundred years."

It wasn't the ship that concerned Adan. He was wondering if he would ever get the stench of it out of his soul.

But he had no choice.

Chapter XIII

With only her eyes expressing protest Ah-wa-o brought El-i-chi's clothing to him. She had to help him get into his buckskin trousers, for it hurt when he bent at the waist. She also helped him pull the shirt over his head. He stood and slipped his feet into his moccasins, hefted his tomahawk, and narrowed his eyes. He took a few practice strokes. His chest pained him with the movement, but he was able to put force behind his blows.

"It is not my place to offer advice," Ah-wa-o said, "but I beg you not to leave your bed."

El-i-chi had been remembering Rusog's experience with white justice. Only Renno's action in producing the real murderer had saved Rusog from the rope. After his experience with the constable he had no further trust for the white man. And somewhere in Wilmington there were two men who could clear him of the unjust charges. This they would do, or die.

"Will you at least eat something before you go?" Ah-wa-o asked. "You've had almost nothing since you were injured."

It was early yet. There would still be people about on the streets, and El-i-chi's business required the privacy of darkness and solitude. He nodded. Ah-wa-o hurried to the kitchen.

The shadows were lengthening. Already the Jamaican sun was below the conical peak to the west. In the growing shadows below, Renno saw the giant Mingo single out an older man and talk earnestly to him. Then the two men separated, and one by one they sought out other men among the Maroons gathered in front of the entrance to the cavern. Those contacted by Mingo and the man Renno assumed to be his father did not congregate but stood apart in groups of twos and threes. Renno saw Mingo cast a quick glance upward in his direction. Although the drums were still beating evenly, the white Indian was restless. He didn't know exactly what was going on down in the cockpit's flat floor. He could only hope that the warriors singled out by Mingo and the other man were enemies of the voodoo master. Their numbers, however, were small; even if they did choose to fight, they would be outnumbered at least three to one.

But here on the ridge there were two. He could wait no longer. Nodding to Se-quo-i, Renno led the way down a steep track so little used that it was often clogged by the dense greenery. The drums were in his ears, firing his imagination about what might be happening to his wife and son inside the cave.

He reached the floor of the pit and crouched behind a curtain of ginger plants. If Mingo had seen them descending, the big warrior gave no hint of it. He stood with the older man, a grizzled warrior with impressive battle scars, his face toward the entrance to the cave.

"When I move," Renno told Se-quo-i, giving him the English longbow and all the arrows, thus lightening himself, "I will keep to the cover of the huts, there. When I break into the open, drop as many as you can to help clear my path. When I gain the entrance to the cave, climb back to the top

of the ridge and wait. Give me support when I come out with
Beth and Little Hawk."

Se-quo-i noted that there was no doubt in Renno's cool,
concise orders. It amazed him to think that this warrior did
not even consider failure. He felt a bit guilty, for he had been
planning an alternative strategy for the possibility that Renno
might die before reaching the cave—in which case he would
take a slightly different route to the entrance. He had no
intention of retreating.

Suddenly the drums doubled the tempo of their persistent
throbbings. Se-quo-i's stomach lurched. Renno tensed.

"So," Renno said, giving Se-quo-i an arm clasp. He came
to his feet slowly and, bending into the shadows, disappeared
for a moment from Se-quo-i's view behind a hut. Se-quo-i
noted with growing hope that Mingo and the men he had
talked with were drifting idly to take up scattered positions
behind the main group of Maroons and the entrance to the
cave.

Spade Hollinger lit a cigar and grunted with satisfaction.
The night's work was going well: the hold of his sloop was by
no means packed to capacity, but he had just about as many
able-bodied male slaves as he dared steal from Wilmington.
There was only the killing of the Indian to accomplish; then
he could slip away into the night and rendezvous with the last
of the longboats filled with slaves from the plantations across
the river. He had selected two good men for the job, each
just returning to the sloop with one sturdy freedman, the two
blacks still dazed and rubber-legged. Hollinger called his
thugs over, then led them down the gangplank and off the
ship. Abe Watts, his right arm getting stiffer as the night
went on—it hurt like hell to hold it in a natural position and
gave him the very devil if he tried to swing it as he walked—
met the three men in the shadows.

"Take these men to the doctor's house," Hollinger ordered. "Show them where the Indian is."

"Damn, Mr. Hollinger," Abe said, "is that a good idea?"

"It is *my* idea," Hollinger told him, an edge to his voice.
"You don't have to do anything. You've already shown that
you're no match for the Indian, even when he's half-dead.

You just show the boys where he is and stand back and watch professionals at work."

"What if the girl is with him?" Abe asked.

"Boys, if there's an Injun gal there, try not to break her up too much. If it's not too much trouble, bring her on back here in one piece. The Spaniards will pay high for a gal such as her."

Abe didn't like it at all. There were more than a dozen stolen slaves and kidnapped freedmen on that sloop, and if they were discovered, it would mean forfeiting his freedom. The law did not look kindly on slave stealers. He started to voice another protest, but Hollinger's face made him decide just to go on and get it over with. He led the two waterfront ruffians up the dock and into the streets. They walked beside him in grim silence.

There were lamps lit in two parts of the doctor's house, the room where Abe had almost lost an arm while trying to smother the Indian, and the kitchen. Abe pointed to the treatment room and whispered, "He'll be in there. You can get in through the French windows."

"Don't try to teach an old dog how to suck eggs," one of the ruffians snarled. The two disappeared through the shrubbery of the doctor's garden.

El-i-chi paced the room, getting accustomed to the feel of his legs under him again. Aside from severe soreness in his chest from the broken rib and a headache that seemed like the spirit of a wildcat trying to scratch its way out, he was ready. His moccasined feet made his steps silent. He paced from the lamplit room into the doctor's dining room and froze as he heard a twig snap outside the open French windows. He backed silently into the shadows along the wall and waited. He could hear Ah-wa-o doing things with dishes and pots and pans out in the kitchen.

A shadow separated itself swiftly and silently from the shrubbery outside the window. Behind it appeared another, and then two men were entering the room, one behind the other. El-i-chi caught the glint of steel knives. He told himself grimly that knives it would be, drew his, and waited. The first shadow drifted swiftly across the room toward the treatment-room door, caught the spill of lamplight, and gave

El-i-chi his target. He merely had to lean forward, make one quick stroke with all the power of shoulder and arm behind it, and a dying man clutched his throat in a vain effort to stop the gush of blood and to aid his laboring lungs in drawing air.

Even before the body began to slump to the floor, El-i-chi was in movement. The other intruder moved to meet him, and El-i-chi heard a muttered curse as he saw a knife arc downward. He bent low, grunting with pain, threw himself under the slashing stroke, and came up to sink his knife into the man's lower stomach, at the same time finding the wrist of the man's knife hand. For a moment there was strength in the man's arm, and they struggled in silence. El-i-chi twisted his blade, lunging to drive it deeper and upward. The strength suddenly left the arm he was grasping. He stepped back, and the body hit the floor with a dull thud.

Ah-wa-o was humming as she came out the swinging door to the kitchen. In the light that came from the room behind her, she saw El-i-chi, crouched and ready, then saw the two bodies on the floor. Because she was Seneca, she made no sound. She carefully set the tray containing the food she had prepared on the dining room table and moved back to stand in shadow, waiting for word from the man she had come to consider her own.

El-i-chi moved to her side. "Stay," he whispered, "until you hear my signal. When I hoot three times, leave through the back door and go straight to the Huntington house. Take Renna from her bed and awaken the servants and Cedric. Send one man to Nathan Ridley's. Tell him that unless I am back by tomorrow, you and Renna are to be protected at all costs and sent west toward our home with armed men as escort. Tell him that it is I, El-i-chi, who says this, and that my brother will make good any money spent in doing as I order."

Ah-wa-o did not question. She watched him slip out the window on the side of the dining room away from the entry point of the intruders. The entire affair had lasted less than a minute.

El-i-chi was in his element. It didn't matter that he was in the midst of a town. There were shadows. There was cover. He utilized them as only a Seneca warrior could, circling the house to the rear, moving quickly but silently. He did not hear or see anything until he was once again at the front of the house, crouched behind a shrub. The tiny scrape of leather on a pebble as a man shifted his feet reached his trained hunter's ears. El-i-chi moved toward the sound, flitting from shadow to shadow.

In the dwelling next door to the doctor's house a woman was playing the clavichord and singing, her voice sweet and soft.

Abe Watts had no warning. One second he was standing safely in the shadow of a bush, wondering why it was taking Hollinger's men so long, and the next he felt pressure on his throat and could not cry out because the hand at his throat was cutting off his air.

"Feel the point of my knife," El-i-chi whispered in Watts's ear, thrusting the knife hard enough to be felt through jacket and shirt. "One sound, and it will be driven home." He jabbed to make sure the man knew where it rested, at a vulnerable spot, over the kidney. "I will ask you a question."

Abe, blood pounding, scarcely able to breathe, nodded vigorously. To free his windpipe, to be able to take a free breath, he'd be willing to answer any number of difficult questions.

"Did the man Hollinger send you?"

Abe nodded. The hand loosed its hold on his throat. "Yes," he croaked. Now that he could breathe he felt better. He had had his fist closed over his pistol. If he could turn its muzzle backward under his right arm, he could blast this devil off his back and that knife over his kidney with him.

"Why?" El-i-chi demanded.

"To kill you." Abe was thinking furiously as he eased his left hand around in front of his belly and poked the muzzle of his pistol backward. He needed a little more time. He told himself to be easy, easy, not to move too fast lest that knife penetrate his clothing and then his flesh. "And he wanted the girl. He was going to take her down to Florida and sell her to the Spaniards."

If Abe could have felt the wave of anger that ran through El-i-chi, he would have known that he did not have long to live.

"And you're working with him?"

"Yes," Abe confessed. The pistol was almost in position. All he had to do was move it an inch farther and squeeze the trigger. "You're hurting my arm."

"Where is Hollinger?"

"On his boat." Suddenly Abe wasn't so sure he could carry it off. What if the ball didn't hit the Indian solidly? "Look, I know you were attacked there on the docks. Take me to the police station, and I'll tell them that. I'll tell them Hollinger wanted you dead because you found out he cheated at dice."

El-i-chi forced himself to relax. It made sense, Abe's suggestion. He wasn't sure that the man would keep his word, but he was sure that the two dead men in the doctor's dining room, obviously intruders, could be traced to Hollinger.

Abe felt the knife's pressure ease. That was the moment he had been waiting for. But he moved as he turned the pistol that last half-inch before firing.

El-i-chi, alerted by the movement, had been in the act of pulling his knife away from Watts's back. He saw the solidity in the hand and grabbed for it, twisting the muzzle of the pistol aside just as Abe pulled the trigger. Abe screamed. The ball entered his right side and tore through a kidney and then smashed into his spine.

El-i-chi saw that Abe's clothing was smoldering around a ragged, burned hole. He didn't bother to check the fallen man's condition. He hooted three times like an owl and moved to see Ah-wa-o slip out the back door and disappear swiftly into the darkness in the direction of the Huntington house. Then he himself was moving swiftly but awkwardly as he favored his broken rib.

From the deck of his sloop Hollinger heard the shot. He cursed. The fools had been discovered. He gave orders in a hoarse whisper, and men scampered about to loose lines and push the sloop off from the wharf. The current began to swing the bow out into the river. He felt no compunction about abandoning Abe Watts. Abe's usefulness was ended. Even if he exposed Hollinger's plans, the sloop would have picked up its remaining cargo and would be well out to sea before a pursuit could be organized. With the gold he'd get from the Spaniards for this load, he could find a lot of places to lie low. If a man had gold he could live well on one of several Caribbean islands.

As the sloop drifted on the current, her stern being held off by a man with a long gaff hook, Hollinger watched the street entrance to the wharf area. He didn't notice a shadow detaching itself and slipping from piling to piling, timing its movement so that it came over the sloop's stern while the man with the gaff hook was otherwise occupied. By then the current had the sloop. Men used sculls to guide her past the bluffs, where lamplight glowed in a few of the windows of a house perched up there—the Huntington residence.

El-i-chi crouched behind a barrel on the stern. The man who had been keeping the sloop away from the docks made clattering noises as he stowed the gaff hook under the low rail. Then he moved idly toward El-i-chi. It became clear that his intentions were to sit on the very barrel that hid the Seneca. El-i-chi slipped away to lie in the shadow of the rail and watched the man take his seat and bring out a pipe. The lights of Wilmington were being left behind as Hollinger gave orders in a normal voice. A sail went up, and the sloop picked up some steerage and made for the far bank.

Knowing that he had to find a better place of concealment, El-i-chi considered moving forward, but he would have to crawl right under the nose of the man sitting on the barrel. There was only one course of action—the man would have to die. Something out of a nightmare, something from the evil night sent terror into the man's heart as El-i-chi's hand closed over his mouth to prevent him from crying out. His pipe fell from his hand as the warrior's razor-sharp knife made a grating cut.

"What was that?" a man standing next to Hollinger asked when the body slipped from El-i-chi's hands and splashed into the water of the river.

"Fish jumping," Hollinger replied. "Don't be so damned nervous."

A small cabin rose from the sloop's middeck. Hollinger was at the wheel, forward of the house; the others were on the foredeck working sails. The western bank of the Cape Fear was a darker blot in the darkness. Hollinger whistled once, twice, and a faint answering whistle came from the shore.

El-i-chi pulled himself to the top of the cabin and flattened out. He watched a boat detach itself from the shoreline

shadows. Hollinger's sloop drifted as the boat came alongside
and a dozen dazed, moaning black men were forced aboard
and down into the holds.

El-i-chi, his side aching painfully, was not on board to
change the world situation. He wanted only to kill Spade
Hollinger, the man who had paid to have him killed, the man
who threatened Ah-wa-o with slavery. It was, he decided,
going to be a chancy thing, for Hollinger was surrounded by a
half-dozen seamen, and now three more had come aboard
from the boat. Killing Hollinger was not worth dying for.
El-i-chi wanted to stay alive for a little rose who looked at
him in a way that made him feel ten feet tall.

The sloop was again under way, heading downriver on the
falling tide, helped by a night breeze that flapped the one sail
that had been hoisted. A half hour later El-i-chi, after con-
cluding from the conversation on the deck below that Hollinger
would never again show his face in Wilmington, decided to
slip quietly overboard and swim to shore. But the sloop
moved close to the western bank just then, and another boat
came out loaded with three white men and ten black slaves.
The process of bringing the slaves aboard would provide an
excellent distraction, during which El-i-chi could slip into the
water. He prepared himself.

The first black man had to be helped aboard. He could not
put his weight on one leg. He was moaning in pain, and his
eyes were rolling whitely in the moonlight.

"This'un fell and broke a leg," a thug reported.

"Why did you bring him?" Hollinger demanded. "He's of
no use to us." He stepped forward and slit the slave's throat.
The slave's eyes went wide and white, and he made wet
gasping sounds as Hollinger shoved him over the rail.

Something snapped inside El-i-chi. There was no longer
any possibility that he would leave quietly. He took advantage of the loading of the slaves to slip down onto the deck
beside the house. A long arm extended outward, closed on
the throat of the lounging seaman, and jerked. This time the
body's splash was covered by the bumping of the boat against
the hull of the sloop. Once more death moved in silence. He
was cutting the odds, but slowly, dangerously, for the confident Hollinger was using a lantern now, so the forward deck
was lit.

When all the slaves from the boat were grouped on deck, ready to be shoved below, El-i-chi overstepped even his abilities. True, a man died, his throat slit quickly so that he made only gurgling sounds, but a shout went up as El-i-chi was seen. He drew his tomahawk.

Lantern light flickered. The deck was a mosaic of light and shadow. The man who had seen El-i-chi died swiftly as he dashed to meet the tomahawk face-on. A seaman with a cutlass closed from El-i-chi's left, while others were moving toward him with knives and belaying pins. He knew that the cutlass was the most immediate threat and sent his knife winging to bite deeply into the cutlass-wielder's neck.

The Seneca warrior then stood to challenge the rush of at least eight men, Spade Hollinger among them. The action was violent and deadly. These men had never faced a tomahawk in the hands of an expert, and the blade slashed and smashed three to the deck within seconds.

In a moment of respite El-i-chi felt a burst of sadness—he would not see Ah-wa-o again. But then the sadness was gone, replaced by the cool deadliness of a senior warrior. If he was to go down before a swarm of sheer numbers, he would be covered with blood other than his own before he shed the first drop. But now they were all around him, so that he had to whirl and feint and slash when he had the chance. He was the stag at bay, surrounded by a pack of snarling wolves, and Spade Hollinger had pulled back from the conflict, a little smile on his face, to watch the fun.

A belaying pin caught El-i-chi's shoulder a glancing blow. He left the man who had struck the blow almost armless with a parrying slash of his tomahawk, but he knew that it would soon be over, for he could not guard all sides at once. And then he heard a wild, guttural cry unlike any he had ever heard and saw the unarmed slaves throw themselves into the fray, bearing men down with their weight, fighting against clubs and knives with their nails, teeth, and fists.

Other slaves struggled up from below. The confusion gave El-i-chi freedom to flit and strike, and his strikes were deadly.

Then it was over. El-i-chi had had his anger cooled by blood. He stuck his tomahawk into his belt and watched— and he did not try to stop them—as the slaves finished off the crew of the sloop with the thugs' own knives and clubs. He stood panting, his side a sheet of fire, his bloody tomahawk hanging from his hand. A cry from forward sent him running. A slave stood there pointing at the water. There were sounds of a man swimming, and he could see a dark head moving toward shore.

"Hollinger," the slave told El-i-chi. "I know that one."

He was over the rail before he remembered his broken rib, diving cleanly into the water. The impact drove the breath from his lungs, and he had to fight to retain consciousness against the wave of pain. He looked back at the sloop when he surfaced. He could make it back and let the slaves help him aboard. Moving his left arm was so painful to his rib that he could swim only with his right. But Hollinger was there, nearing shore. El-i-chi clenched his teeth against the pain and swam.

It seemed to be an eternity before he felt the sharp impact of his knee on a broken shell and lowered his feet to find the muddy bottom. There was a glow of light from the east. He walked out of the water onto an exposed tidal flat, where deep mud sucked at him and tore the moccasins off his feet. He struggled on. There was movement ahead. The flat was a wide one, and beyond it was a high bank and the tall pine woods. Ahead of him Hollinger was struggling through the mud that was sometimes ankle deep, sometimes to the knees. Try as he might, El-i-chi could not close the distance.

He didn't notice the coming of dawn. Suddenly, it seemed, he could see things more clearly. Hollinger had fallen and was struggling to his feet. El-i-chi pressed on. Hollinger reached an area of more solid footing and turned, his chest heaving. Seeing only El-i-chi, he pulled a long knife and waited.

"So, you will stand and fight after all," El-i-chi said, feeling the solidity of a shell bed under his bare feet.

"You're going to pay for what you've cost me this night," Hollinger threatened, rushing forward.

El-i-chi reached for his tomahawk. His knife was still in a man's throat back on the sloop. His hands closed on emptiness. Somehow, in the water or in the mud, he'd lost his tomahawk.

Hollinger, crouching, came at him. The slaver's blade was held underhand, probing and feinting as if it were not merely a knife but a rapier. When he made a lunge, El-i-chi slipped aside, felt broken shells cut his bare feet, and almost fell. He scrambled with his hand on the ground to escape another charge, and his hand contacted a waterlogged limb, long in the water, encrusted with small oyster shells and barnacles. He jerked the limb from the mud, found handholds, and crouched to face the knife.

Seeing his opponent armed gave Hollinger pause. Then with a snarl he came forward to end it. A sodden tree limb was no match for a knife in the hands of an expert. The limb came whistling toward his middle, and he leapt back, to come back in before—he thought—El-i-chi could recover.

The backward stroke of the barnacle-covered club caught him in the face. A razor-sharp edge of a broken shell sliced into his eye, and the force of the blow jerked the eyeball from its socket. He screamed as his hand flew to his face to feel his eyeball lying on his cheek. He screamed again, only once, before the limb crushed his skull.

El-i-chi picked his way carefully to solid ground. His feet were bleeding from numerous cuts made by broken shells. His side was on fire. He sat on the black dirt of the bank and looked out onto a dawn scene of fire and smoke. The sloop was blazing. Slaves were coming to shore in the boats. Others swam. Some of them paused to look and spit on Hollinger's body before coming to stand a few feet away from El-i-chi to stare at him with wide, white-rimmed eyes.

"No more slave he be in dat boat," a man said, showing large, white teeth in a grin.

"No," El-i-chi agreed.

"You save us from sugarcane," another slave observed. "Man, he las' 'bout two year in the Spanish cane."

El-i-chi said nothing. Soon almost forty slaves were standing just below him on the edge of the mud flat.

"You Indian," a man remarked.

"Yes."

"I hear Indian take in black man, let him live free. You take us to your place?"

"I can't do that. It is far away, with many white men between."

"Sir," a lanky man said, "I am a freedman from Wilmington. I think you should let me see to your wounds."

"I'm all right." El-i-chi stood and regarded them. "You fought well. Why, when you had a ship under you, did you not take your freedom by way of the sea?"

"Where we go?" a man asked. "Down there, the cotton field of Georgia and South Carolina. Down there, the Spanish sugarcane. Out there in the island, slave markets send us back to someplace maybe worse than this."

"I think you should all go home," the freedman remarked.

They began to drift away. Those who stayed were from Wilmington. "Your feet will be mighty sore," the freedman told El-i-chi. "Nothing gets any sorer than an oyster-shell cut. You aren't going to walk back to Wilmington that way."

"Are you thinking to carry me?" El-i-chi asked with a grin.

"Not me, sir. Maybe two of these young men," the lanky man suggested.

"We'll need to stop at one or more of the plantations," El-i-chi said. "I'll need statements from the slaves who were stolen."

He walked. The pain in his feet was not as severe as the pain in his side. They had gone only a mile when they were met by two white men in a buggy. The word had spread: slaves had been missing at work time. But then they came straggling back, some of them wet, all of them with a wild story about kidnappers and an Indian who fought with the strength of a god.

El-i-chi did not have to walk back to Wilmington. Wearing improvised bandages around his feet, he rode in a buggy. Behind him came a wagon carrying Hollinger's body. He had signed and witnessed depositions from slaves—taken down by the freedman, who could read and write—and from their owners.

The doctor applied something that stung like fire to the cuts on his feet. Ah-wa-o forced food and drink on him until he had to beg for mercy. Nathan Ridley summoned the magistrate and the chief constable, who listened in awe and quickly agreed that nothing more would be heard of any murder charges. The newspaper printed a story that had the town buzzing. The freedman who had been rescued by El-i-chi magnified the fight on board the sloop with each retelling.

"Suddenly," Ah-wa-o said, "we are very popular. We have ten invitations to call, seven more for dinner."

El-i-chi grunted.

"He's not going anywhere," the doctor said. "He almost drove that broken rib into his lung. He's going to be right there in that bed for about two weeks."

Next day, while Ah-wa-o was downstairs seeing to the preparation of El-i-chi's breakfast, Renna came into El-i-chi's room. She looked at his face; his bruises were spectacularly purple and black.

"Like flower," she said, pointing.

"You look very pretty," El-i-chi said. His niece was in a frilly little dress of yellow.

"Flowers down there," Renna told him, pointing toward the back garden.

"Let's go see," El-i-chi said.

A frantic Ah-wa-o, having almost spilled the breakfast tray when she found El-i-chi's bed empty, ran into the back garden to find him sitting in a lawn swing while Renna picked flowers and leaves and delivered them to him.

"You're not supposed to walk," Ah-wa-o said worriedly.

"Renna carried me," El-i-chi said. "Didn't you, Renna?"

"I did," Renna said, smiling at El-i-chi.

"Well, carry him back upstairs," Ah-wa-o said.

Renna, stricken, looked toward El-i-chi for assistance.

"Where, woman, is my breakfast?" El-i-chi asked gruffly.

They sat in the back garden for most of the morning. Renna went into the house with a servant for her lunch. Ah-wa-o, pleased to see El-i-chi so at ease, could not take her eyes off his face.

"What are you thinking, little rose?" he asked her after a long silence.

"Of home. How the women are gathering the new corn, and how it tastes. How the mountains look like low, dark clouds far away, and how clear the skies are."

"We'll be going there soon," El-i-chi assured her.

"It's been so long."

"Yes." He was picturing the sea, with all of its uncertainties. He could not even imagine the faraway islands where things such as coffee beans grew. "One day soon we'll see a ship coming up the river. You and Renna can watch for it.

Bells will ring when it is sighted, and we'll go down to greet Renno and Se-quo-i."

"And Beth," she said.

In Government House in Spanish Town others were thinking of the American Indians and the flame-haired English lady. The governor had a red-coated colonel standing tall in front of his desk.

"All these weeks and you, sir, can tell me only that their trail leads into the Cockpit Country?" the governor demanded.

"It was not an easy trail to follow, sir," the colonel said. "Some of our tame rustics, probably escaped slaves themselves, followed it until, they said, it entered the land of Me No Sen You No Come."

"Blast those Maroons!" The governor seethed. He was thinking of the woman and what a waste of flesh it was to have her taken by wild Negroes. She'd been such a delicious-looking morsel.

"I considered, sir, that you would not want to inflame old fights by sending soldiers into the Maroon strongholds."

"Yes, yes," the governor said. "But damme, sir, that woman was an Englishwoman."

"Living in America, sir. Actually I think her citizenship would be somewhat in doubt. She was married to that odd white Indian, you know."

The governor was silent. It was, he concluded, one terrible mess.

"Of course, sir, if you give the order, we'll send men into the pits and clean up those black fellows once and for all."

"The devil, you say," the governor spat. "You haven't got enough men to cover two hundred square miles of impenetrable wilderness, where every tree is an ambush waiting to happen. If you had fought in America, you'd know."

"Sir," the colonel said, "I did. I was with General Gates in South Carolina. I know a bit about fighting shadows in woodlands and swamps. We know the approximate locations of the principal Maroon settlements. The worst we can do is make it hard for them by destroying their homes and scattering them. That would at least stop their interminable raids into settled areas to steal animals and kidnap decent, God-fearing people."

"I beg your pardon, Colonel," the governor said sincerely.

"I was unaware of your war record. I don't think that now is the time, however, to mount a campaign against the Maroons."

"The captain of the Englishwoman's ship is making a nuisance of himself. He's demanding that we do something. He has his cargo loaded, and aside from his concern for his employer and her, uh, friends, he's screaming that his cargo will rot if he has to stay here much longer."

"*Hmm,*" the governor mused. "Well, I suppose you'll just have to break it to him. Tell the gentleman that the chances of his ever seeing his friends again are very small and that he might as well take his ship to sea before he loses several tons of prime Blue Mountain coffee beans."

"Yes, sir." The colonel saluted smartly.

Alone, the governor rested his chin in one hand and frowned. Damned nuisance, all of it, and the worst of it was that the woman's trade venture just might have opened up some good possibilities if she hadn't gone and gotten herself snatched up by blacks hungry for a smooth white female body. He'd had plans. He had already sent messages to people on the islands and in England who had the vision to look at the overall good rather than merely at the profit and loss statements of the trading companies back in England. Too bad. Open trade with the United States would have benefited the country he governed and, not incidentally, himself, for he, too, had some trading interests.

But, he supposed, if there wasn't too much of a diplomatic flap when the ship's captain went home and reported the death of his employer and those with her, there'd be another chance. Maybe not in the guise of a delectable red-haired lady, but another chance.

Chapter XIV

The sound of the drums was muffled as it came from deep within the master's cave. Renno could feel his body preparing itself for combat, his heart pumping only a bit slower than the accelerated throbbing of the drums. He felt light on his feet. He covered ground smoothly, quickly, using the huts as cover until he was only a short dash from the mouth of the cave. He looked back toward Se-quo-i's place of concealment and made one quick motion with his hand.

Se-quo-i, he could see, had an arrow ready. The Cherokee drew the bow, straining a bit.

Renno flashed into motion. He had taken a dozen running steps and was well on the way toward the cave when he heard the first reaction, a wild shout of alarm. Three Maroons moved more swiftly than the others and rushed to cut him off. He saw one man lurch while in full stride as an arrow

buried itself in his side just above the hip. The man was
tumbling even as another arrow made the sound of an angry
bee and took a second man full in the back. The third man,
young, strong, proud of his running speed, was too swift for
his own good, for he went down from a smashing blow of
Renno's tomahawk. Renno delivered the blow without breaking stride.

He heard shouts behind him and thought he recognized
the strong, bull-like voice of the giant Mingo, but he didn't
look back. The cave's opening was just ahead. The ground
rose slightly and then sloped down into the dark maw of the
cave. He plunged downward and burst into the entrance. He
slowed only when darkness closed around him. His foot slipped.
He halted, the sound of the drums louder. Behind him there
was a glow of light from the entrance; ahead was only blackness. The air inside the cave was cooler. Underfoot was a
slippery accumulation of guano, the droppings of untold generations of bats.

Renno had never been in such a cave. He groped his way
forward by putting one foot in front of the other warily. Soon
he did not even have the dim light of the entrance as a
checkpoint, for he had found a wall and was following it, so
the entrance was hidden from his view as the wall curved. He
was in the most complete blackness of his experience. His
usually superb sense of direction was confused. He had only
the sound of the drums to guide him, but their booming,
throbbing cadences seemed to come at him from all directions.

Outside, the Maroons, their senses confused by the nar-
cotic effects of the ganja, were shouting and making abortive
charges in first one direction, then the other. Among them
men were dying as a hidden archer rained arrow after arrow
into their ranks. To add to their confusion, Mingo, the most
powerful warrior, was standing between them and the cave,
his spear at the ready, yelling incomprehensible things about
overthrowing the master. Maroon had not yet fought Maroon.

Se-quo-i, drawing and firing as quickly as he could, was
running out of arrows. He saw a group of ten Maroons
shouting and pointing in his direction. The light was failing.
The sun was gone, and the night shadows were coming
quickly. Se-quo-i slowed his firing, making the last three
arrows count. The group of Maroons, depleted by three,

were climbing toward him with wild cries. He secreted the bow in dense brush and slipped away from his position, circling to the left, running in the shadows, making his way toward the cave.

"Now we will have to fight," Mingo said to his father, who stood at his side. He lifted his head and bellowed, "All who stand for freedom, to me!" The scattered groups of his supporters began to move in his direction to form a defensive line, spears outthrust.

Libertador, the master's chief war leader, was not among the Maroons who had been left outside to guard the entrance. He was a privileged man. He was—and for this Mingo was thankful—inside the cave to participate in the master's dark rites. There was no one to take the place of a leader like Libertador, so a considerable length of time would pass while the befuddled Maroons organized and shouted themselves into a frenzy of ganja-induced courage. It took courage, even with superior numbers, to advance on a man of Mingo's size.

Se-quo-i slipped unnoticed into the cave. All eyes were on Mingo and his followers, who stood straight and still, a threatening line of death. Se-quo-i experienced the same disorientation as Renno. Soon he was in total blackness with only the echoing of the drums in his ears.

Renno stumbled over a stalagmite and almost fell as his feet slipped. The drums increased their tempo yet again. He had a feeling that time was running out while he was lost in a darkness as black as evil. The floor of the cave was filled with the stalagmite buildup of centuries.

"Spirits of my fathers," he whispered, "guide me."

He felt a breath of air at his face. From far away, the sound seeming to come from the bottom of a huge barrel, he heard Little Hawk yell, "You leave her alone!"

Again he felt the stir of air. He brushed his hand in front of his face. His imagination peopled the darkness with evil spirits. Something brushed his cheek, and he heard a high-pitched squeak. He moved toward the sound. There was a flutter of leathery wings against his face and another squeak.

He knew new hope. Ah-wen-ga had said, "The mouse that flies will guide you." He moved toward a short, high-pitched squeak and did not encounter any obstacle. The bat was leading him through the maze of stalagmites.

He heard a scream and was sure it was from Beth. He broke into a run, heedless of obstacles, and ran into a huge, rough mass of accreted stone. He moved aside, and suddenly wings were beating at his face and the squeaks were frantic. He halted in his tracks, a sense of danger causing a burst of adrenaline. He felt forward with his foot but encountered empty air. A rock displaced by his foot bounced down and down and after a long fall splashed into water.

"I will follow," he whispered. The brushing wings and the squeaks led him around the pit, and then he felt rock under his feet. He was on a cleared pathway through the century-deep accumulation of guano. The feel of bare rock and the squeaks of the bat allowed him to move more swiftly now.

Se-quo-i had no guide. He was far behind, feeling his way deeper into the cave.

At last the shouts and war cries and the fear of what the master would do sent the Maroons forward toward the defensive line anchored by Mingo. Panicked, a few threw their spears, but the defenders dodged them. Only one man was struck. He took a spear point in the thigh and went down.

Mingo lunged to meet a bold one and buried his spear point in the warrior's stomach. He jerked the spear out, and then the Maroons loyal to the master were so near that he was forced to use his thick shaft as a club. Beside him his father was using skills that had made him one of the most feared men among the Maroons. Mingo did not have time to regret that he was spilling the blood of his brothers. For years he had chafed under the evil rule of the master, while his once-proud people were reduced to the level of slaves, doing that evil man's bidding at the risk of their souls.

The spirit aura of the white man from far away was good in Mingo's eyes. He had determined, even before the Maroons began to move toward him, to stand or die in his efforts to end the evil power of the master. Now he thought only of killing and surviving.

The open fires gave a red glow to the narrowing passageway as Renno rounded a bend in the chamber of the cave. He almost cried out as he heard Beth scream in agony. He ran, heedless of any danger. The floor of the cave sloped down, and the shaft narrowed. He burst through and had to stop quickly to keep from plunging off a narrow ledge into the huge chamber below. Fires lit the large area. Around the fires black men and women danced and writhed in passion.

Beth was tied to a wooden stake in front of a voodoo altar. The skulls of former victims gleamed whitely in the flickering firelight. Little Hawk strained at his bonds at a stake a few feet from Beth. A chill ran through Renno's blood as he recognized the man who stood in front of Beth. Hodano!

Beth was dressed in a loose, white garment. With her arms tied behind her, her breasts strained at the thin material. Hodano held a crude doll, also dressed in white, with a bush of red hair on its head. Hodano had decided to begin his enjoyment with a small experiment in one of the basic techniques of voodoo. He had directed a voodoo priestess to prepare a *gris-gris* doll in the image of the flame-haired woman. He laughed with delight when he discovered that it worked. He jabbed a sharp spike into the doll, and the woman at the stake flinched and screamed in real pain.

Hodano did not laugh often. The sound came to Renno, and it was as if jagged, dried bone had grated against rock. Beth's scream tore at him. He leapt down a drop of some ten feet, landed lightly, and positioned his weapons—tomahawk in his right hand, the familiar Spanish stiletto in his left. He had already planned his route to the altar. He did not draw attention to his presence but ran silently, sometimes stepping on the backs of the celebrants, leaving consternation and confusion in his wake as he dashed toward the altar where his wife was tied. A reeling, drunken Maroon tried to block his way, and a simple swipe of the tomahawk sent the man to whatever hereafter had been promised him by his evil gods.

Libertador, the warrior who had captured Beth and Little Hawk, had been given a place of honor near the fire where the master would gain power from the white boy. The muscular, handsome Libertador had always had his choice of the voodoo priestesses, and this time he had selected two to ease

his hungers and to help him add his fires of passion to the
aura of the rites.

The master had not yet begun his ceremony with the
small white boy. He was intent on watching Hodano, and
Libertador was astute enough to recognize a glint of jealousy
in the master's beady eyes. He wondered why he was not
allowed to end the interference of the odd, ugly shaman from
the distances across the waters, but, he allowed, the master
knew what he was doing.

Libertador did not see the initial rush of the stranger
dressed in nothing more than a loincloth and apron. He
heard the growing sound of surprise from the dazed men and
women as Renno ran and leapt toward the enemy he had
thought to be far away and toward the stake where Beth was
tied, her face pale and beaded with the perspiration of pain.
Libertador bellowed something that was a mixture of surprise
and warning as he reached for his machete. Four of his
followers heard his shout and began to rise, slowed in various
degrees by their indulgence in the ceremonial drinking.

Quicker to react were two white-clad voodoo priestesses
attending the master. They had remained sober. They were
of a height, slender, and well formed, their feminine curves
evident through the gauzelike, clinging gowns.

The master, too, was surprised. He hissed an order, and
each of the two priestesses leapt toward the racing attacker,
keen-bladed knives appearing in their slender hands from
among the folds of their garments.

Now the cave reverberated with the harsh attack call of a
hawk. The cry was repeated, with less volume, by a small boy
lashed to a stake.

Renno had never faced women in battle and had never
killed a female. Yet his pace did not slow. He swerved in an
effort to avoid the two white-clad priestesses who blocked his
path to Beth and Little Hawk, but when they darted into his
way and stood, teeth bared, daggers at the ready, he roared
the challenge of the principal totem of his clan. The sound
was so fearsome that some of the women screamed in terror,
but the two priestesses blocking his way were unmoved.

Renno knew that swiftness of action was his only chance.
He had to secure the safety of his wife and son before anyone

could react and in pure malice kill either Beth, Little Hawk, or both before he could reach them. With a muttered prayer for understanding by his manitous, he feinted to one side, saw the dagger arms of the two priestesses move as one, and then he swung with his tomahawk and lunged with the stiletto, so the two were falling even as he rushed past, blood staining the white garments.

He reached Little Hawk's stake first, loosed the boy with one quick slash of the stiletto. "Behind me," he said. Then he was moving toward Beth, only to see a strong black warrior moving toward him, backed by three others, all armed with machetes.

Hodano had turned toward the chamber entrance at the first mutter of voices, to see his old enemy charging into sure death. Half his mouth twisted into a smile, and his snake's tongue flicked out. The spirits were, he felt, on his side. He could not have asked for more—now he had the great Renno *and* Renno's woman and son. This would be a day to be remembered, the day of his ascent to greatness. His only concern was that Renno would be killed outright by the Maroons.

He watched the master glide away into darkness as Renno dashed toward Little Hawk, and then he himself moved back, more than willing to be amused by Renno's futile struggles. It would be entertaining to have Renno display his great power by killing a few of the Maroons. A victor is made greater by his vanquished enemy's might, so that when Hodano stepped in to kill Renno and transform him into a zombie, his simple domination over a man who had killed many would add to his stature in the eyes of the Maroons.

Libertador had not become the second-most-feared warrior in the land of the Maroons through rashness. He lagged behind just enough to allow one of his adherents to be the first to face Renno. The Maroon screamed intimidatingly and swung his machete. Libertador noted Renno's reaction, his deflection of the machete with his tomahawk, and the swift, deadly thrust with his left hand, which sent steel into a man's heart, then the instant recovery. There were at least forty Maroon warriors in the chamber, and, Libertador felt, even if they were all drunk, their sheer numbers would handle one man. He could wait.

A Maroon charged Renno, his spear held at waist level. Renno danced aside, let the shaft of the spear slide along his side, then ripped out the throat of the attacker with his tomahawk. The spear clattered to the stone floor as men began gathering behind Libertador. The odds were great, and Renno roared something that was half-prayer, half-battle-anger. He heard an answering war cry and, as he parried a powerful stroke of a machete, caught a glimpse of Se-quo-i charging toward him through the milling, muttering women. Within seconds he heard a man utter his last as Se-quo-i attacked from the rear of the warriors surrounding Renno. So now it was two against many.

Actually, for a few brief seconds, it was three against many. Little Hawk, jumping around at the combatants' knee level and yelling encouragement to his father, bent to seize a fallen spear. At that moment a large, sheeny-skinned black warrior charged, his machete at the ready, intent on taking Renno from the rear. Little Hawk tried to raise the heavy spear, but the butt of it was lodged in a crack in the stone of the cavern's floor. Little Hawk angled the spear and found purchase, while the Maroon, his eyes on Renno, ran into the spear, driving it deep into his chest with his momentum. The shaft snapped, and the dying man continued to fall forward, landing atop Little Hawk and bearing him to the floor. The weight drove the cry of triumph out of the boy's throat in a gasp. He couldn't move. He struggled, but he did not cry out.

Se-quo-i fought his way to Renno's side. Renno turned to put them back to back. "I told you to go."

"You were not too specific about direction," Se-quo-i said mendaciously just before his tomahawk sliced deeply into black flesh.

"The boy," Renno gasped as he delivered a deadly blow and parried another. "Take the boy, and I will help you reach the entrance."

He was not accepting defeat with that thought. It was purely pragmatic, practical. Once he had been told that his son would be a great chief. Therefore Little Hawk would not die. From past experience, however, Renno knew that often the manitous needed the help of mere man to further their designs. He was not thinking of abandoning Beth. No. He would fight to free Se-quo-i and Little Hawk of the press of warriors around them, and then he would return for Beth. His thinking process took much less time than the telling. It was on a subconscious level, for his every reflex, his every sense was involved in staying alive and in killing the enemy. The manitous had once told him that the flame-haired one was his future, but they had not specified the length of that future. If he was destined to go down under the sheer weight of numbers here in this dimly lit cavern so far from his home, then so be it, for that was the will of the manitous. But as long as he was alive, he would be with Beth.

"What do I do with these while I get the boy?" Se-quo-i gasped as he struggled to fend off the rush of three Maroons.

"Thus and thus," Renno replied with a forehand and backhand slash of his tomahawk, leaving Se-quo-i with only one man to confront.

The floor of the cave was littered with dead, yet still they came. Renno stumbled over a body and had to react swiftly to avoid a downward slash of a machete. A spear whistled past him and aided him in his work by impaling an attacker on the other side of the struggle.

Se-quo-i could not see Little Hawk, and for good reason. The boy was still trying to squirm his way out from under the first man he had ever killed.

A shout went up from the rear of the chamber. Se-quo-i loosed a war whoop. Renno glanced toward the shouting and saw a bloodied, black giant pushing aside weeping and wailing women.

"Fight on, little friends!" Mingo yelled, wading into the rear of the Maroons surrounding Renno and Se-quo-i.

Se-quo-i almost died when a priestess leapt onto his back. Her first dagger slash brought a line of blood across the front of his shoulder. He threw the woman off, and she lunged for him again. Se-quo-i, never having killed a woman, hesitated long enough to allow the priestess to direct a fatal blow toward his throat. Her arm was smashed by Renno's tomahawk, and a follow-up blow finished her off.

Caught between two men who fought like demons and the

giant Mingo, the Maroons began to pull back, some of them plunging headlong into the darkness of the entrance cave.

Renno faced Libertador. The war leader had been acting as motivator, yelling his men into battle, and now he was angry, having lost at least a dozen of his finest warriors to the power of one man. He held his machete in two hamlike fists and crouched, his attentions focused on the one who had done the most damage.

"Hold, little friend," Mingo bellowed. "This one is mine."

But Libertador, his reason gone, was beyond hearing. His only desire was to feel his blade sink into the flesh of the one who faced him with his tomahawk, circling, feinting. With a great cry Libertador charged.

A man should never fight from sheer rage. Renno knew this, and he recognized the lack of reason, the loss of control, in this large warrior who faced him. He took the charge head-on, then slipped aside at the last moment, ducking under a powerful downward chop of the machete. He killed Libertador with one swift blow to the back of the neck as the man's momentum carried him past. The blow severed the spinal cord. Renno whirled. There was an eerie silence. Even the women who had been weeping and wailing were quiet.

Se-quo-i stood, panting, bloodied, at his side. Mingo was a few steps away. Hodano stood beside the stake where Beth was still tied. She had watched the battle with a combination of terror and pride, calling out warnings to Renno, all unheard in the din of action.

Hodano held his huge tomahawk. It was raised in a position to smash into Beth's skull. That dry laugh made the cavern echo and reeçho eerily.

"It does not matter, these," Hodano intoned, waving his free hand to indicate the Maroon dead. "Kill all of them and still face your own death."

Renno leapt toward the shaman. Hodano lifted his arms, and his split tongue chanted a harsh, rhythmic spell. Se-quo-i lifted a hand as if to ward off evil. Mingo, awed in spite of his courage and his bulk, seemed paralyzed. The fires dimmed, and darkness not of this earth lowered from the dripping, stalactite-covered ceiling of the chamber. And from that darkness, floating on air, there emerged a beast from Renno's night terrors. The creature of his nightmares, the beast was long of tooth and claw and carried the stench of carrion. The women in the chamber moaned in terror.

"Now die," Hodano hissed, pointing his oversize tomahawk at Renno, who had halted his forward rush.

A long, huge, clawed paw shot out, and Renno felt the shock of impact as the flesh on his arm tore. The beast sent him tumbling. He rolled to his feet and swung with his tomahawk as the paw shot out again, but his blade passed harmlessly through the paw as if it were air. He was sent tumbling again by the force of the blow of the paw and leapt to his feet to run to one side, needing time, crying out silently to his manitous for help against this spirit beast. Se-quo-i leapt to Renno's aid and was brushed aside with one smoking paw of the spirit beast. A terrifying roar filled the cavern as Renno dodged and struck out without effect.

"Be slow, spirits," Hodano commanded.

The huge beast of evil, not fully seen by those who watched, roared and began to stalk Renno. The white Indian halted, deciding that here he would make his stand. As he lifted his weapons to the unseen sky, his heart was heavy, for he remembered Ah-wen-ga's warning that he would be alone here in this foreign land. He fervently prayed to the manitous, and there seemed to be a change in the charged atmosphere of the cavern. A light flickered in the darkness, enabling Renno to see them, dozens of them—the spirits of the peaceful, gentle Arawak, dressed in their gay, bright costumes of feathers.

"My brothers," Renno breathed.

Hodano, sensing the presence of other spirits, roared in anger, ordering the spirit beast onward. Renno crouched in readiness. The beast lumbered forward—eerie, unreal, a horror not even imaginable. Then the charged air exploded with an answering roar, and at Renno's side was another strange, huge animal. It bore a resemblance to a great, black bear, but it was as if drawn by children. This bulky beast was a spirit bear born of Renno's mind and given form by the power of the spirits of his Arawak brothers.

Hodano shrieked in rage. The two giant spirit beasts seemed to fill the chamber, but when their movements overlapped the presence of mere humans, no physical contact was felt. The animals closed, and their roars were deafening. When the spirit bear clamped his mighty jaws on the malformed neck of Hodano's evil creature, Renno rushed forward.

Hodano, urging his spirit creature onward, had made the mistake of moving away from the stake where Beth stood tied. Renno leapt between the shaman and Beth. Hodano uttered a harsh scream and attacked, his giant tomahawk glowing with an unearthly fire. Renno countered, and his weapon seemed also to take on spirit qualities, so that when his blade caught the downward blow of Hodano's, a shower of red and blue sparks exploded outward from the clash of metals.

Hodano's one good eye gleamed redly at Renno. The blows and counterblows rained unnatural cold fire on the faces of those who watched. Se-quo-i watched the death struggle between the two spirit beasts and the monumental battle between Hodano and Renno, then turned his full attention to Renno as Hodano nearly decapitated him. The ferocity of Hodano's stare burned into Renno's brain. He felt himself growing weak, falling back, barely able to block Hodano's wild blows.

"El-i-chi," Renno whispered, longing for the good medicine of his shaman brother. "Brothers," he whispered, as his strength seemed to be drawn outward down through his arms, to pour out of his clenched fingers and toward Hodano. He could barely lift his tomahawk. "Brothers!" he called to the Arawak spirits.

The air sparkled, and he felt his power returning in a flow that sent his weapons hammering and slashing, forcing Hodano back, back, between the women, who made way for them. Hodano barely managed to block a killing blow from Renno's tomahawk. The flat of the weapon glanced off Hodano's shoulder with a numbing impact.

As Renno recovered, Hodano raised his head to the evil one. "You desert me now? Then damn you!"

Hodano surged forward in frenzied desperation. One blow penetrated Renno's defenses and left a bleeding slash on the white Indian's knife arm, but then Renno was moving forward, his weapons drawing a pattern of death that was irresistible. Hodano gave way. He knew there was a pit behind him, where the headless bodies of sacrificed victims fell for a count of twenty before thudding into the bottom. He edged around, drawing Renno into following his movements until Renno's back was to the pit. And then he made his charge, intending to send Renno toppling into the pit. He would lose the white Indian's powerful spirit, on which he had based his ambitions, but he would live, and his magic would overcome the master, the other Indians, and the traitor Maroons. He bawled his defiance and rained blows, forcing Renno back, back, and then, seeing his chance, made one last supreme effort. He could feel the spirits of the dying Maroon warriors in the air, and he sought them out to draw a spirit into his mouth and feel new strength.

Behind Hodano the great near-bear loosed an ear-splitting roar of rage and slashed out mightily in one killing blow of his long-clawed forefoot. The night creature, Hodano's creation, was slashed open from shoulder to malformed thigh, and from that gash green, putrid matter gushed, and then small, terrifying winged creatures flew up to disappear screeching in the darkness. The night creature folded in on itself, collapsed, and vanished.

All was quiet as Hodano made his ultimate effort. He put his remaining power, augmented by swallowed spirits, into a blow to cleave Renno's skull and send him plummeting into the pit. He screamed as Renno countered, stepped aside, and used the momentum of Hodano's blow to send the shaman tumbling into the abyss. Hodano fell silently. Renno stood on the brink, listening for the impact of Hodano's body. That sound never came. . . .

He heard a roar behind him and turned to see the spirit bear embrace the flames of the highest ritual fire. Multicolored fingers of light blazed outward, then vanished, leaving only the flickering light of the fires, the moaning of a wounded man, the breathing of the women who had remained to watch.

With one slash of his bloody stiletto Renno freed Beth. She clung to him wordlessly, her green eyes wide, not able to believe fully what she had seen.

Se-quo-i heard Little Hawk's voice, not calling for help but

merely calling attention to his plight. The boy was quickly
freed of the weight of the dead Maroon. Renno, seeing his
son bloodied, felt a jolt of fear, but Little Hawk ran to him
crying, "I killed one for you, Father."

"Please take me away from this horrid place," Beth whispered. She was shaking violently and feared that she would
go mad. She clung to Renno. Mingo led the way, carrying a
torch.

"The master fled," Mingo reported. "Perhaps it is not
over."

Renno gripped his tomahawk more tightly. At the entrance
he told Beth to wait. He walked up the slope from the dark
maw of the cave.

The dead were scattered over the ground. Mingo's father,
one arm wounded, stood with his followers facing the cave. On
a rise to one side stood the master. He was surrounded by
sullen, angry warriors.

"Hear me," Renno said. "I have come here only to reclaim
my own. Enough blood has been shed. This great warrior"—he
put his hand on Mingo's shoulder—"has fought by my side to
free you from evil. Take this chance for peace."

The master lifted his arms. The darkness began to thicken,
to close out the light of the moon and the stars and the fires
of the village. "Kill," the master ordered. Some of the warriors around him started forward.

Renno felt the power of the manitous flowing back into his
limbs. There truly had been enough killing. He lifted his
arm, and as the master, sensing danger, began to float away,
his feet a full two feet off the ground, Renno hurled his
tomahawk with all his strength, yelled to direct its path, and
saw it sink to maximum depth in the wrinkled black skin of
the master's face. The master's body went limp and fell to
impact with a soft thud.

The warriors who were moving to attack halted in confusion.
Mingo shouted: "No more! We are rid of evil. Now we
have peace. Any who dispute that my father is now chief of
Maroons, let him speak and face me fairly."

"Mingo!" a woman cheered, and soon the air was filled
with voices chanting Mingo's name. A warrior who had been
at the master's side made a brief speech, condemning the evil

master. Pledges of peace were exchanged. There was joyous dancing around open fires.

Little Hawk had made a nearly miraculous recovery and wanted to watch the celebration, but Renno, knowing that Beth was exhausted and shaken, pulled him away, taking him and Beth to Mingo's hut, where a smiling, pretty black woman made them welcome. Mingo's two boys—one of them Little Hawk's age, the other older—were bright and friendly. Mingo herded them out, realizing that Renno and his family needed privacy.

When they were alone, Renno motioned Little Hawk to a pile of palm fronds covered with a blanket, and within minutes the boy was sleeping the sleep of a victorious warrior.

"Can't we leave now, this minute?" Beth begged, clinging to Renno in spite of his blood-smeared body.

"With the morning," Renno answered gently. He prepared a bed for her and held her until she slept.

Mingo's wife was waiting outside. "I will watch over them," she offered.

Renno found Se-quo-i standing at Mingo's side, watching the dancers. The big man clasped Renno's arm and pulled him into the firelight. "Hear me," he bellowed. The drums and the dancing stopped immediately. "This warrior from a far land has delivered us from the evil of the master and the one who came from afar. For this we owe him our thanks."

There was a roar of approval.

"My little friend," Mingo said, turning to look down into Renno's startlingly blue eyes, "we were brothers in battle. Now, with your consent, we will be brothers in blood."

"Gladly." Renno did not enter into such relationships lightly, for blood brotherhood carried responsibilities, but this giant had fought well and bravely and had helped him to save the lives of his wife and son.

For a simple ceremony it took much time. First there was dancing, and Se-quo-i recounted the events of the battle inside the cavern. Then the account of the battle outside the cavern was told in great, oratorical style by Mingo's father. Then there was more dancing and wild drumming, and then Mingo used Renno's sharp Spanish stiletto to draw blood from his wrist. Renno did the same. Their blood was joined with Mingo holding Renno's hand high.

"Now we are brothers," Mingo declared. "I will fight at your side, and I will defend and avenge you and yours should harm come."

"We are brothers," Renno echoed. "I will fight at your side, and I will defend and avenge you and yours should harm come."

When Renno returned to the hut, Beth was moaning in her sleep. Little Hawk was asleep, as limp as a rag. Renno stroked Beth's forehead and lay beside her to sleep the few hours until dawn.

They were under way shortly after sunrise, escorted by Mingo and six warriors. Mingo's wife, Uanna, and sons had insisted on going, since Mingo's mission would consist of more than merely escorting his blood brother. She wanted to see the white man's cities, and so did her sons. Since Mingo was on a mission of peace, he had given in. Their send-off was joyful, with music and shouting and dancing. Beth was pale and weak at first, but with each mile of distance covered, removing her from the horror of the cave, she rallied.

Mingo's sons carried burdens of food that appeared to be far too large and heavy for the boys to handle. Surprisingly, they managed. Uanna carried cooking pots on her head.

The journey was made easier when they struck the north-south road and marched along it, garnering many stares from those who traveled the road, to the outskirts of the capital, Spanish Town.

Once or twice during the trip Beth had expressed fear that too much time had passed, that the pirate, Adan Bartolome, would have given up and killed Roberto de Mendoza. She had been a bit puzzled by Renno's lack of concern.

"He will be waiting," Renno assured her.

Since their band presented a ragged and perhaps menacing appearance, Renno sent a runner, hired outside Spanish Town, with a message for the governor. The governor himself met them with a carriage at their resting place. He was escorted by two squads of armed redcoats, for he had been told that the party consisted mainly of Maroons.

"Ye gods!" he exploded when he saw Renno and Beth. Then, "I'm sure you have an interesting story to tell, but first, what's the meaning of this?" He raised his eyebrows questioningly at Mingo and his six warriors.

"My father, Mingo the Elder, sends greetings to the white chief," Mingo announced, "and gives his assurances that there will be peace between us."

"Jolly good," Sir John said. "Does this mean that your people will cease their raids into our settled areas?"

"It does," Mingo said.

Sir John looked at Renno, then at Beth, now clad in Maroon rags. He whistled under his breath. It was, he guessed, going to be quite an interesting story.

Chapter XV

~~~~~~

Sir John Peter Grant knew that primitive peoples were impressed by ceremony. He knew also that it was desirable to end the threat of Maroon raids from their impregnable wilderness strongholds. He therefore scheduled an impressive parade of the local garrison, complete with drums, fifes, and bagpipes. Many gifts were presented to Mingo and his family, and the Maroons were dressed in new, if oddly assorted, clothing. Uanna, slim and proud, had been aided in her selection by Beth, so she was striking in a simple white gown.

Tanyere and Bitty One, Mingo's sons, stood proudly at their father's side as the governor made a speech praising the wisdom of the Maroon leadership and promising an era of peace. At the feast that followed the ceremony, the Maroons' table manners drew some attention but did not ruin anyone's appetite. Beth was then given the floor to tell of her ordeal and the battle inside the cavern. When she told the tale without mentioning the spirit beasts or anything that hinted of the supernatural, Renno's lips twitched in a smile. If he had been telling the story to white men, he too would have left out any mention of the battle between Hodano's evil spirits and the manitous of the Arawak. The white man, for all his advances and his knowledge, had certain areas of ignorance.

"And so," Beth finished, "by the grace of God and by the strong arms of my husband and his friends, we are safe."

Renno and Beth had, in fact, discussed certain aspects of the events in the cavern on the trip back to Spanish Town, and each had given the other some food for thought. Beth, who had seen the spirit beasts and had felt the effects of Hodano's evil power, tried to reconcile the facts to her belief in what she called one God.

To Beth it was a puzzle. If Hodano had represented evil—as he most certainly did—then that evil had to be from the archfiend himself. That given, then Renno's manitous were representatives of that which is good or godly. Why, then, if one God ruled all and determined all, had she never had direct spiritual contact with angels? It was against all her teachings to believe that this man, her Renno, who lived in a savage land and who had killed many, many times, was blessed by the same God who taught "Thou shalt not kill."

Moses Tarpley had been summoned from Kingston shortly after the arrival of his friends in Spanish Town. His relief and pleasure in seeing everyone alive was heartwarming. He reported that the *Seneca Chieftain* was heavily laden with prime Blue Mountain coffee beans and ready to sail for home as soon as Renno's group boarded. Everyone, Renno included, felt that it was high time.

There was further business to be discussed between Beth and the governor, however. Grant asked for a meeting with her. She invited Renno to accompany her, but he told her that business was not his concern. She thus sat alone now in the governor's library with a glass of fine Spanish wine and listened to a very interesting proposition from Sir John:

"It seems that you are in a unique position to bring about something that would be beneficial to yourself, to the United

States, and to Jamaica and other British islands in the Caribbean. The success of this first trade mission of yours to our island—combined with the impact of your family name, your beauty, and the novelty of such a woman in trade—would at least catch the interest of the old men who determine policy back in London."

The possibilities advanced by the Jamaican governor dazzled Beth but also left her with a serious personal decision that would have to be made. If she traveled to London to advance her cause, a very long separation from Renno would result. As she made her farewells to Sir John, the governor handed her certain documents he had signed requesting further trade with her company. He also promised that more documents representing similar requests from the governors of other British islands would be delivered as quickly as possible to her establishment in Wilmington.

When Beth found Renno, he did not question her about her talk with Sir John, so she said only, "The governor had some very interesting ideas about how to expand trade between the islands of the Caribbean and the United States."

Mingo's wife, Uanna, was fascinated by the white man's town, and she begged her husband to delay their return to the Cockpit Country in order to accompany Renno to Kingston. Uanna had been told that Kingston was even larger than Spanish Town, and her desire to see that community was strong.

Mingo, who loved his woman very much, had been enjoying all the attention he was getting both as the tallest man anyone had ever seen and as a "diplomat" on a mission from the Maroons. He agreed to her pleas with alacrity, and soon he and his family were treading the decks of the *Seneca Chieftain*.

Mingo bombarded Renno with questions about the sea and how long it would take to sail to the white Indian's country of the virgin forests. What sorts of animals roamed the wilderness, he wanted to know, and where, and how did they taste? He shook his giant head at the number of weeks required to travel from the North Carolina coast to the lands of the Seneca and Cherokee.

"It is said that our ancestors in Africa hunted game," said six-year-old Tanyere.

"Mingo, why don't you come with us?" Little Hawk sug-

gested. He had come to be great friends with Tanyere and
Bitty One.

Mingo considered. "To hunt one time, to take food as our
ancestors once did, would be a great thing, but we cannot
walk back home and we have no great ship, such as this, to
carry us over the waters."

Twice more, as the ship was being readied for departure,
the boys begged Mingo to take them to North Carolina with
Renno. Beth, thinking about the problems inherent in bringing near savages to an established society, remained silent.

"We could hunt deer not far from Wilmington," Little
Hawk said. "Couldn't we, Father?"

Renno nodded.

"Tell Mingo to come," Little Hawk pleaded.

"I think," Renno said with a smile as he looked up at the
Maroon's seven-foot height, "that Mingo is big enough to
make up his own mind."

"It would be a great thing to be like our ancestors," Mingo
mused, "and to eat meat that is the result of the hunt and not
of a slaughter near the pigsty."

"Then come," Renno encouraged. "We will hunt in North
Carolina, and then you and your family will return to Jamaica
aboard one of the Huntington ships."

Beth looked at Renno quickly.

He smiled. "There will be other Huntington ships traveling to Jamaica, I take it."

"Yes," she said. "Mingo, you and your family are welcome.
As a matter of fact, there will be a ship sailing within a few
weeks of our return to Wilmington."

Little Hawk and the two Maroon boys did an impromptu
war dance on the deck. Moses Tarpley yelled at them to keep
out of the way of the working seamen. Within an hour after
leaving the sheltered harbor, when the ship began to roll and
pitch on the small waves of an ideal blue-green sea, both
Mingo and Uanna, emptying their stomachs over the rail,
were cursing whatever gods had influenced Mingo's decision.
But their boys, untouched by seasickness, remained in high
good humor.

When the *Mano Negra* left George Town on a course given
to Adan by Bastian Vanderrenner's man, the sinister-looking
Noir, Adan was desperately seeking an out. He had caught

another whiff of Vanderrenner's slave ship, and to think of
spending weeks, months, perhaps years, with that stench
under him made him wish that he'd never met the Dutchman. The crew, however, seemed reconciled to the idea;
transporting slaves from Africa was a profitable occupation.
One or two trips, the men felt, and they could open a pub,
buy a farm, or go into another business on shore.

Adan had another problem: the time was near for the
Americans to give him a sizable amount of gold on their way
back from Jamaica. Oddly enough, their destination as set by
Noir—a course that kept them within sight of Vanderrenner's
ship—would take them to the very island where Adan's ren-
dezvous with the Americans was to take place. It seemed to
Adan to be an incredible coincidence that the Dutchman's
hideaway was there, albeit on the opposite side of the island.
He began to make plans as to how he could slip away from
Vanderrenner long enough to collect the ransom money.

The island was, Adan found, an ideal place to hide. Only
one who knew the approaches to the hidden cove could have
piloted a ship through the shallows and the coral reefs. And
once inside the cove, not even the tall spars of a ship were
visible from the sea. If he had chosen to continue a career of
piracy, this little cove would have been a perfect place to
rest or to run to if things got dangerous.

The first thing Adan did once both ships were tucked safely
away in the cove was to send a pair of his most trusted men to
wait for the Americans on the opposite side of the island.
When the American ship arrived, one man was to notify
Adan. By that time he would have worked out a story to tell
Vanderrenner. The gold for the ransom of Roberto de Mendoza
had taken on a new importance for Adan: he was locked into a
relationship with the slave trader, true, but with gold he
could buy his own trade goods, pay for the alterations
belowdeck to make places for the slaves, and then work out a
better percentage with Vanderrenner. Fifty percent was too
much to give the Dutchman simply for the relatively small loan.

Carpenters began working on the *Mano Negra*. Life on the
island was comfortable, for Vanderrenner had quite an establishment there. There were island-type houses, open to the
breezes. There were slave pens for holding large numbers of
slaves to fatten them up and make them more market-worthy

after the trying voyage from Africa. There was rum in plenty, made there on Vanderrenner's holdings. There were sleek-bodied black women trained to do their duty for Vanderrenner's chosen few, the favors of the women being denied the ordinary seamen.

Adan spent many evenings with Vanderrenner, listening to accounts of previous voyages, raids on black villages in Africa, and the riches to be had. Vanderrenner had another holding on a river in West Africa, a fort from which his men ventured out to steal slaves or to buy them from the more powerful tribes of the area. Adan, beginning to realize the extent of Vanderrenner's strength and power, had second thoughts about trying to deceive the Dutchman. One night he finally told his own story, and Vanderrenner laughed.

"You concern yourself about such a small amount of gold?"

"Well, the difference is, you see, that it's my gold," Adan said with a smile. "If it's all the same to you, I will take it."

"Take it," Vanderrenner invited, "if the ship comes before we are ready."

Adan was pleased that Vanderrenner had not demanded half of the gold. "I have planned to pay you for the alterations to the *Mano Negra* and for the trade goods with the gold. Then I think we should talk further about what percentage of my profits you will take."

"If that is your wish," Vanderrenner agreed. "Certainly if you are able to finance your own beginnings in the trade, you deserve to earn more of the profits. Get your gold and work with me, and I will take only twenty-five percent."

"I think, sir," Adan said, lifting his glass in salute, "that I can come to like being your partner."

An incident the following night made Adan doubt the accuracy of that statement. A member of the *Mano*'s crew, well stimulated by raw rum, seized one of Vanderrenner's black women and was in the process of ripping away her clothing when he was discovered. The man was dragged, somewhat battered, before the Dutchman.

Vanderrenner listened and nodded when he was told that the man was stopped before he had raped the woman. He smiled coldly, and a pistol seemed to materialize in his hand, as it had in the pub in George Town. His first shot struck the *Mano* crewman in the genitals, the second impacted directly between the eyes.

Adan leapt to his feet, shocked. He opened his mouth to
protest, but it was too late. He looked at Vanderrenner
questioningly.

The beautifully attired Dutchman stood and addressed all
the men gathered. "A man is entitled to enjoy the fruits of his
own labor. He has no right to steal the fruits of another man's
labor. If any of you want a woman, then buy one. I have
bought these, and they are mine. I will not have them
becoming all poxed up from contact with dregs who have not
enough gumption to provide for their own needs." He sur-
veyed the assemblage, to see the men drop their eyes rather
than meet his defiant gaze.

The pistol disappeared into his clothing as he added, "If
there are any who want to give this carrion a burial, so be it.
Otherwise, toss him into the bay to the crabs and fishes."

It was not Adan's nature to fear a man, but he had to admit
that he had a certain respect for the Dutchman. He decided
that he would never cross the man unless he had a loaded
pistol already in hand. He could not match that almost magical ability to produce instantly a weapon from its hiding
place. And although he regretted the loss of his man, he
knew that in a venture such as he was going to undertake,
discipline was essential.

The passage northward and around Cuba was a pleasant
one for everyone on board the *Seneca Chieftain* except Mingo
and Uanna. Beth did have one scare: one morning when she
came on deck she heard piping voices overhead and looked
up to see Little Hawk and the two Maroon boys perched high
in the rigging. The *Chieftain* was heeled over before a fine
breeze, so that if one of the boys had fallen, he would have
plunged into the sea.

"Little Hawk!" Beth cried. "Come down at once, and bring
the others with you."

"I wouldn't worry," Moses Tarpley advised. "I'll make fair
hands out of them before we reach port."

Beth found Renno forward, leaning on the rail and staring
moodily down into the sea as it rushed past.

"Boys climb," Renno observed.

Beth could not know that Renno's shortness resulted from
his deductions that her talk with the governor of Jamaica was

going to have a long-lasting effect on their lives. She opened her mouth to voice a retort. She was, after all, genuinely concerned for Little Hawk's safety. Instead she remained silent and left Renno there alone.

In the privacy of their cabin, though, their love was as of old—or perhaps even sweeter, more intense, since both were remembering how near death had come to them.

Renno had several things to occupy his mind. Beth and their future, of course, concerned him. The future of his people was a question that was always with him. And in the dark of night, before he slept, he relived that final moment of the battle with Hodano and tried to find an explanation as to why he had not heard the shaman hit the bottom of the pit.

He put all those thoughts aside and readied his weapons and alerted the crew when Moses announced that the land low on the horizon ahead was the island where they were to meet the handsome, laughing pirate.

Moses anchored the *Chieftain* in a beautiful bay. Almost immediately smoke rose from a signal fire on the island, and Renno took a party of seamen and went ashore. Two bearded, ragged men stood just above the high-water mark. Renno stepped out of the boat, alert, his eyes searching the line of dunes and growth.

"Where is your captain?" he asked.

"Our orders are to see the gold, and then the cap'n will come," one of the men replied.

"Tell your captain that we will not wait long," Renno said. "If Roberto de Mendoza is not on the beach by sundown tomorrow, we will sail."

One of the men nodded, then disappeared, walking swiftly.

Renno took note of the makeshift camp. There were signs of only the two men. He got back into the boat and told the men to take him back to the ship.

There was activity on the beach shortly after sunrise of the new day. During the night Renno had made certain secret preparations, which had involved numerous trips by boat from the *Chieftain* to the shore above and below the camp, where a fire had burned until almost midnight.

Now, at dawn, as he and Se-quo-i prepared to take the boat to shore, Beth said, "You're not taking the ransom money."

"So," Renno acknowledged. He had given Moses Tarpley his instructions: the ship was anchored so that she lay broadside to the beach, and her guns were ready. An extra lookout was in the rigging, keeping an eye on the sea.

Renno and Se-quo-i were rowed toward shore by four of the *Chieftain*'s crew, each chosen for his fighting ability, each well armed. Renno could see six pirates surrounding a slim, slumped figure dressed in torn and faded clothing. They were positioned just in front of the line of sand dunes that separated the flat beach from the stunted maritime vegetation of the island.

As the bow ground its way into the sand of the shore, a pirate detached himself from that group and advanced. Renno stepped out of the boat and stood with his arms crossed.

"I have a message from the captain," the man said. He held out his hand and opened his fingers. A dried and shriveled human ear lay in his palm. "There are new conditions. You will give the gold to me now. There is the man Mendoza. You will note that there is a knife next to his remaining ear, and it will be delivered to you if you do not hand over the gold immediately. As you watch, small pieces will be cut away from Mendoza until we have the gold."

Renno moved so swiftly that the spokesman had no chance to retreat. found himself gasping for air as Renno's arm closed around his neck. He felt the sharp blade of Renno's stiletto at his ear. The man screamed, and then he was freed. His hand went to the side of his head, and he screamed again.

"A gift requires a gift in return," Renno said cordially, handing the pirate his ear. Then Renno bent to pick up the shriveled ear that had fallen into the sand. He turned and walked back to the boat. "Tell your captain that I will see him face-to-face with Mendoza."

Renno leaned against the bow of the longboat and watched the bleeding man stumble back to the group in front of the dunes. There was agitated talk, and then the group withdrew out of sight. He waited. The sun had scarcely moved when Adan Bartolome appeared, walking briskly over the dunes. Renno let him walk all the way to the high-water mark before he pushed away from the boat and faced him.

"I think this is a matter of trust," Adan said.

"So," Renno grunted. From long experience he had learned

that if he assumed Indian stoicism and remained silent, men would talk and often say more than they had intended.

"You saw Mendoza. He is there. I will take the gold, and then he will walk to you under his own power."

Renno was silent.

"For God's sake, man!" Adan shouted. "I admit it! The ear was from a man already dead. Mendoza, I assure you, is in perfect health."

"Then that is very unfortunate for the messenger you sent."

"I apologize," Adan said. "I suppose I was feeling a bit dramatic. But now I think we can conclude our business as friends."

"My friends do not kidnap," Renno said. Although his eyes did not leave Adan's face, he noticed a movement in the growth beyond the sand dunes. Several pirates broke cover and dashed toward the beach from two spots, coming toward Renno's boat from up and down the beach. Renno heard the click of metal as pistols were readied and most likely aimed at his men, but still he did not move.

"I would like to conclude our business without violence," Adan said with a charming smile, "but you see how it is."

"So," Renno said. He stood, motionless, his eyes blazing blue fire as Adan's crew began to close on the boat.

"I will take the gold now," Adan said.

Renno lifted one hand. Adan, suddenly unsure of himself, turned slowly. The *Chieftain*'s crew came as a body from behind the dunes, muskets and cutlasses ready. Se-quo-i stepped to Renno's side, and the four seamen in the boat leveled their pistols at Adan.

"Wait!" Adan cried out, raising his hands palms out toward Renno. "Wait, we can still work this out!"

"Very simply," Renno agreed. "All you have to do is give me Roberto de Mendoza."

Adan's mouth opened, but no words came out. He swiveled his head. His men had stopped their advance and had turned to face Renno's well-armed men with some evident nervousness.

"But then," Renno added, "I *am* face-to-face with Roberto de Mendoza."

Adan's shoulders slumped. "How long have you known?"

Renno shrugged. "I was not certain until this moment."

Adan lifted his hands and shoulders in an expressive Latin gesture of defeat. "It seemed like a good idea at the time," he confessed. "Here is my sister married to a very rich English lord—and I? I have nothing. It is only a little bit of gold that I ask."

Renno was coldly silent.

"I wonder," Adan-Roberto said, "if that generous offer from the lady with the beautiful hair is still open?"

Renno's cold anger was fading. "Tell your crew to stand down, to secure their arms."

"I thought that my rich Englishman brother-by-marriage would not miss such a small amount of gold." Adan turned and raised a hand. "We do not fight," he shouted. "Secure your arms." He turned to face Renno. "No hard feelings?"

Renno rarely used his fists as a white man uses them. For one thing, such a blow quite often broke fingers and was not nearly as effective as other means of action. But this time he did, moving with lightning speed. Adan felt a sharp shock on his chin and found himself sitting down heavily on the wet sand.

"Was it the family resemblance to my sister that made you suspect?" he asked, looking up as he rubbed his chin gingerly.

Ignoring the question, Renno turned to face the sea and waved his arms over his head. Soon boats put out from the *Chieftain.* Adan's crew meanwhile had begun to disperse by twos and threes.

"Your ship is anchored on the other side of the island?" Renno asked.

"Yes," Adan replied. "Look, your lady was right—I'm not cut out to be a pirate. I admit I deserved that blow to the chin, although it hurt like the devil. If you hold no grudge, do you suppose it would be all right for me to ask the lady for employment?"

"In a stolen ship?" Renno inquired.

Adan shrugged. "It is a Spanish ship. The Spaniards have no friends."

"Come with me and ask her yourself."

Beth was waiting anxiously aboard ship. When she saw only Adan in the boat with Renno and Se-quo-i, she was puzzled. She was astounded when Renno said, "May I introduce Señor Roberto de Mendoza, brother of your sister-by-marriage, Estrela."

Beth didn't know whether to be angry or relieved. She had come to like this man who wanted to be a pirate. When she asked questions, Adan elaborated on what he had told Renno: his father had died deeply in debt. Beth could sympathize with that, for her father had almost lost everything down to and including the good name of the family.

"But why didn't you simply go to William and Estrela for help?" she asked. "Why did you try to steal from them?"

"Pride?" Adan suggested. "Stupidity? Perhaps I felt that since your brother's wealth was taken from New Spain, then I, as a citizen of the country, had a right to a portion of it."

Renno, standing to one side, hid a smile. Adan's logic was juvenile and convoluted, but there was something about the affable Spaniard that he also liked.

"I have a good ship and a good crew," Adan told Beth. "If I should bring that ship to Wilmington in a little while, could you find work for us?"

Beth hesitated. She, like Renno, was wondering about the complications that might arise from the fact that Adan, or Roberto—it was difficult to think of him by that name—had stolen a Spanish ship. She made her decision. After all, Spain was no friend of either her native country or her adopted one. "It will not be an exciting life," she warned him. "Trips to the islands with a cargo of rice and naval stores, then trips back with coffee, perhaps."

"I think that I have had enough excitement for a while," Adan said. He had his plans formed: he would sail with the Dutchman toward Africa once the *Mano Negra* had been fitted for the slave trade. During the first storm he would slip away and head for the United States, taking his chances that the Dutchman wouldn't turn him in to the British, as threatened. He felt great relief. He would not have to sail for weeks or months with the stench of closely confined slaves in his nostrils. But mostly he was relieved to think that he would be rid of Vanderrenner. The cold, cruel Dutchman, who did not ever perspire in that tropical climate like an ordinary man, made him feel very uneasy.

Vanderrenner's interest in the gold that Adan was supposed to get from the Americans was actually more intense than he had indicated to Adan. The Dutchman calculated that he could take the gold at any time if, indeed, it were delivered. He used the time of Adan's absence to indulge in a pastime that was the thing nearest to his heart: hand-to-hand combat. The Dutchman himself had been an unbeatable opponent in his younger days and could still handle himself admirably. But his preference now was to have new battlers trained and to earn money by promoting and betting on their fights.

At a small distance from his main installation there was a cluster of three island huts. The area was hidden from prying eyes by a bamboo fence. None of the crew was allowed near the huts, which were guarded by Noir when the Dutchman's ship was in his hideaway. Vanderrenner's latest find lived there temporarily, the Dutchman's hope for gambling winnings and a bit of glory. The hope came in the form of a black man over six feet tall, superbly muscled, with a thick, powerful neck and fists like small hams.

This mighty black man, named Tano, was exercising his muscles under Noir's direction when Vanderrenner arrived at the little complex of huts. Tano was naked except for a loincloth, and his skin gleamed with perspiration as he hoisted a heavy palm-tree log and held it over his head for a moment before throwing it, with a mighty grunt, a very respectable distance.

Noir saw Vanderrenner and nodded with a slight, sinister smile.

"He looks to be in good condition," Vanderrenner remarked.

"About ready," Noir agreed.

"Will he be the great champion that you once were, my friend?" Vanderrenner asked.

The scarred, sinister black man shrugged. "He is quick, and he is powerful."

"But does he have the killer instinct?"

"That we will not know until he is put to the test," Noir commented. "Watch." He walked to the center of the enclosed area and spoke to Tano. Then he backed away and assumed a fighting crouch as Tano began to stalk him. Noir moved, seized Tano in a head grip. With a rapt expression Vanderrenner sat down in a chair and enjoyed the rippling of black muscles, the power, and the agility as the two strained. Noir had been the most effective fighting machine he'd ever

seen, the terror of all, and his fame had spread throughout
Spanish Florida and parts of New Spain, where men prized
their champions and wagered large amounts on such fights.
But age and injuries bring a halt to the career of even the
most skilled fighters.

Noir held his own well with Tano, the most powerful black
Vanderrenner had found in many trips to Africa, but youth
and quickness ultimately prevailed. The younger man held
Noir high, as if he were a toy, and was in a position to break
Noir's back over his knee. Then he lowered Noir to the
ground and turned, panting, to face Vanderrenner.

"Excellent, Tano," Vanderrenner commended. "And you
have trained him well, Noir. Yes, I think he is ready."

"I fight well for you," Tano said. "Kill many men. Then
you give me freedom, like Noir."

"Yes," Vanderrenner agreed. "Yes, I think you will kill
many."

Nothing would do for Little Hawk but to see the island.
Like many of the lesser islands of the Bahamas chain, it was
without fresh water, but there were coconuts to be had, with
their refreshing milk. Beth sided with Little Hawk, thinking
that an outing on land would be good for all of them. She felt
guilty, for she realized that she was merely postponing her
decision by delaying the return to Wilmington. But the skies
were blue, the sun pleasant, and she was happy. To hang on
to that undisturbed happiness for just a bit longer would be
no crime.

Thus it was that Bastian Vanderrenner had the opportunity
to see Mingo, seven feet of manhood in its prime. Disturbed
by what he had been told by Adan's returning men, he
organized a force and marched the short distance across the
island to see a beautiful, flame-haired woman walking with a
white man dressed in a breechclout. The woman held his
eyes for only a moment. Women were not his weakness. He
had all the women he needed, and one such as this redhead
would be, for a man such as him, nothing but trouble. It was
when he saw Mingo that his eyes narrowed with quick admiration. He had seen overly tall men before in Africa. There
was one tribe of men who were consistently near or just over
seven feet tall, but they were usually too thin and un-

gainly. This one, however, was magnificently proportioned, and as he played with two small black boys and one white boy, he moved with lithe grace.

Adan was a bit flustered when the Dutchman walked up to the fire where some crewmen were roasting fresh turtle steaks.

"I have come to meet your friends," the Dutchman said.

Adan looked around, nervous. Vanderrenner had left his armed men hidden out of sight, with some very clear instructions. Only half of the *Chieftain*'s crew was on shore. He knew he should have warned Renno of the Dutchman's presence on the island, but now it was too late.

Renno had not missed the appearance of the well-dressed newcomer. He left Beth and walked quickly to face the big white man across the fire. Adan made introductions, sounding as if he were in a drawing room. Renno acknowledged with a nod.

"I had not anticipated such pleasant company," the Dutchman said. "Had Adan told me he was going to entertain, I would have invited you to my place across the island."

Renno nodded. He had alerted Se-quo-i, and the Cherokee was quietly organizing the crewmen. This activity was not lost on Vanderrenner.

"You take precautions," he said to Renno. "Good. I like cautious, prudent men. Perhaps we can do business."

Renno waited, staring into the Dutchman's steel-gray eyes without speaking.

Vanderrenner pointed to Mingo, who was standing with the boys. "I want that slave. Name your price—within reason, of course."

"He is not a slave," Renno informed him.

"No matter. Slave, freedman, I will pay you well."

"Leave us," Renno said. He looked down at Adan. "Perhaps you, too, should leave with your friend."

"Let's not be hasty," Vanderrenner put in. "It's a simple matter. All I want is one black man."

"Then take him," Renno suggested, his eyes boring into the Dutchman's.

"As you will," Vanderrenner agreed. He turned and raised his voice. "Gentlemen, will you please show your teeth?"

A line of men armed with muskets and pistols appeared

atop the dunes. Renno estimated quickly. His men would be outnumbered, but numbers were not always the deciding factor.

"I would guess that the white woman is yours," the Dutchman said. "And the boy? It would be a shame if in the heat of battle something happened to either of them."

"You would not know," Renno warned, lifting his tomahawk.

Adan tensed, for the Dutchman's hand was in a position to draw his concealed pistol with that deadly speed.

"Actually," Vanderrenner said, "I don't want to lose any of my men, and I'm sure I would if it came to that. May I suggest a solution to our mutual challenge? Let your friend the giant face a man of my choice. If he wins, there will be no fighting among us. If he is bested, he is mine." He was sure that the well-trained Tano, student of all of Noir's deadly experience, could overpower the big black without killing him. Then, with the same kind of training, he would have another killing machine that would garner him gold from sporting men all over the Spanish holdings in the New World. A few bouts in Cuba alone would make him more money than a long and unpleasant voyage to and from the slave coast of Africa.

"I agree," Renno said, "but *I* will face your man."

"Oh, that wouldn't do," Vanderrenner said quickly as Mingo approached. "Let's put it to him," Vanderrenner proposed. He turned to the giant. "I am a sporting man. I have a man who fancies himself to be a fine bare-handed fighter, and I have not yet been able to put him to the test. I'd like you to fight him. If you don't, then we'll all have to fight, and a few of us might be killed."

"I fight one man?" Mingo asked.

"Only one, and not to the death."

"Where is this man?" Mingo wanted to know.

Chapter XVI

The sun had passed the midday mark before Tano was brought to the beach. Moses Tarpley, observing unusual activity, had sent the remaining boats with armed men so that the forces aligned against each other were now more equal in number. Had not many of Adan's crew stood with Vanderrenner's men, the numbers would have been equal. Renno had used the time to maneuver Beth, Mingo's wife, and the boys to the seaside where they were guarded by Se-quo-i and members of the crew.

The arena was the hard-packed sand between the low- and high-tide marks. Vanderrenner's men clustered together, weapons in hand; the crew of the *Seneca Chieftain* were grouped with their backs to the sea.

"I do not have to kill this little man?" Mingo asked Renno, but it was Vanderrenner who answered.

248

"I advise you to hold nothing back," the Dutchman said. "This man has some skills. He has orders not to kill you, but if you have to kill to prevent being bested, then so be it."

Mingo looked at Renno with a questioning expression, as if to ask himself, *What sort of rules are these? I, cast as the underdog?* It made him want to laugh.

"Come, little man," he taunted Tano.

Tano stepped toward Mingo, hand extended for a ceremonial arm clasp. Mingo, a foot taller, larger of body and weight, accepted the arm clasp. But before the clasp was broken Tano kicked his knee into Mingo's genitals with a force that drove the wind from Mingo's lungs and dropped him, hands clasped over his pain, face ashen, to his knees.

Tano backed away, spread his hands, and looked questioningly at the Dutchman. Vanderrenner made a subtle gesture, and Tano leapt forward and aimed a kick at Mingo's head. But one of Mingo's hands shot up, seized an ankle, and twisted. Tano fell heavily to the sand but rolled immediately and sprang to his feet. Mingo grunted with pain as he stood.

Tano darted in, agile for his size and bulk, and landed two blows, one that sent a spurt of blood from Mingo's big, flat nose. The other thudded into Mingo's stomach. Mingo grunted and blinked. The huge pain in his groin had weakened him. He felt as if he might vomit at any moment. He backed away as Tano closed in again. He took blows from Tano's fists on his shoulder and his forearm.

"Good, good," Vanderrenner remarked to Adan. "He has courage and stamina. Perhaps he is a little slow, but his ability to absorb punishment and his strength will compensate for that."

Mingo suffered two more blows to the face, blows that landed with surprising power, blows that made white lights dance in front of his eyes. He was breathing through his mouth. Blood gushed from his nose.

"Mingo!" Uanna called out. "You are letting that little man hurt you." Her voice was expressive with concern and surprise.

Although Mingo seemed not to hear, he *had* heard, and his wife's words were a reflection of his own amazement. He grunted. When Tano moved in, fists pumping, Mingo protected his face and watched Tano's feet. He waited until Tano was standing flat-footed on the sand, fists pounding at Mingo's protected arms and stomach. With a roar Mingo leapt in to seize the smaller man in a bear hug.

Tano felt the force of the squeeze and began battering at Mingo's face with his fists, trying also to get one of Mingo's ears between his teeth. He felt the air being forced from his lungs and attempted to bring a knee up into Mingo's groin again but succeeded only in contacting Mingo's massive thigh.

"I don't want to have to kill you, little man," Mingo growled.

Tano snarled and butted Mingo's mouth with his forehead, bringing blood from two sources—Mingo's lips and his own forehead. Mingo dropped to his knees, twisted the smaller man in his grasp, and lifted him to full arm's length as he rose. Then Tano was flying through the air to land hard on the packed sand. He was dazed. He tried to roll, but Mingo had followed, moving with a quickness that widened Vanderrenner's eyes. When Mingo's big, hardened foot crashed down into Tano's stomach, Tano flopped backward into the film of water from a receding wave and lay still.

Vanderrenner, shocked, had hidden his hand in the folds of his clothing. In the excitement of the battle he had not noticed that Renno had moved to stand directly behind him. When Tano did not move, he shouted, "Get up, damn you," but Tano lay still as a wave washed around his head. Vanderrenner shook his head in disbelief. He had to have that man Mingo. He had no skills, but he was the most powerful fighter Vanderrenner had ever seen. He closed his hand on the butt of his pistol and glanced up, preparing to give the signal to his men to attack.

Renno's voice hissed in the Dutchman's ear. "Draw a weapon and die."

The Dutchman tensed, for there was now a cold, sharp blade pressing into his throat. For one moment he considered giving his men the order to fire, but as he swallowed involuntarily, the keen edge of Renno's knife sliced his skin and he felt a small trickle of blood run down to soil the white ruffle of his shirt.

"I had no such intention," Vanderrenner croaked.

"Order your men to retire," Renno said.

It was done; the men retreated over the sand dunes.

"If you would please remove the knife from my throat . . ." Vanderrenner suggested.

Renno stepped back.

"You are not a trusting man," the Dutchman accused, facing Renno, dabbing with a handkerchief at the shallow cut on his throat. "You had my word."

"Go," Renno commanded.

Vanderrenner looked at Adan. His steel-gray eyes told Adan much, for he knew the man. This was not the end of it. "Adan?" the Dutchman said softly.

"I'll be along shortly." Adan feared in that moment he had lost his ship, for most of his own crew had disappeared with the Dutchman's men. Only three of them, the first mate Williams among them, remained on the beach.

Vanderrenner turned and walked away without looking back. Tano was beginning to stir. He shook his head, and when he saw his master leaving, he struggled to his feet, followed for a few paces, and then halted. He turned. "Take me with you," he pleaded.

"Come, little man," Mingo said. "You fight well. You can teach me a few things."

Adan had rushed to Renno's side. "I know the Dutchman. He is not finished."

"Nor am I," Renno assured him, turning to face the sea. He waved both arms over his head. On the *Seneca Chieftain* Tarpley saw the signal and gave one simple order. The *Chieftain*'s guns roared, and just as the Dutchman's men started to charge up the far side of the sand dunes, the heavy balls smashed into the trees around them. A man screamed in terminal agony. A few attained the top of the dune and met a withering fire from the forces on the beach. Another broadside fell among the Dutchman's panicked forces as they ran.

Vanderrenner had counted the flashes of the guns on the ship offshore. She was, for a merchantman, well armed, and he knew his guns could not match her. Besides, his men were in full flight. His biggest regret was that he had lost the most magnificent fighting man he'd ever encountered. He dabbed at his throat, found that the bleeding had stopped, and walked calmly toward the other side of the island.

"Do you suppose we might go and get my ship?" Adan asked Renno.

Renno nodded, then signaled to Se-quo-i. The Cherokee put the women and boys into the boat and sent it off toward the *Chieftain*. He was at Renno's side as the white Indian crossed the dunes, stepped over the dead men lying there, and began to follow the multiple tracks through the splintered trees and the growth.

There was activity aboard both ships when Renno reached the hidden bay. The rattle of the Dutchman's anchor chain could be heard. Sails were going up. And men on board the *Mano Negra* were pouring a barrel of pitch onto the open deck.

"They're going to set the *Mano* on fire!" Adan exclaimed.

Renno drew his bow. Se-quo-i stood at his side. Their arrows flew as one, and the two men pouring pitch fell. Two more, seeing their comrades fall, tried to flee. Because Se-quo-i was a bit slow, one of them dove over the side and into the bay to swim for the Dutchman's ship, which was beginning to get under way with the air of a favoring breeze.

Musket fire rattled, and men pitched forward on board the slave ship. But then she had more sail, and with one last man plunging from high in the rigging to splash limply into the bay, she was out of range.

Several men from Adan's crew had elected to stay behind. They came out of their hiding places, their hands held high. Soon they were on board the *Mano*, beginning to clean up the mess made by the men who had intended to burn the ship.

With the next dawn the *Mano* and the *Chieftain* rendezvoused north of the island and set course for Wilmington.

Mingo rested on a blanket on deck for most of the day. One of his eyes was swollen shut. His lips were bruised, and he walked stiffly.

"This little man," he told Renno as evening came and a glow of phosphorescence made a thing of beauty of the *Chieftain*'s wake, "has been trained by the Dutchman to kill other men in bare-hand fight."

Renno was silent. Tano stood, his eyes down, beside Mingo. They were an impressive pair.

"He is a slave," Mingo continued. "I will take him home with me and give him a good woman." He laughed. "Not that he would have trouble getting women."

"I will serve you well," Tano promised. "And my life and my heart will be yours for delivering me from the Dutchman."

"You will serve no man as master," Mingo said heatedly. He turned to Renno. "Tell him, my friend."

"In the land of the Maroons you will be a free man," Renno verified.

"Eh, I was free in my homeland," Tano told them. "The son of a chief."

Renno, truly a Seneca, liked a rousing tale as well as anyone. He had only to request, and Tano spoke. One of his brothers, the son of a different mother, had been ambitious and coveted Tano's place as firstborn to his father, the chief of a strong and powerful tribe. Tano was betrayed by his brother to the slave hunters and marched with chains on his arms and legs to a great river, far from his homeland. He had survived the torment of a western crossing in the hold of the Dutchman's ship, the sickness, and the near starvation.

Tano sat cross-legged on the deck, surrounded by men and boys, Renno and Se-quo-i among them. He spoke of the home from which he had been stolen, of the animals of grace and beauty and power he had hunted there, of the antelope and grass eaters of all types, the lion, the elephant.

Little Hawk's eyes were wide as Tano tried to use his fragmented English to describe an elephant, but the boy still couldn't visualize a beast of such proportions.

The stories of that far place with its jungles, wide plains, and multitude of odd animals kept Renno from his bed, so that when he went to his cabin after a bath in salt water Beth was asleep. Uncovered in the tropic heat, she was wearing a filmy white nightgown. A sheen of perspiration was on her upper lip. Her flame-colored hair was spread on the white pillow. Renno stood at her side and let his eyes enjoy her beauty. He felt good. A mission that had seemed to be simple on the surface had brought deadly danger to those he loved, and now it was over.

He was thinking of summer in the Seneca-Cherokee village, the sweetness of the melons, the lazy, hot days, and the coolness of the clear streams. Ena and Toshabe would be preparing wondrous dishes with the summer fruits and vegetables. An image of Emily flashed into his mind and superimposed itself over Beth's sleeping face. He saw Emily's pale

hair and her loving smile, saw her at her cooking with Little
Hawk crawling around the longhouse—only a baby but made
wary of the open fire by training. He had thought that he was
long past experiencing the unutterable pain and grief that he
felt. Emily would always be in his heart, but he had thought
that the loss had been absorbed into him. He shook his head,
and there was only Beth.

He joined his sleeping wife, and she turned to him, her
eyes fluttering open. "So you are here at last," she whispered. Her lips tasted of sleep, but soon she was as awake as
he.

The days passed. Adan's ship caught up with theirs and
they traveled the remaining distance in tandem. At last they
heard the ringing of the bell that announced the coming of a
ship up the Cape Fear. The river passage afforded Renno a
view of the back garden of the Huntington house, where he
saw a small white child waving at him. He did not realize,
until he recognized the straight, slender form of Ah-wa-o at
the child's side, that it was Renna. Not to recognize his own
daughter! But she was dressed in yellow frills and lace, white
man's clothing.

You are Seneca, a voice said in his mind. *Seneca!*

So easily did all the old problems return. Nora Johnson
would want Renna and Little Hawk to spend time with her in
Knoxville. There his son and his daughter would be taught
more of the white man's ways. For long moments he seemed
to be divorced from this place and time, not truly on the deck
of the *Seneca Chieftain* as she slowed and prepared to come
alongside the wharves where Cedric Huntington stood waving his hat and shouting. Instead Renno felt far away in the
deep forests. He felt lost, not knowing which way to travel.

"We're home," Beth enthused, her hands, warm and soft,
clutching his arm.

"Home?" he asked.

Her smile faded. She looked away and began to wave to
her father.

Cedric's German-made carriage wheeled onto the docks
just as Little Hawk, determined to be the first on land,
rushed down the gangplank that had barely been set in place.
He ran to kiss Ah-wa-o and embrace his sister and was

chattering up a storm telling Ah-wa-o all his adventures. Renno ran to take his daughter into his arms, and then he saw El-i-chi running full tilt from the Huntington office. An arm clasp and the meeting of their eyes said it all as the two brothers thanked their manitous silently for their reunion.

For the next two days and two nights the atmosphere in the Huntington house was odd for Cedric and Beth, as they felt overrun by exotic visitors. Stories were told, and each had his or her turn. Renno's fists clenched as he heard of El-i-chi's battle with the slaver. Cedric had a bit of trouble tuning his ears to the speech of the two giant blacks, Mingo and Tano.

The old man was charmed and intrigued by the darkly handsome Roberto de Mendoza, alias Adan Bartolome. Adan, as Roberto had come to prefer to be called, added his own adventures to the telling of tales with accounts of his would-be piracy that had Cedric and the others laughing heartily.

El-i-chi had to let out a few whoops at exciting places as Beth and Renno described the battle of the cave and Hodano's downfall. Little Hawk and Mingo's son Bitty One acted out the titanic battle between Mingo and Tano, and El-i-chi looked at both black men with narrowed eyes, measuring his own chances against them in bare-knuckle combat.

Beth missed the second day of feasting and storytelling. She was back in her element, and the cargo of the *Chieftain* brought a price that pleased her. Two ships were back from England as well, so her days were filled. She was at her accounting books late into the night, so Renno slept alone, waking to turn and take her into his embrace when she finally tumbled exhausted into bed.

Mingo demonstrated a flair for learning the woodcraft required to stalk a summer deer in the deep forests west of the Cape Fear. He killed two, with nothing more than a spear. Tano demonstrated the techniques he had once used on the African plains, and thus there was venison in plenty in the Huntington house.

Mingo accepted a gift of money from Beth, and Ah-wa-o shopped with Uanna. Mingo shook his massive head at the piles of her purchases—cloth, cooking utensils, and some things Mingo thought were nothing more than foolish excesses. Tanyere and Bitty One were dressed in white man's clothing, much to their disgust.

Unknown to Renno, Beth and Cedric were a bit concerned. They were hearing some very nasty talk about having Negroes living in their house, even if they were in the servants' quarters in the English basement, and about having savage blacks and a Spaniard sit down at their table.

"Mingo fought at Renno's side," Beth told Cedric. "Because of him we are all alive."

"But, but—" Cedric sputtered, and then subsided.

The uncomfortable problem for Beth was easily solved by Uanna. "I do not like this place," she told Mingo. "It is time for us to go home."

The *Chieftain* was being loaded. When Beth announced that the ship would be sailing for Jamaica in three days' time, Mingo breathed a sigh of relief.

"We are brothers," he told Renno as final preparations were being made for the ship to leave dock. Uanna's purchases were safely stowed. Tanyere and Bitty One were in the rigging, helping the sailors hoist sail. Tano also lent his considerable strength to the chore.

"For all time," Renno confirmed, clasping the giant's arm.

The *Chieftain* disappeared on the falling tide. The day was warm, but there was a hint of freshness, a premature hint of the autumn to come. Renno looked westward with longing.

In the privacy of her large bedroom Beth loosened her clothing. Renno, always amused at the way white women trussed themselves up, observed, "I could undress you in seconds by cutting with my knife."

"But then I'd have to have new clothing every day."

They lay side by side with a cool breeze blowing over their naked bodies. "Isn't it pleasant, just us, just the family?" Beth asked.

Renno would not answer, for the restlessness was in him. The call of his people was not to be denied much longer. Since that night when Emily's face had superimposed itself over Beth's, he had been trying to picture Beth in his longhouse in the village. Try as he might, he could not see her kneeling beside an open fire to prepare the evening meal. They had not spoken of the future, both being content to enjoy each day and each night as it came.

"Renno?"

"Yes."

"You have some idea of what Sir John proposed."

"Perhaps," he admitted. He knew that the talk between Beth and the governor had to do with the possibility of opening unrestricted trade between the United States and British possessions in the Caribbean.

"I don't want to face this, not yet," she said, turning to press her face into the curve of his shoulder. He felt a tug of compassion, for her face was wet with tears.

"It is to be faced."

"I want only to be with you," she insisted. "I can do it, you know. After all, I've lived in the wilderness with you. I didn't whine and complain when we walked all the way from Canada."

"No, you did well."

"It's so beautiful, your wilderness," she whispered. "Take me there. Take me there this minute. Let's get up and get our things and all the others and leave now, this minute."

"If that is what you want," he said, knowing it was impossible. Cedric's health was still frail. The old man was winded and weak from a half-minute romp with Renna or Little Hawk.

She burst into tears, and it was a long time before he could soothe her. Her body heaved with the force of her sobs. "Oh, damn this world," she said at last.

He had never heard her use such words and had never seen her sob with such intensity. "The choice is yours," he whispered.

"I am torn," she wailed. "Why must I have a father, a country, and a business? I wish that I had been born Seneca and that you loved me as a Seneca and that I was the mother of your children."

He was silent.

She sat up and wiped her eyes. She was at the height of her youthful beauty, with proud, firm breasts and skin smoother than the inside of hickory bark. "I—I—can—can't go," she sobbed. "You know how I want to. Oh, how I want to!"

He had known. He went cold inside.

"My father—"

"And Sir John's proposal."

"That, too," she admitted. "Renno, it's a chance to help the

United States. The English blockade is strangling us. Open trade with the islands will help everyone. I have to go."

"To England."

"Yes. And soon, before the winter storms begin," she said. "Go with me, please."

"No."

She clung to him. "I know. I know. You have your duty too."

She was quiet for a long while, clinging to him as if she would never let go. "My darling," she whispered, "what I am going to say hurts me more than I could ever describe. But I can't ask you to go on like this. You have your place in this world, and it is not with me here in Wilmington or in England. Do you think you could simply forget me?"

"No."

"Thank you." She smiled weakly between her tears. "But you must feel free. You can't be expected to keep making that long, difficult journey to come to me when I cry out for you. Be free of me, Renno." The words seemed to damage her throat, they came with such difficulty. "Renna and Little Hawk need a mother. If it is your choice to rear them as Seneca, find a kind mother for them."

"No," Renno repeated. "*You* are my wife. We will continue as we are. When I can, I will come to you. When you have fulfilled your own obligations—"

She laughed. "Thank you. I think I would have died had you—"

"We can speak of the death of your father without being cruel, for all old men travel to the West when it is their time. That will come, and your responsibility will end. But we may not have a natural solution to your involvement in business. The political affairs of the white men are like a quagmire, and you may sink deeper and deeper and be unable to pull free."

"No," she protested quickly. "This one trip, that's all. I owe that much to both England and the United States, for in the long run peace between the two will benefit all. But just this one trip. When the time comes I will sell everything or leave it in William's keeping—or maybe even Nathan Ridley's—and the money will be used for us and perhaps for your people. There will be enough to give Renna and Little Hawk the finest educations."

"In the schools of the white man?"

"You yourself have said many times that for your people to survive, they must become as white men."

She was not certain whether his silence indicated disagreement or thought. "Once the manitou said that your son would be a great chief. What better chief than one who knows the ways of both peoples?"

"So I have said," he agreed.

"When will you leave? Can you stay with me until the *Seneca Warrior* is ready to leave for England?"

"That I can do."

The letter written to warn Renno of the dying words of old Casno came, and Renno once again was taken in spirit to the west, to the villages of his people and the Cherokee. He mused to think that it had taken so long for the letter to arrive. And at the end of the letter there was a note added by Roy Johnson:

We miss you, my friend, and long for the company of our grandchildren. I am sure that Little Hawk, especially, will learn much from his travels. You will find all well here, and there will be a pleasant surprise for you in the village. On second thought, the news is too good to keep, but you must act surprised when you see your sister and see that Ena's stomach is heavy with child.

Renno gave a great whoop of joy. El-i-chi, who had been in the back garden feasting his eyes on his little rose, came running to share the news, and then the two warriors, one clad as a white man, the other in buckskins, were stomping in a dance of happiness with such force that it made the pictures on the walls fall out of plumb. Ah-wa-o joined them in the house, due partly to the ruckus and partly because it had started to rain with a sudden vengeance.

The late-summer storm lashed the coastline, closing Wilmington in under warm, tropical air and heavy rains. It seemed to Renno that Beth had been deliberately stalling, for he knew that the *Seneca Warrior* was laden and ready, her holds filled with rice, indigo, and cotton.

It was cozy in the house. El-i-chi and Ah-wa-o tended

Little Hawk and Renna. Se-quo-i spent much time in the library. The tropical air stalled over the mid-Atlantic coast, and the weather remained wet and gusty for well over a week.

Moses Tarpley, taking the *Seneca Chieftain* south, Jamaica bound, kept his eyes on the weather at all times. It was still early for the huge, roaring storms that came in from the vastness of the southern waters far beyond the islands, but he stayed alert, always ready to run for shelter. He rather enjoyed seeing Mingo's sons scampering up and down the rigging with his sailors, and he told Mingo that he could make proper seamen out of those two. Mingo allowed that the place for his sons was back in the Cockpit Country.

For two weeks the winds were fair and favorable, and the *Chieftain* had passed Spanish Florida's northern areas. Then she ran into a long, low swell that got Tarpley's attention immediately. The ship began to glide and swoop over the swells during a brightly starred night, but with the morning there was a bank of low clouds to the southeast. The winds began to be erratic, gusty. Tarpley, not liking the signs, checked his position carefully. By late afternoon the ship was bouncing on disturbed seas. Overhead, low clouds scudded swiftly to the south, being sucked into the clouds that now were dark and ominous to the southeast. Light showers played over and past them.

Moses gave a new course to the helmsman and ordered the men to hold all sails for maximum speed for as long as possible. The seamen were restless; they congregated on deck and watched the scudding clouds and looked morosely toward the darkness in the sky. The men were not frightened, for they knew that the captain was making for shelter, and a fine sheltered harbor it was—one that some of them had seen before, on the trip back from Jamaica.

A man who had been on the *Mano Negra*—she was now chartered to the Huntington Shipping Company and working coastal runs under the leadership of Captain Roberto de Mendoza—guided the *Warrior* into the protected, hidden bay. Tarpley didn't like the idea, but he had no choice. He left the open sea with the winds spelling *huracán,* a storm that would, at best, leave his ship battered and damaged. He offered a little prayer that the cove would be empty. His prayers were not answered. The Dutchman's dark ship lay there, masts stripped, heavy hawsers anchored to points on shore to keep her in position during the coming storm.

Tarpley saw no activity on the Dutchman's deck, but there was smoke from the area where huts had been built. He put his men to work anchoring the *Warrior* under an armed watch. He would have to take his chances facing the Dutchman, for he was sure now that the storm was to be a full-fledged *huracán*. As the men stretched strong hawsers to shore and anchored them to deeply driven pilings, the winds were blowing with a force that made the rigging sing. By the time they had her secure, the rain was a solid curtain, and the winds came howling with a power that sent trees toppling and brush ripping from the earth to fly like dark, wingless birds.

For eighteen hours the storm battered the island. Only the protected bay saved the *Warrior*. In the midst of that terrible time there was a period of calm, and Moses could see the stars in the sky above before the clouds and the rains came again and the winds reversed direction and came roaring down on them once more.

While an exhausted crew slept—having been on duty to pump the torrents of rainwater from the *Warrior*'s bilges, then watching and having to replace one hawser that pulled a piling out of the ground—the Dutchman's well-armed men came aboard, braving the dying fury of the *huracán*. The first that Tarpley knew of the boarding, he was being shaken awake and was looking into the muzzle of a pistol. He heard shots and shouts from on deck.

"It seems," said the Dutchman, standing with his pistol aimed at Tarpley's left eye, "that fate is kind to me, for you have brought back to me that which was stolen and an extra gift as well."

Tarpley growled and felt for his pistol that was under his pillow.

"Don't bother," the Dutchman advised. "We have what we want and are leaving. Only a few of your men were foolish enough to resist. You'll have enough crew to continue your voyage unless you do something foolish."

The Dutchman went to the door. "Stay in your cabin,

Captain, until you hear us leave your ship. I really don't want
to shoot you for a few slaves."

"Slaves? There are no slaves on this ship."

"Captain," the Dutchman said with a tight smile, "I found
my own man, Tano, on board. He *is* my slave. And in
repayment for having stolen him from me, I am taking the
others."

Tarpley ran to the door almost immediately after the Dutchman had left and looked out. A bearded seaman showed
rotten teeth and tensed his finger on the trigger of his pistol,
so Tarpley went back inside and closed the door. When he
went on deck a few minutes later, he found that four of his
crew were dead, others wounded. And the Dutchman's ship
was moving past, using the last of the dying storm winds to
make swift time to the open sea.

Tarpley's decision was a difficult one, but he chose his
course because he knew Renno. The white Indian had made
a pact of brotherhood in blood with the huge Maroon. He
tracked the *huracán* northward, under all sails, and arrived in
Wilmington to find that the waters of the storm had damaged
the docks, and the winds had unroofed several houses in
town.

While the storm raged, the occupants of the Huntington
house were kept busy mopping water blown under doors and
around windows. Huge oak trees smashed down near the
house.

"I am very glad I didn't leave two days ago," Beth commented during a moment of respite. "We'd have been caught
in this storm in the open sea."

"It was the will of the manitous for you to stay," Renno
said.

"They must know how much I love you and how I hate to
leave you," she suggested.

After the storm Beth and Renno went to the docks to
survey the damage there. A pretty schooner had been holed
when blown from her moorings, and she lay near the bank of
the river with only her masts showing. The Huntington offices sustained only some minor water damage. They were
both quite surprised when the bell announced the coming of
a ship and were more surprised when it came into view.

* * *

"We didn't have a chance to fight," Tarpley told Renno. "We were all exhausted after battling the storm, and the Dutchman's thugs came aboard in the night. We lost four men in the fight, and one more died on the way back here."

Renno had not asked the question that was foremost on his mind. He knew in his heart that something was wrong, for it was not like Mingo and his two lively boys to be invisible.

"He wanted his fighter back," Moses said. "And he took Mingo and his family."

"Where?" Renno demanded, going cold with rage.

"They were pretty open about it. Some of the men heard the Dutchman say that Mingo and the others would have to take a trip across to Africa."

Renno remembered how Tano had told of the dark continent, and his eyes narrowed.

"He'll be heading for the Bight of Biafra," Moses said. "That's where the river is that Adan told us about, where he has his fort and his slave pens."

"Can you find this river?" Renno asked.

Tarpley frowned. "Yes, but it's a long trip and we're just getting into the season of the big Atlantic storms."

"Renno, it is so far, and Africa is so big," Beth protested. "He may be gone with a ship full of slaves by the time you could get there."

"Oh, he'll stay awhile," Moses guessed. "Only a fool sails the South Atlantic after September. It'll take him awhile to gather enough slaves to fill his ship too."

"Renno, no," Beth begged.

"We are brothers," Renno told her. "But it is far, and in a land where I would be a stranger."

He turned and walked away. He had been isolated for too long from all that had been his world. He longed for the familiar forests and the comforting presence of the spirits of his ancestors. He walked out of the town toward the north. It was a steamy day, the air laden with moisture. In the dense tangle of underbrush he found the going hard. But he pushed ahead until he could not hear a sound other than that made by the wind and the small animals of the woods.

Mosquitoes buzzed around him. He gathered mud from the bank of a small stream and coated his exposed skin to prevent their bites. He sat there as night came, and he heard the bark of a fox quite near and then the dying squeal of a rabbit. A fox. A small animal. Not the wolves of the wilderness. Not the satisfying sound of the grunt of a bear hunting acorns or the roaring challenge of that animal, angered. A fox. A sharp, quick yip.

"Give me wisdom," he prayed.

His people. His family. Renna and Little Hawk had been away from their own kind too long, as had he. Se-quo-i, even though he busied himself with his studies, also longed for home. El-i-chi? He was El-i-chi, and content as long as his rose was near. That she was their sister-by-marriage was something else to be dealt with.

And he was Renno. He was a man born to greatness, a man who was capable of carrying heavy responsibilities.

He straightened his shoulders. The manitous were not ready to speak, so he would have to make his own decision. Once made, that decision would be carried out.